The CROWSBROOK DEMONS

by Claire Horsnell

Printed and distributed by IngramSpark.
www.ingramspark.com

Library and Archives Canada Cataloguing in Publication

Horsnell, Claire Marie, 1977-, author
The Crowsbrook demons / Claire Horsnell.

ISBN 978-0-9937020-0-6 (pbk.)

I. Title.
PS8615.O779C65   2014   C813'.6   C2014-901216-0

Spilled Ink Books
www.spilledink.com

Copy edited by Heather Martin
www.heather-martin.com

Printed in the United States of America.

The
CROWSBROOK
DEMONS

Chapter 1

There was something odd about the two men who had just entered Adam Carpenter's office, and he couldn't put his finger on what it was. They looked normal enough. Mr. Smith and Mr. Jones—Adam's executive assistant Felicity had shown them in and introduced them—were immaculately dressed in elegant and expensive suits with brightly polished silver cufflinks. Adam usually appreciated things that were elegant and expensive. He had collected a number of them since he went into business for himself. A Mont Blanc pen gleamed discreetly on his desk, and his shirt cuffs covered a mid-range Movado watch, though it haunted his credit card bill every month. He had watched Smith and Jones carefully when they came into his office and was pleased that they didn't seem to notice the props. He liked people who were not easily impressed.

That wasn't what unsettled him. And it wasn't their demeanour. They smiled politely when they each shook his hand in turn. Firm handshakes. Quick, formal. He pushed the thought away. Maybe he was imagining it. Maybe it was a fear of success trying to manifest. Self-sabotage. He'd read about that kind of thing in the business psychology paperbacks they sold at the airport. Not that he really needed to travel—property development, at his level (he gritted his teeth), didn't really demand it—but Julia insisted that they "get away from it all" a couple of times a year. He didn't know what she wanted to get away from. As far as he was concerned, they lived in the middle of nowhere.

All that was about to change, though. Thanks to Mr. Smith and Mr. Jones.

They worked for a company called Asilida, and the firm was an exclusive one. They didn't work with just anybody. Adam was already successful, but his career needed a boost to take him to the level he felt he deserved, and contracting with Smith and Jones—

Well, that would do it, at least if Carrington, his city-boy mate, was to be believed. But Adam still had to make this work.

"Mr. Carpenter," said Mr. Jones in a voice as smooth and even as a slab of granite. "It's a pleasure to meet you."

"Likewise," said Adam. They were both older than he was— he guessed that they were in their mid-forties. Old enough to know what they were doing, and young enough not to dismiss new thinking out of hand. He prided himself on his ability to assess people accurately—that was how he'd closed his first big deals, and how he'd avoided a couple of projects that turned out to be utter duds.

"Have a seat." Adam gestured to the dark-brown leather chairs on the other side of his desk. They nodded thanks and sat.

Mr. Smith opened his briefcase and took out a burgundy leather portfolio. He closed the briefcase with a snap. "As you requested," he said, "we have prepared a summary of the project our organization has developed to fit your needs."

Adam opened the dossier. He flipped through the sheets— budgets, plans, schedules—and snorted involuntarily. "You're joking, right?"

Mr. Smith inclined his head a couple of degrees.

"Not at all," he said. "We never joke about business, Mr. Carpenter."

"This is ridiculous." The timelines on the project were completely unfeasible for a start. Carrington would have a ball with this. And his father would—rightly enough in this case—make worried noises about his son getting into a business he knew nothing about. He hated proving his father right.

"Please be assured, Mr. Carpenter," said Mr. Jones, "that the manager who will be handling this project has a great deal of experience in these matters. It is, of course, of fundamental importance to us that our clients are satisfied with the bargain they receive. However, you must trust our judgment. For your own satisfaction."

Adam could feel his irritation rising.

"I'm not interested," he snapped. "*Mr. Jones*. I'm a property developer, not a factory owner." The development they were proposing was entirely outside of his area of expertise. He couldn't manage—

There it was again. Self-sabotage. Of course he could do it. But still—

Mr. Smith smiled. His teeth were very white and very straight. "Mr. Carpenter," he said, "this is the project that our organization has tailored to the needs and requirements that your associate detailed. I understand that Mr. Carrington based the outline with which we were provided on direction given by you. I can assure you that the project will suit."

"In fact, you're extremely fortunate," broke in Mr. Jones. "The head of our division has taken a particular interest in your case and has committed himself to see personally that it is successful."

Adam looked out of the window and tapped his fingers on the desk. They could talk the talk all right.

"Our lawyers have prepared the paperwork," said Mr. Smith. He pushed a second dossier across the polished wooden desk. "I think you'll find it's all in order, Mr. Carpenter."

Adam made a mental note to tell Felicity to speak to the building management about fixing the heating in his office. One minute the room was fine, and the next it was freezing. In October. Ridiculous. Those idiots couldn't get anything right.

He looked down at the portfolio again.

It was crazy. It would never work. Thank Christ it hadn't cost him anything so far. He flipped through a couple of the pages, not reading.

Carrington had warned him—no, not warned him, *told* him—that this was how these guys worked. Unconventional, perhaps, but they got the job done, he'd said. Carrington's success was proof of that.

And he wasn't going to be out of pocket. It wasn't as if they were asking for huge amounts of money up front. Carrington had said something about their payment being more ideological. "You'd think I was mad if I told you," he'd said. "So I won't. But you won't regret it. Really."

Adam flipped another page. The numbers swam before his eyes, but they did seem to add up. Carrington was right. It didn't seem as if he had anything to lose.

What the hell, he thought. They'd be off schedule within days. He could always shut the thing down in a week, if they weren't where they said they'd be. He doubted they would be. But he was curious to see what would happen.

"Sure," he said, closing the portfolio. "Let's give it a shot. See what you can do."

Jones smiled. "Thank you, Mr. Carpenter."

Smith coughed, delicately, and retrieved a pen from the inside pocket of his suit jacket.

"Mr. Carpenter," he said. "There is, of course, just *one* last thing…"

• • •

Ted, the driver of the 575 bus to Crowsbrook and points east, saw one of the glass double doors to the school slam open hard against the wall and Jessica Elliot, known as Jez—Ted had been driving the school bus since she'd started at Arden High a good six years ago—came belting through them. One of the teachers peered through the same doors a moment later, presumably to discover the source of the noise, but Jez was long gone, running hard and expertly dodging the uneven concrete paving slabs of the path to the bus stop. She was weaving between two temporary classrooms (temporary since the early 1940s; it took a while to get things done at Arden High). Ted knew how the kids would react if anyone tripped over the treacherous slabs—one false step, and the poor bugger'd be the canteen entertainment for a fortnight. The girl dashed out between the wooden gateposts that were crying out for a coat of cheap creosote, and took a flying leap onto the bus. The doors closed behind her with a malevolent hiss.

"Thanks, Ted." She exhaled hard. There was a reason she'd never make the hockey team.

Ted grunted and pulled away from the curb. Jez stumbled toward her seat at the back, in the corner. It was right over the engine and stank of leaking fumes and old cigarettes and brake fluid. She dumped her bag on the floor and sat down with her A-level biology folder on her lap. Outside, it was starting to spit again. It splattered lightly on the filthy windows.

• • •

Four p.m., on the nose; Jez was lucky she'd made it. There was already some drama at the front: Year Seven bitch queen Vicky Rice tearing into one of her slaves for using the wrong lip gloss. Some Year Eight boys were chucking an almost-dead Pepsi can around. The smell of Paul Barlow's after-school joint drifted down from the top deck. Diesel fumes. Dirty clothes. Armpits. Spray deodorant. Cheap scent from Boots. Shampoo. Tangy Toms. Gym bags. Bubble gum. Damp swimming kits. Fart. The 575 threw a tidal wave of rainwater up over a group of kids waiting for the bus to Northcote, the next village after Crowsbrook, where Jez lived. Jez rolled her eyes as the girls outside squealed in horror; she threw on her earbuds and turned up the volume. The Buzzcocks slouched into life. It wasn't quite enough to block out the chaos, but it would do for now.

"...he didn't even *see* me..."

"...*wicked* goal..."

"...Mrs. Willis *hates* me..."

"...he's just being a complete arsehole..."

"...this weather..."

"...I need to get new shoes for the weekend..."

"... *dare* you to eat it..."

 "...oh, that one was *bad...*"

Bloody kids.

Twelve months to go. Twelve months until her exams were done and she would be out of here, moving, if everything went according to plan, to a city large enough to have more than one screen at the cinema and a couple of night spots where your change didn't stick to the floor if you dropped it.

Oh, and medical school. If she got the grades, which she probably would.

She opened her folder and crossed out another day on the calendar glued to the inside cover, then leaned back in her seat and closed her eyes. The mostly empty Pepsi can hit her on the forehead and flecked her face with flat pop, while the Year Eight boys hooted and hollered apologies. Outside, the October landscape was turning from brown to grey, and everything was wet.

I hate this place, she thought.

• • •

Sarah Trevelyan struggled to stow her luggage in the rack above her head: a suitcase with only three of its four wheels intact, and a large purple backpack that sat incongruously with her calf-length black coat. She pushed an elderly blue and brown carpet bag under her seat, through a tide of empty gum packets and chocolate wrappers.

She had a good view of her three bags; she didn't need anyone walking off with them. They contained pretty much all the stuff she had left. She curled up against the window and closed her eyes. The carriage smelled vaguely of vomit.

A change is as good as a rest, isn't that what they say?

She gave herself a mental slap. *Spare the platitudes. Just stay awake and watch the damn luggage. You don't want to lose anything else.* She bent down and rummaged in the bag at her feet, hoping she had enough cash for a cab from the station to the cottage she apparently now owned.

After searching it thoroughly and picking out all the change, she'd come up with ten quid. Maybe it wasn't too far. She flopped back in her seat and pulled a crumpled letter out of her shoulder bag. It was printed on thick, cream-coloured letterhead. She unfolded it, and skimmed it for the forty-second time.

...regret to inform you...Dorothea Trevelyan, sister to your grandmother and former guardian Elsie Trevelyan (deceased)...

peacefully, in her sleep...due to inherit her cottage and all its contents...

Then there was a long paragraph about paperwork. Sarah hated paperwork.

"Hello," said a voice from behind her. She jumped. A small, dark-haired child was peering at her around the edge of the seat. He looked about seven. "What's your name?"

"Sarah." She looked down at her letter, and hoped the kid would take the hint.

There was a pause. She looked up. He was still there. She sighed inwardly. "What's yours?"

"Jack."

"Well, aren't you the little extrovert. I like being quiet and by myself. Doesn't appeal to you, I suppose?"

Jack looked at her, blankly.

"I'm reading *Harry Potter*," he announced.

Sarah looked at him, baffled. "Oh," she said. She was vaguely aware that he was probably expecting her to say more. "What's it about?" she finally managed. She knew damn well, but she hoped it would keep him talking for a bit while she thought of other things to say, preferably something that would make him go away.

"You don't know what it's *about?*" said Jack, incredulously. "Everybody knows what it's *about*." He sighed. "It's about a boy who's a wizard and goes to school and learns magic and stuff. Everybody knows what it's *about*," he repeated.

Sarah shrugged and pressed her lips together, put the letter away, and started rummaging in her bag for something longer to read as the train lumbered to life and began moving slowly out of the station. "Just making conversation, kiddo," she said. "Where's your mother?" She looked hopefully around the carriage.

"Over there," said Jack, with a windmill gesture that encompassed a space stretching roughly from the next carriage to Iceland. "Silly," he added. And then: "She *said* I could go for a walk."

"And talk to strangers? She said you could do that as well?" said Sarah, raising one eyebrow. "Not a good idea, Jack. Bet she didn't say you could do *that*." She pulled a book bound in stained dark-brown leather out of her carpet bag and settled back in her seat.

"I can do that," said Jack. "I can do *anything*. I'm allowed."

"Well, you shouldn't," said Sarah. She looked at Jack with irritation. "What if you meet a..." She delved in her mind for a moment, and then thought back to Harry and the Hogwarts crew. "What if you meet a witch or something?"

"Witches aren't *real*," said Jack. He rolled his eyes. "Silly."

"Whatever," said Sarah, opening her book. "But they are."

"They're not real. You're a silly."

"You know best, I suppose," said Sarah, without looking up. "Silly, silly, silly, silly, silly..."

He stopped, as Sarah raised her head slowly; her face twisted, transforming from that of an average-looking woman of about thirty to one belonging to an ancient and foul-looking crone: her skin paled into a gangrenous shade of green as warts pushed their way up from underneath; her cheeks drooped and hung loosely off her skull. Several of her teeth vanished; her face sank inward and crumpled; and the tip of her nose drooped like a fairy-tale hag's. Blood vessels in her sclera exploded like fireworks, turning her eyes bloodshot.

"What did you say?" she cackled.

Jack looked at her, wide-eyed with horror. His breath was ragged and his mouth opened and closed a few times, like a surprised goldfish. He eventually found his voice and let rip a scream that would have done Fay Wray proud, and then tore off, roughly in the direction of his mother.

Sarah went back to her book. Her face had returned to normal.

"Told you so," she muttered under her breath. "*Silly.*"

There was the faintest gleam of a wicked smile in her eyes.

• • •

Adam Carpenter sat in his office as the light grew dim outside. He was staring at the box that Smith and Jones had left. A present, they had said. One of those corporate gifts that no one really wanted. The box was nice, though. It was made of polished wood. He didn't recognize what kind. It appeared to be expensive, however, and it was decorated with an inlaid pattern that looked like some kind of alphabet.

So this was it. He'd closed the deal.

He made a mental note to thank Carrington, though it killed him a little bit. Carrington, that bastard. A big swinging dick, they called his type in the Square Mile. Adam could have gone into investment banking—he could have, he knew enough people from Oxford, he was even quite good with numbers—but his father had never trusted those types. "Bean counters," he called them. Adam pointed out repeatedly that trading internationally in contracts on the floor of the stock exchange was not the same as accounting, which was just glorified bookkeeping, but his father always shook his head. It wasn't real work, he said. Not like building things, which was honest work. Adam's father was an electrician. Took pride in not being one of "those cowboys."

Adam had gone into property development.

It could be glamorous. If you got to build skyscrapers in Dubai. Not if you were stuck in the English provinces trying to convince the squint-eyed mouth-breathers on the local councils of the business advantages of out-of-town shopping centres and glass-clad industrial parks. In that case, it was a lot of hearing Carrington make jokes about bad comb-overs and reality TV shows.

Well, whatever. Carrington *had* set up the meeting with these chaps, but it was the least he could do. Among those who knew, he had implied, their reputation for making fortunes, names, careers, *legacies*, was impeccable. "And let's face it," he'd added with a smirk. "You could use help."

Adam had been running his own company for two years now. Two years on Tuesday, in fact. He was doing all right. He hadn't had the stellar luck that had earned him his "Golden Boy" nickname when he'd worked at Bullfinch and Sons, before striking out on his own, though. Straight out of university, and he'd pulled two deals in a row that had netted the company about four and a half million quid. He'd built himself enough of a raise and a reputation over the next decade to strike out on his own He was doing all right. But only *all right*.

Asilida. They hadn't been easy to get in touch with. Firms of that calibre didn't need to make themselves known to everyone, and they wouldn't necessarily take your calls if you did find out about them, either. But Carrington had done a couple of deals with a company vaguely associated with Smith and Jones's lot in 2007—he wasn't specific about the details, but he *was* one of the few to come out of the car wreck that was 2008 with no shit sticking to him, and a job at the end of it. And an extra couple of million, while his colleagues were packing up their office toys into cardboard boxes and heading home to work on their CVs.

Luck of Old Nick, that one.

Adam sighed.

He'd looked through the portfolio when Smith and Jones had left and—well, they knew their stuff. Everything had been taken care of; despite the lunatic timelines, the project was bound to succeed. It couldn't fail, not if—

Well. It couldn't fail. He would show them. Carrington and his loudmouth crowd of braying twats. His father.

This deal would be the making of him. There was no going back. You had to make sacrifices if you wanted to get anywhere in life. His father had at least taught him that.

Adam leaned forward in his chair and undid the clasp holding the box shut. He could hear a faint humming coming from inside. He lifted the lid.

Nothing happened for a moment.

Then he felt something land on his face. On his ear. On his neck. The light brush of insect legs.

They moved too quickly for him to brush them off; he barely had time to feel the delicate spikes on his skin before the creatures crawled into his nostrils, into his ears, down his throat.

Flies. Small flies.

He felt the sickening sensation of the things moving inside his skull before a deafening buzzing filled his ears and the world went black.

Chapter 2

The bus shuddered to a halt in the quiet village square. Jez shouldered her dark-green army surplus bag with the doodles on it, clutched her file full of biology notes to her chest like a breastplate, and stepped out of the cloud of other people's smoke and bubble-gum fumes into near silence. The bus gave a mechanical grunt and hiss and grumbled off up Smith's Hill. The shouts and squeals of the other kids getting off the bus were the only sounds in the darkening October evening. A woman in a navy-blue wax jacket and wellingtons walked a dog that was mostly collie past the village primary school. Jez glared at it all with contempt.

Dead, she thought. *It's totally dead here. Like a bubble sealed off from the real world.* She gave the woman with the dog a withering glance. It was Rose Pound, who ran the village shop with her husband, Jake. *I bet* she's *never read* The Origin of Species, thought Jez, and immediately felt guilty. Rose was all right.

She started the five-and-a-half-minute walk from the bus stop to the house she shared with her dad on Green Lane, one of a row of six old farmworkers' cottages that backed onto a field and a whole lot of nothing. Half a minute might not seem like much, but when you were trying to grab your books, your lunch and your lab coat while tying back your still-wet hair and throwing enough powder on your nose to stop anyone from commenting on the glare until you got to school, it made all the difference. She walked past the Nag's Head, a small country pub that someone in the eighties had painted rose pink. Past the village school that Jez had attended until she was eleven. She had read everything in its tiny library, which was kept in a cupboard by Mrs. Hadley, who had grey hair set in unnatural corkscrews, and lived in Bewley, the next village over. Past the bus shelter, with the proclamations of the village kids hollering in chalk and markers from its walls: "Andy M is a TOOL," "Emily is a Slag," "I luv Jamie IDT INDT," and the ancient proclamation "Sherry loves Bazza 1984" muttering from the corner like a nostalgic great-aunt. Past Mrs. Bastable's cottage, with her ill-tempered Jack Russell rattling around inside it like a noisy canine pinball. Past Miss Forge's cottage, almost hidden in a forest of carefully cultivated rose bushes, done blooming for several months now. Past the Eatons' cottage. Past the Birkins' house.

In less than one year, Jez would be out of there. No more listening to fart contests on the bus, thank God. She was going to an actual city, to live somewhere with people in it she hadn't known since, you know, *birth*. With live music that wasn't just Paul Barlow and whatever musicians he was talking to that month playing hair metal covers in the Red Dragon pub in Arden. She glared at the trees and the neat gardens, consumed with hate.

She was so deep in her reverie that she didn't hear the footsteps behind her.

She felt a sudden hard smack on her shoulder that almost threw her off balance, and whirled round snarling, ready to do battle. She saw a guy who looked about her own age; he was tall and thin, with untidy reddish hair that defied the efforts of both product and gravity. Jez's rage turned into a frustrated sigh.

"Jesus, Sam," she said. "Don't *do* that."

"You need to pay more attention. You can't move to the big city and walk around off in your head the whole time."

"Won't be a problem. If I'm in the city, I won't be thinking about how much I hate living in a shithole where nothing ever happens and where eight out of every ten people you meet are related. Also, what's the worst that can happen here? I'm not going to get mugged by Mrs. Bastable's Jack Russell."

"He's an ornery little bastard."

"I could totally take him." She kicked grumpily at a pebble in front of her, sending it into a shallow puddle with a splash. "Where were you on the bus?"

"Upstairs. Had a small transaction to conduct with Barlow. Procurement of fine herbs for relaxation and health. Why the hell are you so miserable?" Sam pulled a squashed packet of cigarettes out of his bag and lit one expertly. "One thing that struck me today: maths may aggravate my eczema, but for you, my dear, I was willing to risk my complexion, and if my calculations are correct, it is, as of today, less than one year until you will be leaving the bosom of the arse-end of the *colon* of nowhere for rainier climes, all being well, no?"

"That's right."

"I'll join you in two. Years, unfortunately, but we'll go for sushi." Sam exhaled a plume of smoke. "Jesus Christ, two more years of this. Surrounded by people who think Rilke is a sofa from Ikea."

"You've said. Also, *Gareth* doesn't think that." Jez gave Sam a knowing look. Gareth Lake was in the same English class as Sam.

Sam sighed. "This is true. But Gareth could tell me that *Hamlet* was the tragic tale of a small pig, forced to avenge his father's death at the hands of a cruel and treacherous farmer with inclinations toward bestiality, and he would still be, as the kids say—" he paused and coughed "—*hawt*. Damn it, that boy will be the death of me."

"Maybe you should tell him sometime. We've been over this."

"Yes, we have. And you, my dear, do not Get It. Not that simple. Changing the subject now," said Sam. "I was happily wallowing in despair at the thought of two more years in this dump."

"Do you need a Catalogue moment? Do you want to go through the Catalogue?" They had developed the Catalogue—or, as Sam referred to it, a List of Reasons Not to Give Up and Die—the previous summer while sitting on the swings on the playing field at the top of the village and smoking weed, with nothing else to do.

"I think I just might. Just don't start with Joy Division; I'm still too focused on what you said about the upcoming seven hundred and thirty days. Three hundred and sixty-five of which you will have already been gone for, excuse my grammar. *De*-pressing." Sam tapped his cigarette.

"Okay. Hold off on the Joy Division. Um." She paused for a moment and took a deep breath. "You can always come and visit. Anyway. Happy Mondays. James. OMD. The Stone Roses. The Smiths. New Order. Your turn."

"The Charlatans, Inspiral Carpets, the Buzzcocks, Oasis."

"I freaking *love* Oasis."

"I know." Sam sighed. "Me too. Okay. Joy Division. See, I feel better already."

"More than one club."

"Valid." Sam stabbed at her with a finger. "But too vague. Let's stay on point here."

"The Band on the Wall. The Roadhouse. A gay scene for Sam."

"Gay scene for Sam: good call, very important." Sam thought for a moment. "*Coronation Street.*"

"Sam, you are officially forty-seven."

"The writing's amazing. Oh! Oh! Elizabeth Gaskell! *Hard Times! The Guardian!* L. S. Lowry!"

"You know we're going to have to become City fans. Perpetual underdogs." Jez was smiling now.

"Neither of us likes football."

"I'm told it doesn't matter." She glanced ahead. "Whoa!"

"*Whoa* to you too," said Sam. "What gives?"

"Look, look!" Jez pointed. "Cab outside Miss Trevelyan's old place!" She squinted, hunched over, and bent her fingers like claws. "Fresh blood in the gene pool! Fresh blood! Fresh blooooooooood!"

"No 'moment's silence out of respect for the deceased'?" Sam folded his arms. "Jezebel. For *shame.*"

"She died, like, two months ago, Sam. And she was ninety-four." Jez pictured Miss Trevelyan: tiny, gimlet-eyed and wiry. "She didn't look ninety-four. I hope I look like that when I'm ninety-four."

"Well, she was a witch." Sam ground out his cigarette under his foot, and then picked up the dog-end and placed it in a small Ziploc plastic bag containing five more butts. "Can we talk about going north again?"

"*Now* who's speaking ill of the dead?" They had reached the gateway of the small cottage that had belonged to the late Miss Trevelyan, but in time only to see the red front door slam shut and the cab pull away. "That wasn't a nice thing to say, Samuel. Damn it!" She leaned on the gate. "Now we'll have to set up shifts of pitchfork-wielding villagers to watch the house day and night until we find out who's in there."

"It's not speaking ill of the dead when everyone was calling her that when she was alive. Everyone in primary school, anyway. Are you just bitter because you were campfire-yarn deprived?"

"No." Jez looked at him, her chin up. "And I know the stories. Miss Trevelyan: banned from St. James's Church for unspecified reasons, usually having something to do with churchyard nudity; never killed spiders; footprints on her roof; blah, blah, blah. I also heard a great one about how if you mix popping candy and Coke, your stomach will explode. Oh, wait, that one turned out to be *total bullshit*. Not like Miss Trevelyan being a witch or anything. *Totally* different."

"Just a question, mate." Sam leaned his elbows on the late Miss Trevelyan's white-painted gate, and they peered through the windows as best they could. The cottage was dark. "Stress thee not."

Jez held up her hands. "Not stressed. Not stressed at all." She pulled her army bag further up her shoulder. "I spent two-thirds of my free period this afternoon listening to Saskia French telling the common room how crystals are going to help her get from a C in history to a B. *Crystals*, Sam. Bits of shiny rock. Excuse me if I'm a bit urban-legend-psychobabble-bullshitted out."

"That always has such a great effect on your vocabulary." Sam pushed himself off of the gate and they started walking toward the junction where the road led to Sam's house. "Are you coming over later?"

"I have a pile of coursework that could sink a battleship," said Jez. "But if I can bring it with me, you're on. Usual time. Make a playlist."

"And *done*," said Sam. "See you later. Watch out for witches. "

• • •

Adam was running on the treadmill in his home.

He had fallen asleep in his office after Smith and Jones left; that had never happened before. He had woken up in his ergonomic chair about an hour later by his estimation. Embarrassing. Thank God Felicity hadn't found him, and that he'd stayed in his chair. If she'd discovered him lying on the floor, she'd have called an ambulance and there'd have been all kinds of fuss, when he'd just had a difficult meeting and taken an unscheduled nap. Nothing to worry about. He felt fine. Better than fine, actually. Maybe he should start scheduling naps: he was certainly running harder and faster than he usually did at this time of day; he'd been going for half an hour and felt as though he could keep going for another four. It was amazing what a little rest could do.

Yep, time to start building power naps into his day on a regular basis. Things were going to go up and up from here.

His phone chimed. Usually, he wouldn't have stopped for anyone, but Smith had told him to expect the call when he and Jones had left the office. Adam slowed the machine to a walking pace and picked up.

"Mr. Carpenter," said an even voice on the other end. "This is Mr. Brown. A colleague of Mr. Smith and Mr. Jones. They informed me that the contract has been signed and all is in order. We have, of course, already begun working on the development in question."

"We concluded the deal this afternoon," said Adam. "What could you possibly have done since then?"

"Please trust me, Mr. Carpenter," said the voice. "I will be your main point of contact. We have a lot of work to do, of course; there is no time to be wasted. We expect this development to be extremely successful, and, if I may, our organization is very happy to have begun a project that is close to our hearts, but you will understand that naturally there is a certain amount of..." The voice paused for a moment and coughed, delicately. "Of necessary bureaucracy, if you will. Administration."

"Yes," said Adam. "I'm really happy that you're doing the organizing, and not me."

"You trust us," said the voice. It was a statement, not a question.

"Of course," said Adam. Carrington had told him about the way these guys could handle seemingly insurmountable problems. It was as if any obstacles vaporized into the air.

"The *ultimate* insider's club," Carrington had called them.

Partly, Adam just wanted to see what they could do. Access to City insiders, politicians, even ministers, for someone with Carrington's background, was easy. Changing the minds of a local council? *That* was a challenge. Adam had grown up here and had heard his father talk about the "enemies of progress," as he called them, who opposed anything new, opposed innovation just for the sake of it. Who wanted to keep everything in the Dark Ages. Adam had a fair bit of experience with them himself, though mostly through his lawyers (*former* lawyers, he reminded himself; Brown was working on his behalf now). Local bureaucracy was the worst: reluctant men in tweed jackets, and women made of steel with hair to match. *Good luck to the ultimate insider's club,* he thought.

"Your investment," said the voice, "has already ensured the success of the project, Mr. Carpenter."

There was a pause. He hadn't really invested anything yet; just signed the papers. Adam suddenly felt cold. But he'd worked up a sweat running, of course. And the house was old and full of drafts. He cranked the machine a little; he didn't want his muscles to cool down.

"As the agent for this project," Brown continued, "I will be meeting with the town administration tomorrow. We will proceed from there. I shall report on the success of the meeting late tomorrow. Good evening, Mr. Carpenter." There was a click at the other end of the line, and Adam's phone flashed.

If *it's a success*, thought Adam. He'd been dealing with small-town bureaucracies for years and had never found them anything other than intractable and suspicious. Yet there was something about these people that had him convinced. And Carrington—

It was a big risk to Adam's reputation. It had to pay off. You put your heart and soul into your business.

Adam hit the speed button on the treadmill again and started running.

• • •

Sarah stood in the living room of her late great-aunt Dorothea Trevelyan's cottage and looked at the back of the front door.

Three locks, she thought. *It's not paranoia when they really* are *out to get you.*

It was dark. The curtains were drawn, and there was little light left in the October sky to filter through the gaps. Sarah reached toward the shadowy outline of the light switch. As she flipped it on, something ran over her hand. She flinched in surprise, and instinctively flicked it away, blinking in the dim electric light.

A spider the size of a ten-pence piece fell to the floor unharmed and scuttled away. Sarah watched it go.

"If you wish to live and thrive," she said, out loud, "let a spider run alive."

One of her grandmother's sayings. Sarah had never been a huge fan of spiders. But live and let live, and all that. She gazed around the cottage.

For a place that had been shut up for the past two months, it was spotless, although you had to look hard through the clutter to notice. The front door opened directly into the living room, all four walls of which were lined with bookshelves. An old-fashioned lamp stood on a round table made of dark wood in the corner by the window; the table was covered in papers. A wrought-iron spiral staircase to Sarah's left wound up to the second floor, and there was a dark-green curtain hiding the entrance to what Sarah assumed was another room at the back.

She put down her case by the front door, took off her shoes and went over to the table. The scent of wood polish and dried flowers permeated the room.

She turned over a few of the papers on the table; mostly handwritten notes, pages of them, in a neat, tiny, and complicated script that Sarah recognized as similar to her grandmother's. You could read it, yes, but you couldn't just glance at it and see what it said. Sarah decided to leave the papers for another day, and stacked them carefully in order. She'd have to go through everything. She looked at the bookshelves.

While she looked, a spider ran across the papers behind her.

"Dorothea Trevelyan," she said. "What *have* you left for me?"

Although she had been raised by her grandmother, Sarah had no memories of meeting her great-aunt: Elsie had always been tight-lipped about the rift between her and her sister, only putting it down to "differences of opinion."

"Dorothea," Elsie would say with a sniff. "Got some strange ideas, that one." And that would be the end of it.

Sarah crossed the room and stood in front of the curtain. It was heavy, and someone had made several discreet repairs to it: there were three patches, all below knee height, hand-sewn into its folds. Sarah felt a wave of unease move through her, but dismissed it.

She reached out her hand and pulled back the curtain.

It hid a large windowless alcove off the main room. She switched on the light and saw—

Well.

The high table standing at the end of the room was covered in a white cloth that had peculiar symbols embroidered around the edge. Two silver candlesticks stood at the back. On the right side was part of a set of antlers and what looked like a piece of animal skull. To the left was a large sea shell. In the centre, on a plate, stood a crystal wineglass with a five-pointed star engraved on it. In front of that was a censer. Hanging on the wall above all of it was another five-pointed star, this one made out of twigs bundled together.

There was only one word for it: *altar*.

Sarah stood absolutely still for a moment, staring.

Then she ducked out of the alcove and went into the kitchen—badly in need of refurbishment, but still clean and functional—and rummaged around in her great-aunt's cupboards until she found what she was looking for: a small jar of unusual-looking dried leaves and a charcoal disk. She returned to the alcove, lit the disk with a lighter from her pocket, placed it in the censor, and sprinkled a pinch of the leaves on top. A rich aromatic scent filled the room, as the smoke curled upwards. She closed her eyes and slowly drew a five-pointed star—a pentagram—in the smoke with the tip of her finger.

"Thanks be," said Sarah, out loud, "you bastards."

Whatever happened between Gran and Dorothea, it wasn't because Dot left the family business, she thought.

She went back into the living room, and threw herself into an ancient, soft, and tatty armchair. The threadbare tapestry of the upholstery on its arms had been covered with crocheted doilies, to wring every last inch of life out of it.

She could have just reupholstered it, thought Sarah, closing her eyes and rubbing her temples with her fingers. *Or bought a new one. A second-hand one, obviously.* Gran and Auntie Dot had apparently been two of kind in that regard.

Sarah sat there with her eyes closed for a good ten minutes, maybe fifteen, thinking of the journey, the rain, the fact that there was almost no food in the cupboards, her grandmother, her great-aunt, her old home in the southwest. Eventually, she took a deep breath and opened her eyes.

And saw an envelope with her name on it lying on the occasional table next to the armchair.

She picked it up and turned it over in her hands: the paper looked old, but it was thick, good quality. The envelope had been sealed with wax.

Of course, thought Sarah. *Because no one in my family would ever just lick an envelope.*

She broke the seal and drew out the letter. It was in the same neat, complicated handwriting that covered the sheaves of notes on the table.

My Dear Sarah,

My time is running out, and therefore I will be brief.
The solicitors will take care of the paperwork, but I leave
you this cottage; it has been used for centuries by a family
business almost as old as ours, and I think that there may
be a family connection, but I have not had time to trace its

full history, though I know that its wards are strong. The contents, of course, are yours also; of most use to you will likely be the artifacts contained within the trunks upstairs, along with my journals. I have spent much of the past thirty years travelling in order to amass this collection; for this reason, I did not try to find you after the passing of my sister. I hope that you can forgive me this, but I am sure that you will eventually understand that, under the circumstances, it was necessary to accomplish as much as possible in preparation for the coming troubles.

As I travelled, I traded knowledge for knowledge, and insight for insight. This was, as you may imagine, contrary to the wishes of my sister, your grandmother, who was firmly of the belief that our family's knowledge—and the secrecy that has traditionally accompanied it—has been the strength that has sustained us over the centuries; she will have taught you the importance of secrecy, which I do not dismiss, but I believe that the discreet and selective exchange of ancient knowledge will prove of utmost importance in the dark times that lie ahead. In the nine years since my sister's passing, I have seen much, and I am ever more convinced that the evil of ages is rising; if I interpret what I have seen in the glass correctly, then you will be aware of this also, and I am sorry for the losses that you have already suffered; when I became aware of your plight, I was too far away to be of help, and upon my return, it was made clear to me that my time was shortly to come, and it became necessary to prepare. Please know that, although I have not seen you in close to thirty years, I weep for what you have lost, and I hope that one day you will be able to forgive my absence in your time of trial.

I believe truly that the tragedy of this summer is a sign of things to come. You will need to be ready.

You are young. I wish you courage and strength.

Your great-aunt,
Dorothea Trevelyan

P.S. Please take care of the spiders. They will be grateful.

It was dated two days before Dorothea's death. Mid-August. There was another envelope underneath it, also with Sarah's name on it, containing one hundred and sixty-three pounds and eighty-four pence.

Sarah put the letter down. She was shaking.

Dorothea had seen it all. Everything that had happened over the summer: she had *seen* it. And now she was saying there was more to come. And worse.

How the hell could you "take care of" a spider, anyway? Buy it groceries? Take it shopping?

Jesus, she thought. *It would have to be bloody spiders, wouldn't it?* Sarah knew rationally that they played a valuable role in the ecosystem, that they were revered in folklore, that their webs had been used in traditional healing for centuries, that they were supposedly attuned to otherworldly vibrations and activities. But they were still horrid.

If the letter—if the *spiders*—had already waited for two months, though, the dark days probably weren't *that* imminent. Sarah hauled herself out of the chair and went over to her suitcase, flipping it open, so the top rested on the back of the door.

Everything in the case still smelled faintly of smoke. There hadn't been a lot left, after the fire. A few books. Enough clothes to get by: a couple of thick, plain sweaters, two pairs of jeans, a long black skirt for going out (she hadn't been out in years, except to the pub, with Eleanor), and some T-shirts. A packet of incense. She dug deep into the bottom left-hand corner and came up with what she was looking for: a packet of teabags.

Think of it as a new start, she imagined Eleanor saying. Always found the silver lining, that one.

Yeah. Wasn't really looking for a new start though, was I? It was thrust upon me, as you might say.

That was when she saw the cobweb on the staircase. It hung between the first and second steps and it was perfect: all it needed was some dew or frost to highlight it, and it would have been a solid contender for "Cobweb of the Year," if spiders had award ceremonies. But in a house so clean—

Sarah stared at it, frozen.

If her grandmother had taught her one thing, it was that you could never discount anything strange as insignificant.

Time to go upstairs, Sarah thought.

She flicked the light switch at the bottom of the staircase; the bulb flashed for a moment and then went dead. *Great.* She went back into the kitchen; in the third drawer she opened, she found two slightly bent white candles and a box of matches. She lit one of the candles, and used a few drops of wax to place it on a saucer that had obviously been used for the same purpose before.

Don't worry, Auntie Dot, she thought. *I won't drip wax on the carpet.*

The metal lace of the staircase was more solid than it looked. Part of an old nursery rhyme came into Sarah's head as she climbed:

Will you walk into my parlour?" said the Spider to the Fly,
'Tis the prettiest little parlour that ever you did spy;
The way into my parlour is up a winding stair,
And I've a many curious things to show when you are there.
Oh no, no," said the little Fly, "to ask me is in vain,
For who goes up your winding stair can ne'er come down again."

She could hear a soft rustling, like a light breeze through dry leaves. As she climbed, it grew louder; it was coming from behind a closed door on the right side of the hallway at the top of the staircase. Sarah put her hand on the doorknob, turned it, and pushed. The door swung open silently. As she entered, she felt the light threads of a cobweb on her face. She winced and brushed it away.

The rushing noise was loudest here. Sarah put the candle down on a chest of drawers.

The room was tiny and had obviously been used by Auntie Dot as a sort of spare-room-cum-storage space. There was a single bed in it that was covered by an elderly patchwork quilt, and the small chest of drawers to the left. There were the trunks that Dorothea had mentioned as well: solid, wooden boxes edged in studded leather, and padlocked.

And the room was crawling with spiders.

A seething mass of arachnids scuttled across the walls, the ceiling, the floors, each other. The ceiling was covered with cobwebs, inches thick in some places. A large, black specimen crouched at the centre of an especially thick clump of web in the corner. Another was sucking the juices out of an earwig, paralyzed and wrapped in gossamer. There were hundreds—no, *thousands*—of the things. All moving.

Sarah stood there, frozen.

Take care of the spiders. Well, she had found them, which was a start. But the old nursery rhyme still clanged in her head.

For who goes up your winding stair can ne'er go down again.

Sarah picked up the candle and went out, quietly closing the door behind her.

Chapter 3

The next morning, the damp and heavy air rushed in as Sarah opened the front door, and she shivered and pulled her scarf around her as she stepped out into the October drizzle. The sky was overcast, but the clouds were high and the wind tugged at her clothing.

Going to be like this all day, she thought.

She made her way along the narrow lane, past the cottages, and turned into the road. The trees were dark and wet on either side; their branches met at the top, forming a tunnel that filtered the light so that it felt, to Sarah, like light streaming through the upper windows of a cathedral.

Take care of the spiders. But how?

Maybe Auntie Dot was losing her marbles by the end, thought Sarah.

She knew in her heart that that wasn't it.

The village store was in a gap in the trees. She walked up the path to its door, past a notice board covered in brightly coloured pieces of paper advertising whist drives, beetle nights, babysitting, dog walking, and a goat for sale, complete with a faded photograph of the dispirited-looking beast chewing a piece of car tire. A bell clanged as she pushed the green door and walked into the shop. It smelled of fresh meat and old cheese and green vegetables. Sarah picked up a wire basket with red handles and began hunting for breakfast. Bread. Eggs. Bananas. Corn flakes. She filled the basket and went up to the till, behind an agitated woman berating the shopkeeper.

"—absolutely unacceptable. It's outrageous! I don't know how they can even consider it. It's completely illegal."

"Well, I'm sure they'll go through all the proper processes," said the shopkeeper, a heavyset man with short grey hair, wearing a red and white striped apron.

"Well, we've got to stop it! Richard started working on it as soon as he heard. We're both going to the meeting. And we'll definitely be organizing a protest. And a table, in town. To tell people, you know? This is how they get away with things like this; nobody knows about it until it's too late."

"I think that's a good idea," said the shopkeeper. "It really doesn't sound that pleasant, does it? Big factory like that. And we're in the middle of the greenbelt. They're not supposed to build here."

"Oh, they don't care, do they?" said the woman. She had long red hair and was wearing a cloche hat. Sarah saw a copy of the *Guardian* in her wire basket. "It's all about the money with them, isn't it? Pay off the right people, and you can put a tyre fire in the back garden at Buckingham Palace. Disgusting. Can I put a petition in the shop?"

"Fine by me," said the shopkeeper, a little absently. "See you later then, Maureen." Maureen, whoever she was, strode out of the shop, making the bells clang like old-fashioned fire alarms.

The shopkeeper turned to Sarah and pressed his hands together with a smile. "What can I do for you, love?" he said. The electric fly trap behind him buzzed.

"Just paying for these." She started unloading her groceries onto the counter.

The shopkeeper looked at her hard for a moment.

"I hope you don't mind me asking," he began. "Did you just move into Foxglove Cottage? Miss Trevelyan's old place?"

"Yes," said Sarah. She felt uncomfortable. Years of being in the family business had taught her to keep a low profile, and she didn't like being recognized anywhere, let alone somewhere she'd just arrived. This was not a good start. "I'm her great-niece."

"Makes sense," said the shopkeeper. "Pat, from down on Green Lane, with the dog, said someone had turned up last night in a cab. Don't imagine there's a lot of food lying around there after a couple of months. Dot Trevelyan was a tough old girl. Kept herself to herself, but she was always pleasant enough. When she was around."

Sarah mumbled thanks.

"I never really knew her," she managed, tapping her fingers rapidly on the counter. "I only met her once. When I was really small." *Before Gran and Auntie Dot* really *fell out.* "I don't really remember."

"Oh, I see." The man nodded sympathetically. "Long-lost relative kind of thing. Just here to put her things in order, are you?"

"Um." She was panicking now. "Yes. No. I don't know. She left me the house. I don't know how long I'm going to stay."

She just managed to avoid saying, *But I don't have anywhere else to go.*

"Oh, well, it's in a lovely part of the village. Very pretty place, too. Could really make something of that place. I mean, the outside. I've never been inside. Don't know anyone who ever has been, actually. Miss T. was rarely there and didn't hold much with visitors. Anyway, welcome to Crowsbrook. Although it's not the best time of the year to visit." He gestured outside. "Weather's just going to get worse for the next three or four months. Does nothing but rain, but we try to make the best of it. There's a Halloween party at the Scout Hut at the end of the month, though—mostly for the kids, but they put on a pig roast and have mulled cider for the grown-ups. You should come along. There'll be a lot of people there who knew your aunt. Thirteen pounds eighty-four, please."

Sarah nodded. She wanted to grab her shopping and run.

"Are you all right?" The man looked at her, concerned. "You look like it's all been a bit much for you."

"Yeah." She clenched her teeth. *Stupid, stupid, stupid.* "It's just been a crazy few days. Few months, really." *My house burned down and everything I own now fits in a suitcase. Except for the house that I own but that still feels like someone else's. Probably because it's full of someone else's stuff. Oh, and a shit-ton of spiders I don't know what to do with. And the forecast is for Ancient Evil with intermittent Awfulness. Terrible, isn't it?*

"Oh, dear. You do look like you've been having a hard time. Maybe a bit of fresh air'll do you good. Get you away from unpacking, for a start. I'd go for a walk if I were you. Supposed to be very good when you're feeling upset." He glanced outside again. "And it's not raining that much. If you've never been here before, you should go down to the Foxglove Pond. It's very pretty. Cracking in the spring, when the foxgloves are out. Must be thousands of them down there. All wild." He fished behind the counter and came up with a tattered but clean white towel, covered in pink roses. "They're finished now, of course, but there's a bench. You should go and have a nice sit-down in the fresh air. Before it gets too muddy. Wouldn't want to be out there in November, I can tell you."

Sarah took the towel.

"I'm Jake, by the way," said the shopkeeper. "Jake Pound. The wife's Rose. You should come round when you've got settled in, like. Have a bit of dinner."

"Thank you," said Sarah. She was panicking less now. Maybe she could stay under the radar by hiding in plain sight. That seemed to be what Auntie Dot had done. "You're very kind."

"Our pleasure," said Jake. "Got to all look out for each other."

Sarah tried to smile.

"Yeah," she said. "All got to look out for each other." She picked up her shopping and turned to leave and then stopped.

"Actually," she said. "I have a question. Do you have an empty jar I could take with me, please?"

Jake paused for a moment, thinking.

"Think so," he said. "Not in the shop; I'll have to go out back for a minute. The wife keeps 'em for putting jam in. She just made a big batch, but there might be one or two left over. You should take a jar or two of her jam," he added. "We don't sell them in the store; health and safety and all that. Good tombola prizes, though. Hold on." He disappeared through a curtain made of green and white plastic ribbons. "If anyone comes in," he hollered, "tell 'em I'll be back in a mo." There was a faint sound of footsteps and then everything went quiet.

I told him too much, thought Sarah.

The other voice in her mind came back clearly. The other voice that used to be Eleanor's. *You didn't tell him anything. And you're part of a family business. Your family have always kept their secrets, but they've never isolated themselves.*

I'm in a new place. I need to find out more.

You need to trust people again.

Sometimes, the other voice was so unlike her own, it was scary. But it was all in her head. Had to be.

Jake burst through the ribbons brandishing an empty Golden Shred jar. "This do?" he asked.

"Great," said Sarah, taking it from him and putting it in her bag. "Thanks." *Please don't let him ask what I want it for.*

"Happy to help," said Jake. "Rose was glad to get rid of it, actually; didn't want the spares cluttering up the house until the strawberries come in. Asked if you wanted to take the car off our hands as well; damn thing's been parked in the back garden since Alan—that's our son—got his new one; no one wants it. Awful old thing, it is."

Sarah thought about it for a moment. She'd never had a car.

"How awful?" she asked, looking at Jake intently.

"Come and see it, if you want," said Jake, with a shrug. He held the plastic ribbons aside and Sarah stepped through the doorway into the back of the shop.

"Straight through and out the back door," he said, from behind her. Sarah picked her way between flats of tinned tomatoes and dog food and macaroni and cheese, and a high stack of empty crates that smelled like cabbage; in a moment, she came to a plain door covered with chipped and peeling paint. She turned the handle and opened the door; after the dark of the passageway, even the dull October light made her blink.

And there it was. Sitting on a gravel path, in a small garden, surrounded by dormant raspberry bushes and mulched-over vegetable beds. A lime-green, slightly rusted Austin Allegro.

Sarah stepped toward it, enchanted.

No more buses. No more cabs. No more brats on trains.

"It's not pretty," said Jake. "But it runs all right. And it's built like a tank. They all were."

For the first time in a long while, Sarah felt like smiling.

"How much?" she said.

"I dunno," said Jake. "Hundred and seventy-five? It's got a full tank of petrol." He placed his hand on the bonnet. The passenger-side wing mirror fell off with a clunk. "Oh."

Sarah picked it up and turned it over in her hands. "Didn't break," she said. "Our lucky day."

"Make it a hundred and fifty," said Jake, with a shrug.

Sarah felt in her bag for the envelope her aunt had left for her.

"Cash all right?" she asked.

• • •

She still wanted to go to the Foxglove Pond, though. There was something she had to do. She paid Jake, and said she'd pick up the Allegro when she came back. She didn't plan to be long.

The Foxglove Pond was away from the main road—which was really only a two-lane country byway—down a footpath overgrown with moss. It was slippery, and the light was different here. The trees grew thick and close and the path twisted through them steeply downhill. Sarah lost her footing; a shower of stones bumped and tumbled in front of her. The leaves were falling and many of the naked branches of the trees reached toward the sky like—

Like arms reaching out from a burning building... The thought came unbidden.

She walked face first into a thin branch growing across the path and swore.

Down, down, down wound the path, until she reached the bottom, where the Foxglove Pond lay hidden in the gloom of the wood. The light burst in through a gap in the canopy of trees like a skylight and glittered on the water. The pond was large and still.

She looked down. The ground was covered with the sage-green leaves of foxglove plants beginning to moulder for the winter. *Digitalis purpurea.* Good for the heart.

Dead Man's Bells, they used to call it, she remembered her grandmother saying. *Bloody Fingers, in Scotland. Put one of those bells on your finger, it looks like—*

Jake had been right. It was very pretty. And very quiet. Sarah spread the towel on a fallen tree trunk that someone had planed down until it was flat, to make a seat. She sat down.

Take care of the spiders.

The branches whipped and creaked over her head.

"And I have many curious things to show when you are there."
Like arms reaching from the flames...
The flames...

Once, when she was about four or five, Billy, the cat that lived with them (her grandmother had told Sarah never to refer to a cat as *her* cat), had run away and hadn't come back for three days. On the evening of the fourth day, they had heard a scratching at the back door. Sarah opened it and screamed. It was Billy, but he was a mess. One of his back legs was obviously broken, and he was covered in blood. He mewed gently as Sarah cried, and he died quietly while she was petting his head. He looked exhausted, as though he had crawled a long way after the accident had happened, whatever it was. Her grandmother looked sad and said that he had probably been hit by a car.

"Sarah," she said. "It's horrible, but you better get used to it. There's a lot of sadness that comes with the family business."

Like the Mafia, Sarah thought later. *Except if you're in the Mafia, no one thinks you're certifiable.*

No wonder Gran and Auntie Dot had mostly kept to themselves. She missed Eleanor.

A large bird—a crow—taking off behind Sarah startled her out of her reverie; it flapped upwards through the thick brush. She shivered.

One for sorrow.

She got up and pulled her coat more tightly around her. Then she took the jar out of her shopping bag and knelt down by the pond and filled it, before screwing the lid on tightly and beginning the long trek up the hill and back to the village shop to pick up her new car.

• • •

Auntie Dot had been nothing if not organized. Aside from the spice rack, one cupboard in the kitchen—one *large* cupboard in the kitchen—was devoted to the family business.

Sarah found a large plain glass bowl and a black velvet tablecloth, which was wrapped around an old-fashioned looking glass. After piling her aunt's papers on the floor beside her, she spread the cloth over the table in the living room and placed the looking glass on top of it. She then poured the water from the pond into the bowl and put the bowl on the mirror. She lit a candle and sat down to wait.

At first, all she could see was the reflection of the book-shelves in the dark surface of the water. She focused on her breathing, making it deep and regular.

Connect. She could almost hear her grandmother's voice. *Connect, Sarah.*

She made her mind go blank. All that existed was her breathing and the smooth reflection of the water. And then—

Trees. Hundreds of trees with their roots torn up. The heart ripped out of the Earth.

Sobbing. A woman sobbing. No. Not a woman; a girl. And blood.

A pattern, whirling before her, coalescing into strange blobby flowers, red, blue, and black on green.

Hair caught on tree branches.

Weeping. She could hear weeping.

Flies. So many flies.

And then a face; a terrible face, distorted. No. Not distorted. Disfigured. Broken. Caved in. Twisted. And she knew that it was coming, coming for her.

She drew her breath sharply and the images vanished. The water in the bowl sloshed at the sides.

Scrying was a bit of an art, her grandmother always said. It wouldn't give you any answers, but it would tell you what to look out for. And between the pictures and the spiders, well, it was pretty damn clear that something was very wrong.

Or rather, that it was about to be.

Dorothea was right. Something was coming. Something bad. She needed to find someone else—someone local—and ask what was going on. And as pleasant as Jake had been, he wouldn't have any answers for her.

Luckily, she knew where she could find someone else.

• • •

Mr. Bastable, the leader of the council, coughed testily and shuffled the sheaf of papers on the desk in front of him. There was a large fly buzzing next to the window. *Trying to get out, the little bugger*, thought Mr. Bastable. The insect—the buzzing— was annoying him beyond belief. He could barely concentrate on what the man in front of him was saying.

The past few days had all been a bit of whirl. Everyone was in a rush these days. The man in front of him had con- tacted him for an emergency meeting of the planning council. It seemed highly irregular, but the chap had produced a sheaf of paperwork—most of which seemed to have the council's own logo on the top of it—that had shown that everything was in order and the meeting could go ahead. It didn't seem quite right, but the papers were all there. It had given him a headache.

The letters swam in front of him, but the fellow had argued very convincingly. *Very* convincingly. Although Mr. Bastable could have sworn there was something a bit odd about him, he couldn't put his finger on what it was.

And now here they were. "Just a formality," the man had said.

Greenbelt, development, factory, so what?

Mr. Bastable's mind kept sliding off the topic at hand. He had indigestion and wanted a cup of peppermint tea and a nap. What was it about this chap that wasn't right?

He brushed the thought aside. What was the fellow saying now? Something about the factory. Damn that fly to hell. A maggot factory. There'd be hundreds of the little bleeders everywhere. The fly caught the light for a moment and turned a brilliant, iridescent green. Unusual. Never seen anything like that before, Mr. Bastable hadn't. It was as if he were trying to hear the man from another room: he was listening hard, and occasionally would catch a word or a phrase, but mostly, the words were just out of reach.

Sharp bugger, probably. Immaculate suit. Probably Italian. Mr. Bastable had heard things about men who wore Italian suits.

Factory, jobs, yes, yes, yes. Well, it wasn't as if there was anything else for the kids to do in this town. They all either moved away or got jobs at Tesco. But a factory...it would be like in the old days. Bring a little life back to the town. Give the kids a chance. Bloody kids. Do them good, a bit of hard work in a factory. Even a maggot factory.

He wished someone would let the fly out.

"Well," he said sharply. "Process is process, but I think this all seems in order. Let's move on, shall we?"

The man in the possibly-Italian suit smiled.

"As you say, sir," he said. He proffered an official-looking form. "If you could just sign here."

. . .

It had been dark for hours when Sarah left her cottage and followed the signs to the village church. It was an ancient stone building, with a crenellated tower, perched on top of a hill; in the moonlight, it looked like a small castle, albeit one defended only by a waist-high, ivy-covered wall. The churchyard was full of yew trees; their thick foliage blocked out most of the light and made it difficult to see anything beyond the outline of a few crooked headstones. Not fresh graves either, if the angles of the monuments were anything to go by.

She thought, briefly, of her great-aunt, buried next to her sister, Sarah's grandmother, down in Cornwall.

Okay. Here we go.

She knocked three times on the post of the lych-gate and entered the churchyard. The church had been built according to the old ways, on an east-west axis, and Sarah headed to its left, to the north side.

They're afraid of the north side. She could hear her grandmother's voice. *They used to bury the outsiders there. Strangers. Stillborns. Suicides. The ones they had cast out of the Church. The poor.*

It was also the side furthest away from the road. Bonus.

She found a space between the graves, spread a black bin bag on the ground (no sense in trying to concentrate with a wet bum), pulled a large kitchen knife out of her bag, and used it to draw a circle around herself in the grass on the ground. She took some herbs from a small pouch and sprinkled them around the circle, and then lit a small charcoal disk with a cigarette lighter, and dropped it into the censer she'd taken from her aunt's altar. She dropped a few resin-like beads onto the charcoal, and they began to smoke furiously.

She knocked three times on the ground. Her knuckles made a wet, squelchy sound.

"I'd like to speak to the Watcher," she said, loudly and clearly.

Sarah's grandmother had never been one for elaborate chants and incantations, preferring, on the rare occasions she'd had to summon spirits, to call them up with a sharp "Hey!" Sarah, being in a new place, figured that a modicum of politeness couldn't hurt. Besides, it was like calling a customer service helpline. You never knew who you were going to get. You just had to hope you didn't reach someone with an inflated power complex and a grudge against humankind.

A chilly breeze whistled through the churchyard. Sarah shuddered and knocked again.

"I'd like to speak to the Watcher, please," she repeated. She closed her eyes and hoped everything was working properly.

"Well," said a voice. "What do you want?"

An elderly man stood before her; he looked perfectly normal except he was devoid of all colour, as if he'd stepped out of a black-and-white movie. He was also—if Sarah looked hard—slightly translucent. He was dressed in a raincoat, a striped pullover, and corduroy trousers and supported himself with a walking stick. There was a tweed cap on his head. Sarah could see what was left of his hair through it.

"You're the Churchyard Watcher."

"As of three weeks ago," said the man. "Eternal rest, my arse."

"It's only for a while," said Sarah.

"Bollocks." The man coughed. "This is a *young person's* job. People used to die a lot younger."

"Yes." She hoped to keep this interview as short as possible; she didn't think many people would be walking their dogs through the churchyard in the middle of the night, but you never knew. "I'm sorry to hear you're not enjoying it."

"It's death," said the old man. "Are you supposed to?"

Sarah sighed. "Look, I have a couple of questions. I need help. I need *your* help."

"Oh." He looked at her more closely. "Are you any relation to Dottie Trevelyan? Family business and all that?"

"Yes, I'm her great-niece. Sarah."

"Edgar Badgerley," said the old man. "It's very nice to meet you." He didn't sound as though he meant it. "I had no idea," he went on. "When I was alive, I mean. About the business. No wonder she kept to herself."

"Is she there?" asked Sarah. "Because I could really—"

"If you're in the family business," said Mr. Badgerley, "you know the rules. There's ways to get in touch with your relatives on the other side. This isn't one of them." He sniffed. "I do have a job to do, you know."

"I know," said Sarah. "You're a link between the human world and the immortals. And you've been in Crowsbrook for a lot longer than I have; I only arrived yesterday. That's why I came to you. Have you noticed anything out of the ordinary in the past two months?"

Mr. Badgerley gave her a withering look.

"For the first five weeks of the past two months," he said, drily, "I was in palliative care. Didn't get out much. The past three weeks? I'm still getting used to what's ordinary and what isn't."

"Yes," said Sarah. "I understand. But—I mean—no one's said anything? No one's commented?"

Mr. Badgerley sighed.

"Rules are rules. It's not my job to be a messenger between the dead and the living. I look after the churchyard and attend to the needs of the dead. It's like being a bouncer and a waiter all in one. I'm eighty-three, you know." He coughed. "Was."

Sarah clenched her teeth. "Please? I'm not asking for specific messages. Just rumours. Anything strange."

Mr. Badgerley looked hard at her.

"Well," he said eventually. "Dottie Trevelyan was a good woman, even if she was a... well. If you're in the family business, I suppose it's a little different."

Sarah waited.

"They say," Mr. Badgerley began, "that there are a lot more spiders in the churchyard than there ever were before."

He stepped over to the nearest yew tree, illuminating the dark branches with soft light. Sarah gasped. The branches were thick with cobwebs.

"Never seen anything like this. I don't know if that's what you mean."

"That would—that would—yes," said Sarah. "That would count. As strange."

"The only *other* thing," said Mr. Badgerley, " is—well, I suppose you'd call it gossip. Hearsay. And I don't know much about what's going on. Being the new boy and all." He paused to wipe his nose with a spotted handkerchief. "The only other thing has to do with...well—" he pointed "—look for yourself. Over there."

Sarah squinted. It was hard to make out where he was pointing in the darkness.

"What am I looking for?" she asked.

"In the corner," said Mr. Badgerley. "*Luckily*, it's not obvious."

Sarah stood and took a couple of steps in the direction the Watcher was pointing and peered into the darkness. The stones in the corner looked oldest of all. The names and dates on them had mostly been worn away by centuries of weather. But the smallest one, in the corner—

Her eyes grew wide.

The gravestone in the corner had cracked from top to bottom. It was a new crack: the edges were sharp.

And it was covered in blood. As if the stone had split and bled.

Sarah gasped.

"What happened there?" she said.

Mr. Badgerley sighed. "Not only are rules rules," he said, "but this is the north side. Which is not populated by people who played by the rules in life." He pulled a spotted handkerchief out of his pocket and blew his nose. "Good grief, it's colder up here than I remember."

"Someone's trying to get a message through," said Sarah. "Against the rules. Which means it's likely about something important and probably dangerous."

"I don't know about that." He glared at her. "The churchyard is a bit isolated, to tell you the truth."

"It's a closed circuit," said Sarah. "Consecrated ground. Deliberately set apart; very few beings can cross the boundaries. Except mortals, of course. *I know all this.* Can you help me, or not?"

Mr. Badgerley wiped his nose again with the spotted handkerchief. "You're in quite the rush, missy," he said. "If I were talking to the only person who could help me, I'd be a bit more polite."

Sarah pushed her hair out of her face.

"I'm sorry," she said. "But I have about as many spiders living upstairs in one room in my house."

"If you wish to live and thrive..." said Mr. Badgerley.

"I know," said Sarah. "So it worries me that they're... hiding."

"Hiding?" He folded his handkerchief and put it back in his pocket.

"What would you call it?" said Sarah. "Where are they clustering? On consecrated ground and in a cottage that's belonged to w—" She checked herself. "To a family business, for centuries."

"Spiders are predators," said Mr. Badgerley.

"They're also sensitive," said Sarah. "To—bad vibrations." It was the least terrifying way to put it.

"Well, you're in a better position to find out what's afoot than I am," said Mr. Badgerley. "What with me being stuck in the bloody churchyard and all. Oh, and being *dead*. Can I go now? They'll be wondering where I've got to, if I'm much longer. And causing all sorts of trouble, no doubt."

Sarah left open the question of how much trouble dead people in a churchyard could get up to.

"Oh," she said. "Yes. Of course." She drew a complicated sigil in the smoke with her finger. "Thank you," she said, as Mr. Badgerley faded from view.

Gone.

Gone.

Maybe it wasn't true.

She hoped it wasn't true. But her instincts—

The first thing to do was to get home and start reading. Dot knew about the spiders; she must have left more notes than she'd put in the letter. Sarah pulled the knife out of the ground and threw it in her bag, along with the censer, the incense, and the cigarette lighter, traced the shape of the circle anticlockwise with her finger, muttering a few words under her breath and turned to go.

She froze.

Standing behind one of the yew trees was a teenage girl. Late teens, by the look of her. Her eyes were wide and she looked…well. Three words sprang immediately to mind.

Ferocious. Terrified. And *dangerous.*

Sarah felt as though her stomach had dropped through the floor.

You can bluff your way out of this one, she told herself. But she wasn't sure she could. So much for hiding in plain sight.

She slung her bag over her shoulder and started striding toward the lych-gate. The girl stepped in front of her, and dropped an army-green bag covered in felt-pen doodles on the ground.

"You were just talking to Mr. Badgerley." She was breathing heavily. "I saw you."

"I don't know what you're talking about," said Sarah. She tried to duck around the girl, but the kid was agile, marking her like a player on a netball court. *Damn it.*

"You were talking to an old man," said the girl. "In a rain-coat. And a stripy jumper. And a tweed cap."

"Get lost," said Sarah, looking the girl squarely in the face. "I can talk to who I want."

"Yes. Yes, you can. Normally. Anyone can. But you were talking to Mr. Badgerley, and he's been dead for three weeks now, and you can't normally do that. And normally, if anyone else were to tell me that this happened, I'd tell them to get lost myself, because normally, you can't talk to dead people. So what I want I want to know is *what the FUCK is going on?"*

Chapter 4

Sarah stared at the girl, and then started walking again.

"I'm going home," she said. "Get out of my way." She could feel the panic rising again. She was losing her touch. First the conversation with Jake in the shop, and now this. But this was much worse. This—

This was outing the family business. She hoped that telling the teenager to piss off would be enough.

It wasn't. The girl started following her.

"Who *are* you?"

"None of your business." Sarah was beginning to get irritated. It was bad that she'd been seen—*what kid takes a shortcut through a graveyard at eleven o'clock on a school night?*—and she just wanted to get back to the cottage and think.

Probably some teenage freak who thinks she's a vampire. She snorted internally.

Don't worry about the kid. Eleanor's voice. *A little dreamwork will take care of it. Give her nightmares for a week and she'll just assume it was something she ate and won't know what was real and what was her imagination. Because those types have a hell of an imagination.*

But Eleanor wasn't here. The girl grabbed Sarah's arm.

"Look," she said, "what you did back there just isn't—"

No, *you* look," said Sarah sharply. She stopped and turned to look the girl in the face for the first time. "What I do is my business, not yours. And I don't have to explain it to any random *Twilight* fan with an incense burner and an industrial supply of eyeliner in her handbag. Go home. Go to bed. Forget you ever saw me. You won't see me again."

Well, that was a bit of a risk, in a village this small. But it was pretty dark. She'd only counted one street light in the village so far and the moon had ducked behind a thick layer of cloud.

"I'm not *like* that." Dear gods, was the kid starting up again? "I *know* people like that. I know people who would give their right arms and their crystal collection to see what I've just seen. But I'm not one of those people. I'm a scientist."

"You can't be a scientist. You're fifteen."

"I'm seventeen."

"You're annoying me either way." They were heading toward the village square now.

" I don't want to tell," said the girl, quietly. "I just want to *know*."

Sarah covered her face with her hands. This was the worst-case scenario. She'd blown her cover completely.

• • •

"So how did you do it?" Jez asked, when they were back at Sarah's cottage. Jez hadn't taken her coat off; she was sitting in the elderly, lace-covered armchair hunched over in her overcoat and socks. She was still shaking.

It was a trick. It *had* to have been a trick. No one could talk to the dead and get a response. Dead people—she had to stop herself thinking the word *ghosts*—didn't get up and walk around, in any form. It was biologically impossible. She had listed the many reasons why in her head on the way to the cottage. No heartbeat. No circulation. No neural activity. Decomposition. She stopped when she realized that cataloguing it was ridiculous.

"It doesn't matter how I did it." Sarah's voice jerked her back into the present. Her syllables were terse. Whoever this woman was, noted Jez, she didn't talk much.

She decided to try to be friendly. "I don't know your name. You didn't tell me. I'm Jez, by the way."

Sarah glared at her. "Sarah," she said. "Don't tell a soul."

"Okay, Sarah. If it doesn't matter how you did it, *why* were you doing it? What do you call it?"

"Jesus, kid, you ask a lot of questions."

"I'm a science nerd," said Jez. "I don't like things I can't explain."

"Then you'd better get used to not liking a lot of science," said Sarah. "Most of quantum physics, for example."

"They can explain more of quantum physics than most people think," said Jez. "Except it gets used by people who have no idea what it's about to explain things that are impossible. You know," she went on, "like *ghosts*." *Damn it.* There was that word. "Why were you talking to Mr. Badgerley? How was that even possible? You know, if you'd told me this afternoon I'd have seen a ghost tonight, I would have laughed my arse off. I don't believe in ghosts."

"Then why are you here?"

"I *told* you. I don't like things I can't explain. And you seem to think it's perfectly normal to talk to dead people. And I can't explain that, either. Normally, I'd assume you were bonkers. It's the most logical explanation. Except I actually saw you talking to a bloke I knew was dead. And I know *I'm* not bonkers."

"All teenagers are bonkers."

"That's a hormonal imbalance. Basically, our brains start rewiring at the age of about ten or eleven and don't really straighten themselves out until we're in our early twenties. It actually sounds a lot more radical that it is. Usually, it's just our ability to assess the emotions of others that are affected."

"Ah," said Sarah. "So you can't tell when you're, say, driving a complete stranger up the pole."

"Exactly," said Jez. She grinned. "It's really useful in that regard."

Sarah sighed and glared at her. "You're persistent," she said. "I'll give you that."

"Thanks," said Jez. She took a deep breath to begin her interrogation again, but felt a lump rising swiftly in her throat. She burst into tears, to her own surprise and Sarah's horror.

• • •

"Whoa," said Sarah. "Whoa. Calm down. Chill out." For a brief moment, she wondered if kids even said "chill out" anymore, but there was a sobbing teenager in her living room and she knew that the proper thing to do was to deal with her first: make her stop crying and then get her out of the house, although the crying fit would delay the latter by—God—*minutes* at least. She scanned the room hurriedly and retrieved a box of tissues that was perched on the edge of one of the bookshelves. It had pictures of pink starburst lilies on it, on a blue background. Sarah pulled a tissue out of the top and held it out to Jez with a stiff arm. "Do you want a tissue?"

Jez took it without saying a word. She kept sobbing.

"I'll put the kettle on," said Sarah. It was a cliché, she thought, but she thanked whatever gods might be listening for providing something handy to do in a crisis. "We'll have a nice cup of tea. Warm up, after being in that drafty churchyard." A heavy sob suggested to her that talking about the churchyard might not be the best thing to do, so she scurried into the kitchen to fill her great-aunt's heavy stovetop kettle and put it on the hob. A spider dangled from the spout; she removed it carefully and put it on the countertop. It scuttled away.

NOW what? What are you going to do now?

It's fine. It'll be fine. If she tells her friends what she saw, they'll think she's crazy; if she tells any adults, they'll assume she's seeking attention.

There's still a weeping teenager in your living room. Two weeks of nightmares isn't going to cut it anymore. I'm FUCKED.

The whistle of the kettle brought her back to the moment. The sobbing from the other room seemed to have subsided a bit. Sarah dug two mismatched china mugs out of the cupboard, threw in some teabags, and poured the hot water over them. They hissed and bubbled as the air in them escaped.

"Milk and sugar?" she said, sticking her head back into the living room. Jez was curled up in the armchair, her arms around a tatty red scatter cushion, her face buried.

"Milk," she said. Even through the cushion, her voice was thick with moisture. "No sugar. Thank you."

Sarah ducked back into the kitchen for a moment and came out with the mugs.

"Here we are!" she announced, in a voice so cheery it bordered on the psychotic. "Nothing a nice cup of tea won't help."

Jesus. Can you hear yourself? Going for Girl Guide Leader of the Year, are we?

Still, the girl seemed to have calmed down a lot. Jez took the tea and glared at Sarah.

"Thanks," she said. She stared into the middle distance ahead of her.

Sarah was beginning to lose her patience again.

"So," she said. "Is this one of those mood swings that teen-agers are also known for? Attack of the killer hormones, something like that?"

Jez said nothing.

"What's this all about, then?"

"You've ruined everything," said Jez. Her voice was sullen.

"I—what?"

"You ruined *everything!*" Jez was almost shouting now. "Before I saw you in the graveyard, I had a pretty good idea of what was what. What there was evidence for. What could be proven scientifically. And talking to dead people makes no sense. And there's no evidence for it. I tried to take a picture, but—"

"Your phone battery died." Sarah finished the sentence.

"So that's an actual thing too?"

"Kid, are you the only person who's never seen a ghost-hunting show?" Sarah was genuinely surprised.

"I thought they were *fake!*" wailed Jez. "I didn't think they were *real!*"

"They're not," said Sarah. "Mostly."

"Then *what is real?*"

Sarah took a deep breath and sipped from the mug. It was green and white, with a picture of a cat on it. The tea was strong and scalding.

Her grandmother had been clear. Never, ever tell anyone about the family business. About the other world that existed alongside of the world you could see. Never. Full stop.

"They can't handle it, Sarah," she'd said. "Not anymore. They've forgotten how to deal with it, and they can't measure it, or quantify it, or prove it'll do what they say. You have to keep it a secret."

Sarah had only broken the rules once. She had told Eleanor. And she had paid for that mistake. They both had.

She looked again at Jez's bag. Jez's green bag with the doodles on it. Then she frowned.

The doodles looked familiar.

It was a pattern of red and blue and black blobby...flowers?
Whatever they were, they were really stylized. But she'd seen the
pattern before.

Dot believed that an evil so powerful was coming that it
justified breaking the rules by which her family had survived for
centuries. She had known about the fire. She had known about
Eleanor. And she had seen everything in the water and the
looking glass—the same glass that Sarah had used.

The pattern that Sarah was looking at was the same one
she'd seen in the water from the Foxglove Pond. And if there
was something else her grandmother had taught her, it was
never to ignore a sign.

This girl was important. Somehow.

Was it enough?

"What's that?" said Sarah. "On your bag. Those flowers.
Did you draw those yourself?"

Jez gave her a withering look and sniffed.

"They're not *flowers*," she said. "They're *atoms*. It's called
digitalis. It was discovered by this doctor in the eighteenth century; one of his patients had a bad heart and he was all out of
ideas, but the patient took this folk remedy from a plant and
got better." She blew her nose again. "I'm going to be a doctor. I
drew it on my bag as a reminder that if you want to help people
and you're all out of options, sometimes you have to take a risk
and hope it works out."

"Yes," said Sarah. "Sometimes you do. And sometimes it
doesn't. That bloke lucked out."

She made up her mind right then.

"Everything you could believe in before is still real," she said. "Nothing has changed. The laws of physics still apply. The laws of common sense still apply. Most psychics are frauds. People who think crystals can cure terminal illness are flakes. The future is incredibly difficult to predict accurately. But there are other things—"

She paused. There was no going back now.

"There are other things that are older. Ancient—*ways* of doing things. Like folk remedies, in a way. But they have their own sets of rules. And that's what you're dealing with here."

"How come no one knows about them?"

"They used to," said Jez. "But why do you need to know that the churchyard is protected by a Watcher when computerized dissection and donor programs in anatomy schools have put grave-robbers right out of business? Why do you need to know that ghosts exist when you can be scared of global warming and international terrorism and Rupert Murdoch? People learn to focus on other things, especially once they're less likely to drop dead from plague, the common cold, or a cut that went a bit funny." She took another sip of her tea. "But there are still monsters under the bed, whether you believe in them or not."

"People are stupid," said Jez. Her voice was angry.

"People feel like they have no control over their lives," said Sarah. "Superstition is mostly a series of rituals designed to give people the illusion that they have some control over the completely random things that happen to them."

"Does it work? These *rituals* or whatever. Are you trying to tell me that they actually work?"

"It depends," said Sarah. "And it's a long story and it's late and I don't feel like getting into it. The short answer is that there are more things in heaven and Earth than are dreamt of in your philosophy, as a smart guy once said. And the laws of physics remain unchanged. So be good, eat your greens, wear your wellies, and mind you own business: it's the recipe for a nice life. You go back to dealing with science and I'll deal with my stuff." *And you can bet your arse that I'll be more careful in future.* "What the hell were you doing in a churchyard past eleven on a school night, anyway? Not to sound like your mother."

"My mother's dead," said Jez. Her voice was flat now. "I was going home. I was visiting Sam. My friend."

"Boyfriend?"

"*Friend.* Sam's gay, not that it's any of your business. We were doing homework."

Jez kept staring. *Bloody kids,* thought Sarah.

"It's late," she said. "And it's Wednesday. You should probably get going. Don't you have school tomorrow?"

• • •

Jez got up wordlessly and put her empty mug down. "Thanks for the tea," she said. "Thanks for explaining everything." She realized as she said it that Sarah had actually explained very little.

"No worries," said Sarah. "You understand, of course, that you can't tell anyone about this." It wasn't a request.

"Yeah, whatever." She stood and picked up the green bag.

Sarah looked at the bag thoughtfully. "You've lived here for a long time, right?" she said.

"All my life," said Jez. "And it bites. I'm leaving next autumn."

"Do me a favour, will you? Let me know if anything weird happens?"

Jez glared at her. "What's weird? You mean like the whole churchyard thing?"

"Let it go," said Sarah, sharply. "I mean anything else out of the ordinary. People acting oddly. Weird things happening. Anything you can't explain without stretching or bending reality."

"There won't be," said Jez. "Nothing ever happens around here. It's dead."

"I can tell you're looking forward to leaving," said Sarah. "And good luck. But please. Do me a favour. Keep an eye out."

Jez looked at Sarah, who looked tired and deadly serious.

"Why?" she asked.

"It's late," said Sarah. "I don't want to get into it right now. It's probably nothing," she lied, "but it's really important." *Probably never see the kid again*, she thought. She stole another glance at the atoms drawn on the green bag. There was a long pause.

"Okay," said Jez. "I'll keep you posted. But don't hold your breath."

She left the cottage and went home, but she couldn't sleep.

• • •

The next day, the bell for lunch drilled through Jez's head like a demonic alarm clock.

The corridor outside the chemistry lab erupted into chaos as teenagers spilled out of classrooms and headed toward their form rooms and the cafeteria. Jez clutched her folder tightly to her chest and cut through them like an icebreaker. There were some advantages to being in your final year. You knew a lot about how the currents flowed.

She was headed directly for the Year Thirteen common room, going to get a seat in the corner, maybe catch up on some lost sleep before a triple period of biology in the afternoon. An old nursery rhyme came into her head:

From ghoulies and ghosties and long-legged beasties
And things that go bump in the night
May the Good Lord deliver us.

Was it a nursery rhyme or a prayer?

Yesterday she hadn't believed in any of that stuff. Today— Well. Today was another day.

Buggered if I start using crystals to improve my exam results, though, she thought.

She was at the common room door now. *Well,* she thought as she opened it, *whatever bogies exist out there, I'm still not at Hogwarts.*

The common room was basically a classroom that had been given over to the Year Thirteens as a kind of study space and (not acknowledged) chill-out area for between classes and lunch times, so they didn't have to study in the library with Mickey Amble and his crew flicking spitballs and gum and other things that you didn't want to know about at the nearest table within range.

She opened the door.

Harry Potter it wasn't.

The common room was painted in flamingo orange and was filled with spare classroom chairs on their last legs and tables that had been considered too dilapidated for everyday school use, but had briefly passed through the art room on the way to their final resting place, and were consequently covered in dribbles of ink and paint and the occasional smear of encrusted oil pastel, which would ruin either your sleeves or your coursework, or both, if you weren't careful. The elderly sofa in the corner was the prime spot for sleeping, reading, or throwing yourself in despair, if you were Holly Cooper and trying to out-Goth Marina Butterworth, Goth Queen of Arden High. One wall had been covered in film posters by Brian Kirby and a democratic majority of his arty film buff mates; the poster for *The Pillow Book* was covered with graffiti by Alex Appleton and a democratic majority of her Marxist feminist friends. There was a leak in the ceiling, under which Jo Whitley, editor of the school magazine, had placed a red plastic bucket, brought from home.

It was the coolest place on the school grounds. And right now the couch was free. *Thank Christ.* She strode across the room and staked her spot, sinking into the soft cushions. Mrs. Jarsdel, the head of the Maths Department, had donated it to the Year Thirteen common room a good six years ago. It had been almost worn out then, and had taken some hard knocks since. Eva Norton had patched up the upholstery before leaving to pursue a brief career as a model (no one had seen or heard of her for years) and now it was perfectly formed for lounging or catching up on sleep. Jez closed her eyes.

"Jez!"

Well, that lasted a long time.

She opened her eyes again. It was Cat. Cat Greenwood, eco-crusader, flyer queen and Jez's best-friend-who-wasn't-Sam. Oh, and biology partner, although where Jez aspired to expand the limits of human knowledge, Cat was mostly studying biology in search of things to save. She had a pile of flyers in her right hand now. "Are you free on Saturday? It's really important."

Whatever pro-environment event Cat was organizing was always "really important." But, Jez allowed, in scientific terms, she usually had a point, even if it was generally beaten into you with a power play of manipulative emotion.

"I dunno," said Jez. "Depends how much work I get done. What's it for?"

"It's dis-*gus*-ting," said Cat, with force. "Some property development firm wants to build a factory right on the edge of Crowsbrook. It's prime greenbelt land and it's not zoned for industry. I don't even know how they managed to get this far, but the notices are up. And it's totally gross, too. It's going to cause air pollution and it's going to stink for *miles* around. It's absolutely *appalling*."

"Well, if it's greenbelt land, it shouldn't get very far," said Jez. "I haven't done geography in a couple of years, but even I know that."

"It's a *total* mystery," said Cat. "They probably paid off the council or something. We have to mount a legal challenge."

"What with—our pocket money?"

"I'm *serious*, Jez." Cat's wide eyes showed that she was, indeed, not kidding around. "My dad's working on it already." Cat's dad was a lawyer who had made a ridiculous amount of money in corporate law before meeting Cat's mother, who had been chained to a tree at the time. (Cat had skipped school for a week when *that* little gem came out.) He'd had what he referred to as "a spiritual epiphany," and had immediately started working pro bono for whichever environment groups had a solid case. Rather than rebelling against her parents, Cat seemed to be trying to outdo them. "We have a table on the high street from nine until six on Saturday. Mr. Williams is coming and every-thing; my mum phoned him last night and he was all outraged and stuff. Can you come for a bit? Say, between one and six?"

Jez groaned inwardly and glanced through the flyer that Cat proffered. The case seemed pretty clear cut: one thing Cat's father was known for was being rock-solid with his facts. Cat was right: it was mystifying how it had ever got this far in a town that seemed otherwise wholly dedicated to fossilising itself, after all the fun had been dried out of it. But that was a whole Saturday. Half a weekend, plus homework time...ugh. Still, it was really messed up.

It couldn't happen, though. There was no way. She looked at the map on the back of the flyer, showing where they wanted to put the development. It would be almost at the edge of her village.

Her village.

She remembered how much she hated the place.

This wasn't good, though. She looked at the flyer again. It didn't seem to make any sense.

"*Pleeeeeeeeeease?*" said Cat. "You're much better than I am at explaining the science to people so they can't argue back. We *need* you, Jez."

Well, there went Saturday.

"Okay," Jez said. Her voice was full of reluctance, but Cat hooted anyway.

"Yes! Thanks, Jez," she said. "This totally counts as 'maintaining the biosphere.'" It was one of the catchphrases of Mr. Williams, their biology teacher, who was a firm favourite throughout the upper school, although most students were as terrified by him as they were fascinated by his classes. He'd been to a few of Cat's protests before, as well. "Can you bring Sam?" Cat continued. "Can you rope him into it?"

"I'll see what I can do," said Jez, already knowing the answer. Sam hated protests and demos, but if it meant he could get out of spending a Saturday afternoon on a muddy field watching Arden United lose with his father, he'd sign up like a shot. "Oh," she went on, looking at the glass-panelled classroom door, and watching her chances of grabbing forty winks disappear like smoke in the air, "speak of the Devil."

Sam waved frantically at her through the glass window of the common room door. Despite having been born a scant three weeks after Jez, he had managed to time it so that he was in the school year below her; consequently, her common room would be off-limits to him until the following year, when she would be long gone. She sighed and, with a huge effort, hauled herself off the blissful comfort of the couch. By the time she'd crossed the room, her spot had been filled by Marina Butterworth, *Dracula* in one hand, cheek in the other, her long dyed-black hair falling in disarray over her shoulders.

"I need a cigarette," said Sam, as soon as she opened the door. "Let's go. Wow, you look like shit. Are you okay?"

"I love you too," said Jez, glaring at him. "I'm fine. I just didn't get much sleep. Hey, wanna spend your Saturday handing out flyers for Cat?"

"My God, *totally*. Her timing is perfect. Arden are playing Ashworth's Grove and the forecast is for steady drizzle. What is it this time?"

Jez handed him a flyer.

"A *maggot* factory?" said Sam. He gave the flyer back to her. "*Gross*."

• • •

It was at three-fifteen that the lack of sleep really hit her. The lab was warm and quiet, and its sweet, almost sickly smell of formaldehyde and plants, and (today) a residual hint of Mickey Amble and his twelve-year-old chaos agents, was like an unpleasant sedative. Jez could hear a large fly buzzing against the window. Her eyes felt heavy, and a couple of times, she felt her head jerk forward as she slipped into unconsciousness for a microsecond. Mr. Williams's voice was soothing and even; he was talking about the finer points of gas exchange (oh, if Mickey Amble could have been there) and paced up and down, as was his custom, on the raised platform behind the bench at the front of the lab. There was a running joke around the school that by the time he retired, Mr. Williams would have worn a groove behind the bench so deep that the front row would only be able to see the top of his head. But although retirement couldn't be more than seven or eight years away at most (to most of the students, Mr. Williams was impossibly old) he showed no signs of slowing his pace or, God forbid, of wishing to sit down while he was lecturing. Jez made a mental note to read up on gas exchange after the class. She had given up on taking notes for the afternoon and was focused on trying to stay awake.

"Sir," interrupted a voice two benches behind her, "can I let that fly out of the window? It's really bothering me." Mr. Williams's students knew better than to ask if they could kill flies in his classroom—that kind of request was likely to be accompanied by a fifteen-minute lecture on the necessity of all forms of life, especially insects, in an ecosystem, plus an extra take-home essay on the subject, even at A-level. Mr. Williams believed strongly in teachable moments.

"Get used to it," muttered Cat from beside Jez. "There'll be a lot more of them if they start building maggot factories left, right, and centre in the neighbourhood."

Mr. Williams stopped his habitual pacing back and forth behind the bench. He turned slowly and looked at Cat and Jez with the hard stare he usually reserved for the likes of first-years who giggled during the reproduction class. The stare was legendary. It could stop Mickey Amble and his mates in their tracks. Even the older kids were wary of it, although by the time they were in Year Thirteen, most of them knew enough not to do anything that would carry the slightest risk of it falling upon them. Cat, who had been one of Mr. Williams's best students since she started high school, stared back, open-mouthed.

"Did you say something, Miss Greenwood?" Mr. Williams asked, in a voice that could cut steel.

Jez looked at Cat. Her friend's jaw still hung open, and she was in a wide-eyed state that was more shock than panic.

"I'm waiting, Miss Greenwood."

Jez couldn't bear it any longer. "She said there'd be a lot more flies around if they build this maggot factory that's planned in the greenbelt land up by Crowsbrook. Except they probably won't, because—"

"I'm not interested in your opinions, Miss Elliot, and I didn't ask you." Mr. Williams was almost snarling. "The factory is an important facility, and represents a much-needed opportunity to improve the economic situation of the area. Do you know how many jobs will be created, how much wealth will be generated, from that single facility?"

Cat was still gobsmacked. Jez stared, mouth open.

"There's a lot of money in maggots?" she managed, eventually. "Who buys maggots? Apart from fishermen and possibly hospitals with a lot of gangrene patients?"

"Anglers," muttered Cat. "It's less gender-specific."

"I don't want to hear another word about it," snapped Mr. Williams. "Andy, let that bloody fly out of the window and have done with it. And you can all write a three-page essay on gas exchange tonight and turn it in tomorrow. Teach you some bloody discipline. Now turn to page four hundred and twenty-three, and read chapter forty. In silence."

The pages rustled as the class, in shock, obeyed.

• • •

The fly buzzed in the background, grating on Jez's conscious-ness. She glared toward the window. There it was, the little bugger.

As she watched it, she frowned.

Normally, a fly on a windowpane would butt up against it, again and again and again, failing to understand the basic exis-tence of the glass that prevented it from reaching a world that it could see as clearly as—well, as a fly could see anything. But this one wasn't doing that.

This one—it looked a lot like a bluebottle, except that it was an eerie, iridescent green and *huge*, at least three-quarters of an inch long—was making the same loopy, haphazard path again and again, along the length of the windows that ran along one side of the lab. Back and forth, back and forth. Almost as if it were pacing. *Almost,* thought Jez (though she knew better), *as if it had a* purpose.

That was weird, thought Jez. But she couldn't help feeling that this wasn't the kind of thing that Sarah had meant.

Andy opened the window to let the fly out. It didn't seem to want to go.

Chapter 5

Adam was running again. He'd been running for half an hour now, on the treadmill in his home gym. The gym was one of the things he'd invested in doing properly. He hated running in the rain, and the treadmill meant that he could run any time of the day or night, in all weathers. He could track his progress, day by day; see if he was running faster, or further, or both. The only sound in the big house on the edge of the small country village was the whirr of the treadmill motor and the thud of Adam's feet. He didn't listen to music while he was running. It took him out of the moment.

He let his thoughts wander.

He had made the deal. He always had a vague feeling of uncertainty when making deals, but somehow, that was better: that feeling made him pay attention to detail, take nothing for granted. Like an actor with stage fright, he went through the project in his mind, accounting for every detail, justifying every decision, until he was sure everything was note-perfect.

This deal was different, though. This deal—

This deal would be the making of him. If everything went well. The risk was bigger, the stakes were higher, but the payoff...the payoff would be everything.

And oddly enough, he wasn't worried at all.

His running shoes thudded against the belt of the treadmill.

He believed in himself. One thing he and his father had in common. Well, not exactly. His father believed in hard work. "Hard work makes a man." The mantra from his childhood. Drummed into him from the time he started school. *If you put your back into it, you can do anything,* his father told him. If you put your brain into it, though, you could get so much more done. Delegating. Instructing. *Commanding.* So much more.

Commanding? Where had that come from? That wasn't usually his style. But maybe it was time to kick up his game a little, under the circumstances.

Well. Directing, if not commanding. Someone had to be in charge. To take charge. And he had. You had to be more aggressive these days if you wanted to succeed. Carrington had taught him that.

His father was part of an outdated generation. And he was an electrician. A good one, but still at the behest of people telling him what to do. Even if you owned your own business, you would never have that much power. Never make that much of a difference.

(His father would argue that the difference between good wiring and bad wiring was the difference between taking your power supply for granted because you never had a problem with it and dying in a house fire, but, then, his father had no ambition.)

Adam had ambition, though. And whatever his father said about reputation, Adam knew something else as well: no one cared if the people you worked with looked up to you; no one had ever cared if they liked you. It was the people in your circle that mattered. Where you were invited. *That* was what made you a success. And Adam realized that that was harsh: a man could work hard and build something wonderful and *never* be admitted to those circles, never have that kind of power and access. He'd watched it happen to his father. All that hard work for nothing. Nobody knew who he was. He *was* a nobody. Couldn't see dear old Dad down in the Smoke, having lunch with a couple of boys from the Commons, someone connected to a junior minister, if he had the time; couldn't see him with the lads from the big banks (Adam could see his father shaking his head: "Don't trust anyone who can't explain what they do in five words or less"; well, five words wasn't enough to explain the world in the twenty-first century, was it? Did he even realize that, the old fool?)

Thud, thud, thud.

Adam was going to be different. Connected. His father was a self-made man, but times were different now. His father was born in the right place at the right time. Made a bit of money; enough to live on and enough to have a little something to set aside. Adam got in to university (one of the two his father actually recognized) and did poorly. But that didn't matter. That was where his eyes were opened.

He remembered meeting Carrington on his first day. There had been a commotion in the corridor outside his room. He'd left the door ajar. A lanky blond eighteen-year-old burst in and slammed it, breathing heavily and laughing as quietly as he could. He was obviously part of an epic game of hide-and-seek or something similar.

"Oh," he said, when he saw Adam and his open suitcase. "Don't tell anyone I'm here."

There was no one else in the room, so Adam said, "Of course not."

"I'm *hiding*," said the other student.

"Oh," said Adam. "I'm Adam."

The blond man looked at him for a moment and then burst out laughing.

"Good one," he said. "*Adam*. I'm Nicholas Carrington." Adam was struck by the feeling that he should have known the name already. "Just arrived?"

"Yes," said Adam. "Today, actually."

"From where?"

Adam told him.

"The *provinces!*" said Carrington, with delight. "We'll have to take good care of *you*. Where on Earth did you go to school?"

Adam told him. It was an elderly and well-established private school, a small one and not famous. He had got in on a scholarship, which had been easier to do than his mother had feared. He had never really considered the school's status until Carrington smiled politely.

"Oh, well," he said. "We'll take you out for a drink anyway." His game of hide-and-seek forgotten, he opened the door. "Come and meet the chaps."

That had been more than fifteen years ago.

Adam had been running for over an hour now. Getting further in less time. He liked running. It let him think.

The new project was going more smoothly than he'd dared hope. Carrington was right: these guys were good. Very good. And fast, too. One meeting with the town council and apparently they'd been persuaded to move the zoning boundaries to allow for development. It was open to challenge, of course, but who around here had that kind of time or money?

No one would challenge him. It was something that, suddenly, he just knew.

If this worked, he could put developments wherever he liked. With these guys working for him—

This was the one that was really going to put him on the map. This was the big one. And about time, too. Sure, he was doing *okay*. But he could be so much more.

So much more.

His muscles rang as he ran on. He didn't feel tired at all. In fact, it felt as if, after a long time asleep—months, years, even— he was finally beginning to wake up.

• • •

"It's just down here."

Marina Butterworth made her way down the winding path of mud and stones toward the Foxglove Pond. She had changed, when she got home from school, into a calf-length black skirt with a frill around the bottom and a black velvet jacket. Her boots had been carefully selected so that she could make her way down the steep slope to the Foxglove Pond without any trouble. She didn't want to fall in front of Gareth.

Gareth Lake. Year Thirteen's answer to Lord Byron. Secure enough to wear eyeliner and cool enough to get away with it.

Marina would joke with Annabel Wilson about her unrequited crush on Gareth, but in her heart, it was so much more than just a crush. It was bigger than she was, pushing beyond the edges of her body to reach out into the world, to reach that little bit closer to him. It was a boulder that she carried around permanently, between her heart and her solar plexus. She had carried it with her for three years.

She'd never really been afraid to talk to him—they liked the same music, the same books. She had just always been afraid to ask—

She couldn't even think of it. Couldn't think the words. She just felt them, in every cell of her body. Because if he said no…

If he said no…

No.

She couldn't bear it.

But she had asked if he wanted to come down with her to the pond. She liked to go there by herself sometimes when she wanted to write poetry, because she was a poet too, and would he like to come down with her? They could write together, in silence, in the woods, and it would feel a thousand miles away from the mundane world of homework and housework and Saturday jobs and keeping your marks up and finding someone else's chewing gum under your desk. Silence in a world that was dark and beautiful.

She had written it down. It sounded better that way. And he had said he would come with her. And as they walked from her house down to the pond, she was quietly terrified, because being with him was enough, and at the same time, it was never enough, never would be enough.

She stumbled on a loose stone—accidentally, for real, accidentally; shit! Shit!—and flung up her hand for balance. Gareth caught it. They stood still for a moment, facing each other.

"Thank you," she said, feeling like a young lady in a Victorian novel. There was an awkward silence, but he didn't let go of her hand.

"Why is it called the Foxglove Pond?" he asked. She was grateful to him for breaking the silence, and sad at the loss of the moment. They continued down the slope, hand in hand.

"Oh," said Marina. She hesitated.

There's a story. I heard it ages ago. I don't remember it well. I think there was a demon involved. And a witch. No. She couldn't. If high school taught you anything, it was that if you weren't sure whether something would sound stupid, you should keep your mouth shut.

She shrugged. "Some folk tale. Or fairy story, or something. It's probably online somewhere."

Gareth pulled out his phone, tapped at it for a minute or so and then frowned.

"Battery's dead. Weird. I'm pretty sure I charged it this morning. Piece of shit."

"Check it out later. Live in the moment." She half smiled at him and he half smiled back.

Down, down, down.

They reached the bottom of the path and stood for a moment in the half light of the semi-clad trees. The smell of rotting leaves was sweet in the damp air; the only sounds were the dripping of water from the branches of the trees and an occasional crow high above them.

The pond was absolutely still. Gareth looked at it in wonder.

"It's beautiful," he said, and smiled properly at Marina this time. The joy made her ache.

"Let's go sit down," she said, leading him by the hand to the fallen tree and thanking God that she had remembered to bring a towel that they could sit on. She'd planned her outfit carefully, and she didn't want to ruin her skirt, which was her favourite. She spread the towel and sat down, heart racing. Gareth sat down next to her, and after a terrifying silence— *what happens now? he must like you, or he wouldn't have come down here with you; don't expect anything; don't anticipate; don't hope; you know he likes you; don't*—he put his arm around her. Marina's heart exploded, and she leaned her head quietly on his shoulder.

Everything was quiet. Everything was still. She wished it could stay that way forever.

• • •

Sarah knelt in the graveyard in front of the cracked gravestone. She had brought a bucket with her to wash off the blood—no sense in leaving it there for someone else to find, even if it was hidden away on the north side in a corner. The sharp edges where the stone had split were jagged and unnerving.

The stone was old. Too old. It was sandstone, or some other kind of sedimentary rock—not the smooth granite of the newer stones that spoke of insurance policies and sensible planning. This stone was a stone of pure necessity, a stone that had been available at the time. It undulated under her fingers as she ran them across the surface, but the letters had long worn away.

"Who were you?" she asked out loud. "What exactly are you trying to tell me?"

In the ivy hanging off the wall just above the gravestone, a cluster of spiders watched her.

• • •

"The worst was the time my Auntie Gloria decided that she wanted to see what I looked like with a bit of colour. So she basically put me in a headlock and attacked me with a blusher brush."

Gareth laughed, and Marina's heart leaped. He wasn't laughing at her. This was the good kind.

"That's nothing," he said. "The first time I tried doing my own eyeliner, I ended up looking like Alice Cooper, but not in a good way. I blinked too much and got it all up round my eyelids, but I thought it looked great because it was so messed up. But really, it just looked a mess. My sister caught me before I went out. Told me something I'll never forget. She said, 'Kid, you may be a weirdo, but even weirdoes have rules.'"

"There's a right way and a wrong way to do everything," said Marina, grinning.

"It's true!" said Gareth. He struck a pose. "It takes a lot of experimenting with the wrong way to be this cool. I hope you appreciate it."

Marina giggled. "But of course."

They smiled, and the silence lasted a little too long. Then Marina found herself leaning toward Gareth, anxiety gone. She knew this was perfect, it was the moment, it was so *right*, and then his mouth met hers and she thought her heart would melt. The boulder she had carried for so long turned to gold and its weight vanished.

He was a good kisser, too. Not that it would have mattered. But she was glad. And the moment lasted almost forever.

Almost.

A faint humming noise interrupted them. They both turned at the same moment to look.

It seemed to be coming from under the water. A few ripples appeared on the surface, in the centre.

"What was that?" said Gareth. "I didn't think you could hear the road from here."

"You can't normally," said Marina. "It's probably just a big truck or something." She felt torn out of the moment. Gareth's body was warm next to hers, and she felt safe with his arms around her, but she had never seen water move like that before. A kernel of unease hatched in her stomach.

She had never heard the road from down here before.

The humming grew louder. They could feel the vibrations through their feet; in the city, a person feeling the same kind of rumbling deep in the heart of the Earth would have assumed it was an underground train. But out here—

A few large bubbles of air floated to the top of the pond in the centre and then burst.

"Looks like something's going on with the pond," said Gareth. "Are there fish in there?"

"Fish don't hum," said Marina, and then felt stupid. The joy in her heart had been replaced by a tightness in her stomach.

Something wasn't right.

More bubbles, still more, rising furiously. The water in the centre of the pond looked as though it were boiling. Vapour—*steam?*—floated from the surface.

"This is a little messed up," said Gareth. Was there a touch of nervousness in his voice?

"Yeah," said Marina. She was scared now. "Gareth, I think we should go." She stood up, and he started to follow.

"I don't know," said Gareth. She could see him breathing more heavily now. Bubbles were beginning to form at the edge of the pond; it looked like the water in a saucepan, just before it comes to a rolling boil. Gareth stepped forward and held his hand over the water.

"It's *warm*," he said, turning to Marina in amazement and horror. "It's like it's some kind of crazy nuclear shit or something."

The vibrations under their feet were growing stronger. A crow flapped out of the brambles next to them, cawing and making the leaves rustle ferociously.

"We should go," said Marina. Her voice was shaky. "Gareth, please, let's get out of here. This is weird; this is too weird."

Gareth dipped his finger into the water. He screamed.

There was a loud fizzing sound, and a terrible smell like meat left on a barbecue for too long. When Gareth turned around, holding up his hand, Marina saw that the skin had melted from the index finger of his right hand and the drops of subcutaneous fat were running down his palm, leaving trails of scorched flesh in their wake. The smell of burning flesh filled

Marina's lungs; it smelled a little like frying bacon. Smoke was trailing from Gareth's burned hand as the flesh of his finger continued to melt. Marina cried out; she was feeling dizzy. A white flash of bone caught her eye, and she could feel her stomach turning over.

"Acid! Fucking acid!" he screamed.

The water—acid—at the centre of the pond was rising. Something was coming up from the depths.

"*Run!*" yelled Marina.

Gareth was breathing heavily, whimpering in pain.

"I can't," he croaked. "My hand—my fucking hand—I can't." He fell to his knees at the side of the water.

"You have to!" shouted Marina. She grabbed his other hand and tried to pull him to his feet. His sobs could barely be heard over the noise coming from the pond. Marina glanced over his shoulder and saw, rising from the pond, an apparition that—

—couldn't be real

—couldn't possibly be real.

She screamed.

The thing had a body that was vaguely humanoid, but the legs and arms—*were they arms?*—of a giant insect. It rose out of the pond on a pair of sticky-looking wings. Its head—its face—broke Marina's grip on her mind. The eyes were fly's eyes, but they contained a malevolence that no insect that she had ever seen possessed. That an insect *could* possess. Jutting from the middle of the triangular face was a proboscis two feet long, ending in a lethal point.

Marina's eyes were wide with horror as the creature hovered and turned. Weeds from the pond trailed from its feet and wings. She opened her mouth, but her throat was too dry to scream.

When it moved, it moved fast. Faster than she could have imagined. Instinct took over, and she let go of Gareth's hand; her legs were stiff with fear but she managed to get her muscles working. She was about ten feet up the slope when she heard a wet crunch and a gasp.

She turned back and saw the beast's proboscis protruding from Gareth's chest. Blood was already beginning to soak through his shirt, and wisps of smoke drifted up from his prone form, where the acid from the creature dripped on his flesh. His mouth opened wordlessly and he gasped.

The last expression on his face was a mixture of pain and shock, but also of sadness. He looked directly at Marina as the consciousness ebbed from his eyes until they were dull. The creature pulled out of his body with a hideous sound of shifting bones and organs. Gareth collapsed forward with a dull thud.

The creature behind him looked directly at Marina. Her heart broke for the dying boy she loved, and her mind cracked with terror.

Her last coherent thought was *why didn't I run? Why didn't I run when I had the chance?*

She started off again up the hill. Her muscles, charged with adrenalin, screamed as she pushed up the steep slope. She could hear the thing behind her, the hum of its wings, the crashing of the trees it powered through; it snapped thick branches as if they were no more than kindling. And it was getting closer.

She felt a pincer-like grip clutch at her shoulder, and a sudden sharp pain as acid burned through her velvet jacket. She opened her mouth to scream. She never managed it.

There was a terrible tearing noise and then—

Nothing. Everything was still, save for the dripping of water from the twigs around the Foxglove Pond, and two widening circles of red pooling around the bodies underneath the wet branches.

• • •

Two hours. That was a personal record. Adam stared at the computer on the treadmill. The thing had eventually turned itself off, for safety reasons. He'd have to set up a manual override for his next run. Not only had he run for twice as long as he usually did, he'd gone faster and covered more ground. It was brilliant. He wasn't tired at all. Was it the relief of signing the contract? He imagined it must be. You couldn't be considered successful if your body gave up at the first hurdle, and he was determined to stay successful as long as possible. Especially after the commitment he'd just made.

He felt great.

"Hello, you."

He turned from the treadmill. Julia was standing in the doorway. She looked fantastic. Most women looked like dogs after a hard day at work, no matter how long they spent in the bathroom trying to retain that morning freshness. But Julia somehow managed to carry it throughout the day. Her chin-length brown hair, cut into a sharp bob, shone as if she'd just stepped out of a salon. Her figure, in her mid-thirties, was still as tight as when Adam had met her ten years ago. He felt a familiar stirring and smiled at her, like a predator.

"Hello, darling," he said, with a twinkle in his eye. "Get over here."

Chapter 6

The next morning, just before morning break, Jez ploughed down the crowded stairwell that led from the chemistry lab, scattering barely awake Year Sevens to the left and right of her. She paused briefly to glare at Mickey Amble and his mates as the empty Coke can they were using as an impromptu football flew past her head, before she headed toward the common room to recoup. She felt a familiar whack on her shoulder. It seemed slightly less forceful than usual.

"Sam," she said, without bothering to turn around. "How are things, me old duck?"

"How are *things*?" Sam looked at her as if she had asked him if he'd had breakfast with Shakespeare. "Were you late this morning? I didn't see you on the bus."

"Yeah," said Jez. "I overslept." *Because I'm still sleep deprived from having a hysterical meltdown in the cottage of new-blood-in-the-village woman, who talks to dead people, and not in a sort of weird I-miss-my-dead-husband way.* Yeah, right. "I went straight to the chemistry lab. Why? Did I miss something good?"

Sam looked serious.

"No. No, you didn't miss anything good. You missed something *big*, though. You don't have any classes with Marina Butterworth, do you?"

"Bat-head Butterworth?" said Jez, rolling her eyes. "No."

"You have to chill out, Jez," said Sam. "She was murdered last night. Down by the Foxglove Pond." He paused and swallowed. "So was Gareth."

Jez felt as though all the air had been sucked out of the corridor. She turned to look at Sam. He wasn't smiling, and he wasn't the kind of person to joke about something like this, either.

"Seriously?" She felt the blood drain from her face. "Holy fuck."

"Seriously. Official line is: be careful, don't talk to strangers, be indoors before dark, keep on the lookout for anything strange. The rumour mill is in fucking *overdrive*, though. Two dead Goth kids? Oh, my God—it was a double suicide. It was a murder-suicide. It was Marilyn Manson. One of them was a vampire… I need a damn cigarette." He took a deep breath. "One of Russell Norris's tedious snotty mates who's cousin's friend's dad's a police officer says that the bodies were such a mess that policemen who'd been on the force for thirty years were throwing up. Although, if they've been on the force for thirty years in this town, they probably haven't had to process much more than four burglaries a year and the odd speeding ticket, so it's not surprising."

Jez looked at Sam. He was staring straight ahead; his jaw was tight and his lips were pressed together.

"I'm sorry," said Jez. She didn't know what else to say. It was hard to take in. Gareth and Marina. *Murdered.* Gone. Just like that.

She felt a lump rising in her throat.

"That's fucked up," she managed.

"*Yes*," said Sam again. "Yes. It is incredibly fucked up."

They were silent for a moment.

"Some little *shit*," Sam continued, through clenched teeth, "was wandering around the corridors this morning saying that when they found them, they'd pretty much been turned inside out and burned with acid. Who the *fuck* makes shit like that up?"

"I don't—" said Jez, "I don't know. I don't know, Sam. I don't know what to say."

"You know what? Don't say anything," said Sam. "I need not to be here. Let's face it: Gareth may have been a bloody awful poet, but he was..." He trailed off and swallowed hard. "You know what?" he went on. "He did actually *like* Marina. Didn't think she was just some freaky Goth kinkster that he could cop off with for shits and giggles. I hope he fucking told her that. He'd been whining about it for long enough. I hope he told her before—"

He stopped speaking and ground his teeth together.

"I hope he fucking told her," he said again.

Jez didn't say anything for a long time. They kept walking.

"Hey," she said, eventually. "Let's go to the cafeteria." Briefly, a vision of Sarah's living room, and the books, and the flowers, and the old armchair floated before her eyes.

"Let's go and get a cup of tea," she said.

• • •

They sat on hard plastic chairs in the cafeteria, elbows resting on the grey Formica tables, cradling hot disposable cups of tea. The cafeteria was usually the turf of the younger kids, who hadn't figured out that the food was awful, or that you'd eat quicker if you brought your own instead of lining up. It was also the stomping ground of Mrs. Rumble, part dinner lady, part secret police, who ruled her turf with an iron hand wearing rubber gloves.

"Shouldn't you be in class?" she croaked at Jez.

"No," said Jez. "We're free until just before lunch." It was true too. Mrs. Rumble sensed the authenticity of Jez's assertion, and lumbered off to torment some Year Eight girls who were arguing about the calories in salad.

The grey morning light lumbering from overcast skies through the windows and the sound of the October wind whipping through the trees outside hadn't subdued the mood in the caf, despite the announcement in assembly that Jez had missed. She guessed that a lot of the kids hadn't known either Marina or Gareth. In truth, she hadn't known either well herself. Marina had come to Arden High, and Crowsbrook, a year and a half ago when her dad changed his job. Jez hadn't disliked her; she'd felt, frankly, indifferent. She looked out of the window at the gruesome weather. Behind her, one of Mickey Amble's mates dropped a full tray of fountain pop and chocolate cracknells on the floor, sending smashed china and cocoa-covered corn-flakes flying in a tsunami of spilled Coke. Mrs. Rumble was on him like a pit bull on a toddler; the three Year Eight princesses behind him giggled and snorted and tossed their hair like contemptuous candy-floss coloured ponies.

She's missing all this, thought Jez.

The common room would be a vortex of hysterical wailing; Jez knew through experience that grief spread like rumours among teenage girls, and she didn't want to see people who had not only not known Marina well, but had actively disliked her, weeping waterfalls in her spot on the sofa and declaring her loss a tragedy.

It was all so sudden. So *weird.* Everything was weird. The scene in the cemetery. And now this.

"Sam," she said, hearing the awkwardness and hesitation in her own voice. "Can I talk about something else for a moment?"

"I," said Sam, still staring hard at his cup of tea, "would welcome talk of something else. Heartily."

"It's kind of freaky, and it's going to sound like I'm making it up."

Sam raised his eyes to meet hers. "Are you?"

"No." Jez looked straight back at him. "No, I'm not."

"Then hit me."

Jez chewed on the side of her finger for a moment. It was a bad habit that she'd almost broken when she was fourteen. She caught herself and dropped her hand to the table.

"Last night," she started, "I was coming back from yours and I took a short cut through the churchyard. That's the way I always go home from yours. I mean, you know that. I was almost at the gate, and I heard voices. And it was past eleven, and there's no one usually about at that time, so I thought it was a bit weird, so I turned around to see what was going on."

She paused and took a sip of her tea. It was weak and lukewarm, and she winced internally.

"This is the weird part. I went back into the churchyard and there was a woman sitting on the grass, having a conversation with—" She ran her hand through her hair. "I know how this is going to sound. But she was talking to Mr. Badgerley. From Crows Lane."

Sam looked at Jez as if she'd declared that she'd not only masterminded September 11, but was also responsible for WikiLeaks and the death of Amy Winehouse.

"Mr. Badgerley from Crows Lane," Sam repeated. He pressed his lips together and ran his tongue around the outside of his teeth. "I was under the impression that he was dead."

Jez bit her top lip and drummed her fingers on the table. "Yes," she said. "He is dead. Except that doesn't appear to have stopped him getting on with things."

Sam looked at her in disbelief.

"Fuck you," he said eventually.

"Sam, I'm serious. And it has *fucked* me up, believe me. I'm a *scientist*. I don't believe in all that oogie-boogie crap. And I *saw* it. With my own *eyes*, Sam. You have to believe me. I know how this sounds."

There was a long pause.

"I think," said Sam, through gritted teeth, "that your timing's a bit off on this one." He dropped a napkin into his unfinished cup of tea. "Why, in the name of the Flying fucking Spaghetti Monster would I want to hear a story about dead people getting up and walking around when Marina and *Gareth* have just been shoved off this mortal coil by some fucking Norman Bates–Michael Myers wannabe? Did you maybe think there wasn't enough bullshit floating in this *sewer* of a school this morning?"

Jez felt her stomach falling through the floor.

"Sam," she said. "I swear I'm not making this up. You *know* me."

Sam stood up sharply. His chair fell backwards behind him with a clatter.

"I have to go," he said. "I'll see you later." And he left the cafeteria.

Jez sat there, staring into space. Outside, the wind whipped the twigs of a nearby willow tree against the window.

Ghosts. Murder. Double murder, even. It was all so unlike here. Nothing ever happened here. It was so—

Weird.

Okay, well, maybe this wasn't on the same plane as dead people appearing in the churchyard. But it was something very out of the ordinary. And it had happened within two days of

Sarah asking her to keep an eye out. "Anything out of the ordinary," she'd said. Well, hell, this counted.

The chances of Sarah not having heard about Marina and Gareth, when the murders had happened less than a mile from her front door, were pretty small. But it might be worth talking to her about all the rumours. And mostly— mostly, if she was being honest with herself, she wanted to talk more about Mr. Badgerley. About how the universe worked. About the *systems*. Sarah had mentioned systems, hadn't she? Sets of rules? Jez was good with irrefutable rules. Scientific rules. *Universal* rules. (Not school rules. School rules fell into two categories: some had a point; most insulted your intelligence.)

Mrs. Rumble lumbered by and growled an order at Jez to pick up the chair Sam had knocked over. Her mind miles away, Jez stood up automatically and set the chair to rights.

Sam. She felt anxiety building in the pit of her stomach. He'd never walked out on her before.

Didn't think that one through, did you?

Crap. She'd have to go and apologize to him later. And hope that he wouldn't ask what she'd been talking about. She didn't want to explain any further, and if there was any chance she could talk with Sarah, who at least knew she was telling the truth, then there was no point upsetting Sam anymore than she already had.

Marina and Gareth. Marina and Gareth. Marina and Gareth.

For the first time since her mother died, she silently offered up something that was close to a prayer.

Marina and Gareth. If you're still around somewhere, please know that I really hope they catch the guy who did this.

She was struck by a thought, and her head jerked up violently. Her tea sloshed precariously against the sides of the disposable cup.

Sarah can talk to dead people.

That settled it, in her mind. She would visit the cottage again after school.

• • •

The knock on the door surprised Sarah. The girl with the green army bag standing on her doorstep didn't.

"Kid," she said. "Jez. What can I do for you? Don't you have science to do or something? What do kids do these days, anyway?"

"You said to tell you if anything was weird," said Jez. "Things are weird. Very weird."

They stood there looking at each other for a moment.

"How weird?" said Sarah.

Jez shrugged. "Weird," she said. "Can I come in?"

Sarah stood aside, holding the door open and gesturing with one arm.

Jez came into Sarah's living room. The room was messier than it had been before; the table was now covered in piles of books and papers. The books looked very old. Most were bound in leather. A few had tatty paper slip covers on them.

"You know about the murders, right?" Jez started. Sarah raised an eyebrow.

"No…what murders? I haven't been out all day."

"Marina Butterworth and Gareth Lake. Marina lives in the village. *Lived* in the village, I guess. She's not from here. They were murdered last night. Near the Foxglove Pond. It's a pond near—"

"I know the Foxglove Pond," said Sarah, quickly. Her mind was racing.

"Okay. Well," said Jez. "There's all sorts of crazy rumours floating around school." She realized she didn't actually know that much about the murders. "I. Um. I thought that counted as weird. Because nothing ever happens around here. And you can talk to dead people. So I thought that you could ask them who killed them."

"That would be really helpful." Sarah sat down. "Have a seat. Unfortunately, it doesn't work like that."

"Why not?" said Jez, in exasperation. "Don't you have a responsibility to? To try and find out, I mean?"

"If I could, I would," said Sarah, pushing her hair out of her face. "But I can't. There are only a few ways that you can talk to dead people, and you probably know as many as I do. And you know roughly how reliable *they* are." She sat back in her chair. "Not very, in case you're wondering. Thanks for telling me about this, though. This definitely counts."

"I don't really know a lot more than that," said Jez. She sat down in the tatty armchair next to the front door. "And there's nothing in the papers, because it only happened last night. I listened to the radio, but that didn't tell me much either. But people at school were saying whoever killed them was a real psycho, that he really messed them up and covered them in battery acid or something. But that could just be school. People believe all sorts of things..."

"Especially when they're frightened," finished Sarah.

"Not at school," said Jez, wrinkling her nose. "At school, people believe mad stuff all the time. Urban legends and all that."

"But you don't."

"No," said Jez. "There are kids there that still think you can't get pregnant if you shake up a bottle of Coke and sit on it right after. Or that food you drop on the floor doesn't get dirty unless you leave it there for more than seven seconds. One of the ones that's hot shit today is that the devil lives in the Foxglove Pond, and that's how it got its name and that Marina and Gareth were murdered in a Satanic ritual." This one had been flying around the bus while Jez had been travelling home, and she hoped to God that Sam, who had completely ignored her and sequestered himself with Paul Barlow and his collection of fine herbs on the top deck, hadn't heard it. "That one's true. I mean. That is how it got its name. But it's just a story. Obviously."

"Just a story," said Sarah. She looked out of the window; large gobs of rain were beginning to splatter against the glass. The sky was dark grey. "What kind of story?"

"I don't know," said Jez. "A folk tale." She picked at some lint on her skirt. "I don't really think that has anything to do with what happened."

"So," said Sarah, "what's the story?"

Jez shrugged again. "I don't remember all the details. I just heard it when I was a kid, in the Brownies or something. On a camping trip. It's like a ghost story. I don't even know when it dates from. Some kid could have made it up, for all I know." She pulled out her phone. "I'll look it up."

She tapped a few words into the search engine, clicked on the first result that came up and passed the phone to Sarah.

The Foxglove Pond in Crowsbrook takes its name from a folk tale that dates from the Middle Ages.

The Devil was tormenting the small country village, bringing plague, killing animals, and destroying crops. No one knew for certain why the village had been chosen for such torment. Almost no one was safe—rich or poor; peasant or lord; maiden, mother, or crone.

The only person who was spared the torment was the village carpenter. People were afraid of him. It was said he had sold his soul for worldly riches, and it was true that he grew richer and richer, while the villagers around him lost everything.

Eventually, when the villagers could take no more, they went to a wise woman who lived on the outskirts of the village and asked her what to do.

"There is nothing I can do," she said. "You cannot kill the Devil. The Devil will always be with us, one way or another."

But they pleaded with her to save the village. They brought their sick children. They showed her the bodies of animals that had been burned and torn apart. Eventually she relented.

"I cannot get rid of the Devil," she warned them, "but I will do what I can do."

At the next full moon, she went out into the woods at midnight and gathered herbs and water from a fresh pond. She shut herself up in her hut, and wove a spell that was more powerful than any she had worked before. She toiled on it day and night with little rest.

The villagers brought her what little food they had at night and left it at her door. In the morning, it would be gone, but no one saw the wise woman for a month.

On the night of the next full moon, there was a storm, the biggest storm there had ever been in the village that anyone could remember. The lightning flashed and the thunder rolled. Many ancient trees were felled and burned by lightning, and the villagers cowered in their huts and prayed to be delivered from evil.

In the morning, everything was still. The wise woman gathered the villagers together in the village square. She looked older than anyone had remembered, and she was very, very tired.

"I have trapped the Devil," she said. "He will stay among us, but he will not be able to hurt us. Not for a long time. I have imprisoned him at the bottom of the pond in the woods. He will not be able to escape until he has counted every grain of sand at the bottom of the pond."

With that, she fainted. The villagers could not revive her. She fell into a deep sleep that lasted for three days, and then she died. But the villagers were never again molested by the Devil, and peace and prosperity came to the village.

Later that year, the foxgloves bloomed around the pond in their hundreds. It was said that the wise woman had planted them as a warning, on the night of the storm, a sign to the animals to keep away from the evil trapped in the pond.

"Yes," said Jez. "That sounds about right. Witches, devils, superstitious villagers—welcome to Crowsbrook. Is that from the seventies or something?"

Sarah twisted one of the rings on her right hand absently.

"Fancy a trip down to the Foxglove Pond?" she asked.

"Ha," said Jez. "No. Not with some psycho running around out there. And it's raining." It was coming down hard now, and a strong wind was blowing. "Also, it'll be crawling with police. They'll never let us down there."

"We'll take an umbrella. I have a feeling the police won't be a problem. And there'll be two of us."

"There were two of Gareth and Marina."

"True," said Sarah.

But, she thought, *the mistake that most children make when they go into the big, bad woods is that they don't take the witch with them.*

She stood up.

"Well, I'm going," she said. "You can come or you needn't."

• • •

The gap in the trees that signalled, to those who knew, the beginning of the way to the Foxglove Pond, was sealed off with police tape. It ran along the edge of the wooded area as far as Jez could see, and then disappeared into the trees. But there was no one in sight.

"We can't go in there," said Jez. "What if we disturb evidence or something?"

"We won't," said Sarah. "Besides, when they say 'keep out,' they don't mean me." She ducked under the yellow tape.

"I'm pretty sure this is massively illegal," muttered Jez as she followed, but Sarah was already marching off toward the sloped path and didn't hear her. She ran to catch up. "You're supposed to be the grown-up!" she hissed at Sarah.

"And yet," said Sarah, turning to look at her, "despite the fact that you think this is 'massively illegal' and we shouldn't be doing it and I'm not stopping you leaving, and you said that you didn't want to come, you're still following me. Is that because *you* finally have the chance to be the grown-up, or because you're bored out of your skull and this is the most interesting thing that's happened either to you or to this village in about—" she paused and looked Jez up and down "—*ever?*"

The silence hung between them, punctuated only by the dripping of rain from the trees.

"You can come with me," said Sarah. "But you need to realize that if you come with me, you're coming because you decided to." She turned back to the path. "Let's go. We need to be quick."

Jez had never liked the Foxglove Pond or the woods that surrounded it. The narrow path, the trees that closed in overhead—for an outdoor space, it was very claustrophobic. Although it was mid-October and they found themselves ploughing through a mouldering sludge of mud and rotting leaf pulp, the branches were thick enough that they provided almost complete shelter from the rain that was pelting down. Not that they could have used the umbrella anyway: the path was narrow and overgrown on both sides. Jez followed Sarah as the older woman pushed the brambles and thick grasses to the side, and let them spring back after her. The steep path was slick with mud.

This is where—

This is the last place Gareth and Marina ever saw.

She felt her throat swell with emotion.

Don't cry in front of her again. She'll think that's all you do.

Sarah picked up a broken branch in the path ahead and tossed it to one side.

"Stop moving stuff!" hissed Jez. "What if there was a clue on it?"

"Wow," said Sarah, "you're really not a forensic scientist, are you? I'd imagine there wouldn't be much left by this point." She gestured toward the sky.

"By this point?" Jez was stunned. "They were killed last night! Why isn't this place *crawling* with police?" There was an unspoken question behind it: *what if we see remains? A few drops of blood, some strands of hair, a scrap of torn flesh?*

"I would imagine," said Sarah, and her voice was dry, "that someone has made sure that the police have just enough to think they can get their man. Keep it interesting for them. And keep them out of the way."

"*Someone?*" said Jez. "Who would do that? The killer? Are we talking about some kind of genius psychopath Hannibal Lecter–type, here? I mean here? In the village? Why would any psychotic genius come to the village? It's not like it's a hotbed of intellectual stimuli. Why—"

She stopped. The memory of Mr. Badgerley in the church-yard floated before her eyes.

"Oh. My. God." She clutched at Sarah's shoulder. Sarah frowned. "Was it someone dead? Can dead people do that? Why am I even asking that question?" She felt stupid. "That's the most irrational thing I've ever heard. Or said."

"Relax," said Sarah. "Your friends weren't killed by someone dead."

"Well, that's good," said Jez. "I mean, they weren't exactly close friends." She wondered if she should explain the complex network of hierarchies, alliances and vendettas that made up social life at school. "Because. You know. Dead people wandering around committing murder would be totally mad. So it's good to hear that... they're not."

"No," said Sarah. She bent over to look at a patch of acid-scorched grass as they reached the bottom of the path and stood before the Foxglove Pond. "I think they were killed by something much worse."

Jez bent over to look at the grass. It reminded her of the time in Year Ten double chemistry when Cat had tried to hide an experiment with hydrochloric acid that had gone wrong by pouring the solution into the lab's collection of spider plants.

"That looks like an acid burn," she said. "Really strong acid, too. Why would anyone have acid down here?"

Sarah didn't answer. She wandered off toward the pond, picked up a twig, dipped it briefly in the water, and sniffed at it. Nothing happened. She gazed across the pond, thinking.

And froze.

"What are you looking for?" asked Jez. "I can't help you find it if I don't know what to look for."

Sarah was standing stock-still, eyes fixed on a spot in the trees, on the other side of the pond.

"You don't have to help me find it," she whispered out of the corner of her mouth. "Be *really* quiet. This is important. Don't say a word. Don't scream. Don't make any noise at all. And look over there. Tell me if you can see it."

Jez looked across the pond to where Sarah motioned with her arm. She couldn't see anything except trees and underbrush.

"By the rock," Sarah whispered.

Jez's eyes opened wide.

Next to the rock was what looked like part of the biggest insect she had ever seen. It was mostly hidden, and it wasn't moving. But it was there. It sat motionless, in a curl, with its wings wrapped around it. Terror shot through her body like a bullet.

Time stood still. She couldn't move. She stood there for what seemed like hours.

That thing could not exist. It wasn't just a new creature. It was a new species. And yet—and yet, in her heart, she knew that it wasn't new at all.

It was old. Very old.

The thing flinched and shifted in what she assumed was its sleep. There was a crackling noise like rocks grinding together.

"We have to go," said Sarah, under her breath. "Now. As quietly as possible." She turned around and began tiptoeing slowly toward the path down which they'd come.

Jez's legs felt like jelly. She turned and began to follow Sarah. The grass made her tremble as it brushed against the sides of her legs with a soft hiss; it had never seemed so loud to her. They moved slowly across the mud. Every step seemed deafening to Jez; every time her foot hit the mud with a splash, she expected it to be the last sound she ever heard.

Something clutched at her hair. Adrenalin shot through her like lightning. Instinctively, she put her hand to her head and felt something rough and hard and—

A branch. Just a branch. But she was stuck halfway up the slope. Panicking, she pulled hard, and winced as strands of her hair came away. A couple of twigs snapped. She looked behind her; nothing.

The quiet was too much. She ran up the rest of the slope, muscles screaming. It took a century to reach the top. She reached the police tape, out of breath.

Sarah was already standing there, mouth pursed. staring at something. She held up the tape for Jez to duck under.

"What is it?" asked Jez, panting. "What are you looking at?"

Then Jez saw it. Behind the yellow tape announcing POLICE—DO NOT CROSS was a thin strand of barbed wire. Jez didn't remember seeing it before; *we must have ducked under it when we went under the tape*, she thought.

"Was that there before?" asked Jez. "That wasn't there before, was it?" She put out her hand tentatively and touched it, drawing her fingers away almost instantly.

"Get on the other side of this wire," snapped Sarah, "NOW!"

They ducked under the wire. Sarah looked visibly relieved. They were both out of breath and covered in mud from the knees down.

"Well," said Sarah. "Will you look at that?"

Tied to the wire was a piece of red string, with nine knots in it. Jez ran her fingers over it and then inspected them. No residue, although it was a little wet, like everything else in the woods. It just looked like ordinary red string. Her heart was racing.

What had she seen? She was beginning to doubt her own mind. A monster? A real, live monster? Or just some optical illusion, a rock in the lessening light, a branch curving against the water?

There was no way that what she had thought she had seen could exist. No way.

Except for the fact that Sarah had seen something too.

Sarah took a deep breath.

"I think," she said, "that we should go back to my house, and have a cup of tea and calm down a bit. What do you think?"

"That thing," asked Jez. "What was that thing? It can't have been—"

Sarah started walking, brushing off the words like so much rain.

"No! Come back!" cried Jez. "You can't keep showing me weird stuff and then not explaining it!" She ran after Sarah, who was striding evenly in the direction of the village.

"As far as I know," said Sarah, "I haven't *shown* you anything. Either it or you has happened to be in the right place at the right time. Or wrong time, depending on how you want to look at it. Please stop making noise."

She was thinking. Hard. The thing at the pond was old. It had to be the same thing from the folk tale. It had been trapped, and it had served its time. And whoever had trapped it had trapped it for a very long time. And now it wasn't trapped anymore.

But it wasn't free either. Which meant that someone was in charge of it.

"Is that thing going to come after us?" Jez was wide-eyed.

"Not now. Probably. But you're annoying me. *Again.*"

"*You're* annoying *me*." Jez was furious. "Why did you let me come with you if you won't explain anything? That doesn't make any sense. How do you know that thing won't come after us? How does that thing even exist? What is it? An alien? A genetic experiment? A biological weapon?"

"It's a demon." Sarah kept on walking.

"Right. A demon. Of course it is. How do you know all this stuff, anyway? You sound like a mad person."

"I'm not mad," said Sarah. "Why are you asking so many questions?"

"Because why would anyone assume something was true just because someone else told them it was?" Jez held up both hands and shook her head. "Jesus, if I did that, I'd be at home using crystals to improve my grades like that bubblehead Saskia French."

"That won't work."

"*No shit*," spat Jez. "Why did you even say I could come with you if you weren't going to tell me anything about what you were looking for or what we were doing?"

"I think you're bored."

"I think you're *lonely*."

Silence fell between them, heavy as the foggy October air. Sarah took a stick of chewing gum out of her pocket and offered some to Jez, who refused, before unwrapping the stick and popping it in her own mouth. Her eyes wandered down the line of police tape and settled on a medium-sized white sign, a little way down the road.

"Let's go and look at that," she said, pointing to the sign. She strolled off to have a look. Jez folded her arms and ground her teeth.

This woman was obviously mad. You weren't supposed to wander around crime scenes the day after people had been murdered in them. And yet...

There had been nothing there to indicate that that was where Gareth and Marina had died. Nothing at all. And that wasn't right. It was a long way from right. Something was very, very odd about this.

She followed Sarah, who was staring thoughtfully at the sign while she chewed her gum.

The billboard was about three feet by two feet and supported by two wooden posts. The lettering was black on a plain white background. It read

FUTURE SITE OF AN EXCITING NEW DEVELOPMENT BY
CARPENTER PROPERTIES
AN ASILIDA PROJECT

Jez strolled up behind her, jaw still set tight.

"Did you know about this?" asked Sarah.

"What?" snapped Jez. "Oh. Yeah. They want to build something here. A maggot factory, I think. I've got a flyer in my bag. There's a protest on Saturday."

"What's Carpenter Properties?"

"I don't know. They're local. Their signs are all over the place round here. They build houses and renovate buildings and things."

"What's Asilida?"

"*I don't know!* Why would I know?" Jez thought for a moment; something in her mind rang a bell that cut through her smouldering anger. "It sounds familiar, though." She pulled out her mobile and glared at it. The battery was flat. *Again.* "I'll check it out when I get home," she said. "Or you could. Why can't you look into it?"

The rain, which had dried up to a few odd drops as they emerged from the woods, began to fall again in earnest.

"All right," said Sarah. "Maybe I will. I'm going back to mine. If you want to come, when we get there, I'll tell you what I think about that thing down by the pond."

They walked the rest of the way in silence.

In the woods near the Foxglove Pond, the strands of Jez's hair that had caught on the twigs floated in the breeze that crept through the trees, undulating in the air like seaweed attached to a rock, moving in a slow current of water.

• • •

"First up," said Sarah, when they were back at the cottage and holding steaming mugs of tea, "you understand why I'm reluctant to talk about these things, right?"

"Because you sound mad."

"Because I sound mad, yes. Also, how long do you think this place would stay a tranquil country village if everybody knew that there was a demon in it? How calm do you think Joe Public would manage to stay if regular people knew demons actually existed?"

She sipped her tea.

"You're seventeen. I'm going to do you the favour of assuming you're an adult, which I imagine most people still don't. You're obviously intelligent. You know what people are like."

Jez shifted uncomfortably in her chair.

"Thanks," she said. "I think."

"Also, you know that if you tell anyone any of this, they'll think you're mad."

"I know," said Jez. "I tried to talk to my best friend about it and he got cross and walked away."

Sarah rolled her eyes. "That wasn't smart."

"Are you angry?"

"No point. It is what it is, and it would have been better if you hadn't. But I could have told you what would happen. Don't try to tell anyone else." She blew on her tea, sending steam whirling. "I think that something really bad is happening. Or about to happen. In your village."

"Something bad just did happen. Two people died. *Kids.* How much worse can it get?"

"Believe me," said Sarah, "it can get a lot worse. And I don't even know for sure what's going on. How do you feel about spiders?"

"Okay," said Jez, warily. "I used to want to be an entomologist. Studying insects. And I know spiders aren't insects. But I'm okay with things that have more than four legs."

"Good. Because there's currently about four thousand of them hiding out in the room above your head. If you don't believe me, I can show you when you've finished your tea; I know you like empirical evidence. I'm pretty sure they're hiding from something, but I don't know what, although I'm also pretty sure that it has something to do with the demon down at the Foxglove Pond, and I'm ninety-nine percent sure that that's the thing that killed your friends."

"Gareth and Marina. They weren't exactly my friends." Jez felt a sudden sting of guilt. "Well. Kind of. I didn't know them very well. But I liked them. I guess." She tapped her fingers on the arm of her chair. It was surreal, as though a curtain had been pulled away from everything she knew was true to show not only the workings that she knew operated in the universe, but a whole other system of mechanics and gears that worked in defiance of everything that was sane and predictable and verifiable. "What do you mean, you have four thousand spiders upstairs? How is that even p—" She caught herself and stopped.

"I don't know," said Sarah. She gestured toward the piles of books and notes on the table. "That's what all this is. Research." She stirred her tea absently. "The red string really helped."

"How?"

"Someone else knows about the demon and wants to keep it down by the pond for the time being. The red string is part of a charm to keep it contained. And it seems to be working."

"How can you tell it's working?"

"Because no one's died horribly since last night." Sarah plonked her elbow on the arm of her chair and rested her head on her hand. "Someone knows how to control this thing. This isn't high school Deicide fans trying to summon the Devil. This is someone who knows what they're doing." She looked at Jez. "That thing by the Foxglove Pond isn't actually the Devil."

"Oh," said Jez. "Well, that's good. Just a random, low-level, killer demon, then. So, if no one goes down to the Foxglove Pond, we'll all be okay?" There was the beginning of an edge to her voice.

"For now," said Sarah. "I'm sorry I can't be more helpful."

Jez shook her head without saying anything. For the first time in a long time, she was scared—not in the abstract, not by the threat of ecological disaster, or cancer, or an asteroid hitting the planet, all of which she'd written about, turning in assignments that had earned her A grades all through high school, but by something real, something tangible, something *direct. A predator*, she thought. *That thing is a predator. And it's getting ready to prey on us.*

She shuddered.

"You can talk to dead people," she said. "Can you ask Gareth and Marina what killed them? Just to make sure?"

"Why?" said Sarah. "We just walked around a wood that was the worst kind of crime scene less than twenty-four hours ago, and no one stopped us. There wasn't even anyone there. I know that correlation isn't causation, but do you think it's worth disturbing the dead to find out what we basically already know?" She leaned forward. "'Rest in peace' isn't some greeting-card sentiment," she said. "Don't you think they've been through enough?"

They were silent. Minutes passed. Finally, Jez spoke.

"I have one more question." She raised her eyes from the floor and looked at Sarah directly. "I probably should have asked it before. How do you know all this stuff?"

I'm not getting into this now, thought Sarah.

"Oh, you know how it is," she said. "I just read a lot."

Jez knew she was lying, but decided, for now, to leave it at that.

Chapter 7

The flies were everywhere.

On Mrs. Bastable's Jack Russell's food bowl, buzzing around his head, making him bark incessantly, and aggravating her already splitting headache. Assuming that he needed to go out, she eventually stumbled down to the kitchen and opened the door for him into the garden, not noticing the slipped latch on the garden gate that led to the road until after she heard the screeching of brakes and a short, muffled howl from outside the house.

On Ryan Ogden's newspaper, on his kitchen table, as he flipped a pair of them away to concentrate on the football scores as he digested his breakfast. Enzymes broke down sugars and proteins into their component parts and sent them on their way through his bloodstream to his organs, their cells dividing and dividing, until the right combination of mutations would cause them to divide faster and faster and faster, all unbeknownst to him. He got up from the table and went to brush his teeth before heading out in the van to visit his first customer of the day.

On the alphabet building blocks belonging to Sally Jenson's daughter, Becky, landing lightly on each one before spiralling away and upwards, just as Becky's temperature would, until her cries interrupted her mother's phone call with her sister, and brought her running into her daughter's room to find her limp and sick and wailing, with something the doctor would later call "a virus" but which she would be oddly unable to shake.

And something was watching. Something was feeding on the misery as it grew.

• • •

Adam was in the kitchen, chopping garlic. It wasn't often that he made it home before Julia, and he was determined to make an effort. He had started early. He was going to make the dinner. He would surprise her, and they wouldn't have to order take-away. Also, he felt that he had to make the most of his new-found energy. Normally, after a day of work and an hour of running, all he'd be able to manage was a hot shower and a couple of hours on the sofa in front of some bad telly, before he was ready to crash. He'd been clocking up twice that on the treadmill, and he didn't even feel like a sit-down. He must have broken through a barrier with his training. He'd never had this much energy before.

He glanced at the recipe book. *A lemon. Do we even have a lemon?*

The phone rang, and Adam swore under his breath. He washed his hands and picked it up. "Hello?" he said.

"Adam," said a voice on the other end. "It's Felicity. I'm sorry to call you after hours; I didn't know if you'd heard. There was a murder last night. There have been rumours floating around all day, but I just heard it confirmed on the news. They found two bodies down on the site that the Asilida guys are developing for you. Two kids. Seventeen, both of them." Her voice was a little shaky. "Did you know?"

"No," said Adam. He thought for a moment. "Do we even own that site yet? They've only been on the job for a couple of days. Is it our problem?"

Something poked him in the back of the mind, like a thorn. *That's not what you're supposed to say.*

There was a pause on the other end of the phone.

"I—I don't know; they're taking care of it. It's in the port-folio; hold on." Adam heard her turning pages in the file. "Technically, they acquired the site on behalf of Carpenter."

"How is that even possible?" snapped Adam. "I met with them three days ago."

"I guess they work fast," said Felicity. "The paperwork's all here. It's really weird. It all looks fine to me. I mean, I'm not a lawyer, but there's nothing missing that I'd expect to be here. But... there's no way they could have done it that quickly."

It *was* strange. But Adam had been told, the first time that Carrington mentioned Asilida's parent company (he didn't remember the name), that they worked *fast*. He decided that he didn't want to go into it with Felicity right now.

"Hmm," he said. "Are we liable?"

"Jesus, Adam, they were *murdered*. No. No, we're not liable. I have to go." She hung up.

Adam went back to his garlic. *Damn* it, this was potentially inconvenient.

They were kids.

There was the thorn again. It was like having the dentist poke around in his mouth after it had been frozen. He could feel a vague nudge, but nothing more. He was aware that this wasn't the appropriate response, but somehow, it didn't seem to matter. *We're not liable. We can move forward as planned.*

You couldn't let a thing like this derail your plans. It was tragic, yes, but life should go on.

Still, he wasn't sure that everyone would see it his way. People were idiots. Sentimental. He gave the garlic three more cursory chops, pursed his lips, and picked up his mobile.

Brown answered immediately.

"Mr. Carpenter," he said. "What can I do for you?"

Adam felt instantly reassured by Brown's unflappable demeanour.

"It's probably nothing," he said. "My assistant just called me. She told me there had been some trouble on the prospective site—said something about murder? Have you heard anything about this?"

"Indeed," said Brown. "Most unfortunate. Two teenagers: Marina Butterworth and Gareth Lake, both seventeen. Both students at Arden High. You will be happy to know that we have cleared the site. There will be no further trouble."

"What do you mean, 'cleared' it?" said Adam. "If there was a murder there, it'll be closed off for... I don't know, weeks? Months? There'll be a police investigation, for Christ's sake." He felt a sudden twinge of pain, like a stomach cramp. "Is this going to affect our schedule?"

"Not at all," said Brown, evenly. "We have made the necessary arrangements and assisted the relevant authorities. The site is clear. We can move forward."

Adam was silent for almost a minute before he realized his mouth was open. He closed it and swallowed.

"That's not possible," he said, eventually. "Things just don't work like that."

"I can assure you, Mr. Carpenter, we can move forward."

"How?" said Adam, simply. "How can you possibly— how—do you know how much...how much *stuff* you would need to circumvent in order for the project to move forward this quickly after something like a murder?"

"Of course, Mr. Carpenter," said Brown.

Adam was silent.

Holy shit, he thought. *Carrington wasn't exaggerating. There is* nothing *that these guys can't do.* His mind was blank with the magnitude of the realization.

"You work miracles," he said, after a long time.

"We arrange matters for maximum convenience to our clients," said Brown. "Once a client has signed a contract."

"That's what the contract says," said Adam. "That stuff about 'maximum convenience.' If I asked you to explain to me the full implications of that, what would you say?"

"You've read the contract, of course," said Brown.

"I have," said Adam. His mind had gone from blank to racing wildly; there were so many thoughts in his head that he felt as though he were struggling to gain purchase on any of them. If Brown was saying what Adam thought he was saying, then the possibilities—

The possibilities were truly endless.

He cleared his throat. "But this is purely a business arrangement, of course."

"Mr. Carpenter," Brown said, with a note of reassurance in his voice, "please understand that, once a client has signed a contract, we will do our utmost for that client. We are happy to go the extra mile. Always."

"So…" He was afraid to ask the question that was now pounding in his brain. "Let me get this straight—"

"Anything," said Brown. "Anything at all. Anything you want."

"*Anything?*"

"Of course," said Brown. His voice was more soothing now. "Our contracts may be exclusive, Mr. Carpenter, but we feel our service is worth it."

Anything.

He could have anything at all.

Adam's mind struggled with the idea. It was too big. Too impractical. There must be a catch. He couldn't possibly have *anything* he wanted. There were always limits. There *had* to be limits. The laws of physics alone set limits. *Anything* was simply not possible.

He must have misunderstood.

He stared at the kitchen counter in front of him: the garlic shredded on the chopping board, the sharp knife reflecting the overhead lights, the recipe book open in the holder. It was *The Whole Beast*, by Fergus Henderson. Adam never trusted himself to remember recipes. He always liked to work from the book.

With his phone still to his ear, he went to the fridge to check something.

"Anything," he said into the phone, staring into the fridge. "You said anything."

"That is correct," said Brown.

"I need a lemon," said Adam. "Right now." As soon as he said it, he felt like an idiot.

There was a pause.

"A lemon," said Brown, as if he were repeating a list to himself. "Any particular variety?"

"Do they come in varieties?" said Adam, shrugging. "I don't care. I need a lemon. Any kind of lemon. Now." Although, it was a pretty ridiculous request, he reflected. They would probably just send someone over to Jake at the shop and drive down with the fruit from there. It'd be quicker to get it himself. But he was curious to see how far their commitment to client service really went.

"It will be with you shortly," said Brown, and hung up.

Adam sighed with relief. That *was* it, after all. They'd just get one over to him in a taxi; shameful waste of money, but an impressive gesture. He was grateful he hadn't asked for anything more ludicrous. Or salacious. They really ought to be more careful, offering clients *anything*. God knows what some people would come up with. This one time, Carrington went to Amsterdam and claimed that he'd hired—

Well, anyway. These chaps might be a little unhinged socially, but he couldn't argue with the results they'd provided so far. In fact—

The doorbell rang.

Adam frowned. He wasn't expecting anyone. He laid his mobile down on the counter and headed toward the front door. *Probably one of those tossers going door to door, offering to repair your drive or clean your windows*, he reasoned. *Everyone knows you should never buy anything from the door. How the hell do those guys make a living?*

He opened the door. There was no one there.

He looked down the drive to the road. You could see the road quite a long way in both directions from Adam's door, but right now, there wasn't a vehicle in sight.

He went to step outside, to look left and right, to see if some kid was hiding just beyond the door frame, just out of sight, silently laughing like a maniac *(cherry-knocking, they used to call it, banging on the door and then running away, but he'd give the little shit something to think about if he caught him)* and his foot connected with a small package on the doorstep.

He picked it up, stuck his head out of the door, and looked left and right.

There was no one in sight.

He weighed the package in his hand. It had an all-too-familiar weight. It was slightly smaller than his fist, and wrapped in generic brown paper and string.

String? Who uses string in the age of Sellotape?

There was no way that this could be—

No, he thought to himself. *There's no way.*

Jake's shop was a five-minute drive and a twenty-minute walk from Adam's front door. There was no way that anyone could have moved anything from the shop to Adam's house more quickly. And it was the closest shop by a long way; the next closest was probably one of the big hypermarkets on the edge of town; a fifteen-minute drive and God-knows-how-long to walk. But there was also no way that anyone could have dropped off the package and driven off without Adam at least seeing the car.

He looked at the brown paper package in his hand as if it were a grenade. Then, in a frenzy, he pulled off the string and ripped apart the brown paper.

Inside the package was a lemon. It looked perfect. Its colour was bright and its shape was even; its skin was moist and fresh. He sniffed it: the fresh citrus scent exploded in his nostrils, invigorating and lovely.

He went inside and closed the front door, his heart racing. Almost without thinking, he picked up the mobile and tapped in the number.

"Mr. Carpenter," said Brown, almost immediately.

"There's a lemon on my doorstep," said Adam. He felt like an idiot again.

"But of course," said Brown. "With our compliments."

"Thank you," said Adam in a weak voice. The pig's head on the cover of his recipe book grinned at him. For a moment, Adam thought the pig was laughing *at* him, a nasty glint in its tiny, ink eyes. Adam looked more closely. But the pig was just chasing its own tail, as it would for as long as the book existed.

Must have been a trick of the light.

"Will there be anything else, Mr. Carpenter?" said Brown, on the other end of the phone.

Adam swallowed. "Not for now," he said. His throat was dry. "That'll be all for now."

"Of course, Mr. Carpenter. Thank you for your business. And of course, if you need anything at all, please don't hesitate to call. I am at your disposal, all hours. But you know that."

"Yes," said Adam. He was numb. "I know that."

"Until next time, Mr. Carpenter," said Brown. He hung up.

Adam sat down at his kitchen counter, thoughts of dinner, Fergus Henderson, and Julia forgotten. He realized he was still holding on to the lemon. He placed it carefully on the counter.

He began to think about the possibilities inherent in "anything at all."

• • •

At six o'clock, Sarah stood outside the village shop in the driving rain, staring at the noticeboard. Brightly coloured pieces of A4 paper covered in Times New Roman fluttered and rustled in the wind. Drawing pins were obviously at a premium: a large section of the board had been turned into a kind of patchwork of overlapping notices for babysitting services, dog walking, and car washing. She looked at a notice left over from the summer; it was advertising a barbecue, in aid of the local scout group. "Rain or shine," proclaimed the notice. The ink sprawled across the page in a multicoloured explosion of water damage.

A gust of wind caught the papers, lifting a hot-pink sheet advertising an upcoming jumble sale. Underneath it, Sarah saw what she was looking for. She caught the jumble sale notice and ripped it down. Hidden behind it was a plain white offi-cial-looking form. At the top, it said

PLANNING SITE NOTICE

There was a consultation meeting scheduled for that after-noon, at seven o'clock.

That was fast. That was *weird*.

"Hello again," said a voice from behind Sarah's shoulder. She jumped and turned to see Jake Pound standing behind her in his red and white striped butcher's apron. "You feeling better today?"

"Yes," she said. "Thanks." She lifted the pink jumble sale notice. "This came down."

"They never have enough pins, eh?" Jake *tsk*ed and pulled a small box of drawing pins out of the pocket of his apron. "I've got a secret supply for people who know to ask, but I don't advertise it. Mum's the word, Miss Trevelyan." He winked sol-emnly and handed her the box. She thanked him and pinned the jumble sale ad back to the board, leaving the planning notice in plain sight.

"This is a bit sudden, isn't it?" said Sarah, gesturing toward the planning notice. "I thought you were supposed to have the meeting before the construction boards went up. And we must be in the greenbelt here, no?"

Jake looked at the notice as if he were seeing it for the first time. "Hmm," he said. "I suppose so. Although I can't see it going ahead for a while. Not with those poor kids being mur-dered and all. I expect they'll want to hold off until they've got all the evidence they need from the place. Shame to see the old pond go, though. Been there since the Dark Ages, they tell me. 'Course, I only remember back to the Gunpowder Plot." He laughed at his own joke. Sarah smiled. Jake looked more closely at the planning notice and frowned.

"Doesn't seem right," he went on. "I'd go to the meeting, but I can't leave the shop. Still, they do what they want anyway these days, don't they?"

Sarah made a noncommittal noise. "You didn't see who put this up, did you?" she asked.

"Could have been anyone," said Jake. "Looks like it's been there for a while. And I can't see the noticeboard from inside the shop."

"It can't have been here for a *while*," said Sarah, mostly to herself. "It's pouring. There's no water damage on this at all, and it's not even covered in plastic."

Jake looked more closely and shrugged.

"I don't know," he said. "It's a public board. People put things up all the time. I just take 'em down every once in a while when the board gets too cluttered." He looked at the papers fluttering in the breeze. "Probably due for a tidy-up, come to think of it."

Sarah pushed her hair off her face as the wind whipped it around her. "Can I take this with me?" she asked Jake, gesturing to the planning notice.

Jake frowned. "Well, it's fine with me," he said. "But I don't know. Is that legal?"

"Say I wanted to borrow it," said Sarah. "Just for half an hour. You know where I live. I'll bring it back. Thirty minutes. That's all. It was covered by the jumble sale sign anyway."

Jake pursed his lips and let out a long breath somewhere between a whistle and a sigh. "Well," he said. "I can't see the harm. Not if you're planning to bring it back. And there's not long before the meeting anyway. Going to go, are you?"

"Oh, yes," said Sarah. "I'll be going. Civic duty and all that."

"All right, then," said Jake with a nod. "But you bring it back, Miss Trevelyan." He winked.

"Brownie's honour," said Sarah. She was getting good at this. She gave him a military salute before folding the planning notice carefully in four, putting it in her bag, and heading for home.

She was halfway there when she was struck by a thought. She looked at her watch. It had been fifteen minutes since her conversation with Jake. She turned around and retraced her steps back to the shop. The wind was stronger now: the top branches of the trees thrashed back and forth furiously. The notices fluttered and shook. The pink one was pinned down on four corners; the air slid behind it and made it swell and release like the hyperventilations of a hysteric.

Sarah looked closely at the notice.

It *couldn't* be.

The corner of a plain white piece of paper was sticking out from underneath it.

Her mouth fell open. She stopped a short way from the board.

There was no way—

Why would anyone pin a notice under—

She took a step toward the board. There was a loud *crack* from across the road as a large branch snapped from an ash tree, and crashed down to the ground. Sarah jumped.

Why would anyone pin a new notice under *another notice?*

She took another step toward the board and swallowed hard. Her heart was beating fast now. She clenched her jaw tight. She knew that she had to look. She just didn't want confirmation.

Of what?

She didn't want to think about it. She suddenly realized that she was drenched in rain and shivering. She took another step toward the board and reached out a trembling hand. She took a deep breath and ripped away the pink jumble sale notice. The soggy paper clung to her hand.

Hidden behind it was a plain white official-looking form. At the top, it said

PLANNING SITE NOTICE

There was a consultation meeting scheduled for that afternoon at seven o'clock.

Sarah drew in her breath sharply. Her eyes were wide and her pulse was racing. She stood there for a moment, in the rain and howling wind.

"That was quick," said a voice from the door. "God, look at you. You're bloody soaked. Come in here and I'll get you a towel from the back."

"Jake," said Sarah. "Was anyone in the shop since I left? Did you hear a car or anything?"

"Can't hear anything over this wind," said Jake. "Not with the freezers running as well. And nobody ought to be out in this weather. I was only joking," he went on. "You could have waited. You didn't need to get all wet."

"So no one was here?" The look in her eyes pulled Jake up short.

"No," he said. "No one's been in the shop, anyway. Is every-thing all right?"

"I don't...I don't know." She struggled for words. "Can I borrow that towel?"

"Course," said Jake. "Come in out of the wet. I'll go and grab it for you." He ducked back into the shop.

Sarah made her way toward the shop door numbly. Her hand slipped on the wet doorknob, and she gave the door a wild shove that made the bells that hung above it jangle frantically.

"All right?" called Jake, from the back. "Rose is just putting on the kettle for you. We'll be with you in a minute. Have a seat behind the counter."

Sarah wound her way around to a couple of battered bar stools next to the till. She sat down, trying to get a grip on her racing mind.

Another thought struck her. It stood out like a rock suddenly rising in the middle of a rushing torrent of water. She rummaged in her bag until she found what she was looking for.

It was still folded neatly into four. Trembling, she unfolded it once.

Then again.

It was blank. As she stared at it, words bled out of the paper and into view:

GO HOME. MIND YOUR OWN BUSINESS.
OR YOU'LL END UP LIKE THE CHILDREN.

The words looked as though they were written in blood. She knew—she had no proof, but somehow, she *knew*—that the blood, if you could test it, would belong to Gareth and Marina.

She stared in horror at the crimson words soaking onto the paper. The blood began to run down the paper and sizzle, burning through the sheet. Sarah barely had time to drop the sign before it began to dissolve, fizzing furiously. It hit the floor and disintegrated in a wisp of smoke.

She was still looking at the spot on the floor when a woman with dark curly hair emerged from the back of the shop a few minutes later with a hot cup of tea in one hand and a large green bath towel over one arm.

"All right, love?" she said. "I'm Rose. Jake said you got caught in the rain. Crumbs, will you look at the state of you! Forget your umbrella, did you?"

Sarah mumbled something about the rain coming on quite suddenly, and took the towel and the mug.

"You're very welcome to stay. of course," said Rose, "but we don't want to keep you, if you've got things to do. And you'll want to get out of those wet clothes, I imagine. We'll run you home when you've got the worst of it off; it's only a couple of minutes. You don't want to end up poorly. Jake said you're going to this planning meeting tonight. Good for you. They just do what they want these days, don't they?"

Sarah tried to speak. Her throat was dry. She coughed and took a sip of tea.

"Thanks," she said. "Yes. I'm still going to go to the meeting."

Wouldn't miss it for the world, she thought.

Chapter 8

The meeting was in a much smaller room than Sarah had
expected, though it was about as bland: beige walls and tedious
office boardroom chairs and tables lined up in rows with mostly
bored-looking citizens behind them, doing their civic duty.
There weren't very many people there, even though it was seven
o'clock. Sarah recognized the woman that she'd encountered in
the shop on her first day. Maureen, she thought Jake had called
her.

Maureen wasn't bored, though. She was angry.

"I don't know what the heck you think you're doing,
Norman Bastable," she said right off the bat, addressing the
leader of the small group of councillors ensconced behind the
table at the front, "but you must have maggots *in* the brain,
as well as *on* the brain if you think this is a good idea. Putting
a maggot factory smack dab in the middle of the Foxglove
Pond? The lot of you are out of your minds. Have you thought
about the pollution? The increase in traffic in Crowsbrook?
The effect it'll have on the kids? The *smell*, for goodness' sake?
It's not an industrial area. It's a residential area. And yet it's
got this far already. You people can stop it; you should have
stopped it weeks ago. I don't know why we're only just hearing
about it now, but you're going to have one heck of a fight on
your hands, if you try to push this through. And don't think

it doesn't look bad." She took a deep breath. "I've known you a long time, Norm…Mr. Bastable. You too, Annie Casey. And I have to say that, on a personal level, I always thought you were upstanding people. But pushing this through—pushing it through with minimal time for consultation with the public— with the people who *live* in Crowsbrook, for goodness' sake— looks *bad*. Very bad. And I can assure you, that if procedures are not followed properly, I for one won't be shy in asking some very awkward questions."

Sarah believed her. Maureen didn't look like the kind of person who would be shy about asking difficult questions. But district councillors taking kickbacks wasn't the problem. Much as Sarah hated to admit it—even to herself—the incident with the meeting notice outside the shop had unnerved her. She wasn't surprised that there were so few people there. She suspected that someone was working hard to make sure that people either didn't know or didn't care what was going on.

Someone, or something.

Sarah stifled a yawn. The whole atmosphere in the room was beige. Didn't stop Maureen, though; she seemed like the sort of person whose opinions, once formed, had the solid foundations and lasting construction of a small gothic cathedral. Still. Sarah studied the councillors. Was it her imagination, or did they look oddly…*blank?*

"Thank you, Mrs. Greenwood," said Mr. Bastable, an older, fat man in a tweed jacket and thick glasses who was sitting behind a table at the front of the room. For someone who had apparently known Maureen Greenwood for a long time, he seemed strangely unmoved by her impassioned speech and her intimations of wrongdoing. "Your points will be taken into consideration."

"They'd better be," sputtered Maureen. "*Totally* illegal, what these developers want to do. Outrageous. You can't put a maggot factory in the middle of the greenbelt, for goodness' sake." She sat down, still muttering.

A young woman with a toddler on her lap raised her hand and introduced herself as Sally Jenson. She was obviously nervous, and she had dark rings under her eyes.

"Is this—" She coughed a couple of times, and then blew her nose. "Is this factory going to be hiring a lot of people? Because that would be good for the area, wouldn't it? A big factory. Give people something to do, without them having to take the bus for an hour each way to work." She coughed again. The toddler didn't look well either; she looked as though she ought to be home in bed, or waiting to see a good doctor, to Sarah. A large rash covered one side of the child's face, and she was limp and lethargic, like a rag doll.

Wait: job opportunities? Who asks about that kind of thing at a meeting about planning permission?

She sharpened up. Something was going on here. Now. In this room.

She looked around her at the people in the room. To her right, Maureen Greenwood. Sally Jenson and her toddler. Two middle-aged woman with iron-sprayed hair, sitting next to Mr. Bastable behind the table at the front, one of whom must be Anne, or Annie, Casey. In front of Sarah, sat a young man in an immaculate suit; next to him were three men in their seventies: a Fair Isle jumper, an Aran jumper, and a fisherman's pullover. All home knitted, by the looks of them. At the front of the room, a middle-aged man with a briefcase and a slightly more crumpled suit.

"I know most of you here," Crumpled Suit said, with a friendly smile, turning to look at the people in the room, "and you know me. And you know I know Maureen." A couple of people half smiled and nodded. "For those of you who don't know me, I'm Richard Greenwood. I'm a lawyer, and I work independently, making sure, if you'll excuse me," he turned to the councillors at the front table, "that these sorts of corporate abuses are stopped before they tear communities—and, let's be frank—*lives* apart. *Regardless* of whether they provide jobs for the people whose lives they're ruining with ill health and pollution."

Sarah had little experience with lawyers, but her instinct was not to trust anyone in a suit. Still, this man (Greenwood—Maureen's husband, she guessed) seemed to be another lone voice in the fog of apathy that filled the room.

"I will make myself as clear as possible," he was saying. "The legal process—the correct procedures for moving forward legally with a development of this kind—are being completely overridden. This is not how things are done. Even if this development were lawful—which there is a sheaf of evidence," he picked up a stack of papers from the chair next to him and waved them, "clearly demonstrating that it is not—the mere fact that it is being rushed through in this cavalier manner is, frankly, flabbergasting. Again, I cannot make this more clear: if you approve this development, ladies and gentlemen of the council, you will be in violation of both the law and your clear moral duty to observe due process as elected representatives of the community. I do not say this lightly." He put down the pile of papers. "As Maureen added a personal note, so shall I: I'm well aware that we have bumped heads, as it were, before over property development issues, but I have always found the council in the past to be reasonable people. This rough-riding over due process is unbelievable. I appeal to you, ladies and gentlemen, please at least adhere to due process and allow us to make our arguments against this abomination of a development appropriately and as befits a democratic community. To do otherwise, even at the local council level, is to allow a terrifying precedent to take place, and is also an insult to the people that you were elected to represent."

"Hear, hear," cried Maureen, clapping enthusiastically. Everyone else was silent.

Mr. Bastable assured him that his concerns would be taken into consideration.

Something was wrong.

Sarah's grasp of property development law was somewhat hazy (*all right, non-existent; shut up, Eleanor*), but even she could tell that this meeting was a farce. It was just for show. The decisions had already been made, and the development would go ahead. Maureen was speaking again; the man in the crumpled suit was pointing out all the objections, all the problems with procedure; the three men in hand-knitted sweaters were speaking up in favour of the kids being able to get an honest job after leaving school, nothing like working in a factory for teaching you the value of a hard day's work; and the man at the front was merely repeating that procedure was being followed and that all objections would be taken into consideration.

This was not how things were supposed to work. She began to make a list in her mind. Her house was full of spiders. A gravestone in the churchyard had mysteriously cracked open and bled into the ground. Two kids were dead. She'd gone to the Foxglove Pond twice in two days: the first time, everything was fine; the second time, she'd encountered a sleeping insect demon. And someone had—supernaturally—warned her to stop looking into it.

Well, screw that.

Someone wanted to put a maggot factory where they shouldn't. Where it was illegal. Where, if everything were normal, it should be very easy to stop them. But, for some reason, every barrier to doing this massively illegal thing (she was starting to sound like Maureen now, she thought) was collapsing and blowing away like so much ash.

Who would want to do this? And why? And how were they working?

To some extent, *how* wasn't a question. Ethereals were involved. She just didn't know which ones.

Ethereal was the generic term her grandmother had taught her for supernatural beings. It covered everything from poltergeists and phantom Grey Ladies to *chupacabras*, vampires, and werebeasts. It definitely covered insect demons, even napping ones. And only Ethereals had the power to bend reality so that a six-week planning process was finished in two days, and a police investigation that should have taken a month was done and dusted within twenty-four hours.

It was just that usually—well, they *didn't*. Or rather, they *couldn't*. Usually. They would have to be phenomenally powerful to even consider it. There were systems in place so that this kind of thing didn't happen. An uneasy peace. Balance. *Symbiosis.*

Something had happened that had allowed some Ethereal to act—to make changes—in the human world. But what?

Crap. Not only did she not know, she didn't know where to look to find out.

Also, she was *angry.* The last time she'd encountered Ethereals trying to muck about with the mortal world, her life had ended up barbecued. And she wasn't about to let that happen to anyone else.

You're not paying attention. Her grandmother's voice echoed in her head. Sarah snapped back to the meeting and tried to focus.

Look closely. Who's in this room?

Only the man in the immaculate suit hadn't said anything so far. He was sitting two rows in front of her. She studied his back. There was nothing remarkable about it.

Was *he* Ethereal? Many Ethereals were good at disguising themselves, most for innocuous reasons; for many, it was how they survived. But a few, like a few humans, were deeply malevolent. He was out in daylight, which ruled out a large number of Ethereal creatures. He wasn't obviously translucent.

Am I grasping at straws? she thought.

The obvious answer came back to her in a voice halfway between Eleanor's and her grandmother's: *straws are all you have.*

Even if he was a malevolent Ethereal, what could she do? The only weapon she had on her person was a rolled-up meeting agenda, but even if she'd had something more suitable—and you had to pick your weapon carefully if you wanted to do away with an Ethereal—she could hardly enact a double-combo, all-purpose banishing-and-binding ritual in meeting room four, spontaneously, in the District Council offices. She suspected that Mr. Bastable and Mrs. Casey would not look kindly upon that. Even if it *would* be in their own best interests.

She couldn't see anything that suggested the man in the immaculate suit was Ethereal. But something in the room wasn't right. Why were conservative-with-a-small-c townspeople speaking up in favour of a development that would, at best, rip the beating heart out of a small, idyllic village?

She wanted to *know*.

She decided to try something. It was a long shot, but it wouldn't draw any attention to herself. And if Immaculate Suit were Ethereal and bent on destruction, then he wouldn't be able to do anything to her. Not in meeting room four. Not without blowing his cover.

At least, she hoped he wouldn't.

She took a deep breath as quietly as possible and began, as her grandmother called it, to *connect*.

Her conscious mind felt its way down to the carpet of the meeting room, and then plunged through the cracks in the floorboards, through a tangle of wires and plumbing, through the damp course, through the cement foundations of the council offices and into the damp earth below. *Down* it burrowed, through stones and roots and worms and insects and small things trying to grow in the dark. Down through water. Down to rock, smooth rock that had shifted, over time, rock that had once been part of a continent and had shifted, inch by inch over millennia, rock that was still shifting a little every day. Through the rock. Down further, to where the rocks warmed and softened and eventually melted, to boiling seas of molten lava, raging under plates of rock ready to spring into life and tear the superficial world on top to pieces.

To the beating heart of the Earth.

She connected.

She could feel it; she was a part of it: just like the grinding rocks and the swirling magma, she was a part of it, the remnants of an exploded star, billions of years old, remade, recycled, renewed.

She pulled a fragment, a minuscule fragment, of the power of the Earth into her body for a few seconds and then let it loose in the room.

To the untrained eye, very little changed, although everyone present would feel mysteriously energized after such a depressing and unproductive meeting. Maureen Greenwood would go home and write to six relevant members of parliament about the problem, as well as the county ombud. Richard Greenwood, the lawyer, would help their daughter, Cat, with her homework, and then stay up late into the night preparing for the next stage of the fight against the maggot factory. Becky Jenson, with the nasty rash, would later rally a bit, to her mother's relief. But while still in meeting room four, she just woke up and started crying.

The man in the immaculate suit leaped out of his seat and left the room in a hurry.

Sarah slumped in her chair a little. Connecting had taken a lot out of her, and she still had to keep a low profile. But it *was* interesting that he had left. The energy release that was imperceptible to humans, would, to an Ethereal, have been like three fire engines with their sirens blaring and a jackhammer running at full tilt exploding into meeting room four all at once.

She hoped that he wouldn't realize who had done it. Although anyone watching the meeting properly—anyone who knew that family businesses such as hers existed—would be able to figure it out in a jiffy. She was the only other person in the room who hadn't said anything, for a start.

Then again, she'd been sitting behind him. Had she come in before or after him? She couldn't remember. *Damn.*

If she waited until the end of the meeting and filed out with the rest, he was unlikely to spot her. The energy from the heart of the planet would hang around everyone for a while. It was a tiny amount, in the grand scheme of things, but she would have one hell of a headache tonight. She massaged her right temple in anticipation.

The fact that he left still isn't proof, she thought to herself. *It might just be a coincidence.*

It might be, answered her grandmother's voice. *Then again, it might not.*

When the meeting ended, she looked for the man in the immaculate suit as she left the room and made her way through the labyrinthine council offices and back to the street. She didn't see him anywhere.

She didn't notice three very large, very green, very dead flies on the floor near the door as she left meeting room four, either.

• • •

Gravel crunched as Dr. Julia Fletcher pulled her BMW into the driveway leading to the house she shared with Adam. She was tired and hungry. She decided to leave the car round the front; she could always move it if Adam needed to get out later. She wanted to have dinner and watch some bad telly and have an early night and not think about surgery. Maybe Adam could get the take-away on his way home. She'd go to Tesco tomorrow, and fill up the fridge.

She parked the car, and took out her phone to call Adam. As she unlocked the front door and stepped into the house, a wonderful smell hit her: garlic and olive oil and lemons. The citrus scent gave her an instant lift; it reminded her of the time they had been on holiday to Italy—Tuscany—a couple of years before.

"Adam?" she called. "Hello?" It was rare that he was home before she was.

She went into the kitchen. He was standing there with a huge smile on his face. There was a huge bouquet of flowers lying on the kitchen island: starburst lilies, her favourite. Two pots were bubbling gently on the stove.

"Welcome home," he said, beaming. "Happy Friday."

Julia's mouth fell open. She laughed.

"Wow," she said, grinning. "You *have* been busy."

He handed her the flowers with a sweeping bow. "For you, madam," he said with a flourish, and then grabbed her hand. "C'mon. I have to show you something."

He led her through the glass doors at the back of the kitchen and round to the back of the house near the garage. Julia gasped. Parked just outside of the garage was a horse box; inside it was a handsome bay mare. She snorted and tossed her head. Julia looked at Adam in delight and disbelief.

"I thought you might like her," he said. He looked down at his feet and smiled shyly.

"I—I do," said Julia. She stepped forward and the horse came to meet her, lowering her head so Julia could rub her nose. "She's beautiful. But—I mean—you don't just buy someone a horse because it's Friday. Can we afford this? Where are we going to keep her?"

"It's all taken care of," said Adam. "I have a folder inside, if you want to check the details. But I think it'll work."

"This is amazing," said Julia. The horse was exactly as she'd always wished; it was the animal she'd dreamt of owning since she was a child. "Thank you, Adam." She left the horse and kissed him on the lips. "Is this because of the new development? It's going well?"

"It's going really well," said Adam, still beaming. "Everything's going to be different from now on. You can have anything you want."

Julia looked back at the horse. "Wow," she said again. "Just—wow. We can't just leave her there, though."

"I thought we'd have dinner and then drive her over to the paddock," said Adam. "We can borrow the box for the evening. She'll be okay for half an hour, then we can take her to her new home. And you can give her a quick run around, if you like."

"Oh my God," said Julia. She was feeling heady and a little breathless. "You've sorted all this out already? You must have been working on it for days! I thought the deal had only gone ahead this week."

"Let's go back in and have dinner," said Adam. "Don't want it to burn or anything. Or set fire to the kitchen." Although, he reflected, they could always just replace the kitchen now. Brown would see to it.

He felt a slight twinge of pain in his stomach. *Must just be hungry*, he thought.

"Come on," he said, putting his arm around Julia. "Let's go eat."

• • •

Hours later, Jez awoke with a start. She looked at the digital display on the clock next to her bed. The numbers glowed eerily in the dark.

3:22.

She groaned and realized at the same time that she was thirsty.

She had lived in the same house for more than half of her life; she didn't bother to put the light on as she groped around on her bedside table for her glass and hauled herself out of bed to go to the bathroom. She pressed down the handle of her bedroom door gently, and tiptoed past her father's room. She could hear his breathing, slow and even, from the landing.

The light in the bathroom made her wince when she flicked the switch, like a sudden, too-loud blast of music. She filled her glass with cold water and drank. The carpet in the bathroom was soft under her bare feet as she drained the glass.

Turning the light back out plunged her into temporary blindness as her eyes adjusted. She ran her fingers along the wall of the landing until her eyes adjusted to the darkness and her hand touched the frame of the door to her bedroom.

She'd be fine now. She was a heavy sleeper usually, and her curtains were thin; although there were few street lights in the village, the storm from earlier had cleared and the light from the moon leaked through the fabric. It wasn't bright but it was enough to see—

She froze, gasping.

There was something in her bed. Something that hadn't been there before. There was a lump beneath her blue and white duvet. Whatever it was, it wasn't moving, but she could see its outline clearly.

It looked about the same size and shape as a human being.

Fear closed around her like a clamp; she felt her stomach drop through the floor. She fumbled for the light switch, scrabbling on the wall until she found the white plastic square, her hands shaking. She slapped at the switch; the room exploded in light, temporarily blinding her. She blinked as her pupils contracted; when she saw what was on the bed, she cried out, her stomach heaving.

On the bed—*in* the bed, in *her* bed—was Marina Butterworth. Marina Butterworth's body, decomposing, and half-covered by Jez's comforter. Her skin was peeling off in sheets; her lips and tongue were swollen and bloated. Her eye sockets bore the traces of her signature heavy eyeliner, but her eyes had liquefied in their sockets, leaving black, gelid trails over what was left of her cheeks; half of her face had already rotted away and Jez could see her teeth and jawbone through the rags of tendons and sinews that remained.

And the corpse—the thing—*Marina*—was alive with maggots.

Jez's eyes grew wide with terror and her breath caught in her throat. Cold flashed though her body like lightning, followed quickly by nausea. She tried to scream and half-choked on the rising contents of her stomach. A cluster of maggots dropped out of the socket where Marina's left eye had been and fell with a soft patter on Jez's bedsheet.

Jez half screamed and half howled.

"What? What is it?" Jez's father was behind her in an instant, hitting the landing light with so much force that the plastic switch cracked. "What's going on, Jez?"

She turned to face him, sobbing and insensible. She could barely get the words out though heavy, gasping breaths; each one was hard labour.

"In...in...my...in my *bed...*" she eventually managed. She screwed her eyes shut and pressed her head against the wall.

Her father was over there like a shot. He turned to her, looking puzzled.

"But Jessie," he said, using the name that he'd always used when she was little and skinned her knee or had fallen out of a tree or smashed into a wall on her roller skates and come to him wailing. "Jessie, there's nothing here."

Jez froze.

In the warm glare of the electric light, she moved slowly over to the bed. It was empty. The sheets were clean. There were no stains. No maggots. No corpse.

For the second time in a few minutes, she was flooded with fear, which ebbed into relief, briefly, before her stomach was gripped by the tension of a low-lying dread.

"But..." Her breathing was more even now, although her heart was still racing. "She was right *here*. She was in my bed."

"Who was in your bed, sweetheart?" asked her dad, gently. "There's no one here."

"Marina," Jez managed, before collapsing into tears.

Her dad swore under his breath. "Oh, lord. Jessie, it must be so hard for you at the moment. She was in your year, wasn't she? That little girl who died?"

Jez sobbed harder. Her dad hugged her.

"You just had a nightmare, Jessie. It's all okay now. All okay." He stroked her hair. "Everything's okay. There's nothing in your bed."

Jez's heart rate was slowing and her breathing was calmer. But she knew what she had seen. And she knew what it implied.

She was involved.

Before, she had been on the outside of whatever it was that Sarah was trying to deal with; now, whatever that force was had identified her as a source of trouble. Whatever that force was, whoever controlled it, *it knew about her*. And she knew that from now on, it would be watching her.

"Do you want to sleep in the spare room tonight?" her dad was saying. "I can make up the bed, if you want."

She looked at him and saw how tired he was, and how concerned. She took a deep breath.

"Yes," she said. "Yes, please. I mean. I know it was just a dream. I'll be fine." With an immense effort of will, she sat down on the bed and picked up a pink rabbit from the bedside table next to her. "I've got Mr. Pinkles with me. I'll be okay." She forced herself to smile. "But can I sleep in the spare room?"

Her dad frowned for a moment. "Of course." He looked directly at the rabbit. "And I'm relying on you, Mr. Pinkles."

Jez giggled, and this time, it wasn't fake. "Thanks, Dad," she said. "Sorry for waking you up."

"No problem," he said, with a smile. "Any more nightmares, just holler and I'll come running."

"Will do," said Jez. "But I think I'll be okay now."

She helped her dad make up the bed in the spare room. When he had tucked her in, like he used to do when she was small, she waited for him to turn off the light on the landing and close the door to his room before switching her bedside lamp on again. She lay under the covers waiting, although she couldn't have said for what.

• • •

Sarah, as she had predicted, had a hell of a headache. She was lying in bed; the shards of the power she had taken up earlier worked their way through her. It felt as if an iron ring had been placed inside her skull and was slowly expanding; as if, were her head to crack open or her eye to drop out, the pressure would release and the pain would go away.

Wasn't likely to happen, though. The only thing she could do was to wait it out. She let out a short involuntary gasp of pain in the silence.

Silence.

It was silent. The rustling had stopped.

Sarah opened her eyes.

The spiders were in the room with her. The walls, door, nightstand were all covered with arachnids. They pooled around her hands on the top of the bedspread. She couldn't move, for fear of squashing one.

She didn't think that would go down too well.

Sarah looked straight ahead, at the assorted spiders that covered the ceiling.

"I'm supposed to take care of you," she said. "I wish I knew how."

It happened in a heartbeat.

They swept over her, thousands upon thousands of delicate, spiked legs crawling over her skin, *layers* of them, flowing over her arms, in her hair, on her face. She held her breath, partly from shock, partly afraid to inhale for fear of choking on the swarm; she couldn't move. And they kept coming, in their hundreds. She could feel their collective weight through the blankets.

The pressure built in her lungs from the effort of not breathing.

And then, just as suddenly, they were gone, back to the walls, to the ceiling. Sarah sat up, very carefully. There were none on the bed. She looked around her. The spiders seemed to be waiting. They were still.

She realized her headache was gone. She looked at the spiders.

"That's it?" she said. The spiders didn't move.

"You feed off of..." She didn't want to finish the sentence. *Energy* seemed a little too New Age and she could imagine what the kid would say. "That's how you feed," she finished.

As one, the spiders flowed out of Sarah's bedroom door and back into the room in which she'd first found them.

"That's how they feed," she muttered to herself again, looking after them. "That's how she must have fed them."

Drained, she drifted into sleep with a single word echoing in her brain: *familiars*.

Chapter 9

At 7:26 the next morning, Sarah's phone rang. She cursed and rolled over and picked it up. A spider ran out of her hair, across her pillow, and disappeared down the side of her bed.

"Yes?" she said, frowning.

"Something else happened," said a voice on the other end.

"Huh," said Sarah. "Yes. Like what?"

Jez explained about the vision she'd had of Marina's corpse.

"Can I come over?" she finished. "I have something to show you."

"Don't you have school?"

"It's Saturday," said Jez, patiently. "So no. I'm going to a protest against this maggot factory later, though."

"I'm not up yet," said Sarah. She yawned. "Give me thirty minutes."

At 7:55, there was a knock on the door. Sarah cursed again and ran her fingers through her still-wet hair, pushing it out of her face. When she opened the door, she found Jez neatly dressed in jeans and a dark grey coat.

"I have to show you something," said Jez.

"Yes," said Sarah, rubbing her eyes. "You said that on the phone." She moved aside so that Jez could come in. "So what's going on?"

Jez produced a glass jar from her green bag.

"This," she said. "It's dead. I found it in my room."

Sarah peered through the curved glass of the jar. At the bottom of the jar, on its back with its legs jutting upwards at improbable angles, was a large fly, obviously dead. It had the iridescent sheen of a bluebottle, but it was significantly larger— about three-quarters of an inch from head to tail—and shone a deep, eerie green as the light caught it.

"What kind of fly is it?" asked Sarah. "You're the science kid."

"I don't know," said Jez. "I did some online research and looked in the books I do have that have entomology sections, but I couldn't find anything. Maybe it's nothing," she finished, lamely, "but I thought you might want to see it."

"I don't think it's necessarily nothing," said Sarah. She thought back to the meeting and the man in the immaculate suit. "Maybe it's a coincidence. Maybe it's not. Given that we don't really know a lot about anything that's going on, it might be worth taking a closer look. Although I'm not really sure how."

Sarah and Jez looked at each other and then back to the fly.

"Can I dissect it?" said Jez. "Will it be dangerous? I brought the things with me."

"If you're not careful with the scalpel, it will be," said Sarah. "How do you dissect something as small as this?"

"You can do it," said Jez. "I mean, it's possible." She pulled her green bag onto her knees. "I know that correlation isn't causation and all that," she went on, "but seeing Marina—or whatever it was that looked like it used to be Marina—really freaked me out, and I've never seen a fly like this around here before. Well, really, I hadn't before all this started happening. But there was one in the biology lab the other day, and my teacher was acting all weird. Which is probably just a coincidence. It shouldn't take very long. But I didn't want to do it by myself in case something else happened."

"Good call," said Sarah. She looked directly at Jez. "You know this is getting dangerous, right?"

Jez avoided her gaze, studying the fly in the jar intently. "It's just a fly."

"You shouldn't be involved."

"But I'm up to my ears in it now, aren't I?" Jez set the jar down on the table in the living room and dug in her bag for a cloth roll of dissection tools. "And *they know.*"

"Yes. They know you're involved."

"So now what happens?"

"We have to try and stop it," said Sarah. "Do you not watch telly at all?"

Jez glared at her. "Fuck off."

Sarah raised an eyebrow. "Why are you so hostile?"

"TV and real life are two different things," said Jez. She put the roll of tools down and turned to face Sarah. "I'm scared, and I didn't ask to be part of this. And I don't even know who you are, not really. I don't know why you're so mixed up in all this stuff or how you know so much about it all or even whether any of what you say is true. I've been going along with it, because it's the best explanation I've got." Her voice was rising. "And now there's something supernatural or paranormal or whatever going on in *my village* and I have to stop it? How? How do you stop something when the fact that it exists in the first place makes no sense?" She was yelling now. "None of this makes any sense! You realize that, don't you?"

Sarah stood up.

"And I *swear,*" shouted Jez, "that if you go into the kitchen and put the kettle on, I'll come in there and dump tea all over

the floor! You can't keep running away when I ask you questions! What the hell is going on? Really?"

Sarah sighed deeply and pushed her hair out of her face
with both hands. For a moment, to Jez, she looked terribly old.

"No tea," she said. "Right."

She bent down opened a small cabinet made of dark wood
behind her. The door opened with a *thunk*, and she pulled out a
dark-green bottle of Laphroaig and a dusty glass. She wiped off
the glass with her skirt and poured herself a large slug of Scotch.

"Auntie Dot's personal reserve," she said, drily. "I wouldn't
normally offer you one, since you're under eighteen and it's
Saturday morning," she said, "but we're dealing with serious
stuff now, and if you're not capable of acting like a grown-up,
you're not going to last very long at all. Got that?"

Jez nodded.

"Right," said Sarah. "Want one?"

Jez stared at her. It was the first time an adult she wasn't
related to had offered her a drink. And whiskey, at that.

"Yes, please," she managed. "But just a small one."

Sarah pulled out another glass and poured Jez a Scotch.
Jez took a sip. She'd never tried spirits before. The sour taste of
the Scotch and the burning in her throat were horrible, but she
managed not to pull a face.

"Where do you want me to start?" said Sarah.

Jez stared at the floor. "I don't know," she admitted. "Tell
me how you know so much about all this stuff."

"I read a lot."

"Bollocks. I read a lot, too. I hang around with people who
read a lot, and they're *not like you.*"

Sarah took a sip of her whiskey and sat there in silence.

"I'm a witch," she said simply.

Jez rolled her eyes and looked incredulous; she couldn't help it. "Like in *Harry Potter?*"

"No," said Sarah. "Not like in *Harry Potter.*" She took a sip of whiskey and ran her finger around the edge of the glass. "It's my family's business. This is what we've always done. There's no Hogwarts, no professors, no house points for levitating the cat. They used to call us cunning women. Or cunning men. You read a lot. You study. You know how it is. I learned a lot from my grandmother. There aren't many of us left. Not here, anyway."

"How many?"

"One. That I know of. There might be others, but not many. It's a job with a lot of hazards."

They sat in silence. Minutes passed.

"You're a witch." Jez's voice was flat.

Sarah stood up and beckoned. "Come here." She crossed the room to the green velvet curtain and pulled it aside. Jez stepped into the alcove, ducking slightly under Sarah's arm; she blinked as her eyes adjusted to the half light.

The room was lit by candles, and there was a stick of incense burning on the altar, which was covered by a cloth that had obviously been hand-embroidered, probably a long time ago: the cloth was clean, but showed a little yellowing from age. There were two vases of fresh flowers on the altar, and Sarah had polished the silver candlesticks until they gleamed. Jez's mouth fell open.

"It's beautiful," she said, eventually. "What is it?"

"It's an altar," said Sarah. "To the old gods. My family's gods. That thing's been there since Victorian times, although we were wise men and wise women for way longer. A cheap alternative to surgeons and apothecaries. Especially out here, in the country." This was the second time in her life that she had

had this conversation, and she was acutely aware that not only had she been warned by her grandmother against ever having it at all, but that the eventual result of her having it the first time had been more dire than she could ever have imagined.

But you saw the atoms, she reminded herself. *She's important.*

Jez rolled her eyes again; it was like a reflex. *I've got to stop doing that*, she thought. "Gods," she said. "So...you're religious?"

Sarah caught her eye. "Not in the way you mean it. Well, not at all, really. The old gods don't help much with anything. It's just best not to piss them off. And then be grateful to them that you haven't."

"Oh," said Jez. "So they can't help?"

"They could," said Sarah, "but they're arseholes. So they probably won't."

"Oh." Moments passed and Jez felt awkward in the silence; her mind was scrabbling frantically for something to say. It seemed to happen a lot when she was with Sarah. "So. What does being a witch involve, anyway?" She felt like an interviewer on the kind of lame daytime TV chat show she only watched on the rare occasions she was sick and didn't have the energy to read.

"Depends," said Sarah. "Time was, it was love potions and curing warts. Getting rid of demons. Trying to avoid being confused with one, and avoiding the vicar. Knowing your herbal medicines. Keeping the peace between neighbours without letting them know that's what you were doing, but you don't need magic for that."

"Magic?" Jez looked disbelieving.

"Real." Sarah was staring into the middle distance. She felt as though all her skin had been peeled away, exposing her nerves to the mild and slightly stuffy air of the cottage.

"How real?"

"Just take my word for it for now. Chances are, you'll find out sooner or later, the way things are going." Sarah drained the glass of whiskey. "It's powerful stuff. Like any natural force, I guess. It's all about controlling it. You know. Like electricity."

"Is it dangerous?"

"It's like electricity," said Sarah, again. She stared at the carpet. "You can use it to power a life-support machine or an electric chair, or to make a meal for your friends, or to attach clamps to some poor bugger's balls and make him scream until he tells you what you want. Yes, it's dangerous. But if you know how to use it…" She trailed off. "Short answer: you can use it safely," she said, coming back to the moment. "But you'd sure as hell better know what you're doing. Otherwise you might blow a fuse."

Jez didn't want to know what blowing a fuse might entail if you were using magic. Also, something was bothering her. Her curiosity was running hard, in spite of herself.

"What about other things?"

"Like what?"

"I don't know. The kind of stuff that Saskia French is into. Sort-of magic things. 'Occult' stuff, I guess." She made the quotation marks with her fingers. "Tarot cards, for instance."

"They work, yeah. But not in the way most people think. The best way to find out what happens in the future is to stay out of trouble so you're around to find out."

"Astrology?"

"Sometimes helpful, if you're good at it. You have to be very patient and quite good at maths. Don't bother reading your horoscope in the paper, though. Unless you're bored."

Jez nodded, numbly. "I don't. But thanks. Crystals?"

"Shiny rocks. Didn't we talk about that before?"

Jez smiled, in spite of herself. "How about Ouija boards? When I was in primary school, one of the dinner ladies used to go berserk every time she caught Cassie Soles and Emily O'Brien in the washroom with a home-made Ouija board. I swear to God, it would happen, like, once every six months." She thought back to the bleak playground, and Cassie and Emily furtively sneaking off to the toilets with the piece of stolen sugar paper, the letters written on it in felt tip. "Is it, like, from the Devil? That's what Mrs. Tate used to say." She still couldn't quite bring herself to believe in the Devil. Despite all she had seen, it still felt like a cop-out.

"Well," said Sarah. "The electricity thing still stands. But with the boards...that's really more like calling a phone box in the middle of nowhere. You really need to know why you're doing it. Shits and giggles? Curiosity? For help? You might get a good Samaritan. You might get a prankster who wants to mess with your head. Or you might get a complete psycho. If you should have called the emergency services, that kind of thing won't help you." She sighed. "It's kind of complicated. But on the bright side, they're easy to use."

"I see." Jez leaned on the wall of the alcove, transfixed by the altar. The candles flickered, making shadows dance on the walls like macabre puppets. She felt as though the foundations of her world, already loosened by her shortcut through the churchyard and her trip down to the Foxglove Pond, were crumbling faster by the minute. It *couldn't* be true, and yet the evidence of her own eyes gave the lie to her conviction. Her mind felt partially frozen, as if it refused to process what she knew it ultimately must.

"You still haven't told me what it is you do. Now. These days."

Sarah looked at Jez steadily. Her voice was quiet and even and urgent.

"Jez," she said. "There's a whole other world lying underneath the one that most people see, and they don't know about it. Sometimes you can catch glimpses of it, in everyday things that you don't think about—in superstitions and in folk tales—but mostly, people don't know and they don't care. People think that because they have smart phones and flat-screen tellies and Internet connections and antibiotics and chemotherapy that nothing bad will ever happen to them, or that if it does, Science-with-a-capital-S and Technology-with-a-capital-T will just zap the humanness of the human condition out of its misery and everything can go on like it did before. But the truth is that shitty things still happen. You're no less subject to chance than you were before. Just because you can go to Tesco if there's a bad harvest, and slap some Germolene on your finger if you slice yourself open doesn't mean that you're less a part of nature—less *subject* to nature—than you were before. You've just got all this crap in the way so you can't see it. And not seeing that is the problem now. The things from before—the old things, the ancient things—that feed on human misery all still exist. We may have got the upper hand over the last century or so, but they're waiting and they're watching and they're adapting, like any organism under threat. You know how it is. They're biding their time, but they want to come back. And they *will* find a way."

She upended her glass, searching for one final drop, ducked around the curtain and held it open for Jez. "My job *now* is to keep an eye out for where they look like they're managing to get a foothold and to try and stop them."

Jez frowned. "What kind of ancient things are they, anyway? More demons?"

Sarah was sitting on the edge of her favourite chair, by the book cases, with her elbows on her knees. "Sometimes. Sometimes bigger things. Things that could race demons like people race greyhounds." She frowned. "Do people even run greyhounds anymore? Anyway." She sat up straight and slapped her thighs. "Big, scary, dangerous intra- and occasionally extra-dimensional beings. Versus me. Welcome to my life." She got up. "I think I'm going to have another drink."

Jez watched her, frozen. The magnitude of what Sarah had just said was almost unbelievable.

"But there's *one* of you," she said, after a long pause. "Against all that?"

"I didn't say I was winning."

"It doesn't sound like a zero-sum game," said Jez. "They can't be unequivocally powerful or they'd have won by now."

"I like you. You're clever." Sarah took the bottle back out of the cabinet and poured herself another slug, healthier than the first. "Maybe two is too much. Do you think two is too much? Oh, what the hey. I've earned it. And it's not even nine o'clock." She took a big swig and looked at Jez. "This is the last one, though. I didn't used to work alone," she added, almost as an afterthought.

What are you doing? She couldn't really tell whose voice she was hearing anymore. Eleanor's, her grandmother's. *Fuck it*, she thought. The normal rules didn't apply anymore. She'd always followed the rules before, and look where that had got her. Maybe it was time to try Dot's way.

Jez couldn't imagine Sarah around other people for very long. She was intrigued. "Who did you work with? If you don't mind me asking. I mean, if it's not too personal a question." There was something about Sarah that suggested it might be.

"It's all right." Sarah sipped her drink. I worked with a friend. A close friend. Whatever. There isn't really a formal business structure for this kind of set-up. She wasn't a witch. Well, she sort of was. Her family weren't. No family business stuff."

"She was a Muggle?"

Sarah looked at Jez blankly for a moment and then burst out laughing. It was the first time Jez had heard her laugh. Come to think of it, it was the first time that Jez had seen her smile.

"Oh, lord," she said eventually. "I suppose so. In a way. She was studying anthropology when I met her. She moved on, though: secret societies, Aleister Crowley, the Golden Dawn, that kind of thing. But she knew a lot about folklore as well." She looked down at her feet. "She's dead now."

"Oh," said Jez. She knew you were supposed to say more. "I'm sorry about that," she managed.

"Me too. It's an occupational hazard."

"What happened?"

"There was," said Sarah, "a house fire. It didn't start by accident. My previous house. We were in the west country. Cornwall. There's a lot of old stuff down there. Things from the old days. Beings." She stared at her glass. She knew she should stop, but she hadn't spoken to anyone about what had happened. Hadn't *really* spoken to anyone since the fire.

"Fair folk," she said, bringing her chin up.

"Fairies?" said Jez, wrinkling her nose.

"Not mini-Barbie dolls with sparkly dresses and butterfly wings," said Sarah. "You'd never see them unless they wanted you to, and they want you to less and less these days, especially after what happened in Cornwall. And they're warriors, not wish-granters; treat them like a mail-order catalogue, and you're likely to get a knife between the shoulder blades before you know it." She rubbed her forehead. "But you know what they say about bringing a knife to a gun fight. And so do they. So they stay out of the way of humans."

She massaged her temples.

"Anyway," she went on. "One of the clans in Cornwall are the guardians of—" she paused "—a fern. A particular kind of fern. It's—I guess the closest human concept is 'sacred'—to them. And it has the unfortunate side effect of causing eternal youth."

She took another deep breath. This was getting difficult.

"I say 'unfortunate,' because some poisonous human—a speculator, or something, something to do with making an arseload of money out of other people—found out about it. I have no idea how. I would like to find out. But that aside, this piece of slime decided that the best use for this sacred fern, this plant that had been guarded by the fair-folk clan since before time began, that the best use for it was dissecting it in a lab, so that he could synthesise its essential properties chemically and make the world's most effective anti-aging cream." Her voice dripped with contempt. "Because the worst possible thing in this world is looking *old*. Because ancient wisdom is only good for *marketing*. For making a fast buck. He sent in the heavies. He teamed up with the worst kind of Ethereals—'supernatural' beings." She made quotation marks with her fingers. "Ethereals are 'supernatural' beings."

"Not if they exist," said Jez. "Everything that exists is natural by definition."

Impressive, thought Sarah. She tilted her head in agreement. "You're getting the hang of this."

Yeah, thought Jez. *Except I usually use that line to point out when stuff's bollocks.*

"He found out the fern existed," said Sarah. "He made it look like he was going to play things by the book. Sent a delegate from his team of Ethereals to ask the fair folk how much they wanted for the fern. They sent the puppet back with donkey's ears to make a point. So he tried again: told them he was going to buy the land they live on, so it'd be his anyway. This time, they send his agent back in seven pieces, over the course of a week. So he went to war."

She shrugged.

"What were they going to do? They put up a good fight, but they were up against mercenary Ethereals. Ethereals who have done a deal with a human. Ethereals who apparently now have a stake in the human world. I don't know what he offered them, but whatever it is, it's bad news for, oh, everybody else. The fair folk? They weren't a big group to begin with. And lots of them died."

She barely seemed to be talking to Jez.

"You know how much the world loses when something mortal dies," she said, eventually. "Think about what it loses when you kill something that's supposed to be immortal."

Jez realized she was listening with her mouth open.

"How did—" she began. "How did you get involved? If they don't talk to anybody, I mean. Is it, like, everybody magic knows each other?"

Sarah ran her tongue around her teeth thoughtfully.

"No," she said. "It was the house."

The old house. The house she'd grown up in.

"The house had been my family's for centuries," she said. "The house I was living in, I mean. When you run a family business out of one house for that long, it builds up...well. Let's just say it's a very protected place. From Ethereal and human intent. And places that exist between the worlds have always courted a certain amount of respect. There's one in every neighbourhood. The haunted house, the witch's cottage. There's got to be a place around here like that."

Yeah, thought Jez. *I'm sitting in it.* She said nothing.

"The fair folk came to us for protection, and we did everything we could," she said. "We forgot who we were dealing with."

She swallowed.

"They burned the house down," she said, quickly. "The fair folk escaped with most of the plants. But he got one of them. And Eleanor—my friend Eleanor—was trapped in the fire and we couldn't get her out."

She gulped at her drink.

"She died," she said. "She died because of greed and face cream."

Jez didn't know what to say.

"Did you find out who did it?" she said, eventually. "The speculator. Do you know who he is?"

"I have a *name*," said Sarah. "And when *this* little episode is all over, if I find my arse still in one piece, I am going to find out how this fucker found out about us, and *I am going to make him pay.*" She spoke slowly and carefully. "We were not a threat to him. Neither were the fair folk. We were only a threat to his plans. And Eleanor died because of it. And I *will* extract bloody vengeance." She looked straight at Jez. "Nicholas. Carrington. If you ever run into Nicholas Carrington, don't tell him I'm coming."

"I won't," said Jez. "Why didn't you go to the police?"

"Don't be daft. I had nothing on him that I could use. And he's a financier or something," said Sarah. "You know how complicated that stuff is. Well, maybe you don't. But they make it purposefully complex so they can do what they want without getting caught. Carrington's the kind of ambitious human excrement who'd sell his soul to get ahead of the pack, and I suspect he probably has, although from the little I know of him, whomever he sold it to probably got a lousy deal. Anyway." She started clearing books off the table. "Bloody vengeance will have to wait. Didn't you have a fly you wanted to dissect?"

Jez felt deeply uncomfortable. Although she was still unwilling to commit to believing the truth of everything that Sarah said—it went against her every instinct—she couldn't deny the evidence of her own eyes, and the vision of Marina's decomposing corpse in her bedroom was burned into her mind. And she was sure the dead fly in the jar had had something to do with it.

"We can do this safely," she said. She was trying to sound confident, but her voice was full of tension.

"I don't think it's a good idea." Sarah saw the look on Jez's face. "You don't know what you're dealing with."

Jez swallowed hard and picked up the glass jar from the floor where she had placed it next to her chair. She looked at the fly one more time.

The thing was definitely dead. "It'll be fine."

She rummaged around in her green bag for a moment and brought out a cork mat that she'd borrowed long ago from Mr. Williams's biology lab, and a small packet of dressmaking pins. She put one hand on top of the jar and twisted. It opened with a pop. She shook the fly out onto the cork mat. It weighed hardly anything. It lay there, legs sticking up awkwardly. She straightened the fly on the board. "I've researched what it should look like," she said, and fished a crumpled printout out of her bag. "If it looks massively different, or if it's clockwork or electronic or seriously mutated or anything, we'll notice something's wrong. I've dissected stuff before." Jez frowned. "Just usually stuff that was meatier. And bigger." She brought a small candle out of her roll of dissection tools, lit it, and blew out the match. A wisp of smoke spiralled crazily up to the ceiling. She waited for a moment, and then let a couple of drops of wax fall on the cork mat. Quickly, she blew out the candle, picked up the fly with a pair of forceps, and placed it face up on the blob of wax, pressing down on it gently as the wax cooled.

"So it doesn't move," she explained.

"Yes," said Sarah. "Got that. Yes." She edged toward the window.

Jez handed her a small medical face mask. "This might seem a bit weird," she said. "But I think we should totally wear these. I have gloves as well. What do you think?"

Sarah looked at Jez in silence, raised one eyebrow, and put the mask on without saying a word.

Jez pulled the mask over her face and worked her fingers into the gloves with a snap. She sat down at the table and bent back over the fly. It looked similar an ordinary bluebottle, except it was larger. But there was something—and Jez couldn't quite put her finger on it—that made it seem somehow *malevolent*, even in death. The green shone eerily under the office lamp perched incongruously on Sarah's dark wooden table. Sarah pulled up a chair and sat beside her, mask on, looking intently at the fly.

Okay, thought Jez. *Here we go.*

She took a scalpel and carefully slit the fly's abdomen open. A small amount of whitish fluid burst from the body.

"*Crap*," said Jez, out loud. "Too much pressure."

The wave of energy hit them both at the same time, like a silent explosion. Jez was thrown back in her seat; her head snapped back and the scalpel fell from her hand.

The room around her disappeared. She was in darkness. All she could feel was total, abject misery; it was in her stomach, paralyzing her body. Far away, she could hear voices crying. It was as if all the pain she had ever felt had been distilled, condensed and amplified; all her self-doubt, her occasional bouts of self-loathing, all that was usually buried deep within her psyche, rising only at her weakest moments, hit her at once. She was alone. She was unloved. She was a failure, and not because she didn't try or because she didn't work hard: because she was inherently *not good enough*.

Her mother was dead and Jez would never see her again.

Across the years, the agony of those final few months came flooding back: the hospital rooms, the drip of the drugs, the confusion, the waiting, her hope—her eleven-year-old hope— that everything would really be okay, and everything would go on as it had before. She relived the morning she woke up at 4:00 a.m. because her Auntie Rebecca was crying downstairs; nothing ever woke eleven-year-old Jez up except for birthdays and Christmas, but that morning, *that morning*, she knew. She could feel it—something was different, something was gone, and the world felt stiller, emptier, somehow flatter, and there was no comfort to be had anywhere in it.

The pain was immense; she could barely breathe. Everything was darkness; everything was despair. It felt eternal. There was no way out.

• • •

"Jez! Jez!"

There was a voice in the distance, but she couldn't move or open her eyes. It was as if she were suspended in mid-air, in pitch darkness, and her muscles had turned to dough. All she could feel was the anguish.

"Jez! You have to come back!"

She didn't recognize the voice, but it sounded familiar.

"JEZ!"

The realization that there was someone else there, someone out there, was immense. She found herself lying on the floor with her eyes shut; her muscles unlocked and she stretched. The carpet felt scratchy next to her face. She opened her eyes and saw a tangle of chair legs and table legs and the bottom of a bookshelf and a pair of feet. Her head hurt.

"Ow," she said. She pushed herself off the floor stiffly, and noticed the scalpel lying on the carpet. She picked it up and put it on the table before turning to Sarah. "What the hell just happened?"

There was a *pop* from the table behind her. She turned and her eyes widened.

The fly was on fire, flickering with a small, bright green flame. Smoke spiralled up to the ceiling.

"Put it on the plate," said Sarah sharply. She dashed to the nearest window and opened it as wide as it would go. Jez picked up the cork board with the fly still attached and placed it on the willow plate: the fly burned brighter for a moment, then fizzled and went out. It had burned a hole in the cork board.

Sarah was still opening windows.

"What was that?" asked Jez again.

"Are you okay?" said Sarah, coming back to the table. She looked concerned.

"Yes," said Jez. "I think so. I have a bit of a headache, though." She rubbed her forehead. "I never want to feel like that again."

"No," said Sarah. "I felt it too. We were both out cold. I think you caught more of it than I did."

"Out cold?" said Jez. Her eyes widened. "That would have been really dangerous. How long were we out?"

Sarah pointed to a clock on the wall above the kitchen door. Its hands pointed to twenty past one.

"Four *hours?*" said Jez. "That's not possible. Do we need to go to the hospital?"

Sarah shrugged. "I don't think it would be worth it," she said. "How would we explain what happened? They'd just assume one of us or both of us were on drugs and something went wrong. Even if they believed us, I have a feeling that whatever was inside that fly wouldn't be something that would show up on your average blood test." She slapped Jez gently on the shoulder. "When I say we're on our own, kid, I mean we really are *on our own.*"

Jez twisted her ankle around the leg of the chair she was sitting in. Although the pain in her body was gone, the memory of the darkness, the *despair*, was still fresh. Her stomach felt unsteady and oddly new; it reminded her of the times her dad had taken splinters out of her hands when she was small. The shard would be gone, but the hole it left, freshly cleaned and disinfected and anaesthetized with antiseptic cream would feel numb and cool, its deadness a reminder of the accident that had made her scream.

Magic cream, thought Jez. *That's what he used to call it. He said it could make* anything *better.* She felt as though she could use some magic cream right now.

On our own.

The implications of this hit her like a truck. There was no one who would help her. No one would believe her. Even Sam wasn't talking to her. Because of this. Because of all this.

Even if someone believed her, most people wouldn't have a clue how to deal with the truth. No one could give her an antidote to a supernatural neurotoxin (*if that's even what it was,* her scientific mind reminded her, *don't jump to conclusions; you don't know for sure*); no one could tell her how to kill a giant insect demon; no one could protect her against nightmare visions appearing in her home.

Except the woman sitting opposite her. The woman who had started this all in the first place.

"This is all your fault," said Jez, in a voice that was barely audible. She could feel her anger growing as she formed the words.

Sarah raised her head. "Excuse me?"

"*This is all your fault.* You came here and started messing around with things, and now two people are dead, and I'm seeing things that aren't there and don't exist, and Sam's not speaking to me, and apparently I'm in mortal danger, and I just spent four hours unconscious in your house and it's *all your fault!*" She was really yelling now.

"It is *not* my fault," snapped Sarah. "You're Little Miss Uber-Rational; pay some fucking attention. You came through the churchyard by accident. It was a total coincidence that I was there. If you'd been less obsessed with dissecting *every-thing*, you'd have assumed you'd seen a ghost, and gone home screaming, and had a fab ol' story to tell at school, where approximately no one would have believed you. *You* came after *me. You* demanded to know the truth, and I figured you were smart enough to handle it. I didn't make you go down to the pond, either. You could have left at any time." She stood up and leaned forward, hands on the table in front of her. "Now I know you're shitting yourself because for the first time in your life you've actually encountered something real, and it's really fucking dangerous. And that part doesn't get old. This stuff is terrifying. I get it. I live with it *all the time.*" Her voice dropped until it was almost a whisper. "But don't you *dare* tell me that this is all my fault, because if you refuse to take responsibility for yourself and your actions, then you are *fucked* in more ways that you can even imagine at this point." She took a deep breath and stood up straight.

Jez said nothing, staring sullenly in front of her. She kicked the table leg next to her foot, but her heart wasn't really in it. *And besides*, said her more rational self, *it isn't your table.* She was still angry, but her mind was revving wildly in neutral, seeking purchase, trying to get in gear.

"It's not *fair!*" she burst out all of a sudden, and immediately hated herself for it.

Sarah was quiet for a moment. "No," she said eventually. "It isn't. But life isn't. You make the best of it, and you try to make things better. That's all you can do." She turned in the kitchen doorway. "I'm going to put the kettle on. And before you say anything, I'm not just making another cup of tea. I'm going to put together something that'll likely counter whatever was in that insect. One of Granny's finest brews. You want to learn something?"

Jez shrugged. "Sure," she said. She got up.

Jez had never been in Sarah's kitchen before. The walls were painted a surprisingly modern terracotta red, and it was phenomenally untidy: what looked like a week's worth of dishes was piled in the sink, rinsed off and ready to be washed properly, and there were several boxes of cereal standing on the counter, as though they'd been taken out for a hasty emergency meal and promptly abandoned until the next time. Apart from its untidiness, the most remarkable thing about the kitchen was the spice rack, mounted on the wall beside an elderly and stained electric cooker. It went from floor to ceiling, and was packed with small jars, all of which appeared to be filled with various quantities of dried plants. Sarah started hunting among them, pulling them out of the rack, examining them, and returning each jar to its place. When she had five, she stopped and put them down on the stovetop.

"Hex breakers," she said. "Strong ones, too. Thistle, galangal, toadflax, squill, and wintergreen. Probably won't taste great, but they'll do the job." She started dropping pinches of the herbs into a saucepan, and when she was done, filled it with water and turned the hob up to high heat. "Won't take long." "Will it work?"

"It should," said Sarah. She tapped her finger on the edge of the stove and looked at the ground. "In the interests of honesty, I put a little something in there for protection as well. Just in case."

Jez laughed joylessly and shook her head. "Protective herbs," she said. "Jesus. Well, if it works."

"We need to go after these shits, Jez," said Sarah, and then stopped, mid-breath. "Well. I say *we*, but you can still get out, if you want to. The corpse in your bed was meant to scare you, and it did. If you want to stop, they'll keep an eye on you, but they'll probably leave you alone."

Jez shrugged. "I don't even know what we're trying to stop."

"*Someone* has released a bunch of poisonous flies into the area," said Sarah. "*Someone* knew there was a demon in the Foxglove Pond and may or may not have let it out of the *pond*, but wanted to keep it contained so they could play with it later. *Someone* wants to build a factory in the middle of the greenbelt—you'd think people would be up in arms, but they're not. And these flies are everywhere. And my spare room is full of spiders, but they're not acting like normal spiders. And that's *odd*. Where would you start?"

"Well," said Jez, thinking carefully as she spoke, "it sounds daft, but I would start with the people who want to build the factory. I would try and find out who's in charge. Oh!" She ran back into the living room and rummaged frantically in her bag, reappearing in front of Sarah a moment later with a piece of paper in her hand. "This is the demo against the factory. It's today. Christ. I have to go soon. Now."

"A combined project of Asilida and Carpenter Properties," read Sarah out loud. "Well, I agree with you. I think that paying Asilida and Carpenter Properties a quick visit might be an excellent place to start."

Chapter 10

Jez stared at Sarah. The saucepan of tea bubbled noisily. The kitchen filled with a smell like cold medicine.

"How do we do that?" she said. "You can't just walk into an office and go, 'Er, we think you're running around with demons and creating mass hallucinations so can you just stop or we'll do something really nasty. With witchcraft.' That's not going to work."

Sarah checked the contents of the pan. "We're not going to go breaking and entering or anything. We just want to have a look. Find out who's in charge of this operation. What they're like. We can use a glamour."

"What's a glamour?" Jez prepared for battle. "I'm not dressing up like one of those women who work on the MAC counter in Debenhams."

"It's an illusion. You make people think they're seeing something that they're not. It's a lot like makeup, actually: it takes a bit of practice and a lot of concentration, and every so often you run into someone who's got it a bit wrong and makes you cringe. Oh, and when I said 'we,' I meant 'I'; you're not coming with me on this one."

"Why not?" Jez frowned. "I coped with the half-fly demon. I'm not going to embarrass you in an office."

"You don't know how to make or sustain a glamour, and I can't do it for both of us," said Sarah. "Take a break. Go home. Have a rest. Read a book. Pretend you're not involved. Remember, they're aware of you."

"But they'll know what's been going on here anyway," argued Jez.

"Jez," said Sarah, "this cottage has belonged to witches for at least six centuries, if my Auntie Dot's notes are to be believed. It has the same level of protection you'd find surrounding a presidential motorcade, except it's magic. They can't see what happens here. It would be the equivalent of trying to look inside a lead-lined box using X-rays, while blindfolded. Not happening. All they'll know is you were here. They won't know what we've talked about. I think the tea's ready." She took the pot off the heat and turned off the hob, before rummaging one of the chaotic kitchen cupboards for two mugs and a strainer. "It probably won't taste great. Do you want honey in yours?"

"If it'll make it better," said Jez. She stared warily at the greenish brown soup in the pan as Sarah started straining it into the earthenware mugs. She didn't like the idea of being watched, especially if whoever was doing the watching was able to see into her own bedroom. School was bad enough. "How are they watching me?"

Sarah shrugged. "Not sure. Here." She handed Jez the mug. "It's not like they'll be using cameras or anything. They'll only have a very general picture of what you're up to. Chin-chin." She took a big swig of the tea and made a face. Jez took a sip of the tea. The fumes wafting from the cup made her eyes water and the taste was vile.

"Have a seat in there," said Sarah, pointing toward the living room. "I'm going to see if I can find something for you.

And make sure you drink all your tea. Don't water the plants with it. It's for your own good."

Sarah disappeared upstairs as Jez sat down in the chair she'd sat in the first time she'd come to the cottage less than a week ago. It seemed so much longer. She'd never romanticized danger or excitement—all she'd really been looking for, she thought, was a few more rock shows, a few more interesting bars for on the weekends, and a few more people she could hang out with that she didn't want to stab. This was something else altogether. Sarah may not have had peer-reviewed studies in *Nature* backing up her stories about the way the world worked, but Jez had seen enough with her own eyes to trust the witch.

The world that Sarah lived in was terrifying. And it was the world where Jez lived, too. She had a right to know what was going on. No one at the offices would know who Jez was anyway.

She gritted her teeth and glared at the carpet.

"Hey." Sarah came spinning down the spiral staircase in the corner of the room. "I found this for you." She held out a long, heavy chain with a pendant dangling from it: a five-pointed star set in a circle, made of silver. There was an inscription in squiggly letters etched into the circle. "For protection."

Jez was skeptical. "I'll look like a Mötley Crüe fan."

"The look worked for my great-auntie Dot. Go on, take it." Sarah pushed the necklace into Jez's hands. "Wear it under your clothes if you don't want anyone to know. But I'd say you need all the protection you can get."

Jez slowly pulled the pendant over her head. It was heavier than she thought it would be. "Thanks," she said. "I appreciate it."

"No problem," said Sarah, breezily. "Have you finished your tea yet? I've got a glamour to make. And it's going to take a while."

· · ·

Jez's dad dropped her off near the protest.

"Have fun changing the world," he said, and kissed her on the cheek. She rolled her eyes.

"Cat's family's doing the changing," she said. "I'm just here to hang out."

"Well, hope it stays dry for you," said her dad, glancing at the dark grey sky. "Really stormy this week. Do you have an umbrella?" Without waiting for an answer, he produced a plain black telescopic one from the glove compartment. "Don't lose the cover," he said.

"Everyone loses the cover," said Jez, taking it off and handing it back to him. She opened the car door. "Can I go to the Greenwoods' for a bit afterward?"

"If you did your homework," said her dad, "you can do what you like. Within reason," he added. "I mean, I don't want you to—"

"Yeah, yeah," said Jez, waving her hands. "I know. I'm just going to Cat's. Talk about science and stuff." This was actually true. Sort of. Jez wanted to push Cat to see if her mum had found out what was up with Mr. Williams. The incident in the lab the other day had really rattled her, especially considering, in retrospect, all the other weird stuff that had happened.

"Okay," said her dad. "Well, let me know if you need a taxi. I'll drop everything and come running." He frowned.

"Thanks," said Jez, deliberately missing the irony in his voice. "Appreciated. Won't be late," she called over her shoulder as she climbed out of the car, slammed the door and watched her father pull away.

There were a bunch of people milling around the protest site. Alex Appleton and the Marxist feminists of Year Thirteen were clustered around some homemade banners painted on sheets: "F**K ENVIRONMENT RAPE" one said—complete with asterisks so as not to offend anyone, Jez noted. Lee Humbolt, from Crowsbrook, and a couple of his straggle-haired mates were hanging around, because they were totally committed to the cause and definitely not because he had a massive crush on Alex but was afraid to ask her out in case it was too patriarchal and domineering. Jez spotted Cat's mum arranging flyers on a table that had a banner on the front of it saying "NO MAGGOT FACTORY" in big black hand-painted letters. Cat's dad was wrestling with a sheet of plastic, to cover the flyers. Cat was handing signs on stakes to people gathered around the back of her dad's car. Jez guessed that they were students from the university up the road: they were too old to be at Arden High and—this was the kicker—she'd never seen them before. There were six of them: three blokes and three girls, all wearing torn jeans and army surplus coats, each with its own collection of badges. "No badger cull." "No nuclear power." "Give peace a chance." That one looked *old*.

Cat came over and handed her a sign. "Watch for splinters," she said. Jez looked up. Another "NO MAGGOT FACTORY."

"Are we chanting?" she asked, hoping to whatever benevolent supernatural powers might be listening that the answer was no. Chanting really didn't work with small groups of English people.

"Depends," said Cat. "We'll see how many people show up." She glanced at the sky. "Probably not many more than this. A lot depends on the weather. Is Sam going to show up?"

"I don't know." Crap. Sam. That whole thing. "He said he would." Hopefully that was suitably noncommittal; Jez really didn't feel like explaining everything to Cat, since it was trying to explain everything to Sam that had caused her and him to fall out in the first place. Ugh. A drop of water the size of a marble fell onto her head and she looked up. Her heart sank. "Starting to rain." On top of everything else.

"I better help Dad cover the flyers," said Cat, and bustled off in the direction of the table. Not many people were stopping, Jez noticed. They were mostly rolling their eyes and crossing the street. Every so often, one of the students would shout "Say no to the maggot factory!" or "Protect your community!" at shoppers who scuttled by with their heads down. The dampness crept under Jez's clothing, until it felt as though a thin layer of cold had wrapped itself like cling film between her flesh and her bones. She hunched down in her coat and thrust the hand that was not holding the sign deep into her pocket.

"Want to share a brolly?" It was one of the students, one of the girls. She had elbow-length red hair and a northern accent. "You look cold."

Jez nodded. The girl couldn't have been more than three years older than her at the most, but at that moment, it felt like a century. "Thanks," she managed.

"I'm Tasha," said the girl. "D'y'live here? We came up from the university."

"Yeah," said Jez. "I guessed. I'm from here. It's really boring," she added, to prove that she wasn't under any illusions.

"S'beautiful," said Tasha. "What they're planning is disgusting. And totally illegal." She sniffed. "Must be rotten, they want to do that to where you're from."

"I'm leaving next year," said Jez. She'd never really thought of her village—or the country that surrounded it—as "beautiful." There wasn't anything there.

"You'll still be from here," said Tasha. "Did you grow up here?"

"Lived here all my life."

"Must be gutted," said Tasha. "I'd be."

"Where are you from?" said Jez.

Tasha sniffed. "Manchester," she said.

Jez stared at her, feeling as though she'd just run into a wall.

"That's, like, the coolest city *ever*."

Tasha turned and looked at her, her face blank with surprise. Then she started laughing.

"Not joking!" said Jez, hastily. "All my favourite bands are from there! There's so much stuff going on!"

Tasha grinned. "Well," she said. "Yeah. I'll give you that." She picked at a piece of dry skin on her lip. "But you see places differently when you're from there." The wind whipped her hair against her face. "And you see the places you're from differently once you've left as well."

"This place'll always be crap," said Jez, wryly.

"Maybe," said Tasha. "But if you leave, and they wreck it, then you won't have it to come back to. And it won't be crap, it'll be *gone*. You've got to care a bit, else you wouldn't have come out. Say no to the maggot factory!" she hollered at an elderly man in a raincoat, who was clutching a newspaper to himself to protect it from the rain. He turned away from her proffered flyer and crossed the street. "Funny," said Tasha, turning back to Jez, "when I've been here before, it's been more friendly. Weather must be bringing out the worst in people. Stop the maggot factory! Protect your community!"

"How you doing there, Tash?" It was Maureen, Cat's mother. "There's not many people stopping today. It's really worrying."

"S'like no one cares," said Tasha. "It's not even like they don't know about it, and they find out and then they don't care. It's like we're not here."

Not here. *It won't be crap; it'll be gone.* Tasha's words echoed in Jez's head while Tasha and Maureen talked tactics and strategies and direct action and letters to the paper.

What you remember will be gone.

She thought of Sarah, losing everything, starting again, with nothing to go back to.

You'd still have your dad, right? You wouldn't lose everything.

But her mind began to wander around the village that she'd grown up in, the town that stood next to it, the places she'd hung out with friends: smoked weed, read books, talked for hours, walked to nowhere, for no reason; the whole landscape of the first seventeen years of her life; something that she had felt, had *assumed* would be solid and unchanging, even as she hit eleven like a wall, and her mother slipped away in a forest of tubes and IV bags and ice-clean sheets; the world tilted and Jez struggled to stay upright, but the landscape remained the same. And now—*now*—now that the top layer of the world had peeled away, revealing the exposed, livid, dangerous tissue underneath—the landscape was as threatened as her view of the world. The view that said that there was a rational explanation for everything, that everything was governed by rules, scratch that, *laws*, laws of physics and mathematics was not all there was. And, although Sarah had said that those rules were still true, there were things out there that would drive you out of your rational mind if you thought about them for too long because they made *no sense*.

None.

Everything was under threat. She didn't like the town or the village any more than she had before. But she knew she had to do everything she could to save it.

"HEY!" Jez, Tasha, and Maureen looked up.

It was Lee Humbolt.

"That's fucking HIM!"

"What?" said Tasha, looking at Lee and then Jez. "Who's fucking what?"

"That's Lee Humbolt," said Jez. "He's not fucking Alex. He's kind of famous for it. Around here," she added. "Well, around school."

"That's HIM!" Lee was shouting again and pointing.

"Oh, my God," said Maureen, staring at a couple making their way through the now-pouring rain under an expensive golf umbrella. "Lee's right. That's him. That's Adam Carpenter." She turned to Tasha. "He owns Carpenter Properties. And he lives in Crowsbrook. On the opposite side to where he wants to put his bloody factory, of course. Unbelievable." She nodded toward Carpenter. "That man."

Jez followed Maureen's gaze. The man under the umbrella was average height. Average build. Brown hair, cut neatly. Three-quarter-length black wool overcoat. Dark-green golfing umbrella.

He could have been anyone. But he was the guy—

The vision of Marina's rotting body flashed into Jez's mind. *His* fault.

She felt dizzy and sick. He looked so ordinary.

"HEY!" shouted Lee Humbolt. "CARPENTER!"

The man looked up. Alex Appleton's mouth fell open and she stared at Lee.

"NO FUCKING MAGGOT FACTORY IN OUR TOWN!" shouted Lee.

"Holy crap," murmured Tasha. "Looks like your mate might get lucky after all." Alex's Marxist feminist friends had picked up on what was going on and were shouting uncoordinated abuse across the street. Carpenter just stood there.

Jez would remember the look on his face for years. It was completely blank. There was no reaction at all.

"Easy, kids," said Cat's dad, loudly. "Let's keep things civil, all right?"

"Who's that?" Tasha whispered to Jez.

"Richard," said Jez. "Richard Greenwood. He's Cat's dad. Maureen's husband," she said, a bit more loudly. Maureen was still standing near them, trying to reason with Alex and the students. "He's a lawyer who works on this kind of stuff."

"More power to him," said Tasha, nodding. "And that's Carpenter? Of Carpenter Properties?" She looked down at the flyer in her hand in disbelief. "He's got a nerve."

"I guess," said Jez. Her throat had gone dry. The woman with Adam had cottoned on to what was going on and was whispering something to him and trying to get him to come away. But he wasn't moving.

"Maybe I should go talk and have a word with him," Jez heard Richard say to Maureen behind them. One of the students threw an empty Coke can in Carpenter's direction. It landed with a metallic *clunk* at Carpenter's feet.

The noise seemed to jolt Carpenter out of his trance. He looked at the can and then back at the protesters, surveying the crowd.

Lee Humbolt, possibly hoping to build on his earlier success identifying their chief antagonist and raise his chances with Alex a further nanometre, fished an empty beer bottle out of a nearby rubbish bin and lobbed it in Adam's direction. It smashed in the road between the protesters and the couple. The woman leaped back and drew her breath in sharply.

"Adam, let's *go!*" Jez heard her say. But Carpenter didn't budge, and in a moment, the air was thick with all kinds of rubbish flying across the street. The woman with Carpenter was backed up against a wall on the other side, staring in horror.

Carpenter stepped into the road, umbrella held over his head.

"FUCKER!" shouted Alex Appleton. The rubbish continued to rain down. Jez found herself moving instinctively toward the edge of the crowd. Cat had taken over trying to calm Alex down, and was hollering something about working within the system.

"You're not helping anything!" yelled Richard.

And Carpenter stood in the middle of the road and started laughing.

Jez never figured out if it was that or the fact that the rubbish bin was finally empty that stopped the airborne tide of trash. It wasn't evil movie-villain cackling; it wasn't snorts of humorous contempt. It was the laughter of a man who found something genuinely and heartwarmingly funny. The man stood in the pouring rain, in the middle of the street, surrounded by smashed glass and empty cans and leftover biryani and balled-up kebab wrappers and Costa cups, laughing hard enough to split.

One by one, the protesters fell silent. Adam kept on laughing. The woman with him just stared.

Richard Greenwood stepped forward, toward Adam, and took him by the arm.

"It might be better if you moved on," he murmured, just loud enough that Jez could hear him over the frenzied whispering of the protesters behind her. "We don't like what you're doing, but nobody wants anybody to get hurt. We'll do this through the proper channels. We don't want any trouble. Do we? Any of us?"

Adam looked at him for a long moment, and then snorted contemptuously.

"You should move on." Richard's voice was low but firm. "Think of your reputation. Think of your company's reputation. Things are bad enough for you as it is."

"I don't know what you're talking about," snapped Adam.

"Your company," said Richard, levelly, "is attempting to do something hugely illegal, and is so far getting away with it. You can't do that forever."

Adam's face darkened with rage as he stared at Richard.

"Your family are all from here," continued Richard. "Your father was an honest man, who worked hard. He's still well liked. Well trusted. If you—"

"I'm not listening to you anymore," announced Adam. And then, loudly, "You lot should pick this up," gesturing at the rubbish on the ground.

He was angry. His father had nothing to do with this. His father *was* nothing. Not like Adam would be. He wanted to go for a run. He turned and strode away, leaving Julia to scuttle after him, throwing up her hands.

"No maggot factory," hollered a lone voice. But most of the protesters were looking at each other, completely baffled. The rain hammered down. A trio of flies circled the rubbish in a lunatic holding pattern.

"What just happened?" Tasha asked Jez.

"I don't know," muttered Jez. Which was true. But she knew that whatever it was, it was really, really bad.

• • •

When she got home from drying out at the Greenwoods' house, Jez lay on her bed, staring at the ceiling. Sam hadn't spoken to her since they'd drunk tea together in the cafeteria, the day after Gareth and Marina had been killed, and she was torn. She wanted to call him—he *was* her best friend after all, damn it— but she didn't want to have to deal with...

With what?

With everything, her mind said. She'd told Sam the beginnings of what had been happening, and he hadn't believed her.

Well, said a voice inside her head, *your timing was a bit off. You know. With the Gareth thing. And to be fair, if he had told you the same thing on a good day, you wouldn't have believed him either.*

But being able to talk to Sarah about this stuff was one thing. Being able to talk to Sam about it was something else. Sam hadn't lived his whole life in a completely irrational, magic universe, even if he *was* planning to study English.

You should call him, said the voice inside her head. *Call him and apologize.*

What if he's an arse again?

She knew that Sarah would point out that this wasn't her—Jez's—problem.

Screw it, she thought. She grabbed her green bag, yelled at her dad to let him know where she was going, and headed out the door, across the village to Sam's house.

• • •

"Hey," said Sam, as he opened the door. He paused. "I haven't seen you in *forever*." He stood aside to let her come in. "Where the hells have you been?"

He seemed friendly, but Jez could feel awkwardness between them as tangible as the physical door had been. She shrugged, trying to push through it. "Busy, I guess," she said. She liked Sam's house. It smelled of fried garlic. She stared at the bookshelves that lined the hall; they were full of old *National Geographics* and paperback Penguin Classics. Sam's love of doorstop novels ran in the family. "What have you been up to?"

"Not much," said Sam. "But enough about me. The last time I saw you, you were talking about ghoulies and ghosties." *Damn his good memory.* "What, if I may, the fuck was *that* all about?"

Jez inhaled deeply and leaned against the wall. "It's kind of complicated," she said. "How are *you* doing?"

"Better," said Sam. "Most of the time. I've been home for an hour, and I'm not drinking in secret yet, which is progress, of a sort. I'm not letting this go, though. What the fuck were you on about in the caf?" He had progressed from pissed off to ferociously curious. Jez suspected it was a distraction.

"I don't really want to talk about it," she said. It was partly true: she didn't. She was afraid of what could happen.

"I do," said Sam, firmly. "You—Ms. Über-Rational, future Nobel Laureate and Scientist of the Year—suddenly start talking about seeing ghosts, with no previous history of experimenting with hallucinogens or being the kid from *The Sixth Sense*. Have you been hanging out with Saskia French? I think not, since no one has stabbed her in the head, to my knowledge. Jez, what, please, is going on?"

Jez rolled her right foot onto its side, trying to fit it into the cream-and-brown pattern on Sam's mother's carpet. "It sounds stupid," she said. "You're right: it's not rational. But..." She trailed off. She couldn't do it. "Can we go somewhere else? Like, and not talk in the hall?"

"My folks are out," said Sam. "But sure." He turned and headed up the stairs; Jez followed.

Sam's room was a shrine to Manchester bands of the 1990s, and piles of books had collected on every surface; although they regularly did their homework together, Jez had never actually seen him use the large pine desk under the window, since it was always covered in a chaotic salad of novels, papers, old essays, vinyl records, and collections of poetry, with a vintage fedora balanced on top like a precarious garnish. He moved a stack of books from off his duvet, straightened it out and sat on the bed while Jez took the beanbag chair in the corner. The beanbag was ancient and blue, and covered in discreet patches where it had been frequently repaired by Sam's mother, who threatened to throw it out every time it tore.

Sam held out his hands. "So. What's up with you?"

Jez studied her knees hard. She still wasn't sure she could bring herself to tell the truth. "Okay," she began eventually. "This is going to..."

"...sound stupid. Yes," Sam said. "You mentioned. Don't care."

Jez chewed the side of her finger.

"I went home from yours through the churchyard a few days ago," she finally said, in a rush. "I heard voices, so I turned round, because I didn't like the idea of walking around in the dark on my own with people I didn't know around. I saw a woman sitting on the grass, in the wet, talking to Mr. Badgerley, and I knew he'd died about three weeks before that, because my dad told me, because when I was little, I was helping my mum to deliver flyers about a jumble sale for the Brownies, and I ran up his drive to put the flyer through his letterbox and tripped, and ripped a hole in my knee, and I can still show you the scar, if you like, but it made a big impression on me, and so my dad thought he would tell me when Mr. Badgerley died, I guess."

"You can edit some of it," said Sam. But she could tell he was listening.

"Okay. Well. He was glowing. Mr. Badgerley. Not much. Not metaphorically, either. And she—this woman, I mean—was just sitting there talking to him, like it was the most normal thing in the world." She swallowed. "And it really upset me. I mean, *really*. Because it made no sense. Dead people don't get up and walk around. I don't believe in life after death. This is all there is. This *has* to be all there is..."

Her hands were balled up into fists; her nails were digging deep into her palms; and she realized what she'd just said. Sam was looking at her, steadily.

"I was so *angry*," she went on. "I waited until she was done talking, and then she just picked up her stuff and charged out of the churchyard, like nothing weird had happened. So I followed her and asked her what was going on. And..." She fumbled for words. "There's all sorts of weird stuff going on, Sam. Here. In the village. There's something horrible down by the F—"

She stopped herself. The thing by the Foxglove Pond was going too far. The thing had killed Gareth and Marina. She couldn't tell him that. Not yet.

"I saw a corpse in my bed, Sam. It was real. It was there; I wasn't dreaming. And then it wasn't there. It vanished. I don't know what's real anymore."

Sam was staring at the floor.

"Say something," said Jez. But Sam remained quiet.

"Jez," he said finally. "I have no fucking idea what to say. If I didn't know you, I'd assume you had some serious mental health issues, and I'm not making jokes this time: you sound like someone with severe paranoid schizophrenia. But—"

"But?"

"But I *do* know you. I don't think you're the kind of person who would make this shit up. And I'm not a doctor, or a scientist, but I don't think you're ill, either. So I don't know what to think."

"Don't tell anyone."

"No."

Jez picked absently at the side of the beanbag chair. There was, unsurprisingly for Sam's room, a pile of books next to it. "What are these?" she asked, picking up the top one. *Pincher Martin* said the cover.

"Homework," said Sam. "Essay on William Golding." Jez flipped it over and looked at the back. "It's about a bloke dying on a rock in the middle of the ocean for no apparent reason. It's brilliant."

"Sounds it," said Jez, wrinkling her nose. She put it down and picked up the next one. "*Rites of Passage.*"

"Bloke on a boat, stirring up shit among the other passengers. Also brilliant."

Jez picked up the third book in the stack. It was lying face down. She turned it over and froze. A severed pig's head leered at her from the cover. But it was the title that caught her attention.

"What's this one?"

"Jesus, Jez, where were you for English? That's his most famous one."

"What's it *about?*" She stared at him, eyes blazing.

Sam was thrown by Jez's intensity. He looked at her, quizzically. "Um. It's about a group of boys... there's an airplane crash and they end up on an island. They turn into wild savages pretty quickly; there's lots of allegorical stuff about Jesus and order and society and stuff."

"Yeah? What's the pig's head all about?" She waved the cover in front of him.

"Holy spontaneous English literature pop quiz, Batman." Sam rolled his eyes. "Er. They kill a pig so they can eat it, but they end up cutting off the head and putting it on a stick to ward off a sort of supernatural entity they've come to believe in that doesn't really exist. They call it The Beast and they put the pig's head on the stick to keep The Beast away from their camp, and it all demonstrates perfectly the fragility of civilization and the readiness of humanity to revert to a superstitious and animalistic state, etcetera. So my essay's about how he took that theme and—"

"Yeahyeahyeah," said Jez. "What's the Lord of the Flies?"

"The pig's head on the stick. My essay is fucking *brilliant*, by the way. You should totally read it."

"I'm sure it is."

"Oh, and Beelzebub. Which is—"

"*What?*" Jez felt a wave of cold fear creep through her body.

"The Lord of the Flies. It's another name for Beelzebub."

"The *Devil?*"

"*A* devil, technically, I think. I have a feeling he was one of the Seven Princes of Hell, but I also think that once you get promoted past a certain level in Hell, people tend to mix you up with Satan anyway."

"Sam," said Jez. Her hands were clenched again, and she was breathing faster. "There are flies *everywhere*. Poisonous flies. They look like regular bluebottles, but they're bigger, and they're kind of green. I dissected one; I think they're secreting some kind of neurotoxin but I don't have the stuff to test it, and I don't know what I would be looking for anyway. But it's really, really potent. It gives people hallucinations and makes them sick and miserable. If you see one, kill it. Then—" She realized she didn't know how to destroy them. "I don't know. Bury it or something. Or put it in a jam jar and seal the lid until you can get rid of it. These things are *awful*." She winced as she heard herself speak, aware of how ridiculous it sounded. "And they're probably not the worst part. We think someone's controlling them. Or someone released them. And we think that whoever released the flies has something to do with the maggot factory that they want to build over by the Foxglove Pond."

"You told me about the maggot factory," said Sam, slowly. All the sarcasm had gone from his voice and he was looking pale. "And Cat did. I'm sorry I missed the demo." He paused. "I'm saying this in all seriousness now, no matter how many times I've said it in jest in the past. Jez, I think you need to get help."

"Sam, this is *real*," she said. Her hands were clenched so tight that they hurt, and her eyes were earnest. "I don't know how to prove it to you. Come and meet Sarah; she'll show you."

"Who?"

"Sarah. You remember the new woman who moved into Miss Trevelyan's old cottage? We saw the cab arrive. That's her. She was the one talking to Mr. Badgerley in the churchyard. She figured out that the flies are connected with the maggot factory."

"Flies often are," said Sam, but there was no joy in his voice. "Jez, it's just a development. It's a stupid idea, and it's probably illegal so it won't happen anyway, but it's not the work of the Devil. Who's the developer?"

Jez fished in her bag for the now-crumpled flyer that Cat had given her. "Carpenter Properties," she said. "But they've been around for ages. I mean, you see their boards up all the time, and nothing this weird has ever happened before. They're working with a company called Asilida."

Sam pulled his laptop toward him across the bed and opened it. "C'mere," he said.

Jez got up from the beanbag chair and sat next to Sam. He opened his browser window; the Google logo appeared.

"Sam," said Jez, twisting the duvet in her fingers nervously, "what are you doing?"

"I'm looking up Asilida," said Sam. "I want to look at the website. They're just a legal practice. Or a consulting firm or something."

Jez suddenly felt cold. "I don't know if that's a good idea." They were watching her already; she knew that. She didn't want to give them a reason to watch Sam too.

But Sam was already typing. "Is that right?" he asked, showing her the spelling.

"I think so," she said. Her heart was beating faster now; she was fighting the urge to run away. "I think these people have more power than you think." The list of hits appeared on Sam's screen. The top one was just a hyperlink. "Asilida Solutions" it read. There was no description.

"Is that them? Sam pointed.

"It could be," said Jez. She stood up. "Sam, I really don't want to look at their website."

Sam frowned. "Why not?"

"I think they've been watching me." She folded her arms across her chest and hugged her torso tight. "Sarah says they've been watching both of us. Me and her, I mean. I don't think this is going to help anything. What if your IP address gets logged?"

"It'll be logged anyway." He stared at her. "Why would Asilida do that? *Could* they do that? Is that even legal?" Sam's cursor hovered over the link. The arrow cursor turned into a pointing finger. "I don't think it is. It's a free country, Jez. And this is just a corporate website."

"I don't know, Sam." She was speaking faster now. "I've seen some really weird shit over the past few days. Please don't." Sam's hand was still poised over the track pad. He looked at her with a blend of sympathy and horror.

"Jez, what's the matter with you?" he asked. "You're talking like you've lost it completely."

Jez collapsed back down on the bed. Her head dropped into her hands.

"I don't know how to make you believe me," she said, through her fingers. "Because *I* wouldn't believe me, if I were hearing this. I can't prove any of it." *Unless we go down to the Foxglove Pond,* she thought, *and then it's pretty much game over for both of us.* "All I have to back this up is a fucking dead, half-dissected, half-burned fly in a jar. Wanna see my dead fly in a jar? It's totally awesome." She pulled her green bag toward her and fished out the jar. "Don't ask me to open it, though," she went on, "because it's covered in a neurotoxin that can knock you out for hours, and make you feel like shit at the same time. Well, it could before it caught fire. Check it out!" she finished, holding up the jar with a hysterical cheesecake smile, like a housewife in a 1950s cleaning advert.

Sam peered into the jar. The fly was, once again, on its back with its legs in the air, but the incision Jez had made had torn open further when the neurotoxin sacs had burst. It was a darker green now, and not as shiny, and its head was hanging to one side at an awkward angle, swaying back and forth with the movement of the jar as if it were on a hinge.

"I thought you said it had burned up," said Sam. "It doesn't look burned." He peered more closely. "Maybe slightly singed."

"Doesn't surprise me," said Jez, without looking. "Nothing surprises me anymore."

Sam looked more closely at the jar. "It *is* kind of weird," he admitted. He put the jar down on the bed; the glass gleamed in the sunlight that tumbled through the windows. "I've never seen a fly that big before. But by itself—"

"It doesn't prove anything, I know," said Jez. "And this is all anecdotal evidence. I've got nothing else, Sam. But I'm telling the truth." She picked at the duvet cover. Sam was looking at the laptop again. Her stomach clenched.

"I just want to take a quick look at the website, Jez," he said. "It's just a website. And it's a business as well; there's not going to be pictures of dead babies or beheadings or Justin Bieber on there."

Before Jez could protest, he clicked the link. The page loaded quickly: it was a smart, well-designed splash page in shades of grey and green with the company name at the top.

"Hm," said Sam. "It just looks like a boring corporate website. It doesn't even say what they do. 'Solutions.' What does that even mean?" He looked at Jez, who shrugged. She looked again at the web page. She wasn't as nervous as she had been—it was just a website, after all—but the whole thing still unnerved her. Maybe it was just a regular website, after all.

There was a loud *pop* from behind them. They both jumped. They turned around to look at the jar.

There was a large crack in it. The fly was gone, replaced by a small heap of ash. Smoke curled crazily inside the jar.

Sam and Jez were silent for a moment.

"What," said Sam, eventually, "the *fuck* was that?"

The tension had crept back into Jez's stomach and she felt cold with fear.

"Weird stuff," she said, miserably, turning back to the computer.

She saw the screen and froze.

Thank you for your interest in Asilida, read the message on the screen. *One of our representatives will be in touch with you shortly.*

"Sam, did you touch anything?"

Sam's jaw had fallen open. He looked at Jez and then back at the screen. "I didn't touch anything," he said finally. "It must be an error. How is that possible? I didn't even click on anything." Jez was shaking her head. "It must be a problem with the website. I wasn't even touching—"

"Close the window," said Jez. "Shut the computer down. Maybe it is a mistake. Like a glitch or something." Sam tapped a few times on the touchpad and the laptop chimed to show that it was shutting down.

"There," he said, uncertainly. "All gone."

He looked back at the jar, the smoke, and the pile of ash.

"I think we should bury that," he said. "Deep. Without opening it."

"Good call," said Jez. There was a long silence. Both of them stared at the carpet.

"That fly," said Sam, "just spontaneously combusted."

"Yup," said Jez. She felt sick.

"You're not crazy," said Sam. His voice was flat, but Jez knew him well enough to know that he was reeling with the magnitude of what had just happened. "You were telling the truth."

"Yeah."

"That is *seriously* messed up."

"Yes," said Jez. "It is."

"So this woman—"

"Sarah."

"Sarah, right. She knows the Da Vinci code? She can stop all the weirdness happening? Why doesn't she?"

"She's still working on it," said Jez. She knew she had to tell him the truth, but the last thing was the hardest of all. "Sam. You're not going to want to hear this. But we think that these people—the developers, Carpenter and Asilida, whoever they are—may have caused the deaths of Gareth and Marina."

Sam stayed frozen for a moment. "Go on," he said. His voice was hard.

"Sam, it's *fucked up*. Beyond whatever would be normal fucked up when two kids get killed in the middle of nowhere. I went down to the Foxglove Pond with her the day after it happened. It's a murder scene, right? You think it's going to be like something out of *CSI* or whatever. There was *nothing*, Sam. No police. No forensics. No tents; no one collecting evidence or looking for clues. There was some police tape and a bit of barbed wire, and *that was it*. We just walked right down there like we were on a hike or something." She swallowed and took a deep breath. "And we saw. We saw the thing that probably did it. It's not human. I know how mental this sounds, but you have to believe me. It was a fucking *monster*, Sam. Sarah says it can't leave the Foxglove Pond at the moment, but please, please, *please* don't go down there to see. Because that thing is dangerous, and it's being controlled by someone else, and whoever the controlling person is arranged for the murders to be mostly ignored. There's a for sale sign up outside Marina's house. My dad says her folks are moving away, as far away as possible. It's going to be like it never happened. It's *fucked up*."

Sam said nothing.

"You have to believe me," said Jez. Her hands fell limply to her sides; she felt faintly nauseated.

"I went to English class yesterday," said Sam, after a couple of minutes. "Mrs. Crowther was giving back our Hemingway essays. Gareth's was in the pile; I sit near the front and I could recognize his handwriting. And I was dreading her getting to that point in the pile, and then I wondered: why was it even in the pile at all? Why hadn't she taken it out before she came to class? It's not like she didn't know... I mean, everyone knew; it's all everyone was talking about yesterday. They announced it in assembly. It was in the papers. There's *no way* she can't have been aware."

He swallowed hard.

"And then she gave me back my paper, which was the one on top of Gareth's. And I was freaking out, because his essay was right there, and she was going to pull it out and put it to the back of the pile, or whatever, and then, then it would all be real, all over again, but I didn't say anything, because it was in the middle of class, so I went back and sat down. And then she just looked down at the next paper on the pile and called out 'Gareth Lake.' Just...as if *nothing* was wrong with that."

He was speaking faster now.

"And I feel sick, right, like, *fuck*, she actually called on him... and I was, like, what the fuck is going on? And I wait for someone to say something, because *I* fucking can't, and then bloody Saskia French pipes up from the back and goes, 'He's not here today, miss.' And Mrs. Crowther goes, 'Oh,' and *then* puts his paper to the back to the pile, and carries on giving out the rest. Like nothing happened. Like it wasn't a big deal or any-thing. Like he wasn't fucking *dead*."

He looked straight at Jez. His eyes were burning.

"I want to meet Sarah," he said. Jez had never seen him this intense before; she was almost afraid. "I want to see what she has to say, and I want to hear what she thinks, and if she can sort this out, I want to help, because this is—"

"—fucked up," they finished in tandem. Neither of them laughed.

"Jesus Christ," said Jez. "You wouldn't think there'd be a fine line between clinically boring and mortally dangerous, would you? You can't say that Crowsbrook doesn't do things properly."

"When are you meeting Sarah again?" asked Sam. He'd calmed down a lot, but his fists were still clenched.

"I don't know," said Jez. "She said she wanted to go to the Carpenter offices and have a look. She had a lot of stuff to get ready. We can go over there Monday evening maybe? She doesn't have a mobile."

"Who doesn't have a mobile?" said Sam, wrinkling his nose. "You'd think it would be the first thing you get yourself if you're dealing with, you know, supernatural killing machines and stuff."

Jez thought about it for a moment.

"You know," she said. "I don't think she knows anybody that she could call."

"Then," said Sam, "she needs all the help she can get. Even if that's two bored high school kids with one provisional driver's licence between them, and an iPhone. Okay. Monday evening." He turned back to the jar that was still lying behind them, full of smoke. "I'd like to bury that now, if that's okay."

"Not a problem," said Jez.

Sam stood up. "Also," he announced, "if these *fuckers* mess up my iPhone, I shall be seriously displeased."

• • •

There wasn't a full moon on Saturday night. That was a piece of bad luck, but you worked with what you had in this business.

Sarah, naked under the thick cloak she kept about her for warmth leaned over the firepit in the garden of her cottage. There were three spiders crouching on her shoulder.

You want to know the true sign of a witch? She heard Eleanor's voice in her head. *High hedges around the back garden.*

It was close to midnight now, and there were no short-cuts running through the garden to tempt annoying (and, she allowed, surprisingly intelligent) teenagers. Although, to be fair, Jez had been more helpful than she probably realized in the past few days. And, all right, she allowed herself to admit it. It *was* nice having someone to talk to again.

Focus.

She concentrated on her breathing, inhaling deeply, exhaling slowly, focusing her mind away from Eleanor, from the cottage, from the spiders upstairs, from the girl with the green bag, from the dead kids, from the house fire...

All that there was, all that there ever was, all that there ever would be, was the will of the woman sitting naked on the grass, cloak wrapped around her against the October cold, with the wind blowing her hair across her face.

Will and only will. Beyond language, beyond thought.

Sarah began to make magic.

Chapter 11

Adam was sick.

He'd been feeling unwell since before he'd run into the pro-testers in town the previous day. Some kind of flu or stomach bug or something. He was aching and tired. And in the past twelve hours, he'd thrown up everything he'd tried to eat. He'd even sicked up in his home office while he was working into the night, spluttering quietly so Julia wouldn't hear. And this morning, he couldn't even run. His treadmill was still, waiting downstairs, ominous as a medieval torture device, while Adam was lying in bed.

"Do you need anything?" Julia had asked before she left that morning. At least he'd got out of going to visit her sister. Grumpy cow. Face like a box of frogs, she had, too.

"No," he said, frowning. "A new head, maybe. New stomach. Nothing."

"Oh *dear*," she said. She sat on the side of the bed and laid a hand on his forehead. It irritated him beyond end. "You don't have a temperature."

"I thought *you* were the one who's always arguing you're not my mother," he snapped, twisting away.

Julia swallowed and gritted her teeth. "Can I get you a glass of water?"

"No."

She sighed.

"Okay, then," she said, with false cheerfulness. "I'll be off. Pauline's coming in later; I'm sure she'll make you something hot if you want it. Just stick her an extra fiver or something."

Adam grunted.

"Hope you feel better soon, darling," said Julia. She kissed him on the forehead and left, closing the door behind her. The sound was deafening; her heels clicking down the hardwood floor of the landing and then the stairs seemed barely quieter. But she was gone, thank God.

Adam rolled over in the bed, desperately searching for a cool spot in the crumpled sheets. A fever was burning in every cell of his body. His skin felt as though it belonged to somebody else, and his heart was racing. He thrashed in the bed in frustration.

How long had Julia been gone? He couldn't tell. A few minutes? An hour? Her last words to him echoed in his head; he couldn't tell if they were real or something he had imagined. He kicked the duvet to the floor and began to shiver as the mild air cooled his sweating skin.

So hot. So hot. And so *hungry*.

He hadn't been able to eat a thing for two days. Brought it right back up, but at least he'd been able to fake it until this morning. His throat was sore and his mouth was dry and tasted faintly of vomit. He didn't remember the last time he'd been this sick. Didn't *ever* remember being this sick.

God*dammit*, what was under his skin?

Once, when he was in student digs, no one had emptied the kitchen bin for three weeks. It was summer, and the fruit flies swarmed in the kitchen as the smell slowly became riper and riper. By the time his housemate Rich had finally cracked the lid and lifted the fetid sack out of the metal can, thousands of tiny wriggling worms were crawling on the bottom: tiny, thin and aimless. That was what it felt like. Constant, directionless movement, coming from within his body. Alone, it was enough to make him nauseated.

The room swam before him. He was weak. *Weak.* And hot. And thirsty.

He was going to get up and get a drink of water. He could do that for himself; he didn't need Julia fussing and flapping around him like a stupid mother hen. Or Pauline. She'd be worse. He could hear her clattering around downstairs already, mixed with the intermittent electric buzzing of the hoover.

The bathroom was a hundred miles away, at the end of the hall. Gravity pulled him down, down toward the bed.

Fuck it. *Fuck* it. He *would* get the water himself.

His legs felt as though his muscles had turned into solid iron; moving demanded a superhuman effort. He ached all over.

Take it in stages, he thought. *One step at a time. It's all just willpower.*

He swung around so that his legs hung over the edge of the bed. His feet hit the floor. He still lay on the bed, summoning the energy to sit up.

He put his hand on the head of the bed, took a deep breath, and hauled himself up in one excruciating motion. He sat there, panting, lightheaded. The room danced in front of him; he felt as though it were mocking him. Julia's collection of soft toys—*why the hell does a grown woman, a doctor, no less, need so many soft toys?*—jeered at him silently, a rogues' gallery of motley plush and glitter. The powder-blue rabbit she had picked up as a souvenir from some girls' day out to Alton Towers two years ago was in hysterics, while the peppermint-green teddy bear from last summer's trip to the coast just looked disappointed and disgusted. The pink and white clown from her childhood screamed with laughter.

Another deep breath. Another colossal effort. He pushed down hard with his feet and slowly stood up. The room sped up and tilted; Adam stumbled and fought to keep his balance. He could almost hear the laughter from Julia's toys.

He had to get to the bathroom. He was gasping now.

One foot before the other. That's all it is. Come on! Internally, he hurled curses at his weakened body. *Fuck you! Fuck you! Work, goddammit!*

He managed three steps before his knees buckled and he sank to the floor, out of breath. The warm, homely smell of wood and varnish was no comfort.

It's just the fucking flu, for God's sake.

A wave of pain shot through him and he convulsed. The floor below him added to the clammy sensations on the surface of his skin. Energized by his fury, Adam dragged himself to his knees and began crawling toward the bathroom. He grit his teeth and tried to ignore the ferocious aching in his muscles.

Closer. Closer. The bathroom door was open. *Thank God.* Pain shot through him again, and he had to stop.

One more push. Willpower. Willpower!

His fingers reached the cool tiles of the bathroom floor.

...one more foot...

He felt their smooth surface beneath his skin and collapsed.

Rest. Just rest for a moment. Then get your water.

He felt as though he'd been on the treadmill for hours. The tiles beneath him began to feel moist against his skin. With another gargantuan effort, he hauled himself up to the sink and grabbed for his tooth glass. A cascade of plastic clattered into the sink: toothbrushes, dental floss, some small glass pots of Julia's that were full of goo. He turned on the tap too strongly:

water flooded out and sprayed him lightly as it hit the side of the glass before filling it.

Damn, it was heavy.

He left the tap running and drank greedily, swallowing huge, uncomfortable gulps. The movement of the water felt good in his throat, but the taste in his mouth was metallic and dull. Stale.

He relaxed and leaned on the bathroom wall. *This is ridiculous*, he told himself again. *It's just the fucking flu.*

His stomach cramped and he felt a rising in his throat. He scrambled for the toilet and just managed to raise the lid and seat before the water he'd gulped down came pouring out of his mouth. The taste in his mouth was slightly sour; he spat and groaned.

How sick do you have to be to throw up water?

Better get back to bed, he thought, but the effort that faced him seemed overwhelming. He leaned his head back against the bathroom wall and sighed.

"Hello?"

Pauline. She had stopped hoovering downstairs. Her voice floated toward him from the stairwell.

"Hello? Adam?"

Thank God he was wearing shorts. His muscles cramped and twitched, and he flinched.

"In here," he croaked. The last thing he wanted was Pauline fussing over him.

"Oh, good *lord*," she said when she saw him. "You look awful, if you don't mind me saying. You should be in bed." He grunted agreement, but didn't look at her. "Do you want some help getting back there?"

He looked at skinny Pauline; she must have been in her mid-sixties if she was a day. He ran at least five miles every day, and now he was reduced to getting help from her?

"I'm sure I can manage," he said, and then, as an afterthought, "Thanks."

He *was* hungry, though. That was probably what was making him feel weak. He just needed to eat something. Line his stomach. Then he could have a drink of water and a nap, and by the time Julia got home, he'd be better. If not fine.

Toast. That's what his mother would have made him. Toast and a boiled egg. Sick-day food.

"Can you make me some toast, please, Pauline," he said, looking at her directly. Julia thought she had a kind face; he didn't see it himself. She wasn't attractive. Right now, she looked concerned.

"You ought to be in bed," she said.

"Yes," he said. "Probably. Can you make me some toast and a boiled egg, and I'll go back to bed." She didn't usually cook for them—it wasn't her job; she looked surprised—but he was *never* sick. And he was paying her, wasn't he? More than the going rate too, because of Julia's bleeding heart. How long did it take to make a boiled egg and a piece of toast? Stupid woman.

"All right, Adam," she said. She didn't even look as if she minded. 'You go on back to bed, and I'll get that up to you in a jiffy." She smiled at him sympathetically. "D'you want your toast cut into soldiers? My Emma always used to want soldiers when she was poorly."

"Whatever," said Adam. He had to get back to the bed while she was in the kitchen; he knew he wouldn't have long, and he wanted to focus. "Just—I'll be in bed when you're ready. Don't hoover the upstairs today," he added, as an afterthought. "I have a splitting headache. I'll tell Julia." He made a mental note to tell her to knock an hour off the total for next week as well, when she was putting the money in the envelope. No sense in paying for something you weren't going to get.

Pauline tramped off downstairs and Adam looked down the hall to the bedroom door. The world still tilted and swirled, and his body still ached, but he was determined that his cleaner wouldn't see him scrabbling around on the floor like a toddler.

He gritted his teeth, grabbed the heated towel rail with one hand and hauled himself to his feet.

• • •

Pauline went down to the cavernous kitchen. Her feet hurt and her back was starting to ache too. Adam and Julia were the first ones on her list this morning; she hoped she wouldn't be too bad by the end of the day.

Oh, well, she thought. *Give me a bit of a break, boiling an egg. Not like it takes much effort though. Can't do a bloody thing for himself, that one, and she's not much better.*

She felt bad. She was a churchgoing lady, after all. Sunday evenings, not in the mornings where everyone could see, and besides, she had to work in the mornings, fit it round her other job at the big supermarket in town. Not one of those who had to flash it all over the place and make sure it was in everybody's face, but still. She tried. And that hadn't been a good Christian thought.

Don't be so hard on the poor lad, her better self chided her. *He's poorly. And there's no one here to look after him. Can't be much fun for him, not for someone works as hard as he does.*

Her inner pagan snorted.

Doesn't know the meaning of hard work. Sitting in his office all day, giving orders like Lord Muck. And then he comes home to do the same.

You're just cross because your feet hurt, she told herself, and that shut up Bad Pauline, which was what she called that voice in her head.

She hunted in the kitchen for a saucepan. She couldn't see these two cooking that much. Out to restaurants five night a week, she imagined, with a house this size and only the two of them. She hoped they actually had eggs. She'd seen Adam in a temper once before, when she'd put some of his papers in a pile when she was dusting. She didn't want to see *that* again. Like a spoiled child, he was.

She opened the shiny fridge. *Thought so.* It was almost empty: three bottles of white wine, some elderly blue cheese, six different kinds of mustard. Not much you could make a meal with. But there was an egg box right at the back. She pulled it out. There were two eggs left. She breathed a sigh of relief. And they were just about to go out of date.

She put one of the eggs in the pan and turned on the tap; water gushed over the smooth shell, covering it completely. Most of the things in the kitchen were new, less than a year old. Pauline remembered Julia having the kitchen done: bits of stone lying around and tile samples everywhere. *Nothing's too good for her, snooty cow*, she thought. *Get the shock of her life if she had to live in the real world for five minutes.*

God, her feet hurt. The weather must be about to turn or something. They always gave her a warning.

She put the pan on the burner and turned on the gas; a second later, the blue flames clicked to life. She sat down for a moment on one of the tall stools that stood in a row by the breakfast bar, to take the weight off her feet.

Christ, she thought. *Toast. His lordship wanted toast.* There was a toaster on the granite countertop (Pauline had wiped the crumbs away earlier); she climbed down from the stool and began hunting in the cupboards for some bread. Finally, she found a frost-encrusted loaf in the freezer.

Have to do, she thought. She broke off a couple of slices and put them, frozen, in the toaster. There wasn't any butter, but she could cut the toast into soldiers and he could dip them in the egg. Her Emma still liked that. Always had. Her and her chap, Ryan, they'd be about the same age as Adam as well. Been sick a lot more than Himself Upstairs recently, Ryan had, and never complained. Even with all those tests they were doing, sticking him like a bloody pincushion, they were, and he just kept on smiling. She was hoping this trouble wouldn't last. She liked Ryan; some of Emma's blokes had been awful, but Ryan seemed to have it together, and hopefully this one would stick. He was a good lad. Some people didn't know they were born.

On the hob, the water began to bubble.

• • •

The sheets were damp and humid. Adam could feel the wrinkled cotton under his back. But he had made it back to bed. He was sore, but there was a glass of water next to the bed. Not that he wanted to throw it up again. But at least it was there.

Where the *hell* was Pauline? He was hungry now. Ravenous. Maybe he was getting better. Mind over matter. He had made it to the bathroom and back. The journey back had taken him much less time. He would beat this thing. He would beat it. If he slept this afternoon, he could be back at work tomorrow.

Pauline appeared at the door. She was carrying a tray with the boiled egg in a blue egg cup and a matching plate with a slice of toast, cut into strips. There was a steaming cup of tea on it, as well.

"I made you a cuppa," she said, almost apologetically. "Nothing like a hot cup of tea to perk you up."

And then it happened. Adam was overwhelmed by hunger.

He could feel his body moving involuntarily. In the distance, he could hear screaming, the crash of the tray. He felt the heat of the tea on his foot; he didn't care.

This is not me, he thought, in the last, panicked seconds before he broke Pauline's neck with a loud crack. *This is not me.*

At the same time, it was all he wanted.

He didn't remember anything after that.

• • •

From the corner of the room, a spider watched with interest. When everything was still, it moved a little closer to the two figures lying on the floor, first toward one, then the other. It paused for a moment, as if it were taking stock.

The flies descended: six of them, buzzing ominously. They flew to it as if it were rotting meat; the spider disappeared beneath a carapace of emerald green with a shine like metal.

When the flies took off again, all that was left was a small wet patch on the floor. A thick tendril of vapour drifted up from it, and then evaporated.

• • •

It was getting dark when Adam woke up. He was lying on the floor, his cheek pressed against the hardwood. His throat burned as if he'd been drinking acid, and there was a foul taste in his mouth. And something was different.

He felt *full.*

This was the second time he'd blacked out in less than a week. It was getting ridiculous. He'd speak to Tim about it, next time he was at the gym. Tim was a doctor; it'd be a lot less hassle than making an appointment and having to wait in a room with kids with dripping noses and old people with oxygen tanks. Certainly a lot less trouble than talking to Julia, and she was a surgeon anyway; probably wouldn't know what was wrong with him unless he was gushing blood or had a gunshot wound or something. All he needed was a quick confirm that everything was okay, and he'd be done.

He opened his eyes.

On the floor in front of him was a pool of blood and thick tissue that looked like meat that had been dissolved in a blender. What was left of Pauline's body lay prone on the floor in the middle of it. From the shoulders down, her skin and clothes appeared intact, but they rested over a more skeletal frame than they had in life. His eyes travelled upwards, and he felt his stomach churn.

Her face and neck had been—burned? dissolved? What flesh was left ran from deep red to charred black; around her mouth, it had been burned away entirely, leaving her teeth and jawbone exposed.

Her eyes were open and stared, unblinking, at him.

He let out a sharp cry and sprang to his feet; he didn't even notice that his muscles didn't ache anymore.

"What the fuck?" he shouted. "What the fuck? What the fuck?"

He had to get this thing out of here, get it all cleared up before Julia got home.

"What the fuck happened?" he shouted. No one answered.

Clean it up.

"I can't clean it up!" he shouted, to no one. "*She's* the cleaner!"

Idiot. CLEAN IT UP. *And call Brown.*

It wasn't so much a voice. It was more like a persistent thought that wouldn't go away. It was *his* thought. And yet—

No. It was his thought. Who else's thought could it be? It was just his rational self, taking control.

Call Brown. Right. He had to call Brown. Pauline's dead eyes stared at his shins.

Wait, he thought. *Why do I have to call Brown?*

Because Brown knows how to fix *things. Brown can fix anything.*

"Right," he said, out loud.

He sat down on the bed, picked up his phone, and dialled the number that Brown had given him. The phone rang three times, and then there was a click and a voice said, "Mr. Carpenter."

"Brown," said Adam, in a rush. Suddenly, he felt stupid and lost for words. What would he say to Brown? How could anyone understand what had happened? He didn't even know what had happened himself. How could he tell anyone that there was a horribly mutilated corpse in his bedroom, that he had to get rid of it and clean up the mess before his girlfriend came home, that he had to stop anyone from finding out what happened? The man was a business associate, for God's sake. A fly buzzed lazily over the corpse.

Stomach cramps wracked his body. He groaned involuntarily.

"Mr. Carpenter," the voice said. "I understand you have a problem."

"A problem?" croaked Adam. He was doubled over in pain, trying not to look at the dead eyes staring at him from across the room. The smell of blood and—what was that, *vomit?*—was making him feel queasy.

Adam heard a fly buzzing, from the general direction of the corpse.

"A *problem*, Mr. Carpenter," said Brown. "You need a cleaner. And you do not currently have one."

The nausea vanished. Adam froze. He felt as though he were falling through space.

"How," he snapped, "the *fuck* did you know that?" He stood up and looked around the room wildly; he marched over to Julia's shelf of stuffed animals and swept them off the shelf; he started looking behind pictures and opening drawers. "Do you have cameras in here? Bugs? Because I *swear*, if you do—"

"Please calm down, Mr. Carpenter," said Brown. "We have arranged for Dr. Fletcher to remain at her sister's until the matter is resolved, and a team of our most discreet cleaners will arrive at your house shortly to address the main issue."

Adam felt as though he were drowning.

"Please be assured," Brown continued, "everything will be taken care of. Our organization is known for the subtlety of our work."

Adam tried to speak. His throat was dry and raw.

"I don't—" he croaked. He cleared his throat and gave it another shot. "*I* don't know what happened. How do *you* know what happened?"

"You were hungry," said Brown. "Were you not?"

"I *was* hungry," said Adam. "I asked Pauline—my cleaner, I asked my cleaner—if she would make me a boiled egg." He looked quickly back at the mess of blood and flesh on the floor. The egg and the eggcup were lying about two feet apart, but both were intact. The toast was in the puddle of blood. Adam noticed that it had soaked some up. He felt sick all over again. "She made me an egg. I didn't eat it, though."

"No," said Brown. "You didn't eat it."

There was a pause.

"I'm not hungry anymore," said Adam. He felt like a small child.

"No," said Brown.

"Brown," said Adam. A sickening suspicion was growing within him. It was impossible. Beyond impossible. And yet—

And yet.

He *was* full.

"Brown," he said again, his heart racing. "This is mad. It's completely mad. It makes no sense. My cleaner is dead. In my bedroom. And she's a mess; I don't know what happened. I was sick, I went to the bathroom to get a glass of water, I came back to the bedroom, she came in with a boiled egg, and that's the last thing I remember before everything went mad. And you," he gestured, pointing, realizing as he did so that it was futile, "you not only know that there's something wrong when I call, you seem to have a fair idea of how to fix it. So I'm going to ask you directly." He took a deep breath. "What *exactly* is going on here?"

There was a long silence. Adam looked at his phone to check the call was still connected.

"Mr. Carpenter," said Brown, eventually. "You did read the contract we provided?"

"Of course I read the contract," said Adam, rolling his eyes. He felt like a student accused of not completing a basic assignment. "I dealt with it myself." It was true. Carrington had told him not to get outside legal involved in this one; he'd been very specific. "They'll want you to handle it personally," he'd said. So Adam had. The language had been more arcane than he'd been used to, but it had seemed pretty straightforward at the time.

"Excellent," said Brown. "Then you remember. You are the host."

"Carpenter Properties is the host," said Adam. That was the term that had almost tripped him up. They'd used "host" instead of "employer" or "contractor"; when he'd asked, they told him that, in this case, the terms were interchangeable.

"Yes," said Brown. "Carpenter Properties. But as head of Carpenter Properties, you, Adam Carpenter, are ultimately the host. Of our executive."

Adam was growing irritated. "It's the company that's legally liable. So what?"

"Mr. Carpenter," said Brown. "Our relationship is special. It is—" he paused "—symbiotic, if you will. You provide us with certain conditions, and we provide you with certain services. It is the same throughout business, no?"

"Essentially," said Adam. He was growing impatient, and couldn't be bothered to argue the finer points; he was still feeling sick and didn't want to get into a philosophical discussion while he was waiting for Brown's people to come and clean up the mess on his floor.

"It reflects life," continued Brown. "You have been feeling stronger, since we last met in person, I think? More physically able?"

"Until the past couple of days," said Adam. "What the hell does this have to do with anything?"

"Mr. Carpenter," said Brown. He retained his cool, level tone, even as Adam himself was becoming more and more annoyed. "You provide the host body for our organization. Our organization will bring you, if I may be so frank, more success than you could possibly have ever achieved by yourself. We make conflict-ridden relationships work. We make immoveable obstacles disappear. We dispose of crises quickly and discreetly. We feel that acting as a corporate host is a small price to pay for our services."

Adam was taken aback. The project—the factory—had been running more smoothly and more quickly than anything he'd worked on before, he'd give them that.

"You will not need to eat again for some time," said Brown. "When you feel that you do, please contact us if you need assistance. We will, of course, be more than happy to help."

There was a click and a pause, and then the dial tone. Adam stared at the phone in disbelief.

The doorbell rang.

Panic shot through him like a laser. He stepped carefully around the mess on the floor and looked out of the window. An unmarked van with illegible number plates was parked in his driveway.

He went downstairs, checking his path at every step to make sure he wasn't trailing blood, and opened the door on the chain.

"Mr. Carpenter?" said a man's voice through the crack. "We're here from Asilida. Cleaning services."

He let them in gratefully, and sank into a chair in the living room as the team of three men, dressed in identical blue shirts and no-name jeans, headed upstairs with wire brushes and bleach and plastic sacks.

Chapter 12

Monday morning. Sarah was standing in the spiders' room, looking at the trunks. She was dressed in a dark grey pinstriped suit, tights and heels. It was getting on a bit, that suit, and it still smelled faintly of smoke from the fire, but the glamour would take care of that.

The glamour was one of her best. Her hair was now blond and pulled into an updo; her skin was pale as ice and she was wearing dark-rimmed glasses. It wasn't simply a disguise. She looked—physically, she *was*—someone else.

There were three trunks in the room. The spiders had scattered when she walked in; they crouched in the thick layer of cobwebs that now enveloped the ceiling and corners of the room. She couldn't help feeling that they were watching her, while she hesitated.

She just wanted to meet Carpenter. That was all. See what was up; if there was anything…well…anything odd. Whoever had released the flies—whoever had, temporarily, contained the insect demon down by the Foxglove Pond—was likely to be working at a high level with Carpenter Properties. Jez had said that the firm had a long-standing reputation in the area. So she was really interested in finding out who Adam Carpenter—she'd looked him up online at Jez's insistence—really was, and what he was like.

She was wearing a pentacle similar to the one she had given Jez under her office blouse. It would offer her some protection.

And yet, she couldn't help feeling that it wasn't enough. Ethereals teamed with humans would be far more powerful than they would be on their own. If anything she found at the office turned out to be hostile—

It's an office, she told herself. *How bad can it be?*

The feeling wouldn't go away. And that was a bad sign. First rule of the family business: don't let anything that seems odd slide. Don't ignore the niggling feeling in the pit of your stomach. It might turn out to be nothing. Then again, it mightn't.

Throwing energy balls in a public meeting was one thing. This feeling was condensing into two words.

Go armed.

She exhaled through her teeth, knelt down, and flipped open the first trunk. It's just for self-defence, she told herself.

Her own words to Jez came back to her. *You know how much the world loses when something mortal dies. Think about what it loses when you kill something that's supposed to be immortal.* If a human attacked her, she could use small magic— little charms with temporary effect—to give herself time to get away. She could fight back. The Ethereal world wasn't like that. It didn't negotiate and it wasn't easily deceived.

If she was attacked by an Ethereal, she would have to be prepared to kill.

Each trunk was full of objects wrapped in paper. She took them out one by one and laid them on the floor. A rope made of human hair. Three shrunken heads in a string bag. A stake with elaborate carvings down each side, whittled out of some- thing that looked suspiciously like a hip bone. A small Victorian pistol with a set of grimy and tarnished silver bullets. She made a mental note to go through each box sometime and figure out what they were all for. If Auntie Dot was anything like her grandmother, there would be a catalogue somewhere, even if it was heavily coded.

In the third box, she found something promising: a small dagger, with a blade about six inches long. She picked it up and was surprised at its weight; when she looked closely at the blade, she discovered that it was made not of metal, but of a smooth, dull grey stone. The handle was dark wood and fitted neatly into her hand.

"Blue slate," she said out loud.

It was heavy and it was pointy. Heavy and pointy would see you through a lot, even if it didn't do anything else.

She wrapped it back up in the paper and dropped it into her bag. A small spider ran up her sleeve and hid inside the cuff of her shirt.

. . .

Arden High was on the other side of Arden to Crowsbrook, and the school bus went through the town to get there. Jez got off the bus two stops early. She had looked up the address of the office before she left home. She wasn't sure what she was planning to do, but she didn't have any classes until ten.

Maybe I can help Sarah out if she gets in trouble, she thought. *If I recognize her.* Just how different could the witch make herself look?

And how much trouble can she get into in an office? part of her wondered.

Jez positioned herself behind a wheelie bin and a lamppost, and waited.

. . .

Sarah had driven to the edge of town and then walked the rest of the way. Much as she loved the Allegro, it didn't fit with the suit.

The weight of the slate knife was reassuring in her one good leather bag. She still didn't know exactly what kind of Ethereals she might be dealing with; she was assuming the insect demon wasn't on the nine-to-five payroll and wasn't likely to be in the office first thing on a Monday, but slate was absorbent, sucking up life force from anything it…well…stabbed. Most Ethereals stabbed with a slate dagger would be incapacitated for quite a while. She was *really* hoping that she wouldn't have to stab anything. It was a lot less onerous to deal with thoughts of death and revenge when all you had was a name on a piece of paper.

She had sworn bloody vengeance on Carrington, and she would take it. But today? She wasn't feeling the urge for a bloodbath.

The door now in front of her was heavy and black and covered in thick gloss paint that had obviously been built up in layers over the years. A brass plate at the side of the door told her that she was in the right place. She took a deep breath and pushed it open.

Across the street, Jez watched the blonde woman with the updo enter the building.

From an upstairs window in the building Sarah had just entered, a young man in an immaculate suit watched Jez.

· · ·

The receptionist inside was young and obviously overqualified, and also probably just killing time between modelling contracts. *Felicity Allister* announced the name plate on the high desk in front of her. *Receptionist.* "Good morning," she said, with the bright, shallow smile of someone used to being adored for her looks.

"Good morning," said Sarah. "I have an appointment with Mr. Carpenter." She didn't. "At nine-thirty. Eleanor Fitch."

Felicity frowned and flipped through a couple of pages in the appointment book. "Hm," she said. "I can't see you here. I think he's free, though, if he's in. He's been ill for a couple of days."

"Nothing serious, I hope?" Sarah's concern was polite. "I would have thought he would have called me if he hadn't planned to make our appointment."

"Just a bit of flu, I think." Definitely not a professional executive assistant, for all her blue suit jacket and black-rimmed glasses. *You don't tell people who don't have an appointment what your boss has when he's sick, Felicity.* "Have a seat." Felicity gestured across the hall to a waiting area filled with mismatched but unmistakeably old furniture. There were copies of country living magazines on a dark-brown coffee table in the middle of the room. Not the most current issue, Sarah noticed.

They don't give the impression that they're doing well, thought Sarah. *Someone's trying to spruce up the office with glitter like Felicity, because he can't afford the renovations he'd like.* She looked up. There was a cobweb in the corner of the room, although its creator was nowhere to be seen. *Or a decent cleaner, for that matter.* She tried to put the matter out of her mind and focus. She needed to get up to Carpenter's office. There was a set of spiral stairs leading up to the next floor, just beyond the reception. That must be it. A man like Carpenter—a man like she suspected him to be—wouldn't hide in a back office.

She had to get Felicity out of the way. She closed her eyes and concentrated hard. She connected—

—and she was walking past the desk, Felicity couldn't see her, no one could see her, they all thought she was just sitting in the waiting room, but she was wandering through the back of the office; she didn't have long because if someone spoke to her in the waiting room, she'd have to come back, and she couldn't connect properly because she was still half-focused on the glamour; she couldn't go upstairs like this. Already it was getting darker. She fumbled along the walls and found a gap; patting around with her hands, she found a sink, a fridge…the office kitchen.

Something. There must be something.

A kettle, plugged into the wall. A plate. A mug.

She summoned up as much energy as she could muster and pushed the plate off the counter—

There was a crash from the back of the building. Sarah opened her eyes. Felicity was frowning, her head turned toward the kitchen. She got up from behind the desk and disappeared into the back.

Sarah slipped off her high-heeled shoes and headed upstairs in stocking feet. There was the office, across a small landing, just as she had anticipated. Large, roll-top desk, probably antique, but not new, not by any means; dark, hardwood floors—it had to be the boss's office. She slipped inside and pushed the door until it was almost closed.

Now what? She still wasn't really sure what she was looking for. There were files on the desk, she opened one and the top page was just a form with a list of scribbled signatures. She didn't have a camera. She didn't have anything. She felt a little silly.

Then she saw the box. It looked expensive and it was decorated with an inlaid pattern that looked like some kind of alphabet.

She couldn't read it. Not right away. But she sure as h—
Well, she recognized it, all right.

That alphabet. The script on the box. Her grandmother had told her about that alphabet. And it wasn't anything good.

She'd need the books to help with this. Her notebooks, back at the cottage. Fortunately among the few things that hadn't gone up in the fire; maybe one of the few generous acts of the Old Gods. She grabbed a pen and notebook from her purse and started scribbling furiously. copying down the curly inscription.

There was a polite cough from the doorway; her head jerked up. A young man was standing there, in an expensive-looking, immaculate suit. She was pretty sure that, could she see the back of his head, she would recognize it as that of the man who had sat in front of her in the world's weirdest council planning meeting only a few days before.

The most remarkable, most noticeable thing about him, thought Sarah, was that there was absolutely nothing remarkable about his appearance. Had she tried to describe him, the best she could manage was to describe his clothes: dark grey, obviously expensive suit, surgical white shirt, silver cufflinks, stamped with some sort of complicated pattern—
That was worrying.

"Ah," he said. "Welcome to the Carpenter offices." He smiled, but his eyes didn't change. "We've been expecting you."

Sarah froze. She closed the folder and stood up straight.

It's okay, she thought. *You can bluff your way out of this; the worst-case scenario is you'll get thrown out.* There was no way he could see through the glamour. No one, even an Ethereal, should be able to see through a glamour. No one should even be able to sense a glamour. And her glamours were good.

Expecting me?

"I'm sorry," she said. "I have an appointment. My name is Eleanor. Eleanor Fitch. I'm here to see Mr. Carpenter."

"Of course you are," said the man in the suit. "But you do not have an appointment, Ms. Fitch. Also, I believe that it is not customary in England to remove one's shoes when in the office of a person with whom one has a business appointment, nor indeed to peruse the papers of people with whom you have business appointments in their absence unless you have express permission. Which I do not believe you do."

Fuck. Sarah was speechless. "I was worried about the floor," she eventually managed. She slipped her shoes back on, painfully aware that she would break an ankle if she tried to run in them.

"Furthermore," he went on, "I have concerns that you are not, in fact, Eleanor Fitch. I suspect that you are one of the few people still alive who are inconveniencing our operations. I refer, of course, to Sarah Trevelyan."

Sarah's stomach fell through the floor.

He *was* an Ethereal.

"I don't know who that is," she said, lifting her chin and looking him straight in the eye. He stared back, unblinking.

"Do not be afraid," the man went on. "I have no intention of hurting you. We—Asilida—are but a small subsidiary of a much larger operation. You have come into contact with some former members of that operation before, I believe."

Sarah stood completely still. Her fury was growing. And her fear. Why didn't he care what he was telling her if he wasn't planning to kill her?

"Needless to say," the man went on, "your attempts to stop us will not work. We have been working in this field for even longer than your family has been in business. And, trust us, we will continue to do so long after you are dead." He gave the word no special emphasis, but it rang in Sarah's mind like a stone clattering into a metal bucket.

He still doesn't know for sure who you are.

"Why," said Sarah, who was not prepared to give in completely, "would I listen to you? You're mad. And you're threatening me."

The man continued smiling. "It is not a threat," he said. "You are well aware of what can happen when you cross us. And you would not want anything to happen to the girl. Would you, *Eleanor?*"

He knew. Blood shot to Sarah's face.

He knew about the fire. He knew about Eleanor. He would definitely not be on her side. He was one of *them*. Even if he wasn't one of the mercenary Ethereals, he knew.

He was looking at her, steadily, studying her.

"If I may give you some personal advice," he said, looking around the room, "it would be to stop now and leave this town and never come back. We will not stop you, but you should stop yourself. Even if you don't care what happens to you, which you may not—we know you can be reckless—you will at least think of the girl. And the boy, now."

Boy? What boy?"

"Of course you would not want any harm to come to either of them. They are innocents."

"Since when do you lot care about innocents?" spat Sarah. "You're preying on a whole village of innocents. And you lot are going to rip the heart out of it." She wanted to pick up the box files lying on the desk and smash them into the man's smiling face.

"But it is our *raison d'etre*, if you will," said the man. "It is what we do. A contract has been signed. We will do the work; we will take our payment; and we will make our profit."

"Your profit is human misery," snapped Sarah.

"Everyone has to eat," said the man. "Everyone has to feed."

"I said *profit*," snarled Sarah. "It's not about survival. It's not about all rubbing along; it's not about that nature-red-in-tooth-and-claw crap. It's about expansion. It's about growth. It's about taking over *everything*. It's about controlling all of conscious existence. Ruling it."

The man rolled his eyes. "So melodramatic," he said.

"Am I wrong?" shot back Sarah. The man was silent for a moment. Then he shrugged.

"You are *powerless*," he said. "We do not care what you think. We do not care what you do. You will not change anything. You have, of course, failed before."

"I *have* stopped things like you before," Sarah growled.

"At what cost, ultimately?" The man inclined his head and looked at her directly. "Should I remind you?"

Sarah was breathing heavily.

"Was it you?" she said, in a low voice. "Did you know them? Did you and your team of—" she scrabbled for words; she was shaking with rage "—*slugs* cause the fire? Because if you did, if it was you..." She was looking straight at him now, and her eyes were burning.

"No," said the man. "Actually, it was not our organization." He paused and beamed at her. "But humans are not the only ones who need entertainment in our hours of leisure."

Sarah felt her stomach clench.

"You were there," she said. "You were there, weren't you?"

"If you're looking for revenge," said the man, rolling his eyes, "do not waste your energy. I will repeat myself once more: I recommend that you leave town and do not come back, regardless of your family ties to the town. Which, I might add, have inconvenienced us before. Do you know how tedious it is, to count grains of sand for centuries at a time?"

The demon in the Foxglove Pond. Dot was right: there is a family connection.

"You deserved it," muttered Sarah. The man shrugged.

"Your judgments are meaningless," he said. "There is nothing you can do. There is nothing you *will* do. Action will put those you care about in danger. You know this. You have paid the price before."

"Where's Carpenter?" snapped Sarah. She didn't want to think about what had happened before. *Warm. It was so warm in the office. Too warm.* She felt as though she were burning up.

"He is well, for the most part," said the man. "He has been feeling under the weather for the past couple of days, but he is likely to be back at his desk again soon. Though we have advised him to work from his home office until further notice."

"What have you done with him?"

"I really don't see that that's any of your business, Miss Trevelyan." The man opened the door to the office. "Any business conducted between Mr. Carpenter and Carpenter Properties and our organization is in confidence and purely contractual. Since you are not a party to that contract, I see no reason to disclose its details to you." He held the door and stood aside, gesturing for her to walk through. She complied, seething.

"I'll have Felicity show you out," said the man. "Enchanted to meet you."

Fuck you, thought Sarah. She was icy calm. *One of them. He's one of them. He was there.*

She sniffed and touched the end of her nose and then reached into her bag, as if for a tissue. Instead, she whipped out the dagger and jammed it upward, below the man's rib cage.

There was no blood. Only a clear, warm fluid that looked like water, and a little vapour. He gasped and sank to the floor, fighting for air. Sarah pulled the dagger out of his body; it came out clean.

"Slate," he choked out. "*Witch.*"

"You knew that," said Sarah with contempt.

"It won't make a difference," he wheezed. His face was crumpling, skin draped like tissue paper over the bones, as vapour wafted from his body.

"It made a difference to you," she said, and walked out of the office as his body melted into dark water and soaked into the carpet. His cufflinks fell to the ground with a thud.

Sarah bent down, picked them up and looked at them closely. Her eyes widened.

When she came downstairs, she told Felicity that she couldn't wait any longer, and that the man upstairs had helped her. Then she left.

She still had the paper with the letters on it in her bag.

• • •

Fifteen minutes later, Felicity went upstairs to ask Mr. Brown if he would like a cup of tea.

Mr. Brown smiled.

"Yes, please, Felicity," he said. "That would be lovely."

She turned to go.

"Oh, by the way," he called after her. "Can we get the carpet cleaned? There's a nasty stain on the floor in Mr. Carpenter's office."

Felicity looked surprised. It wasn't usually her job to handle the cleaning.

"Of course, Mr. Brown," she said. "I'll get right on it."

"Thank you," he said, still smiling. "Whoever was here before has left a *terrible* mess."

Chapter 13

In her seventh year at Arden High, Jez knew the school as if
it were an unruly pet dog. She could read its moods, knew
the things that got it overexcited, knew when it was, for the
most part, exhausted and needed a nap, and knew when it was
freaking out with anticipation and the promise of something
juicy, a treat—usually in the form of gossip or scandal or a massive act of vandalism, like when they all came back after half
term in February one time and discovered someone had spray-
painted outsized hearts on every ground floor window on the
school grounds.

There was no excitement today, though. Today, it was hostile. To Jez, at any rate. The school as a whole was baring its
teeth and emitting a low growl from its metaphorical throat.
She'd walked into the classroom block late, behind Paul Barlow,
who had known she was right there, but had pushed the door
hard after him so that it came within an inch of hitting Jez
in the face. She cried out; he turned around and smirked; a
sparking cluster of passing Year Eight girls giggled at her, nastily.
When she got to the common room, Saskia French rolled her
eyes and sighed when Jez walked in, and then pressed her lips
together and told her small cabal a little too loudly that *she* was
leaving, and if they didn't want to catch a severe case of Freak,
they might want to think about leaving too.

"If I have a case of Freak," said Jez, equally loudly and staring at the wall, "then yours is terminal." No one laughed. Saskia gave Jez a radioactively filthy look and swept out.

Needless to say, there was no space for Jez on the sofa.

Jez was puzzled. She was the first person to admit that she openly loathed most of the people she went to school with, but it had never really seemed to bother anybody that much. Socially, she just wasn't that important. She found a hard seat in the corner of the common room, plonked down her biology folder and flipped it open.

And then she saw it.

It was in the corner of the common room, by the window, on the sill.

A large, green fly.

For the second time in as many minutes, she experienced a sharp jolt of shock and fear. She looked along the window sill and drew in her breath sharply.

There must have been twenty, butting up against the window pane. They were everywhere. And nobody was giving them a second glance.

She slammed her folder shut and stomped out of the common room, pushing Pete Lennon into Lee Humbolt on her way out. She had biology in twenty minutes anyway, and she could think about something else.

• • •

Sam was restless. It didn't happen often in English, but the combination of Saskia French talking misguidedly about Jane Austen—for, God, it must be *minutes*, he thought—and sitting in a warm room in a world on the edge of not apocalypse exactly, but *something very bad* would be enough to distract the most ardent student of literature.

That's just it, he thought. That's the problem. *The world isn't going to end. Everything is going to go on just as before, except that a lot more people will be miserable and a few more people will make a bit more money and some other people will have a lot more power. And no one will care about some kind of supernatural evil living among us, because they've managed to make themselves look enough like us that no one would suspect anything was up.*

If the world *was* ending, would it be easier to get people off their arses to do something about it? He thought of the family in *Night of the Living Dead,* the family hiding in the cellar while civilization collapsed around them outside, and concluded, gloomily, that it probably wouldn't.

Saskia French sat down, thank God, and Mrs. Crowther was standing up and talking again. Sam forced himself to concentrate.

"—marked your essays from last week," she was saying. "And don't forget, next Monday is a practice exam; come prepared." Ugh. He was so prepared. He was prepared to take the damn exam now if it meant he could leave town, like, *now,* and head north, and never come back. They could tear down the whole fucking town as far as he was concerned. He wanted out.

He heard a faint buzzing from the window. A chill shot up his spine. There was a large fly crawling on the fanlight, near the ceiling.

He heard his name being called and mechanically got out of his seat to collect his essay. It was the one on William Golding. Sam was one of Mrs. Crowther's top students, and this effort would destroy all pretenders. It was a fucking awesome piece of work. He hoped the mark would cheer him up, take his mind off the chaos that Jez had exposed. He flipped to the final page of the essay to find his mark and the comment, in red pen.

His mark was nineteen out of twenty. He whistled with relief internally. Whatever the netherworld was doing, at least they weren't screwing with his A-levels yet.

Then he saw the comments underneath, in Mrs. Crowther's neat handwriting.

You think you're really smart, don't you? If you're actually smart, stick to writing essays about books by dead people, and forget about all that bullshit the Elliot girl was talking about. No one will believe you anyway. And stop obsessing over the dead. Gareth's gone. It would never have happened anyway. Forget about all of this and just get on with your life. There's nothing to see here, Sam.

He looked up in shock. Mrs. Crowther was handing out essays as if nothing was odd. Should he say something? He was pretty sure it was against some rule somewhere, to use the word *bullshit* on a student essay, at the very least.

He looked back at the paper.

Another excellent essay, Sam. I may not agree with your argument, but you make it convincingly and present relevant evidence in context, and it made me want to read the novels again—good job!

He stared at the page in shock. Then he decided to find Jez immediately after class.

• • •

She found him first, in the corridor outside room nineteen, on the way to the common room.

"Sam," she said. "You look like your day is going about as well as mine. Please be nice to me. Everyone's being horrible. And I haven't even done anything. I liked it more when everyone ignored me. And there are flies everywhere. I am freaked the hell out."

They kept walking and quickened their pace. "I think I got a supernatural warning on the bottom of my essay," said Sam under his breath. "It was in Mrs. Crowther's handwriting, but it told me to basically ignore everything crazy that's happened, disregard everything you've said, and get on with my life, such as it is. And then when I looked again, I got nineteen out of twenty and a nice note from Mrs. C. It is safe to say that I, too, am freaked the hell out. Oh," he added, "and room nineteen was full of flies too."

They stopped and looked at each other.

"How much money do you have on you?" said Jez.

"Tenner," said Sam. "Are we on the same page?"

"Let's get a cab home at the end of the day. Avoid the bus. Go back to the village. Find Sarah. Ask for more protection." Her fingers went to the chain around her neck. "Because I don't know what this Ozzy Osbourne stuff is actually doing, but when she said *protection*, I thought she was implying that things wouldn't get worse."

"Well, there's that," said Sam. "And also, we have no idea what's going to happen next, and we can't rule dying horribly out of the equation. And apparently, in this school, if you die horribly, *no one will notice*." He fumbled in his bag for his cigarettes, and then remembered where he was. "God*dammit*, I need a cigarette. Yes. Let's go meet the famous Sarah," he said. "I hope she knows as much as we hope she does."

• • •

"Good ride?"

Adam looked up from his papers when Julia walked in flushed and exhilarated.

"Great," she said, walking over to the couch where he sat with his feet up and planting a kiss on his cheek. "She's perfect.

I don't know where you found her, but it's like I've been riding her all my life. Amazing stuff." She pulled off her crash cap and hairnet; her hair tumbled around her shoulders. "I'm going to go take a shower. Want to have lunch afterwards?"

"Maybe," said Adam, with a weak smile. "I'm not that hungry yet."

Well, that much was true. He wasn't hungry. He was still full from his—from the last time he had eaten. (He tried not to think about it too much; although the clean-up had been phenomenal, the thought of what had happened to Pauline still sickened him, though the feeling was growing milder.) And he felt incredible. He could work for hours, deep into the night; he was down to two hours of sleep a night and he didn't miss it. He was running more than ever before, and didn't even feel tired. Sex with Julia was amazing; it had never been bad, but now—now it was mind-blowing. And the deal was going smoothly.

He just couldn't eat normal food.

He was better now, from the flu, or whatever it had been. But every time he tried to eat solid food—or anything stronger than water—he threw it back up almost immediately. He didn't want Julia to find out. She would only worry. Or, worse, try to examine him; she was a doctor, after all. And whatever was happening to his body, and however great it was, it wasn't normal.

He felt as though he were immortal.

He knew he wasn't. He had reread the paperwork that Smith and Jones had provided, the paperwork that he had signed. He wasn't immortal, no. But he was invulnerable. They would look after him. There wasn't much he couldn't do before the contract was up that would have any consequences at all. And it was a long-term arrangement.

Carrington had told him as much, but Adam hadn't believed him. And he'd asked Carrington what would happen when the contract was up. Carrington had just shrugged, and mumbled something about an option to renew. "You've dealt with this stuff before," he said. "You can just renegotiate."

Adam hadn't found a renewal option in the papers he'd reviewed, but he assumed that Asilida wouldn't turn down further business. Who would?

But that was a problem for the future. Right now, his problem was how to avoid having lunch with Julia. He heard the waterfall of the shower cease. He didn't have long to come up with something.

He went into the kitchen and started pulling things out of the fridge: bread, butter, cheese, lettuce, tomato, even some prosciutto Julia must have picked up from somewhere. He started making her a sandwich. He'd make himself a protein shake. He glanced at the tub of protein powder that was sitting on the counter, and shuddered involuntarily. It was vanilla flavoured. He used to make a really good milkshake; great for after a run. Now, it might as well have been powdered shit.

He was going to have to fake it.

He finished making Julia's sandwich and stuck two little cocktail sticks through it. They had blue twizzly things on the top for decoration. A nice touch. He scooped out the protein powder and dumped it into a large glass, and filled it up with milk, stirring slowly until the power dissolved.

He was feeling nervous already. His stomach churned in anticipation of the impending assault. He stopped stirring, and the milk in the glass swirled dizzily.

"Ooh!" Julia's voice floated in from the doorway. "*Epic* sandwich!" She was wearing jeans and a tank top. God, he thought, she looked hot. Maybe he could distract her from eating with sex. It had worked occasionally before.

"I'm starving," she announced. *Crap.* She looked at the table, then at Adam. "Where's yours? What are you having?"

"Still feeling a bit sick, actually," he said, breezily. "Thought I'd just have a protein shake to keep me going."

Julia looked puzzled. "That's odd. You seem so much better."

"I know," he said, feigning surprise. "I guess the bug just killed my appetite." Which was true. "I feel fine."

She frowned. "Okay," she said. "I'll let you off this time. But you better start eating again soon. Otherwise I'm going to nag you until you go see a doctor. Another doctor."

"Ooh," he said. "Two doctors. Now there's a thought."

She giggled, before pulling up a stool, sitting down at the island and pulling the sandwich toward her. She sank her teeth into it and groaned with delight.

"Damn it, Carpenter," she said through a mouthful of avocado, cheese and fresh bread. "You know how to make a sandwich."

"Doing my best, ma'am," he said, tipping a fake hat and affecting a fake American accent. Anything so as not to have to drink the damn milkshake.

"If that's all you're having," she said, through the crumbs, "you might as well tuck in. What are you up to this afternoon? Still working?"

Adam took a sip of the milkshake. It tasted sour and vile, and burned his mouth and throat like acid. "Uh-huh. The deal, you know."

"Needs must, I guess," said Julia. Adam grunted.

"Someone's gotta put the horses on the table," he said. "So to speak." He steeled himself, and took a big swig of shake. It was like drinking drain cleaner. He smothered a cry of pain. The nauseated feeling in his stomach was getting stronger.

Julia finished her sandwich and her pager beeped. She looked down at it and pulled a face. "I have to run," she said. "Damn it. Great sandwich." She got up. "Make sure you finish that thing." She pointed at the glass, which was still two-thirds full.

"Yes, doctor," said Adam meekly. She laughed and rumpled his hair before heading out.

She went upstairs to get ready to go to work and didn't hear his mad dash into the downstairs toilet to be sick.

• • •

After another run, he sat down with the paperwork again. The contract. Since the guys at Asilida had made all the arrangements for Julia's horse, Adam had been hooked. He was still trying to get his head around it. Anything. He could have anything at all. It was like a cross between eBay and Amsterdam, only better.

He'd been to Amsterdam once, with Carrington, for a mate's stag do. Well, they'd left England with Carrington. They hadn't seen much of him once he got to the red-light district. He turned up when it was time to go back. Didn't say anything for three days. Just smiled. Adam had felt as though, in the world's most notorious party city, the real party had happened somewhere else, and without him.

Well, not anymore. He could throw his own parties. Maybe Carrington would hear about them, one day. Maybe Asilida could work it so that Carrington would definitely find out and Julia definitely wouldn't.

Right now, he was focused on getting to grips with the details of the contract. He was lying on the sofa in the living room, feet up. Making sure there was nothing he'd missed. Nothing he'd misunderstood. He wasn't great with legalese—that was why he had a solicitor, after all—but he was getting the hang of it. He still wasn't sure about this "hosting" business, but if he was right, then his company was ultimately positioned to take the fall if anything went wrong. The host. Like the host of a party. You were in charge, but at this party, someone else was doing the dirty work.

But there was something he was curious about. A word that kept cropping up in the pages of assurances of exceptional service and excellent attention to detail.

Minion.

The Minion.

And he couldn't for the life of him figure out what it referred to. He'd gone through the appendix to the contract—the terms and definitions—and he couldn't find any reference to it. But it was right there, in the paperwork.

He didn't want to look like an idiot. But at the same time, he was curious.

Fuck it, he thought. He pulled out his phone.

Brown, as usual, answered immediately.

"Mr. Carpenter," he said. How come the guy never got flustered or upset or caught off guard? "What can I do for you?"

Adam took a deep breath and then exhaled slowly. "I have a question," he said. "About the contract."

"I would be happy to offer any clarification you need," said Brown. "Naturally."

"It's on page two," said Adam, "about three-quarters of the way down. Do you have a copy in front of you?"

"There is no need," said Brown. "I know the sections to which you are referring. With what may I help you?"

Adam cleared his throat. "The 'Minion,'" he said.

"Yes?" said Brown.

"I don't know what that is."

There was silence from the other end of the phone. It lasted for so long that Adam thought the phone had disconnected.

"Hello?" he said.

"I see," said Brown. He coughed delicately. "It is something of a tradition in our firm." There was another pause, as if he were choosing his words carefully. It was the first time that Adam felt that he might have caught Brown off guard.

"Mr. Carpenter," said Brown, finally. "You have probably noticed that our methods are somewhat unusual, though remarkably effective. We are very good at what we do, and we have been doing it for a very long time. The tradition of the Minion is one way that we honour our heritage, so to speak. It has always been an element, in one form or another, in the contractual services we provide."

"Okay," said Adam. "It's a tradition. I'm sure it works very well." He tapped his fingers on the side of his phone. "I'm just not clear on what it is. Or what it does."

"Are you familiar with the word?" said Brown.

Adam was irritated. He hated being made to feel like an idiot.

"Yes," he said. "It's a kind of servant."

"Indeed," said Brown. That was all. Adam thought about this for a moment.

"But," he said, "if Asilida can arrange pretty much anything, why would anyone need an extra servant?"

"Perhaps," said Brown, "there are things that our clients would wish to have handled with the utmost discretion. Certain desires. Impulses. Tasks that stem from emotions—from *drives*—that perhaps one would not wish to admit to. We provide a Minion to assist in such private matters."

"A personal servant," said Adam. He wasn't sure he was quite comfortable with this.

"If you like," said Brown.

"So…how would I get in touch with this Minion person?"

"Call it," said Brown. "Will there be anything else, Mr. Carpenter?"

It?

"How?" asked Adam. He was thoroughly confused. And was it his imagination, or did he hear the ghost of a sigh of exasperation at the other end of the phone?

"Mr. Carpenter," said Brown, "you are the Master of the Minion. You may call it however you like." He hung up.

"Hello?" said Adam into the dead phone. "Hello?" *Damn.* It was the first time that Brown had been anything other than exceedingly—excessively, even—polite. It was almost as unnerving as his usual impeccable manners. And he hadn't been that helpful, either.

Call it however you like, eh?

Well, he'd seen some pretty weird stuff over the past week. Things he'd never have believed before. Even when Carrington told him. Though, to be fair, Carrington had only ever mentioned the firm's business acumen and legal wizardry. He hadn't talked about—

—Pauline—

—well, about anything else. Anything related.

Call it however you like. There were butterflies in Adam's stomach. He didn't have a clue what to expect. And he had nothing in mind. No—what was the phrase Brown had used?— *private matters* that he needed attending to.

But it was worth a shot, right? Trying it. If he was entitled to the services of the Minion… if it was in the contract, he needed to make the most of the services available to him, didn't he?

He stood up from the couch and walked into the middle of the living room. He coughed.

"Minion," he said, out loud. "Come here."

He waited for a minute or so. Nothing happened. He tried again.

"Minion," he began, "come and do my bidding."

Again, nothing. Adam felt a bit silly. It can't have been like this in the old days, he reasoned. No medieval alchemist would have been reduced to calling up a supernatural servant between a Laura Ashley floral sofa and a week-old copy of the *Radio Times*.

He was amazed at how readily he accepted the idea of the supernatural now. Three days ago, he had still been convinced that Brown's firm was just extremely well connected. It obviously was. But now he knew that there was more to it than that. It was like taking off a blindfold. The possibilities were endless. He could do anything.

And then—just like that—it was as if something inside him that he hadn't known was there took over. He stood up straight, eyes blazing.

"Minion," he thundered. "Come here unto thy master to do his bidding!"

There was a noise that sounded almost like glass breaking. Adam glanced nervously at the French doors behind him. They were intact. He couldn't tell where the sound was coming from. And then—

Then it appeared in front of him. His mind scrabbled to keep a grip on his sanity.

We are its master, something whispered inside him. *It won't hurt us.*

Somehow he knew it was true. Good job, really: his phone was still on the sofa—behind the... whatever it was that had just appeared in his living room.

It was huge. And it was hideous.

It was about eight feet tall and shaped roughly like a human, but its coarse skin was covered in insectoid bristles. It hovered in front of him on oily, translucent wings that gave off an abrasive buzzing sound as they kept the creature—the Minion—in the air. It was heavily muscled, with powerful shoulders.

But it was the head that transfixed Adam. The head wasn't humanoid at all. The eyes were bulbous and multifaceted, without pupils. Between them protruded a...nose? trunk?— Adam wasn't sure what to call it—that extended a couple of feet in front of its face. It looked sharp. Deadly sharp.

Adam's mouth was dry with terror. His heart was racing; he felt as though he were being electrocuted from the inside.

It won't hurt us, said the voice inside him. Minutes passed. The thing did not move.

It won't hurt us.

It won't hurt me.

Adam cleared his throat and tried to speak, but the sound came out as a croak. He tried again.

"Minion," he said.

The creature bowed its head.

"You can understand me?" said Adam. The thing looked so primeval that he hadn't really expected it to be able to deal with language. It looked like a predator, pure and simple.

The creature bowed its head again.

"Can you speak?" asked Adam. He couldn't see whether the thing had a mouth, but he was very quickly learning that anything was possible.

The Minion inclined its head to one side and then the other. No? Depends? Not *yes*, anyway.

"I am your master, correct?"

This time a nod.

"You can't hurt me, right?"

Nod.

Well, that was that out of the way. It was as he had suspected. The horror Adam had felt at first when confronted with the thing—the sheer terror it had evoked in him—had subsided a little. The beast still wasn't pretty, but now it had sort of said that it wasn't actually going to kill him, he felt a bit better.

He also felt stumped. He had called the Minion up primarily to see what would happen because, if truth be told, he still hadn't been quite convinced that anything would, despite Brown's assurances. And now, standing—hovering—in his living room, was his own personal slave, devoted to him and provided in order to satisfy the most private of his needs. The ones that he wouldn't feel comfortable discussing with Brown.

His imagination cranked into life. He thought back to Amsterdam and all the things that Carrington claimed to have done. Bastard. With most people, you could safely assume they were lying, but Carrington always seemed to be in touch with the right people, have the right connections, know the right thing to say...

And now Adam did, too. In fact, it didn't matter what he said. He had his own personal Minion. And he wasn't going to ask it for a fucking lemon, that was for damn sure.

Still. He'd start small.

"Minion," he said. "I need..."

It was no good. He couldn't articulate it.

Your most private desires, Brown had said. He felt pretty stupid talking about his most private desires with an eight-foot supernatural flying thing in his living room, especially when the damn thing couldn't talk back. It wasn't like they could crack a couple of beers to get the creative juices flowing, either. *Damn it.*

Then his mind opened up. There was no other way to describe it. It was as if there were a tunnel between his consciousness and the monster's, and everything that he couldn't articulate, that he was too ashamed to articulate was being drawn out of him. Without him having to say a word. It was terrifying and oddly gratifying. It felt as though the inside of his head was being sprayed with cool, clean water. He felt refreshed.

It would know now. The thing would know. Suddenly, he understood why it couldn't speak. It didn't need to. He thanked Brown silently. The tunnel closed, and Adam knew that he didn't have to worry about telling the creature a thing.

The Minion stopped hovering and stepped lightly onto the hardwood floor. It knelt before its master.

"Thank you," whispered Adam.

There was a terrible, wet sound of tearing meat. Adam leaped back in horror. The monster had split between its left shoulder and its neck; the tear was swiftly running diagonally across its body. It didn't make a sound, but it shuddered as though in intense pain. Adam could hear its bones breaking as the thing tore in two. It lay on the floor writhing: two lumps of still-living flesh.

Holy shit, thought Adam. I've killed it. *How did I kill it?*

The thing on the floor—both bits of it, Adam noted, numbly—twitched once and lay still.

Everything went quiet.

Adam sucked in his breath through his teeth. He held it for a second or two and then let it out in a rush. He looked at the two hulks of meat on the living room floor. *Thank God for*

Brown and his team, he thought. *Better get this cleared up before Julia gets back.* He started to tiptoe around the disintegrated corpse to get to his phone. There had better not be an extra charge for killing the stupid thing. It wasn't like it came with an instruction manual or anything. He'd had one instruction, and he'd followed it to the letter; if Brown tried to hold him responsible for the untimely passing of this whatever-it-was—

He reached the sofa and bent down to pick up his phone. There was a sudden noise behind him like running water. His heart jumped into his mouth and he spun around.

The creature's flesh was melting. But instead of pooling on the floor, it seemed to be running *upward.* The same thing was happening to both parts. They were shifting and reforming into two separate creatures. Adam was at the razor's edge of his sanity.

This world is too much, he thought. *Anything can happen.*

Were these creatures Minions that would have much less compunction about harming him than the one big one had had? Especially since he had killed their…friend? Their *father?*

His hand hovered over the screen of the phone. He was going to call Brown. He had to. And then he saw something that, for all his horror, made him stop dead in his tracks.

The reforming flesh was taking on a distinctly female shape. In both cases. The bodies formed, shaped, indented, swelled. The heads began as blank lumps of flesh, then sprouted hair that grew until it was waist-length, while the facial features formed as if someone, some invisible hand, were moulding them out of Plasticine, crude at first, and then more refined, and then, fully human.

With a shock, he realized that he recognized one of them. Or rather, one of them looked like someone he used to know. Anna Jarvis. The creature standing in front of him in his living room had longer hair, but it was the same honey blond; she still had the same green eyes and fine-boned teenaged features. He'd had such a crush on her when he was fourteen. But she was sixteen and dating a sixth-former with a driver's license and an illegal tattoo. She'd have laughed her head off if she knew how he felt. Luckily—ha—she hadn't known he existed.

This version looked a little older—twenty-three, twenty-four at most—but as her features formed, the resemblance was unmistakable.

He stole a glance at the other one, breathless with anticipation. The other one looked a lot like the dark-haired American actress Mila Kunis. Julia had insisted he go to see that ballet movie *Black Swan* with her a couple of years ago. He'd been bored out of his mind: girl gets dream job, people are horrible to girl, girl goes nuts, whatever. But there was one scene—that one scene...

He'd enjoyed Mila Kunis's performance very much.

And now Anna Jarvis and Mila Kunis were standing in his living room. Albeit with longer hair. He loved long hair on women. He'd never understood why Julia kept hers bobbed.

The noises had stopped. The beings in front of him were complete. They smiled at him, and Adam felt suddenly awkward.

"Er," he said. "Hello." There was a pause. "I'm Adam."

"We know," they said in unison, and giggled, but not nastily.

"You can talk!" said Adam, without thinking. The monster hadn't been able to talk. But he didn't want to think about the monster right now. The two girls stood in front of him, heads to one side, smiling.

"Yes," said Anna. Well, not-Anna. "Human throat structure. It makes it easier. But we're not here to talk, are we?" She looked into his eyes knowingly.

Adam felt dizzy. "I—" he said. "I—"

Not-Mila took one of his hands and Anna took the other, and together they led him upstairs to the bedroom.

"We arranged for Julia to have a few more appointments than usual," said not-Mila, winking at him. "So we can all get to know each other."

With Adam in a daze, they went into the bedroom and closed the door.

• • •

Three hours later, Adam lay in bed by himself, staring at the ceiling. He was still trying to take it all in.

The afternoon had been… He didn't have the words to describe it. But Brown was right. Adam would never have thought to ask Brown for that. Wouldn't have thought it possible. And there was no possibility that anyone would ever find out what had happened. He had heard the tearing of flesh and the crunching of altering bones (and the girls' muffled screams of pain) as the Minion reformed into one being downstairs after they were all done. He didn't need to see that to know that the Minion would go back to where it had come from, and all of the evidence would be removed.

And he could do it whenever he liked.

Not that he didn't love Julia, of course. But really. *Whatever he wanted.* Who could refuse?

It wouldn't hurt anyone if she never found out. He dismissed the thought from his mind and went back to contemplating what Brown had referred to as his most private desires.

The ones he wouldn't want anyone to know about, let alone Julia.

He was deep in thought when the phone rang. The landline. That was unusual. He picked it up.

"Hello?" he said.

"Hi," said a friendly male voice at the other end. "It's Greg Jarsdel. I'm a reporter for the *Arden Spectator*. I was wondering if you'd care to comment on the allegations raised by the leader of the opposition movement to Carpenter Properties' proposed maggot factory, that suggest the process is being rushed through because of inappropriate collusion?"

Adam's stomach fell through the floor.

"Who?" he said. "What allegations?"

"Richard Greenwood, the local environmental rights activist and lawyer. He says that no development could have been rushed through the normal processes this quickly without, and I quote, 'gross levels of collusion and corruption.' Do you have any comment on these allegations?"

Adam's mouth was dry. Then he felt angry.

"Comment?" he said. "There's nothing to comment on. These allegations are utterly false. I don't know how you got my home number, but don't ever call here again." He slammed down the handset.

The lawyer. Richard Greenwood. Greenwood had humiliated him, comparing Adam to his father. He was inconveniencing the building project as well; not that this was likely to stop Brown and the boys at Asilida, but the man was clearly an enemy to progress. Adam had met people like Richard Greenwood before. Self-righteous, knit-your-own-quinoa types; people who had been blessed by the system and still wanted to smash it.

And he had humiliated Adam at the protest. Questioning his education. His *character*. What was this, a Famous Five novel? No one gave a fuck about "character" any more than they gave a fuck about "honour" and all that other public-school, 1940s bullshit. People cared whether you were successful; whether you worked hard; whether you did what you said you were going to do. He tried to think of the last time that he had used the word "honourable" to describe someone, and couldn't.

Greenwood couldn't stop the factory. He couldn't stop Adam's success. But Adam could stop him. Without Greenwood, there would be no inconvenient letters to the local paper about collusion and corruption and greed. Without Greenwood, Adam could walk with his head high in the town that he was about to remake in his own image, among people to whom he was about to bring opportunity. He could bring so much more to the town than could a man like Richard Greenwood, for all his talk of "community" and "environments."

Greenwood disgusted him. In one sudden movement, he tore off the tangle of sheets that covered him and pulled on a pair of pyjama pants; they were dark grey, some silky fabric that Julia had picked out for him and given him as a present. He stomped downstairs into the living room, in a near-trance of hatred.

"Minion!" he hollered. "Come to me! Now!"

There was no ceremony in his voice, but the monster appeared anyway, with a crack that split the air. Its body still bore a red, livid scar where it had split in two earlier in the day.

"Minion," said Adam. "Get rid of Richard Greenwood. I want him scrubbed off the face of the Earth."

The creature nodded once and vanished with a sharp hiss. Simple as that.

Adam looked at the clock. It was getting on for four-thirty.

He decided to go upstairs and relive his favourite moments from the afternoon. Getting rid of Greenwood had taken a remarkable weight off his mind.

At about five, he heard the front door open and close. A moment later, Julia appeared in the doorway of the bedroom. Her face was sheet-white and there were dark circles under her eyes. He had never seen her look so exhausted. She looked like a hag.

"Sorry I'm late, darling," she said, and tried to smile. "Afternoon from hell."

• • •

Greg Jarsdel, sitting at his desk in the offices of the *Arden Spectator*, put the phone down gently.

It had been a risk. Of course it had been a risk. But they'd warned him, the more experienced reporters at the *Spec*, sometimes these things paid off and sometimes they didn't. This time, it hadn't.

None of them had wanted to touch this one. "Total non-story," one of them had called it.

He pushed his chair back from his desk and let out a sigh. It wasn't surprising, really. If Carpenter had thought about what he, Greg, was saying for more than about five seconds, he'd have realized that Richard Greenwood would never have jeopardized anything he was working on by talking to the press before everything was public knowledge anyway. But he wanted something. Something big. So few papers employed actual reporters anymore; he'd been damn lucky to get this job (no one—*no one!*—got hired at local papers these days; he'd only got in because no one else wanted to run the Facebook page for the pittance he was being paid plus a couple of free movie tickets when a blockbuster came out).

He wanted a *story*.

Maybe they were right. Maybe there wasn't anything there after all.

He got up and put on his coat. Then he picked up an old copy of the *Spectator*, rolled it up, killed a large green fly that had been buzzing against the window for hours, turned off the light, and went out.

Chapter 14

The last vestiges of the glamour were still visible on Sarah when she opened the door to Jez and Sam. Her hair was streaked with blond, and she still had on traces of makeup. She looked at her watch and raised an eyebrow.

"Jez," she said, looking at Sam and speaking with a note of concern tinged with acid. "What brings you here?" She tried to smile brightly and failed. "Who's your friend?"

"This is Sam," said Jez. "He knows everything. There's a spider in your hair."

"If he knows everything, he's way ahead of me," said Sarah, putting her hand gently and absently to her head. She stepped aside to let them in. "Sam! Welcome aboard. Ever done battle with the paranormal before? We may have a job for you. No experience necessary, but you could end up murdered by super-natural entities at any point from here on in. Sound good to you?"

Sam shrugged.

"Gareth was a good mate," he said. "Jez is a good mate. And I'm not a fan of getting creepy threatening messages when all I want is to find out if I'm likely to get grades good enough to head north in a year or so. I'd like this to stop. Jez says you know how to stop it."

"What creepy threatening messages?" said Sarah, looking at Jez for clues. "Why would you want to head north?"

"Because we're sick of nothing happening here," said Jez.

There was a moment of silence.

"Well," said Sarah, "stuff is very definitely happening now. It'll probably change the whole town by the time it's done. If you're here because you're serious about giving me a hand, take a seat. I wasn't joking about the unusual and probably certain death part," she added.

"I know," said Sam. "Like I said, Gareth was a mate."

Sarah nodded, curtly. "Yeah," she said. "Gotcha." She went over to the table, which was more than usually covered in a litter of books and papers. "Jez said you know everything, so if there's anything that's confusing, holler. I went to the Carpenter offices this morning. Didn't meet Mr. Carpenter, but I did have a run in with someone he's working with. Someone from Asilida."

Jez looked concerned. She had hung around for a bit after she'd seen Sarah go into the office, but had slunk off after a guy in a suit had stared at her for far too long from a window, grossing her out. "How did that go? What were they like?"

"Creepy," said Sarah. "And definitely Ethereal. I went up to Carpenter's office. He wasn't there, so I started taking a look around. Bloke came out of nowhere. Ethereal. Pretty open about it, as well. I didn't know what kind. He saw through the glamour—still trying to work out how; shouldn't have happened—and gave me a warning."

"A warning?" said Jez, worried. She pushed away the memory of Marina's rotting body. "What kind of warning?"

"He just told me I couldn't do anything to change what was happening; I couldn't stop it...he told me that I had tangled with his organization before and knew what the consequences would be." Sarah looked down and started snatching at papers on the table, slamming them down in some sort of order.

"Your friend," said Jez, quietly. "Eleanor...that whole thing with the face cream."

"Yup," said Sarah. "According to him, that wasn't Asilida, but some kind of related organization or subsidiary or whatever the hell structure they're using these days."

"They?" said Sam. "Face cream?"

"Tell you later," muttered Jez.

Sarah exhaled through her teeth. "While I was in the office," she said, "I found a box. A wooden box. There was an inscription on it. The alphabet's occult."

"How can an alphabet be—" began Sam. Jez stomped on his foot.

"It's human," said Sarah, over Sam's muffled *ow*, "but it was only used for occult purposes. From round about the time the pyramids were being built, but from a bit further north and a bit further east. That's probably where they first broke through. Asilida. Where they made contact with humans. However you want to think of it."

"What does the inscription say?" asked Sam.

Sarah sat down at the table and picked up the top piece of paper. "If I've translated it correctly," she said, "it reads along the lines of 'The darkest of desires shall be given freely unto him who pays the greatest price.'"

"It's hardly Shakespeare," said Sam.

"It probably loses something in the translation," said Sarah, glaring at him. "And there's this." She pushed forward the cufflinks on the table with the tip of her finger. Jez and Sam leaned over for a close look. "That design," said Sarah, "is a sigil. A magical sign. Like a signature: it's a symbol of authorization or power."

There was no easy way to put this.

"That's the sigil of Beelzebub," she said. "So don't think Shakespeare. Think Marlowe."

Sam thought for a moment, and his eyes widened in shock. "Oh, my God," he said. "That can really happen? That's real?"

"Hey," said Jez from the tatty armchair. "Scientist here. Saw *Hamlet* once. Fell asleep. Anyone want to tell me what's going on?"

"Marlowe was a contemporary of Shakespeare," said Sam. "Well, a bit earlier, but not much. He wrote a play called *Doctor Faustus*, about a man who makes a deal with the devil to gain knowledge, worldly wealth, and a shit-ton of pussy."

"Wow," said Jez, "the poetry's really beautiful. So this is what's happened here?"

"My guess would be that Carpenter made a deal with Asilida for worldly success, which is why and how they're running roughshod over all the bureaucratic red tape. They just rearrange reality so that it suits them, and most people go along with it because it looks like a close approximation of what they're used to." Sarah went to the drinks cabinet and hauled out the bottle of Laphroaig.

"So who are Asilida?" asked Sam. "Also, how do you know all this stuff?"

"She's a witch," said Jez, flatly. "For real. And if you make a joke about chocolate frogs, she'll probably punch you in the head. I'll fill you in later."

"Thank you," said Sarah. "As far as I can tell—and the inscription would seem to confirm it—Asilida represents an earthly manifestation of a group of Ethereals that has been around for, oh, *ever*. They feed on human misery, and they exist largely extra-dimensionally; they need some kind of physical connection to this reality in order to conduct their nasty little business in it."

"Carpenter," said Jez.

"Probably," said Sarah. "And whether it's him or not, I'd very much like to know where he is."

"So what's with all the flies?" asked Jez.

"I'm only speculating," said Sarah. "But they're likely the conduit for inducing misery, altering reality, and probably keeping an eye on you as well. Busy little buggers." She poured herself a large slug of Scotch into a glass that looked as if it had held orange juice earlier in the day. "Remember how you felt when you got hit with the full monty? From the fly?"

"What about..." Jez took a deep breath. "What about that thing we saw down by the Foxglove Pond?"

"I would imagine that that is something of a perk for whomever signed the contract with Asilida. A sort of personal slave, if you will."

"Like Mephistopheles in *Doctor Faustus*," said Sam. "A demon who'll do whatever the guy who signed the contract wants." He paused for a moment. "Wait a minute. Does that mean that someone ordered—down by the Foxglove Pond—someone told that thing to—"

"Not necessarily," said Sarah. "There's a local legend that it had been trapped in the Foxglove Pond for centuries. The Asilida organization is really old. My guess is that it's somehow an integral part of their set-up. Could be anything from a mascot to a favourite pet, but either way, it's useful to fling into the deal when you're handing out the worldly wealth; it's a goodwill gesture, right? So, maybe they'd wanted to get it out for a while and when Carpenter—let's assume it's him for the time being—signed the contract, they were about to generate enough human misery through the neurotoxins produced by their little insect buddies to set it free so it could get on with personal slaving. And it woke up and was—"

She stopped herself.

"Go on," said Sam, looking hard at the carpet.

"Hungry," said Sarah shortly.

No one said anything for a long time. Sam finally broke the silence.

"So what do we do?" he said.

"Ah," said Sarah. "I was afraid you would ask that."

"Jez said you're a witch," said Sam. "Can you do magic and make it stop?"

"I don't know," said Sarah, staring into her glass. She ran her thumb around the top and dabbed at an imaginary smear on the side. "I didn't tell you this before," she began, "Jez, I mean. I didn't tell you before because I wasn't sure what was going on and I didn't want to freak you out. There's a lot of stuff I can deal with. I've got three trunks full of weapons upstairs that could take out anything from a werewolf to a wendigo. Not that you get many of those in England," she added. "I've read a lot, and I'm good at—at magic. Basic magic. Small magic. Such as it is." She took a deep breath. "But what we're talking about here is an organization—a subsidiary, I guess they're calling it—of something huge. Something old. Eons older than humanity. And malevolent. The likelihood is that it feeds on unhappiness. On suffering. The more misery it causes, the stronger it gets." She pulled up her head and rested her chin on her hand. "And then there's me. With my three trunks." She sat back in her chair, and stared into the middle distance.

The silence was awkward.

"If they've been around for so long," said Sam, "how come no one's ever heard of them?"

Sarah looked directly at him. "They have," she said. "People used to live with an acute consciousness of them from day to day, with an extra double dose on Sundays."

"They're from Hell," said Sam simply.

"Not *from* Hell," said Sarah. "They *are* Hell."

No one said anything after that for a very long time.

• • •

"Hell's a place?" Jez finally broke the silence.

"No," said Sarah. "Hell is what these Ethereals create and seek to perpetuate. It's not a cosmic battle between good and evil for control of the souls of humankind so the winners can thumb their noses at the enemy for all eternity; it's more like a predator turning to farming, so it has a steady supply of nutritionally optimal food so it can grow and reproduce until—well, there is no until. Just forever."

"Carpenter becomes wildly successful because of the property deal that puts the maggot factory in the town," said Jez, slowly. "Asilida facilitates the building of the maggot factory, and fills the town with flies that generate a steady source of misery."

"When they're done with Carpenter, they get rid of him however the contract specifies," said Sam. "If it's anything like *Doctor Faustus*."

"And then either find someone else, or wait it out and feed off the stockpile of misery they've created," said Sarah. "It's a win-win situation, as long as you're part of the deal."

"It wasn't in *Doctor Faustus*," said Sam. "You don't know what price Carpenter paid for the deal."

"Look," said Sarah. "Some guy selling out a whole town for a bit of extra cash is not a tragedy. It's a fucking crime."

"Can we talk to him?" said Jez. "I mean, most contracts have a void clause, right?"

"Not deals with the Devil," said Sam. "At least, not according to the literature. That I've read," he added, glancing at Sarah. "Your mileage may vary."

"The Asilida guy already told me that I wouldn't be able to stop it," said Sarah. "We're not going to be able to negotiate our way out of this. Even with Carpenter. Can you imagine what it would do to a person to be able to have everything he or she ever wanted with no consequences whatsoever? Not pretty. Try not to think about Carpenter too much," she went on. "There's only one way I can see out of this."

"We have to kill him," said Sam.

Sarah jerked her head up and recoiled slightly. "Yes," she said, eventually. "How did you know?"

"It seems like the only logical solution," said Sam. "Plus, it's what Buffy would do."

"Sam," said Sarah. "I've just met you, but I like you, and I can tell you're smart." She rubbed the side of her face hard. "Think this one through. This isn't the telly. Could you go up to a human being and stab or smother or strangle that person until there's no kicking anymore? Could you? Honestly? Because I'm not sure I can."

"You said you had a trunk full of weapons," said Sam defensively.

"I do," said Sarah. "But I'm not a fan of killing stuff."

You did, though, didn't you? In anger, as well. What does that make you?

"Can we set fire to his house?" said Sam. "Maybe we'll just get—Ow!" He rubbed his shin where Jez had kicked him.

"We won't be doing that," said Sarah, acidly. "And we're getting ahead of ourselves. I don't even know where this bloke lives."

"Why do you have to do it?" asked Sam.

"Who else will? How many people believe in Hell anymore? It's a tabloid metaphor for serial killers' flats and war zones and nuclear plant meltdowns. Smart people think Hell is a bad day at the office; it's a revenge fantasy for upstanding churchgoing folk. And you know what? There is no chosen one: no Slayer, no Doctor, no amazing fucking Spider-Man. There's just me and what I know and my three boxes full of tricks upstairs." She sat down and closed her eyes. "That's why I'm grumpy."

"Can we help?" asked Sam.

"You might die," said Sarah, opening her eyes and looking at him directly. "I really can't emphasize that enough. I had a friend who used to help me, and she died. People die doing this kind of stuff."

"I know," said Sam. "My friend died too. I think we should stop anyone else's friends dying."

Sarah looked at both teenagers.

"No," she said, eventually. "You two should be out of it from this point on. You know too much and that already puts you in danger. Just stay out of it. Go home." She got up and began walking toward the front door.

"What?" said Jez. "Why? Everyone at school is ignoring me. Or being awful. I saw Marina's corpse in my bed. I'm already in it up to my neck." She stood up and whirled round to face Sarah.

"No, you're not," snapped Sarah. "You've been warned. By them. Both of you have been warned; they're on to you. Stop poking around, and trust me: everyone at school will be offering to be your best friend and inviting you to their birthday parties before you know it." She opened the door of her cottage and a blast of damp air shot in from outside. A few leaves blew onto the doormat.

Jez's phone rang. She stared at Sarah in disbelief for a moment, until the persistent tone broke the spell. She dived into her pocket and fished out the phone, checking the screen as she did so. It wasn't a number she recognized.

"Hello," she said, frowning. She was still angry. Then she froze.

"*What?*" she said. Her expression shifted into a look of shock and horror. "Where? Where is he?" She felt as though she could barely breathe. "Okay. Okay." She struggled to stay calm. "I'll head over right away. I don't know. Cab, probably. I can get some... anyway, it doesn't matter. I'll be there soon." She touched the screen of the phone and her hand dropped to her side.

"What is it?" said Sam. "What happened?"

"My dad," said Jez in a small voice. "He's been in a really bad car accident." Her hands were shaking. "He's in the hospital."

"What happened?" said Sarah, sharply.

"They don't know," said Jez. "Someone drove past his car on the side of the road and it was all wrecked... there was no one else there."

The three of them stood in silence for a moment. Sarah closed the door.

"Okay," she said. "You need to get to the hospital. As soon as possible. Can I drive you?"

"No," said Jez. "Yes. No. I don't know." Everything was swimming in front of her.

To Sarah, Jez suddenly looked her age, younger even. *She's just a kid*, she thought.

"I'll call a cab," said Sam, pulling out his phone.

"Thanks," said Jez. The world was tilting again; any more and she felt as though she was about to fall off it altogether. She turned to Sarah. "This is them, isn't it?" she asked, viciously.

"We don't know that," lied Sarah.

"Yeah, we do," said Jez.

"Yes," said Sarah. "We do."

"So is this a warning or what?"

"No. Not anymore."

"Cab'll be here in ten," said Sam, putting his phone back in his pocket. "Are we allowed to help now?" he asked Sarah, cocking his chin upwards.

"Sure," she said. "What can you do? What's your plan? Because I'm at a loss."

Sam tapped at his phone. Jez stared into space.

"What about the Franciscans?" said Sam, looking up from his phone. Through her shock and grief, Jez recognized his expression. It was the same one he wore when he was explaining why one of his essays was brilliant.

"What?" said Sarah. "What have they got to do with anything?"

"The flies," said Sam. "The Lord of the Flies; Beelzebub, all that? So I just looked up 'Beelzebub' and it turns out that in one old demonology text, he's placed in opposition to Saint Francis of Assisi.

"Sébastian Michaëlis," said Sarah. "I don't think that praying to Saint Francis will help."

"Maybe not," said Sam. "But what about the Franciscan Order?"

"Friars?" said Sarah. "How the hell could they help?" She just managed to stop herself saying *the Firm won't want anything to do with the likes of us.*

"Do you have any Beelzebub-specific weaponry in your trunks?"

"I don't think so, but—"

"Look," said Sam, tapping the screen of his phone and turning the screen toward her. "Asilida." Sarah recognized the familiar layout of a Wikipedia page. "*Robber flies*. Even the non-supernatural ones are vicious. They don't just vomit on their food: they paralyze it, stab it, liquefy the insides with acid, and then slurp it all back up again. And these ones are *special*."

A car horn sounded outside.

"Fuck," said Sam. "That's the cab. Jez, I'm coming with you. Sarah, we *will* be back."

Jez held up her hand. "Sam, I want to go by myself."

"Why?" said Sam.

Because this thing warned me once and I didn't listen. Because it warned you too. Because I'm on my third strike, and I don't want you to get caught in the crossfire. Because this is all my fault. She couldn't say it; she knew that Sam would insist on coming anyway. She took a deep breath and lied.

"I just want to be alone," she said. "All this crazy stuff. I just want to be by myself."

Sam frowned.

"Well," he said eventually. "It's your call. But if you need us, give me a shout."

"Sure." Jez tried to smile. "I've got protection," she said. "Remember?" She hauled the antique pentacle out from under her shirt. The horn sounded again. Jez stared at her feet.

"Get outta here," said Sam. "And give my best to your Dad."

Jez gave them a weak smile and disappeared through Sarah's front door. It closed with a firm *click*.

• • •

Cat was making tomato sauce. The onions and garlic were sizzling in a saucepan; she opened a tin of crushed tomatoes, wrenched the lid back, and dumped in the red goo. It landed in the pan with a thick *splat*.

She caught the side of her finger on the rough edge of the tin lid and felt the sickening sensation of the metal biting into her skin before the pain hit.

"*Ow*," she muttered. "Bollocks."

"Cat," murmured Maureen. An absent, perfunctory warning. Jamie, Cat's nine-year-old brother, was sitting at the kitchen table, doing his homework while Maureen watched. "Language."

"Cut my finger," said Cat. It was deeper than she'd thought. The blood was running down her finger. She went to the sink, under the window, and turned on the cold tap.

It was dark outside, and pouring with rain. Cat could only see faint outlines of trees against the sky. The branches clawed at the sky in the wind.

For a moment, it looked as though there was a vaguely human shape moving in the darkness.

Cat peered through the window. It was too high up to be a person. But it was too big to be a bird.

She looked harder. It was difficult to make out any shapes against her reflection. She could only make out the movement of the swaying twigs. A gust of wind blew a hefty splatter of rain against the window, and she flinched.

"Ugh," she muttered, and pulled down the blind. Nothing out there except rain.

"Watch the sauce," said Maureen, without looking up from her laptop.

The vegetables in the pan were bubbling thickly. Cat dashed across the kitchen and turned down the heat.

Dried herbs. Oregano. Basil. Black pepper. Oh, right. Salt. Her mum was determined that she would know how to cook for herself by the time she left for university. It was a whole year away, but her mum maintained that the more practice she had, the better.

There was a muffled thud from above. All three of them looked up.

"That a branch?" said Cat.

"No idea," said Maureen. She stood up, crossed to the window, and ducked up and down, trying see through the darkness and rain. "Horrible out there," she said.

Cat stirred the sauce to make sure it wasn't burning, and then went to the fridge and retrieved a packet of mince, which she unwrapped, and dumped in another pan. The smell of frying meat joined the other scents in the kitchen.

"Huh," said Maureen. "Probably nothing." She went back to the kitchen table and sat down.

The Minion crashed through the window. Maureen screamed; Cat turned and froze in shock.

There was broken glass everywhere. The thing that had crashed through the window was partially tangled in the curtain it had ripped out of its tracks; it was *hideous*.

It wasn't a person. It was too big. And it had goddamn *wings*.

Without thinking, Cat ducked down behind the kitchen door and pulled herself into a ball. Her eyes were wide with terror. She barely had time to register the Minion's monstrosity before it shook off the curtain and broke her mother's neck like a dry branch. Her body dropped limply to the floor with a thud. The creature turned round.

Dear God, thought Cat.

It had some sort of beak, thing, what did you call it? Her brain scrabbled wildly. Jamie was screaming, hysterical with terror. The creature was between her and her brother. There was nothing she could do.

It impaled him, pinning him against the wall. He screamed once more, and then fell silent.

Cat's mind shut down. The creature turned slowly, almost a hundred and eighty degrees, almost facing her hiding place.

The kitchen door flew open, obscuring her from its view. She couldn't see her father come into the room.

"What the hell—" Richard Greenwood began. Then, all Cat heard was a hissing noise, a crunch, and the smell of burning meat mingling with the smell of burning tomato sauce.

As quickly as it had come, the thing vanished through the window; Cat barely registered that it was bundling something with it in its claws. She stayed in her hiding place, frozen and shaking, until the smoke alarm went off.

Her muscles were stiff. She didn't want to see what was on the other side of the door. She stretched out her legs, choking on every breath. They hurt. Cramp. She was shaking so hard that she missed the doorknob the first time she tried to grasp it to pull herself up.

Her fingers eventually made contact with the cold metal and she pulled herself up, swaying along with the door.

To get out, she would have to move around to the other side of the door.

She didn't want to look. The room was full of smoke from the burned pan, and the smoke alarm was still screaming. The wind howled outside; everything else in the house was silent. The smoke made the air heavy, and there was a metallic taste to it.

Cat turned to face the wall behind her, and edged the five feet to the front of the hob. Moving like an automaton, she turned off the burner.

And now she had to get out.

Facing the wall, she moved like a crab back to her original position behind the door and turned to face the pale wood. She closed her eyes tight and edged around the door.

She stepped in something warm and wet.

Don't look. It was as if someone else was speaking to her. *Whatever you do, don't look.*

A muffled sob escaped her body. She turned.

Don't look.

With her eyes shut and her hands spread out to the side of her, she felt for the door frame. Her foot made contact with something solid on the floor.

DON'T LOOK.

It took every rag of focus she had left. She knew what it was. Her father's leg.

She lifted her foot, eyes tight shut, and move forward. Her hands made contact with the door frame. She moved through it, wracked with sobs, half crying, half screaming, and stumbled toward the front door. Out. She had to get out of the house. She had to get away. She had to get as far away from the kitchen as possible. Adrenalin coursed through her; she didn't notice the wind, or the rain soaking through her hoodie. She stumbled down the dark drive to the road that led away from her house and toward the village, still screaming. She kept her eyes on the path in front of her, not daring to look up.

Go somewhere safe, her instinct urged her. But where was safe? Where was safer than the kitchen of your family home?

She heard the faint drone of a car's engine in the distance, and turned. Headlights turned the rain into two streams of sparks in the darkness as they moved toward her.

In the fog of fear and adrenalin and grief, she couldn't imagine how this could be anything other than help.

"Help!" she screamed at the top of her voice. "Help me! *Help me!*"

The car slowed and came to a halt. The window on the driver's side lowered. Cat sobbed, hysterically.

"Oh, dear," said a young man in an immaculate suit with silver cufflinks from behind the wheel. "What on Earth could be the matter with you?"

"Help me," whispered Cat. "Help me."

The young man in the immaculate suit looked at her. She was soaking wet, wide-eyed, grey with fear and grief.

He smiled.

"Why don't you get into the car?" he said.

• • •

Adam started from his reverie.

He had heard something. Hadn't he? The sound of Julia breathing quietly beside him rasped in his ears. She'd fallen into bed almost as soon as she'd got home, claiming she had a splitting headache and hoping she wasn't coming down with whatever it was that Adam had. He probably should have changed the sheets before she came back. Oh well.

He frowned and listened hard. It was probably nothing.

Then he heard it again. He recognized it as the same noise, but was surprised that it had woken him up. It was the achy screech of something sharp being dragged gently across glass. And it was coming from downstairs.

Adam drew in his breath sharply and looked across at Julia. She seemed to be deeply asleep. And she had had a hard day at work. He peeled back the covers and slithered out of bed. The floor creaked loudly, and Julia shifted in her sleep. Adam swore under his breath. He crossed the room in three exaggerated paces and slipped around the door.

screeeeeeeeeeeeeeech

There was the sound again.

screeeeeeeeeeeeeeeeeeeeeeeeeeeeeeeech

From the kitchen. It was coming from the kitchen. Adam stepped over to the French doors and pulled back the curtain covering them.

It was the Minion. It was holding something. Adam peered into the darkness.

The Minion pushed its claws forward. The gesture's meaning was clear.

For you.

This is for you.

Adam stared at the dark bundle. He felt numb. It was Richard Greenwood's severed head. He could feel himself beginning to panic.

Holy shit. He's dead. It killed him. I told it to kill him, and it killed him. What if someone finds out? His stomach clenched and he felt dizzy.

The Minion looked at him, and put its head on one side.

For YOU.

"Thank you" Adam croaked.

He heard his own voice, and was flooded with anger. For a split second, he was surprised at its ferocity, and then he was overwhelmed.

Fool. There are no consequences for you. Your cravenness is revolting. And, of course, it was. He raised his chin and looked directly at the Minion's horrific face.

"Bury it," said Adam. "Where no one'll find it. Ever."

He waited for the Minion to bow and disappear into the darkness before drawing the curtain and heading back upstairs.

Chapter 15

The cab hurtled through the murk of the October evening. Jez sat alone in the back, in silence.

Her dad had been hurt. Badly. The police officer who had spoken to her over the phone hadn't given any details, had apologized for not telling her in person, had said that someone would meet her at the hospital, had said she needed to come right away. She felt her throat tighten as she pictured her dad in the car, in the ambulance, in the hospital.

She had always been an independent kid, but that didn't change the fact that her dad was pretty much the only relative she had left, apart from her Auntie Rebecca, her dad's sister, who was always travelling for her job, and some of her mum's cousins, whom she'd met when she was small and could barely keep track of when their cards arrived at Christmas. And they didn't count. Her mind whirled. What if anything happened to her dad? What if he couldn't walk anymore? What if his neck was broken and he couldn't move at all? What if he *died?*

She would be alone. And it would be her fault. She had persisted. She had gone to the Foxglove Pond—and she had gone because she was bored. Sarah had been right. Jez wasn't a rebel. She'd been seriously drunk—blackout drunk—*once*, at one of Cat's friends' eighteenth birthday parties. Cat's friend was from the college, which was where you went if you were sick of

Arden High but wanted to do more school after your GCSEs, and Jez hadn't known anyone except Cat, who was trying to cop off with Evan Smith because she'd had a soul-destroying crush on him for five months, so Jez kept drinking until she fell over on the way to the bathroom, and that was the last thing she remembered. She didn't do drugs either, except for weed, which didn't count. She'd had several mild crushes and one big one (when she was fifteen, on Josh Cook, who had gone to uni in London to study molecular biology at the end of the year, and she hadn't seen him since, and was pretty sure he had literally never known she existed). That day she'd followed Sarah, she had been fighting the feeling that she was in a holding pattern—waiting for her life to begin, without even knowing it. She and Sam made jokes about getting out, but she couldn't wait. She had wanted more.

She had gone down to the Foxglove Pond because something unusual was happening and she wanted to know what it was. And also because she hadn't really believed that there was a possibility that it was dangerous and she could die, even though Gareth and Marina had died there hours before, because that wasn't how things worked in her world. And that was the crux of it. She hadn't really thought that it would be dangerous. And Sarah had known better.

For the first time, she cursed her scientific curiosity. She'd always felt that it made her more grounded than flakes like Saskia French. Turned out: not so much.

The cab rounded a bend in the road, and the lights and red-brick buildings of the hospital swung into view. Myriad signs pointed out helpful routes for people who knew where they were going. Jez wasn't one of them.

"Where can I drop you, love?" asked the driver.

"I don't know," said Jez. She could feel her chest tightening and an unnerving electric buzz in her stomach, as if her body were full of vibrating wires. She looked out of the window and saw a sign pointing to Accident and Emergency. "Maybe there?" She pointed.

"You're the boss," said the driver, and pulled in, just ahead of the spot reserved for ambulances and other emergency vehicles. "Nothing bad, I hope?"

"It's not me," said Jez, feeling foolish, *of course he can see it's not you, idiot.* "It's my dad. He was in a car accident." She choked up. "I don't know how he is. Or where he is."

The cab driver tutted sympathetically. "Sorry to hear that," he said. "They'll probably be able to point you the right way in there. Hope he gets better soon," he added. "You meeting your mum here?"

"My mum's dead," said Jez. Her hands were shaking as she fumbled in her bag. She found a ten-pound note. *If I get out of this alive,* she thought, *I'm going to have to spend a lot less time browsing the iTunes store.* "Thanks," she said, pressing the note into the driver's hand.

"No problem," he said. "Hope yer dad's doing all right. You have a good night and take care of yourself, our kid."

Jez nodded. She couldn't speak anymore; she was too choked up. She grabbed her bag, scrambled out of the cab, slammed the door, and stood in the glowing white light of the hospital entrance.

• • •

"He's in the theatre at the moment," said the doctor. She had long, dark hair tied back into a pony tail and was wearing hot-pink scrubs that had faded a little from frequent washes. She looked to be in her late twenties. "They took him into surgery as soon as possible after he arrived." She paused. "You won't be able to see him for a while, I'm afraid. It's going to be a long night."

"What happened?" asked Jez. The reception area had been painted a pale shade of greyish pink; Jez suspected that the colour was supposed to calm people down. It didn't calm her down: she felt as if she were being psychologically manipulated by the walls.

The doctor stopped. "You mean no one told you?"

"I just got a phone call," Jez said. "From the police. They told me to come here."

"A *phone call?*" said the doctor. She looked horrified. "They didn't come and see you? How did you even get here?"

"I took a cab," said Jez. She could feel herself choking up again.

"That doesn't make any sense," said the doctor. She frowned. "Not that I'm doubting you. But that's *really* not supposed to happen. I don't know what they were thinking; there must have been a giant screw-up somewhere. Not what you need, under the circumstances. I'm Dr. Chaturvedi, by the way," she said, holding out her hand. "You can call me Sangeeta. I'm on the night shift tonight. We'll take good care of your dad, don't worry. Is your mum here?" She turned her head toward the door, scanning the quiet reception area. A drunk guy with a bleeding head was at the triage station, and a nervous-looking young couple with a fretful toddler were the only other people there.

"My mum's dead," said Jez mechanically. "Cancer. I was eleven," she added. That was what people usually asked next.

"Oh dear," said Sangeeta. "That can't have been easy. I'm sure you're not keen on hospitals, then." Jez was feeling slightly better already. Sangeeta's kindness was soothing; even if it was just professional, it was more reassuring than the interior decor. "Like I said, your dad's in surgery at the moment," she said. "The team's great; they'll totally do their best for him. But it could well be a few hours before we know anything for sure. Are you hungry at all? I can show you where the caf is, if you like. Do you want me to come with you?"

"Maybe," said Jez. "Yes, please. Actually, no. Thank you. I don't know." She was staring at the floor, trying to fit her shoe into the square patterns of the vinyl tiles. "I still don't know what happened," she added.

"Oh, my God," said Sangeeta. "I'm so sorry." She looked at the chart. "I don't know exactly. I mean, it's not really the part I do. But I think I heard one of the policemen say there weren't any witnesses. It looked like a hit and run. They found the car at the side of the road. They couldn't figure out what had happened; they think it was a head-on collision, but they're not sure. I did hear one of the paramedics say that the car looked as though someone had dropped a giant boulder on the front of it. He said he'd seen it once before... it was kids dropping stuff off an overpass, just small things, but when they're high up and the cars are going fast... Sorry," she said again. "That's not what happened here; the car was nowhere near a bridge or an overpass or anything like that. Your dad's very lucky. If something had come through the windscreen..." She looked at the chart again. "Anyway. His left leg is fractured in two places, and he has a punctured lung. The thing that's really worrying us is he also has a bad head injury; he was unconscious when they brought him in." She took a deep breath. "As I said, he's in surgery now."

"Will he be okay?" Jez felt as though she were eleven again.

"Honestly, at this stage, it's too early to say. We've put in a chest tube and they're setting the bones in his leg. He's definitely not out of the woods yet. But the fact that he's made it this far is good. Great, actually." She put her hand on Jez's shoulder. "You look like you could do with a cup of tea."

Jez nodded. Her eyes were welling up. *Damn it, damn it, damn it.* She *would* act her age. She was *not* going to cry in front of a stranger. Not for the second time in a week.

Sangeeta put her arm around Jez. "Come on, our kid," she said. "Let's go to the caf and see what they can rustle up for you."

• • •

"How do you even find a Franciscan?"

"Same way you find anyone else, I imagine," said Sam. "Google. In a pinch, Facebook." He started tapping the screen on his phone again. He turned it to face Sarah. "It looks like there's a guy over in Castleton. Father Dominic Quinn."

"Hm," said Sarah. "Where's Castleton?" She was thinking hard.

"The next town over from Crowsbrook in the opposite direction to Arden," said Sam. "It's about eight miles away. You can get there by bus from Crowsbrook if you have a couple of hours to spare, but the buses stop running at six."

"Okay," said Sarah, pulling on her coat. "I'll drive; you find me a Franciscan. Wait here," she added, and dashed upstairs.

She pulled her carpet bag out from under her bed and emptied the gubbins in it out onto her bedroom floor. Then she went into the spiders' room. They scattered away to the corners. She wasn't taking any risks this time. She needed weapons that had range.

Click. Thud. Click. Thud. She threw open the lids of the trunks one by one. *Click. Thud.*

She rummaged carefully for a good five minutes until she found a pointy bamboo stick, and what looked like a bow and a set of six arrows in a moth-eaten quiver. She picked it up and the strap broke.

Brilliant, she thought. *The only thing I know about this is that it's broken.* Still, pointy and better than nothing. She packed it carefully in the bag.

She looked up. "Coming?" she asked. She raised her arm and waited for a moment.

Six small spiders dropped silently onto her sleeve and hid in her clothes.

Sam was tapping the screen of his phone furiously as she made her way downstairs, and they headed out of the cottage to Sarah's Allegro. Sam stared at the lime-green paintwork.

"Probably best take the back roads, right?" he said, his tone measured. "I mean, if there's something out there crashing cars on behalf of the Devil."

"*A* devil," said Sarah, unlocking the car and opening the door. "We think."

Sam got into the car. Sarah gunned the ancient engine, and the car blasted out of the laneway.

"Take a left out of here," said Sam. "Do you have any music?"

"Look in the glove compartment," said Sarah. "It hasn't really been a priority since I came up here."

Sam fiddled with the latch on the glove compartment. It fell open with a *thunk*.

"*Tapes?*" he said. "Oh, my God. Will we be picking up hairspray and bleach on the way?"

"I can't wait until you and her are out in the world on your own," said Sarah. "This car is what I could afford. I thought you wanted music?" They car suddenly veered drunkenly to the right.

"Finefinefinefine," said Sam. "If you could focus on not killing us, that would be cool." He grabbed a boxless tape at random, and the opening riff of AC/DC's "Back in Black" blasted through the car. "Left up ahead."

They reached the friary in about fifteen minutes, as rain began to spot the windscreen. The house was a Victorian heap behind a low, ivy-covered wall and next to a neo-gothic church with a tall spire. The sky was overcast; the tower's grotesques were silhouetted in the wash of the street light and the rain.

"Now what?" said Sam. "Do we just bang on his door and ask how to vanquish Beelzebub?"

"This was your idea," snapped Sarah. "There might be a reason it sounds stupid. Ever think of that?" She pushed open the wrought-iron gate and headed up the path to the front door. "Coming?"

Sam followed in silence. Sarah raised the heavy brass knocker and banged on the door hard.

"What if he's asleep?"

"It's six-thirty," said Sarah. "Even good Catholic boys don't go to sleep that early." She banged on the door again. The wind stirred the yew trees in the churchyard.

"Maybe he's not in," said Sam. "Maybe we should go."

"Maybe he knows something we don't," said Sarah. "This idea's grown on me. What's the worst that can happen? Looking stupid or crazy is not the worst thing in the world, especially once you turn nineteen." She banged on the door a third time, more loudly than before.

They heard the sound of a bolt being drawn back behind the heavy oak door. A moment later, it creaked open slowly to reveal an old man in his dressing gown. He walked with a stick.

What was left of his hair was pure white, and he peered over his glasses at the two people on his doorstep with curiosity.

"Good evening," he said, in a strong voice that seemed incongruent with his obvious age. He must have been well into his eighties. "What can I do for you?"

"Good luck," muttered Sam from behind Sarah.

"Father Dominic?" said Sarah. The friar nodded. "There's trouble brewing, Father," she continued. "A bad contract near Arden. The worst kind."

"Oh, God," muttered Sam. "We are *so* getting committed."

The friar grunted. "You're part of a family business?"

Sarah nodded. Sam's mouth fell open. The friar grunted.

"I can't help you, you know," he said, not unkindly. "The Firm won't allow it." He nodded toward the dark silhouette of the church. "You know that."

"You can't give us any advice, Father?" said Sarah. "In the name of compassion?"

"Whoever signed the contract isn't part of the Firm," said the friar. "We would have heard about it." He sighed heavily. "You must understand that my hands are tied." His voice dropped. "You're a witch, my dear," he said, more quietly. "And who are you working with, these days?"

"We're not asking for the Firm's help," said Sarah. "We just want advice. We think that the contract is with the Lord of the Flies. Your patron knew—"

"It's pissing down," interrupted Sam. "Can we have this conversation indoors?"

There was a pause.

"Yes, yes," said the friar. He scratched the side of his mouth, and looked out at the now-horizontal rain. "Hm. You'd better come in. Just for a bit, though," he added. "I'm due for a cup of tea and a digestive biscuit at seven o'clock, and then I'm going to take a nap. Friars need their sleep too. Especially when they're eighty-four." He stood aside and hauled the heavy oak door back to let them in.

They stepped into a narrow, low-lit hall lined with bookshelves. It smelled strongly of stale cigarettes. The wallpaper had once been cream but was now fading and discoloured; near the ceiling, it was almost yellow, and in places, it was blistered and peeling. The forty-year- old carpet had a pattern that was only clearly visible at the edges; years of penitent traffic had worn a threadbare path in the middle. The friar led them into a small living room on the left; smoke curled lazily upward from a half-finished cigarette in the ashtray next to an overstuffed brown armchair. The friar gestured to them to sit down in the mismatched armchairs on either side of the fireplace.

"You know I'm Father Dominic," said the friar, settling painfully into his armchair and taking a comforting drag on his cigarette. He winced and cleared his throat with a low, phlegmatic rumble. "You are...?"

"Sarah Trevelyan," said Sarah. "This is Sam. He's helping me." Sam resisted the urge to ask if he could smoke. Devout Catholics made him wary.

"Sarah Trevelyan," said Father Dominic, turning the name over in his mind. He sat up, and peered at her more closely. "Related to Dorothea Trevelyan?"

"Great-niece," said Sarah. Father Dominic nodded.

"Hmm," he said. "I see. " He took a drag on his cigarette. "Dorothea never gave the Firm any trouble."

"Why would she?" shot back Sarah.

"You must understand," said Father Dominic, "that the Firm has had centuries of dealing with family businesses. Not all are tractable, and effectively, they're competition. We must protect our members."

"I'm not here to talk about the politics of the Firm," said Sarah. "We think someone in the Arden area has signed a pact with the Lord of the Flies. The archenemy of Saint Francis. We just wondered if you could give us any advice. Texts. Weapons."

"Weapons?" The friar began to laugh, a wheezy creak that soon turned into a hacking cough. He spat into a handkerchief and wiped his mouth. "As I said, my hands are tied. And the Firm likes to keep direct intervention with its adversaries—its *spiritual* adversaries—to a minimum. It's highly specialized work, and we keep these things under wraps. I'm sure you know that. *Weapons.*" He snorted again, a splutter that quickly turned into a bubbling cough.

"I do know that," said Sarah. "But if the Firm won't get involved, we have to deal with this ourselves. With what we've got. Can you at least give us some advice?"

Father Dominic took a final drag on his cigarette and ground it out in the overflowing ashtray next to his chair. He tapped his fingers on the arm of his chair for a moment.

"I can't tell you anything about weapons," he said. "That would count as occult matters, and we don't deal in that. I don't, anyway. Maybe higher up, they do, but you won't even get past the door with *them*. And you'll already be aware, Miss Trevelyan, of any—" he coughed "—any textual sources that might help you in the situation. "

Sarah rubbed her temple. She'd actually been quite impressed with the boy's idea, but she hadn't held out much hope that the Firm would help. Still, it had been worth a shot.

"I met your great-aunt," said the old friar, clearing his throat again. "Years ago, it would have been. Long, long time ago. Decades."

Something in his voice made Sarah look up. But the friar was staring into the fire.

"I'd imagine you inherited everything she owned," he went on, almost to himself.

"I'm her heir," said Sarah, looking carefully at him, her forehead wrinkled. "I'd say I inherited pretty much everything she owned."

"Hmm," murmured the friar, nodding. He stroked his chin. "In that case," he went on, "I think I have something that belongs to you."

Sarah blinked.

"To me?" she managed. "To *me?*"

"Arrived in..." The friar paused. "August, probably." He struggled out of his chair with a grunt and crossed to the mantelshelf, where he picked up an already-opened white envelope covered in dirty fingerprints. He looked inside, pulled out one sheet of paper, put it back on the mantelshelf, and handed the rest to Sarah.

"Your rightful property," he said. "Not help. All I will say is this." He fumbled in the pocket of his dressing gown and dug out a crumpled packet of Player's, pulled one out, and lit it expertly, inhaling deeply. "Evil is like good, Miss Trevelyan. In the abstract, it is nothing. It can only work through people. And people choose whether to act in a manner that is good or evil." He coughed, deep in his lungs. "If this contract exists, you will need to find the person who signed it. What you do then is up to you. You will have to choose." He tapped his cigarette into the ashtray, adding a few more grains to the mountain of ash piled there. "That, Miss Trevelyan, is all I have to offer."

Sarah stared at the sheet of paper he had given her. Her great-aunt's handwriting was, by now, familiar.

Sarah: Your grandmother taught you to do no harm. If you receive this message, things are progressing as I had suspected they might, even as I hoped they would not. Harm only as you must and the Wise will guide you. Harm as you will, and you are lost.

Shit. That wasn't good. Killing in anger, as Sarah had killed the Ethereal in the Carpenter offices? Wasn't that kind of the epitome of "harming as you will"? Guidance of the Wise didn't come into it.

Sarah stood up. Sam couldn't read her face. He stood up as well.

"Thank you, Father Dominic," she said. She extended her hand and the friar took it.

"Good luck, my dear," he said. "You have quite the task ahead of you."

"I don't understand." Sam broke in for the first time. "Isn't the Church—the Firm—supposed to stop devils and demons from running around all over the place?"

"And witches," said Father Dominic, drily. "But things are rarely as clear cut as they seem. And like Miss Trevelyan, I have no inclination to begin a discussion of church politics at this time of night. I am due a cup of tea and a digestive biscuit. We are here for the faithful, you may be sure of that."

Sam opened his mouth and Sarah stepped on his foot.

"Thank you for your time, Father," she said, smiling. "Enjoy your tea and biscuit." She led Sam to the door and they let themselves out.

• • •

Jez sat in the hospital cafeteria with a disposable cup full of tea. Sangeeta had shown Jez how to work the machine, but she'd been paged and had to run back upstairs. Jez didn't mind. She wanted to be alone. She felt emotionally numb; there was a tense ache in her abdomen.

She sipped her drink and winced as the scalding liquid burned her mouth. She reflected that she had spent a lot of time over the past week drinking tea of varying quality to calm her nerves. It hadn't worked. She was tenser than ever. But at least it gave her something to do while she was waiting. It was the waiting that was killing her.

Would they leave her alone now? Was this enough warning for them? She'd left Sarah and walked away—would the supernatural goons at Asilida assume that Jez had taken their warnings seriously and had been frightened away? Why hadn't she been frightened away before? She didn't give a damn what happened to the village. Or the town. Fuck Tasha. If Jez survived this whole thing, she would be out of town like a bat out of—

Anyway. The point was, what would she do now? This was the question to which her mind kept returning.

She pulled out her phone and texted Sam.

Dad in surgery. No news yet.

She stood up, tossed her cup in the rubbish bin, and left the cafeteria to head back to Sangeeta and the nurses' station.

The hospital's corridors were labyrinthine, a maze of right-angled twists and turns, filled with gurneys and silent, ominous, electronic machines, and patients shuffling and quietly dragging intravenous drips behind them, and the insidious smell of disinfectant. Jez made her way slowly, following the signs for Accident and Emergency. Sangeeta had said that if Jez came back there, she'd find her a proper waiting room to rest in while the doctors worked on her dad. Sangeeta had been right, too: Jez hated hospitals. She felt eleven years old again, and ill-equipped to handle anything that was going on around her: illness, injury, death. She rounded a corner and discovered a woman in tears on a cheap sofa, wrapped in the arms of her distraught husband, while a couple of nurses looked on sadly. Jez quickened her pace and turned down a quieter corridor.

She wasn't even sure what section of the hospital she was in anymore. She hadn't paid that much attention when Sangeeta had brought her up, and she'd been told she could just follow the signs to get back down. It was like being in a rabbit warren. There were barely any windows; she guessed that the windows were in the patients' rooms. She glanced through an open door: she was right. It was completely dark outside.

It was almost silent in this corridor. After visiting hours, she imagined. She checked her phone. Seven o'clock. All she could hear were the quiet beeps coming from the open doors. She passed another room with the lights out and then another.

She passed the third room, where the door was ajar. A flash of movement outside the window caught her eye. She froze.

She must have imagined it. She was on the second floor after all. She knew she should just keep walking. It was crazy. It was all too crazy.

But she had to check.

She stepped carefully to the edge of the door with her shoulder against the frame. She could see the window, but anything outside it would have to be at the right angle in order to see her. She tried to breathe slowly and deeply.

There was nothing outside the window. She waited for a minute. Then another. Then another. Nothing happened.

She exhaled slowly. It had just been her imagination. She realized that her shoulders had crept up around her ears and relaxed.

Another jolt of movement, unmistakable this time, shot past the window. It was real. She was on the second floor and there was something outside the window. Jez's stomach dropped as if she were on a roller coaster; her breath caught in her throat. She fixed her eyes on the window. She could hear a faint buzzing noise coming from outside.

The thing hove into view. She had only seen it once before, but she recognized it immediately. It was the fly-like monster—*demon*, Sarah had called it—from down by the Foxglove Pond. The thing that had killed Gareth and Marina. She had only seen it curled up, in repose. In flight, it was enormous. And revolting. Its proboscis shone with slime in the light from the hospital's windows; the deadly point glittered in the dark. Jez flattened herself against the wall instinctively.

Had it come for her? For her dad?

A thought struck her. Sarah had said that whoever was controlling it had made sure that it couldn't get out of the area around the Foxglove Pond, as long as they wanted. So what was it doing at the hospital?

She pulled out her phone. Her hands were shaking as she tapped the screen; it took her twice as long as usual to type out the message to Sam.

Tell S. the demon thing is at the hospital.

She hit *Send*, and her legs buckled; she crumpled to the floor in a heap. Now what?

She glanced through the door. The thing was still hovering outside the window. It was completely dark outside, and Jez realized with a sinking heart that she must be on the side of the hospital opposite the car park. No one looking up from the ground floor would see the thing, because there was no one on the ground on that side of the building.

She had to go. She had to get back to the emergency waiting room, where Sangeeta would be waiting for her. They wouldn't attack her in a crowd; they couldn't. No one would forget that, even with supernatural help. She *had* to believe it.

She struggled to her feet as the thing outside threw itself against the glass.

THUD.

The sound was dull and laced with a metallic clank. It shot Jez through with adrenalin.

Jez's phone buzzed in her pocket. She pulled it out as the demon outside the window thudded against the reinforced glass for a second time.

"Jez." It was Sarah. "What's going on?"

"That thing we saw at the Foxglove Pond is here," said Jez, in a whisper. "It's trying to break in here. I don't know why, and I don't know if it's after me or my dad. Tell me what to do."

There was a brief pause on the other end.

"Okay," said Sarah. "Meet me at the Accident and Emergency entrance in—" there was a pause as she confirmed with Sam "seven minutes. Stay away from the windows. Try and keep around other peop—"

The phone went dead. Jez tapped at it furiously. The battery was flat.

Get down to Accident and Emergency. Stay away from the windows. Simple plan. There was another thud from the room behind her and she thought she heard something crack.

She had to move now. She turned to her left, the way she had come with Sangeeta to the cafeteria, and froze.

It was at the back of the hospital and had probably, when it had originally been built, been some sort of veranda or patio for patients with consumption or brain fever or whatever it was people had back then to sit in the sun for a bit. Someone had noticed at some point that Ardenshire didn't get a whole lot of sun, especially from October to April, and had come up with the money to box it in.

With glass. The stairwell was on the other side of a well-lit corridor that was made, on two sides, ceiling and wall, of glass.

Jez stared at it in horror.

Then the lights went out.

Chapter 16

Jez trembled in the dark. The thumping had stopped.

Maybe it couldn't see in the dark, but she wouldn't bank on it. Somehow, she sensed that the thing that was chasing her was born in the dark.

Her eyes adjusted to the darkness, and she saw the light switches glowing on the wall. That explained it. They were on a timer in the evening, set to go out if there wasn't any movement for a while. It was after visiting hours, after all.

The door to the stairwell was about ten yards away, on the right. The letters *E-X-I-T* glowed above it, in red.

It wasn't *that* far.

There was a loud *crack* from the room behind her. Jez turned and saw the window sporting a lightning-strike fissure. A flicker of movement in the dark told her the thing was back, and she was still hanging around where it had last seen her.

She needed to move. Preferably without triggering the light sensor and presenting the thing outside with a clear target in a nice glass gift box. She inched long the wall, breathing hard. The light switches glowed in the dark. There was no sound, other than Jez's breathing and the various clicks and beeps of the monitors in the hospital rooms off the corridor. She hoped that no one would come and trigger a blast of light.

She reached the edge of the wall, where it met the glass. *Shit.* She needed to cross the corridor, to be as far away from the glass as possible. It wasn't much distance—about ten, maybe twelve feet?—but she didn't want to be snatched away in a crash and tinkle of broken glass to the kind of torment she didn't want to think about and, ultimately, certain death. She shuddered as she thought, involuntarily, about the creature's rough, clawed limbs grabbing at her, the lacerations of the glass. Too real. She needed to get across the corridor. She began to crawl across, face up, on her hands and feet and bum, inching forward, trying to breath slowly, trying not to flood the corridor with light.

After an age, her foot touched the wall on the other side of the hall. She exhaled hard. Her heart was racing. Absently, she put a fist to her chest and rubbed hard, trying to calm herself.

She felt the weight of Sarah's pentacle under her shirt.

So much for protection.

It would be all right, she told herself, unconvinced. It would be all right. *Sarah's a witch, for God's sake, she thought. She must be able to do something. She said she's dealt with things like this before.*

All you have is her word for it. And a few parlour tricks. You don't know what kind of power she really has.

No, thought Jez, trying to push those thoughts away. *But right now, I have to have faith in her because I don't really have a lot of other options.*

She looked at the exit sign. It seemed a long way off.

She'd managed to get across the corridor without triggering the lights. The chances of her being able to get all the way along it and do the same seemed slim. Either she could slide along an inch at a time on her bum and hope the thing couldn't see in the dark, or she could stand up and make a floodlit run for it, and hope that she was faster than a supernatural flying demon.

Not supernatural, she reminded herself. *It actually exists.*

Yeah. And it's after you something fierce. MOVE.

She looked down the corridor. That was a lot of sliding. She heard something outside. Was it wings? Was it just the wind?

Best guess: it was about four minutes since the phone call with Sarah. They'd be here in about another three.

And just like that, she made her decision.

Run for it.

She leaned her back against the wall, pulled her feet toward her, and rolled her weight forward so that she was crouching on the balls of her feet. She balanced herself with her hands.

Stand up slowly. When the lights come on, you need to move faster than you've ever moved in your life.

She pushed up. Her thigh muscles burned as she inched her way up to a standing position, expecting the lights to flare on any second.

It stayed dark.

She pulled her bag across her shoulder, so it wouldn't fall off.

Still dark.

Three.

Two.

One.

RUN!

The lights crashed on, dazzling her momentarily; there was a resounding *crack* from above. The thing was back, and it could see her. She pounded on, bag thumping painfully at her side; the thing above her threw itself at the glass again, and she heard a musical pinging as a couple of chips of glass came loose from the panel. The exit sign loomed larger; there was a smash from behind her as the pane of glass caved in.

Shit!

She kept running. She could hear voices behind her; they must have heard the crash, someone must have called the nurse, they were behind her, but the door was in front of her, closer by the demisecond.

Her hands were shaking so badly she could barely grasp the door handle; she missed twice and then slammed it down so hard, she bruised her hand. She slammed her shoulder against the door, shot through it, and kept running.

Down the stairs. Down. She heard the door close behind her with a bang. She was shaking as she ran down the stairs; she slipped on the last step and twisted her ankle badly.

Well, she thought, *at least you're in the right place.*

She came to the door at the end of the stairwell and crashed through it into a familiar corridor; she slowed to a limping walk and headed straight for the nurses' station.

"Is Sangeeta around?" she said to the nurse behind the desk. "She's a doctor. Dr. Chaturvedi."

"No," said the nurse. "She's attending to a patient. Can I help at all?"

Jez took a deep breath. "I was coming back from the caf and I got a bit lost," she said. "I think something might have happened upstairs. There was broken glass everywhere." She pointed behind her. "At the top of that stairwell. It just seemed really... I don't know. Not right. I thought I should come and tell someone."

"Good call," said the nurse. His name tag read "Martin." "I'll ask someone to check it out." He picked up the phone behind the desk and tapped a few numbers into it. "Do you know what happened?"

"No," said Jez, absently. She hesitated by the desk, peering down the corridor for any sign of Sangeeta. Nothing. She knew she had to go, but she was desperate for an update on her dad.

Nothing. A car horn blasted a half-quaver outside. Jez looked through the door; it was Sam and Sarah in the lime-green Allegro. Sarah motioned ferociously with her head: get in the car.

It killed Jez to leave, but she knew she had to. There was a possibility that Sarah could keep her safe; the hospital, she knew, couldn't. She took one last look at the emergency waiting room; there was still no sign of Sangeeta. She stepped over quickly to the desk, wincing as she put weight on her ankle, and asked one of the nurses for a pen and piece of paper. She wrote:

Sangeeta. My friends came to meet me. I've gone to get some rest. Will be back first thing tomorrow. Thanks for everything.

She wasn't sure how plausible it sounded—hell, it wasn't what she'd be doing if she had a choice—but she didn't, and she had to make the best of it.

And she needed to keep her dad safe as well. She grasped the pentacle around her neck and pulled it over her head.

Please can you give my dad this? she wrote. *It's like a good-luck charm. Say it's from me, if he wakes up. Please? Thanks again.*

She folded the note around the pendant.

"Excuse me?" she called to Martin behind the desk. He looked up.

"Can you give this to Sangeeta?" asked Jez. "When she's done with her patient? She was looking after me... I have to go. Get some rest. But I wanted to say thank you. For looking after me." She passed the note forward and the nurse took it.

"Sure," he said. "No problem." He looked at Jez more closely. "Are you okay? You look like you're limping."

"I—" said Jez. She stalled. "I have to go." She dashed out of
the hospital's automatic doors and into the Allegro's lumpy back
seat, slamming the heavy car door behind her. Sarah and Sam
turned to look at her.

"You all right?" asked Sam.

"It was…that thing," said Jez. Her hands were still shaking.
"The fly-shaped demon monster thing—it was trying to get in.
After me." She paused. "It started banging on the window when
it saw me." She paused. "Why would it be after me?"

"Doesn't matter," said Sarah. "It is. How's your dad?"

"In surgery," said Jez, again. She swallowed hard. "I gave
him the thing you gave me. The pendant. I left it for him, for
when he comes out of the operating room. I told them it was a
good-luck charm from me. I can get it back," she added, as she
realized how that sounded. "I know it was your aunt's. Was that
okay?"

"That was good thinking," said Sarah. "Where's the giant
flybrid?"

"Don't know. Last time I knew where it was, it was trying
to get through the hospital roof. I think it saw me." Her breath
was coming more easily now, but her hands were shaking. "I
don't know if it got in."

"I'd say no." Sarah looked at the hospital doors. "Otherwise
there'd be a lot more noise coming from in there." Jez glanced
up at the sprawling Victorian building; it seemed serene and
gloomy in the darkness. No screaming, no breaking of glass.
"Which is good."

"That means it's still out here," said Sam. He peered up
through the Allegro's windscreen.

Sarah was drumming her gloved fingers on the steering
wheel. "Okay," she said. "This is what we do. We go back to my
place. You both stay at mine. Sam phones his mother to say that

he's staying with Jez because of her dad. In the morning, Jez comes back to the hospital; we find out where Carpenter lives and…after that, we'll figure it out." She didn't want to think about what "figuring it out" would necessarily entail. "But right now we go back to mine. We'll be safe there." *Unless someone burns it down.*

"That thing's still out there," said Sam, again.

"Yes," said Sarah. "We're five miles from home. My home is safe; I can tell you that for free. But we're going to have to make a run for it. Jez, there's a bag in the back." Jez looked down at the footwell behind Sam's seat: there it was. It was blue. "There's a couple of bits and pieces in there that should help, in an emergency. Put it where we can get at it." Jez hauled it up and did as she was told. "Okay," said Sarah. "Let's hit the road. Keep your eyes peeled; if you see anything, shout. If all goes well, we'll be home in fifteen minutes max. We're unprotected for a full fifteen minutes, and then we'll be fine for the night."

Jez swallowed.

"All right," said Sam. "Let's go." His jaw clenched.

Sarah muscled the car into gear and hit the gas.

• • •

All three of them were silent for the first three minutes of the journey. The road snaked around the back of a residential estate; the street lights were regular and evenly spaced. Jez scanned the sky for movement. Nothing.

Nothing at all.

"This is a good start," said Sam, echoing Jez's thoughts.

Sarah grunted and Sam and Jez looked toward the road. The street lights ended about two hundred yards up the road. After that, it was pitch-black.

Sam swallowed. Jez took a deep breath.

The road went dark. They were out in the country. The hedgerows loomed high on either side of the tarmac, and the trees were growing more thickly. It was difficult to see the sky. The only sound was the Allegro's engine, growling in the dark.

Sarah broke the silence. "I'm going to step on it a bit," she said. "Get us there a bit quicker." She pressed her foot to the floor and the car kangarooed forward. The engine whinged and she changed upwards. The white lines of in the centre of the narrow road were swallowed by the car's bonnet. Another. Another. Another. The engine droned on in the darkness.

"Sam," said Jez, "can I borrow your phone?"

He handed it to her wordlessly. She looked at the time. Twenty past seven. They were almost halfway. She knew this road like the back of her hand; her dad had driven her along it for ill-advised piano lessons for five years, and then intermittently since then; one time, she'd had to go to the hospital herself, when she was hit in the face with a hockey ball during PE. Her nose was fractured and she had been in excruciating pain. But she could have sworn that the drive wasn't as long as this.

She looked at the phone again. Still twenty past seven.

Her eye caught a flash of movement in the headlights and her heart leaped as Sarah slammed on the brakes; all three of them were thrown forward in the darkness as the car skidded and came to a screeching halt. A badger looked at them grumpily from the pool of light thrown forward by the headlights, and lumbered off into the hedgerow.

All three relaxed and sat back in their seats. Sarah exhaled.

"Okay," she said, almost to herself. "Okay."

She changed down with a crunch, and the car grumbled forward.

Seven minutes. Almost halfway. They rounded a treacherous double bend, which Sarah navigated with skill, and entered the

Beaston Woods. Beaston was closer to Crowsbrook, but the woods stretched all the way down to the Foxglove Pond on the edge of the village. Here, the trees grew thick and the road narrowed; with the sky overcast, it was difficult to see through the tangle of naked branches.

"I guess we're more protected here," said Sam. "If it can fly, it won't be able to see us from above."

Sarah shrugged. "More places for it to hide in here. Try not to think about it."

"We're over halfway," said Jez, from the back seat.

"That's good," said Sarah. "Keep your fingers crossed." They lapsed into silence once again.

Jez swiped her finger across the screen of Sam's phone to check the time again. Nothing happened.

"Sam," she said. "When did you last charge your phone?"

"This morning," he said. "Why?"

"It's dead," said Jez. "The battery's flat."

There was a pause.

"Don't panic," said Sarah, her eyes glued to the road. "We don't have far to go." She spoke with a calmness she didn't feel. The trees hanging over the road gave her a feeling of claustrophobia. She would be a lot happier, she felt, if she could see the sky. "It might be nothing."

Something hit the roof of the car with a crash like a boulder dropping on sheet metal. All three of them cried out; Jez looked up and saw that the roof of the car was dented inwards. The force of the blow had ripped the plastic fabric that covered the car's ceiling. Sarah stomped on the gas and the engine screamed as the car shot forward. There was another crash, this time from behind; the rear windscreen shattered and the car lurched, snapping back the heads of its passengers. Jez felt broken glass shower her back; she bent forward and covered her head. Sam turned back. At the top of the frame of the broken windscreen, the monster's bristle-covered head appeared, insect-eyes huge and dark and blank. A two-fingered arm snaked down to the bottom of the window; it crunched on the broken glass and the thing didn't even flinch.

"Hang on," hollered Sarah, "and try to relax!" She slammed her foot on the accelerator; the needle on the speedometer shot up to sixty. When it hit sixty-five, she stomped on the brake. The engine sputtered and stalled.

Jez tried to go limp; she was thrown forward and her teeth crunched together painfully. She felt a sharp pain in her neck as her head snapped back and she threw up her arms, bracing for the crash against the headrest of the seat in front. Her seatbelt cut into her shoulder, and she felt something slice into her leg: a small piece of broken glass from the back windshield. She managed to stop herself from crying out.

Sarah's plan had worked, at least temporarily. The creature was off the roof of the car and lying in the road in front of them. Not dead, though. It was still moving, temporarily dazed.

"We can't outrun it," snapped Sarah. "Jez, give me the bag." There was no room for disagreement in her tone, and Jez passed the bag over without a word. Sarah ripped open the zip and pulled out the blue slate dagger, which she handed to Sam, the bamboo spike, which she passed back to Jez, and the bow and ratty quiver of arrows, which she placed on the dashboard in front of her. "Okay," she said, "This could be a rough ride. Stay in the car as long as possible, and do *exactly* as I say. It's that thing or us; got it?"

"How the fuck do we use this stuff?" shouted Sam.

"Pointy end away from you," yelled Sarah. "Hold tight!"

She turned the keys in the Allegro's ignition and the elderly car coughed into life. In the road, the demon raised itself onto all fours, and then leaned forward into a predator's crouch. It slowly turned to face them, expressionless. Its eyes glittered in the headlights.

Sarah yanked the handbrake up, gunned the engine until it squealed, and then dropped the handbrake. The car shot forward. She flicked the headlights to full beam.

The demon stood up and turned its head away, adjusting to the light. Then it turned back and leaped forward.

"Hang on!" yelled Sarah, and the car hit the demon with a wet *crunch*. The front windscreen cracked, but, amazingly, held. The demon was thrown up over the roof of the car and landed with a thud behind them. Sarah pulled on the handbrake and swung the car round a hundred and eighty degrees, throwing Sam and Jez against the doors. The thing was lying in the road again, stunned, shaking its head. One of its upper limbs was lying at an awkward angle. In a single, twisting movement, it was back on its feet, arm dangling.

"It's pissed now," said Sarah. "Things are about to get ugly." She gunned the engine, and shot the car forward for a third attack. They sped closer to the angry demon. It squared off against the car, showing no signs of moving.

"It's not very clever, is it?" said Sam. Jez glared at the back of his head.

At the last moment, second before impact, the muscles in the demon's neck rippled, its throat twitched, and a glistening wet pellet, the size of a clenched fist shot out of its proboscis toward the windscreen; it crouched and leaped over the car just in time. The pellet hit the windshield with a wet smack; it was the last straw for the strained glass, which caved in with a crash, showering Sam and Sarah in shards. A large piece of glass caught Sam on the forehead, tearing through his skin; blood gushed down his face. Sarah swore. In the mirror, she could see the demon crouching, poised to pounce again.

An audible hiss came from the front seat, accompanied by thin reeds of smoke curling upwards.

"What the hell?" panted Sam.

"Acid!" yelled Jez. "It's acid; it's fucking... it's part fly. Did it touch you? Don't let it get on you!" She leaned forward, looking at a spot on Sam's school blazer. The fabric was burning, melting away before their eyes. The acid bubbled and smoked as the cloth melted away.

"Get that off," snapped Jez. "Chuck it in the road. No, no—mop up the other acid with it, first. Don't spread it around!" Sarah had restarted the engine and was firing the car away from the demon, heading back down the road the way they had come. Sam pulled off his blazer awkwardly, bringing down another rain of broken glass upon himself. He turned the crank on the door to wind down the window; when it was open, he threw the blazer into the road, where it lay, smoking gently. The acid continued to eat through the dashboard and the upholstery of the car's ceiling, filling the car with delicate threads of acrid, curling smoke and the smell of charred plastic.

Sarah spun the car around, and it crouched in the darkness, under the trees, engine grumbling. There was a nasty grinding noise coming from beneath the bonnet, and something was scraping the road underneath them. A chill breeze blew through the blown-out windows, dispersing some of the acid fumes, but bringing with it a spatter of cold rain.

"Okay," said Sarah, half to herself. "Sam, can you drive?"

"Provisional license," said Sam, warily. "Why?"

"I want to try something," said Sarah. She revved the engine. "When I let go of the clutch, you're in charge of steering and changing up. Got that?"

"Wait; what?" said Sam.

"Just do exactly as I tell you," said Sarah, "and everything might be fine." She took her foot off the clutch and the car careened forward. "Now *steer!*"

Sam leaned over and took the wheel with his right hand. The engine's pitch grew higher.

"Clutch is out," yelled Sarah. "Change up!" Sam grasped the gear lever. It felt like stirring a bucket of bricks; the car clunked into second. Sarah picked up the bow from the dashboard and held it horizontally. Sam was getting the hang of steering; the car was wobbling less. The demon hove back into view. Sarah held the centre of the bow underhand in her left hand; with her right, she fitted one of the arrows to the string.

"Change up," ordered Sarah again. They were going faster through the trees. The demon took off; it was hovering in the air, ready for another attack.

"Keep it steady," hollered Sarah. "Change up again!" She popped the clutch and Sam crunched into gear. Sarah pulled the string of the bow back as far as she could, leaning back in her seat and pulling her right arm between her seat and the car door. The demon dropped into a dive, heading straight toward them.

Everything happened in a flash. Sarah released the arrow with a sharp *twang*; it struck the demon in the leg, penetrating its calf entirely; the thing shrieked and reeled away from the car, just as Sam turned the steering wheel wildly. Sarah took her foot off the gas; the car slowed dramatically before clipping a tree on the nearside. The headlight smashed and the car came to a complete halt.

"Okay," shouted Sarah. "Out of the car. Bring your stuff and stay behind me." She scrambled out of the car, bow and two remaining arrows in hand; the others followed. The demon was still hovering; they could see its silhouette in the light of the one remaining headlight. Sarah fitted another arrow to the bow and fired wildly; the creature swatted at the arrow and it went wide.

"Come here, you bastard!" she shouted. The thing turned and shot toward her; it was only a couple of yards away when she fired the final arrow and leaped out of its way. The arrow went deep into the creature's chest. The thing screamed in pain and sank to the ground, spitting acid as it went. Jez, Sam, and Sarah jumped back. The demon thudded to the ground, panting.

"Jez!" shouted Sarah. "Give me that!" The demon sent an arc of acidic spittle toward them; it splashed on the tarmac and sizzled.

Jez looked at the weapon in her hand. The demon was on the ground, fighting to get up.

She thrust the spear at Sarah, arm locked.

"Go behind it!" yelled Sam. "Stab it in the neck!"

Sarah moved without thinking. She grabbed the spear from Jez, stepped in and thrust the spear forward wildly. It hit flesh and went in, hitting something hard. She pushed on it blindly, desperately; blood spurted out of the wound in the creature's neck. Its scream turned into a groan and its head fell forward. Then it was still.

Harm only as you must. She felt a chill in her stomach.

Jez couldn't move. She stood looking at the demon and the witch, mouth open.

"Is it dead?" asked Sam without taking his eyes off it.

"Probably," croaked Sarah.

Harm only as you must.

She took the slate knife out of Sam's hand. "We'll make sure before we go, though." She stepped up to where Jez was standing behind the demon's head and knelt down. "You might not want to watch this."

"No," said Jez in a voice barely above a whisper. "I want to make sure it's dead."

Sarah shrugged. "Okay," she said, and began to saw through the flesh of the creature's neck. The skin was tough; she hacked at it with the knife until she broke through; the blade bit into the soft flesh underneath and slid through it like butter until it hit the bone. Jez turned away, feeling her stomach turn. When she heard Sarah snap the bone, it was too much. She threw up by the side of the road. Sam went over to her and gave her a hug.

"Hey," Sarah said. "I need some help here. We have to get this thing off the road. Drag it into the trees. Come on," she said, sharply. "I need you to focus for a few minutes longer."

Sam picked up one of the now-headless demon's feet; Sarah grabbed the other. Its skin was greasy and covered in bristles. "Wash your hands when we get home," said Sarah as they dragged the body into the trees. "It'll probably decompose pretty quickly. But we don't need anyone driving past and getting curious."

Sam looked at the body lying among the moss and dead leaves. "That was the thing that killed Gareth and Marina?" he asked.

"Yup," said Sarah. She turned on her heel and walked back to the car.

Sam looked at the demon's corpse for a moment, and then spat on it. Then he followed Sarah back to the car.

Chapter 17

"God," said Sarah. "My poor old car."

The front and back windscreens had both been smashed; there was a large dent in the roof where the demon had cannonballed the car, and there was another big dent in the bonnet. The driver's side headlight was smashed, and there was a large acid burn across the paintwork on the front. Sarah climbed into the driver's seat and turned the keys in the ignition. The engine coughed and then fired on the second attempt.

"British Leyland one, Hell nil," said Sarah. "Hop in, kids." She sounded a lot more confident than she felt. She had killed for the second time in a week, and for the second time, had killed something that was supposed to be immortal.

"Can you get it fixed?" said Jez. "Can you magic it right or something?"

"You're still not getting how magic works, are you?" said Sarah. "This is an Austin Allegro. The intervention of supernatural powers isn't going to help it." She slammed the door shut; a couple more pieces of glass fell off onto the tarmac.

Jez got in the back; Sam in the front. Sarah reversed gingerly away from the tree.

"Watch for acid, Sam," she said, glancing across to his side of the car, where a few tendrils of smoke still trailed lazily upward. Sam opened the glove compartment and pulled out a rag, which he wrapped around his hand, and a cassette, which he stuck into the Allegro's tape deck. The opening bars of "Don't Stop Believin'" filled the car.

"This car," said Sam, "is definitely tougher than it looks."

They drove in silence back to Sarah's cottage.

• • •

Adam's phone chimed beside his bed, paused for a moment, and then chimed again. He stirred in his sleep and rolled over. The display on the bedside clock read 12:30. He swore quietly. Who the hell would call him at half past midnight?

He picked up the phone and looked at the screen. Brown. He hit the screen to accept the call.

"Mr. Carpenter," said Brown. "I have news. Updates."

"It's half past fucking midnight," said Adam, testily. "Why now?"

"We felt that you would want to know immediately," said Brown. "The situation is most unusual." For the first time, Adam noticed a note of—was it anger, perhaps, or just anxiety?—in this other man's voice. He frowned and sat up.

"What is it?" he said. "What's happened?" A flash of fear shot through his intestines. *Your most secret desires*. What if Brown knew about Greenwood?

"We understand that you used the Minion to resolve a personal situation," said Brown, the evenness returning to his voice. Adam took a deep breath, preparing to deny, to justify whatever had happened. The Minion had brought him Greenwood's head. That personal situation was resolved all-fucking-right. He felt all the terror of a child caught racing toy cars under the desk when he was supposed to be learning the seven times table.

"That—" he began. "I—"

"That is irrelevant, Mr. Carpenter," continued Brown. "The matter has been resolved. Unfortunately, there were some unforeseen consequences."

Oh, God. The police. I'll go to gaol. Adam's mind raced ahead before he remembered what the Asilida people were capable of. There was nothing he could do that would be punished. Nothing. Still, anxiety brewed in his stomach. Force of habit.

"Go on," he said, a lot more calmly than he felt. He *would* remain in control of the situation. In control of himself.

"Your Minion was thorough," Brown went on. "As it was expected to be. As it has been for centuries, when serving the elite who make up our clients." He cleared his throat. "However. In attempting to complete the task, it —" he paused.

"Stop being so goddamn cryptic," snapped Adam. "Get to the fucking point."

There was an acid-tinged pause.

"In carrying out its other duties," Brown continued, "the Minion was slain. Regrettably, it is no longer available for your use."

Adam's irritability grew into full-fledged anger. This was gross incompetence. These men had promised him anything he wanted, and had delivered, too. And then to stop the service they were providing just as he had accepted its possibilities, had accepted that limitations were a thing of the past for him—it was beyond outrageous. He slid out of bed, strode out of the bedroom, and quietly closed the door behind him. Then, he let rip.

"You fucking incompetents!" he spat. "I've held up my part of the bargain, haven't I? The least you could do is to keep your... *thing* alive for the duration of the deal." A vision of Mila and Anna floated before his eyes, and, inexplicably, he felt a lump rise in his throat. "*Slain?* Like, killed?"

"Indeed," said Brown. "And please understand, we are most distressed by the occurrence ourselves."

"Greenwood *killed* it? That fucking hippie couldn't kill a fl—" He changed tack. "He couldn't kill a spider in the bath."

"Greenwood is dead," said Brown. "As you are well aware. Allow me."

Adam's phone buzzed, and he pulled it away from his ear. A photo message. Then another. And another. He tapped open the first one. A decapitated corpse: Greenwood,. The next: a woman, about the same age as Greenwood: his wife. Neck broken, and disembowelled. The third: a child, a boy, his face and chest burned with acid, down to the bone, organs exposed. He felt numb. Nothing.

"We take our duty to our clients seriously," said the disembodied voice on the other end of the line.

Adam swallowed. "So not Greenwood," he said, still angry. "Then who?"

"You must understand," said Brown, "that we did not anticipate—"

"*Who?*" screamed Adam. "That thing was *mine!*"

Another pause.

"Technically, it was contracted to you," said Brown. "But it is irrelevant now. It was killed by a witch," he continued. "Sarah Trevelyan."

Adam was silent, stunned. Then he began to laugh. He laughed and laughed and laughed.

"A *witch?*" he managed, eventually. "A fucking *witch?* With a pointy hat and a broomstick and a little black pussycat? You have *got* to be shitting me."

"No," said Brown. "I am not."

"This thing kills Greenwood and a bunch of other people, and it's taken out by—" He couldn't even finish the sentence. "Does she have magic powers?"

"Of a kind," said Brown. He coughed again. "She should not be considered— she *is* not—a match for Asilida. There was a misjudgement, and for that we apologize most sincerely."

Adam was still chuckling as Brown talked. He stopped abruptly as the weight of what Brown had implied struck him. "Wait," he said. "You *knew* about her?"

"We did," said Brown. "She was not viewed as a threat."

"You knew about her," said Adam, his temper rising again, "and you didn't stop her, and she killed my Minion. If you didn't anticipate that she was going to do that, what the hell could she be doing to the deal? Is she working to wreck that, too? How did she even find the Minion?"

"She would naturally have been sensitive to the nature of our operation in the area," said Brown, "and she was overly curious, but we had informed her that her actions would have no bearing on our plans. In addition, she is closely associated with an individual who has a connection to Greenwood's daughter."

"Greenwood's—Jesus *Christ!* She was poking around in our business, and she has a connection to Greenwood, and you didn't see her as a threat? And Greenwood has a daughter? Do you have a nice picture of *her* to show me, as well?"

There was another pause, one that seemed to have a lot less edge.

"Currently," said Brown. "I do not."

"Where is the daughter?"

"We kept her," said Brown. His voice had a clear edge now. "We found her. She was in intense pain. Her misery was exquisite. She will generate perfect human desolation for us for the rest of her life. We found her, retrieved her, and—" he paused "—found somewhere to *keep* her. A commission. "

Adam swore again.

"So let me get this straight," he hissed through gritted teeth. "This fucking teenage whore watches what happens to her family, escapes, gets picked up *by you lot*, and is still alive? And can tell the world that there's a fucking monster running around Ardenshire, doing whatever the fuck Adam Carpenter tells it?"

"She will never escape," said Brown, wearily. "She has lost her mind. She has lost the power of speech. In an impossible scenario in which she escapes and recovers her mind, no one will believe her." He cleared his throat. "Would you? We have destroyed her sanity; she can no longer distinguish the truth from her own memories and nightmares. We have made the truth sound like a lie. In addition, she is seventeen: the words of a seventeen-year-old girl bear no weight. And she would know of no connection between all of this and you, Mr. Carpenter. Please be reasonable."

"Why?" snapped Adam. "My fucking assured future is now decidedly unassured because of your idiocy and some bitch reject from seventeenth-century Salem. Where the hell is this witch now?"

"Sarah Trevelyan," said Brown. "You may do well to remember that." There was a touch of acid in his voice.

"You may do well to pull your fucking finger out and start working for me again," said Adam. His voice had gone dangerously quiet. "I want to meet Sarah Trevelyan. At the earliest possible fucking opportunity. Get it?" He hung up and went downstairs to the kitchen. He needed a drink. A real drink.

He was starting to feel nauseated again. Two minutes and twenty-four seconds later, his phone pinged. A picture message. A girl: limp, wide-eyed with terror.

Whatever. Adam tossed the phone onto the kitchen counter. Then he frowned, picked it up again, and looked harder at the picture.

The girl was slumped against a stack of Rubbermaid boxes that were topped with a purple backpack. It looked a lot like the backpack that Julia had taken around Europe when she was a student. She couldn't bloody get rid of anything.

He stared at the phone, nausea and hunger rising.

The girl was in his basement.

• • •

Sarah woke up in her spare room and stared up at the cob-web-covered ceiling. Her muscles were stiff, and it took her a moment to figure out where she was. The springs in the old mattress complained as she stretched and winced. She wasn't getting any younger, that was for sure.

What the hell. The kid needed the bed. She'd been shattered by the time the battered Allegro pulled up at Sarah's cottage; a combination of shock and emotional exhaustion. Sam had folded himself up to fit on the sofa, citing a loathing of spiders and also sensing that Jez needed the most rest of all of them. She'd need to go back to the hospital first thing, find out how her dad was. And they didn't know what else was out there. Jesus, things were complicated.

Sarah hauled herself into a sitting position. She really wanted both the kids to stay in the house. They knew too much. Every malevolent Ethereal in Asilida would be on the lookout for them, and the Ethereals weren't just monitoring them anymore. They were out for blood.

But Jez needed to be near her dad. And Sarah had given her the last protection charm in the house, and Jez had given it to her father. Which had been necessary; Sarah couldn't fault her for that. But still. They had no protection once they left the house. The daylight was good; few Ethereals preferred to do their dirty work in the daylight. But the days were shortening. And she had to find Adam Carpenter. And when she found him—

Damn it.

Harm only as you must. It seemed pretty clear cut. That didn't make it any easier. She had killed twice now, in self-defence. But to kill a human who was not a direct threat to her—for what? For the greater good? Who was she to decide?

She was still pondering the problem when Sam knocked on the door and asked if she had a spare loo roll.

• • •

"No," said Jez. "I'm going back to the hospital. I'm not staying here."

Sarah sighed. "You'll be safer here," she said. It was worth a shot.

"I don't care. I want to see my dad. Jesus." *I want to know if he's still alive*, Jez added, silently. "Just because *you* don't have any family left—"

"How are you going to get there?" said Sarah, faking patience. "I know the Allegro still goes—just—but I can't exactly drive it in the daylight in the state it's in."

"We can take a cab," said Sam. "If you can lend us a tenner, I'll go with her. But we have to go. It's daylight; what can possibly happen in daylight?"

"You don't get it, do you?" said Sarah. "We don't *know* what could happen. Anything could happen." She stirred her tea, absently.

Jez picked up her phone and pulled out it off the charger. "We killed that thing," she said. "There can't be more than one.

I'm calling a cab." She tapped her phone a couple of times and turned away and covered her ear as it began to ring.

"We'll be fine," said Sam, over Jez's voice quietly arranging the pickup. "She needs to go, though."

"I know," said Sarah. She rubbed her forehead with her hand. "I just... I feel responsible. For all of this."

"You're not, you know," said Sam. He put his hand on her arm, and Sarah flinched in surprise. "Neither of us thinks you are."

"If anything happens to either of you," said Sarah, "I will be. This job... I don't think this is the kind of job where you can be around other people much." She stared into her mug of tea and kept stirring.

"We can take care of ourselves," said Sam. "Do you have something nifty we can take with us?"

Sarah shrugged. "I'm all out," she said. "The stuff from last night... it's like your bloody phone; it would need time to charge before you could use it again. And if I worked up something new, it would be dark again before you could use it. And the rest of the stuff in the boxes either needs a bit of specialist knowledge or is stuff I don't know how to use anyway. Which I guess is the same thing." She sipped her tea. "A lot of my job is being prepared. And being paranoid."

"Then how come you're not ready now?"

"There isn't usually three of me." Sarah looked at the bookshelves. "When this is over, I have a lot of reading to do."

Jez put her phone back in her bag. "They'll be here in about fifteen minutes," she said. "Are you coming with me?"

"Sam is," said Sarah. "I'm not. I have to find out where Adam Carpenter lives. Do some work on my kit. Find out if I have anything else that's useful." *Because,* she thought, *if I do,*

I'm going to have to kill him with it. She pushed the thought to the back of her mind.

"They used to live in the village," said Jez. "The Carpenter family. Maybe Adam Carpenter still does."

"He's not going to be in the phone book though, is he?" said Sam. "I don't even know why they make a phone book anymore."

"Shut up, Sam," said Jez. "You should ask at the shop. Jake and Rose know everyone in the village. If he's still here, they'll know where he lives. I mean, it's not like you have a huge number of options; the village isn't that big."

A car horn sounded outside.

"That'll be us," said Jez. She stood up and so did Sam. Nobody said anything for a moment.

"Take care of yourselves," said Sarah. "I mean that."

"Yeah," said Jez. Her throat was feeling tight again. "You too."

"We'll be fine," said Sam. "Don't worry about us. We'll go straight to the hospital. It'll be fine."

The car horn sounded again, a little longer this time.

"See you later," said Sam, turning to go. "We'll come back here when we're done."

"Good," said Sarah. "That's a good idea." The two kids turned and headed out the front door, closing it behind them with a click.

• • •

Adam barely noticed Julia as she slugged through her morning routine; he was consumed by two thoughts: first, that Julia should be prevented at all costs from going down to the basement and, second, that he needed to get down there as soon as possible to see if the girl he'd seen on his phone was actually in there.

She never goes down to the basement, the voice in his head told him. *Don't be ridiculous.* He felt like a kid in bed on Christmas Eve: the anticipation of what was down there waiting for him was electric.

You don't know that she's down there, he thought.

Do you want her to be? the voice retorted. *She is down there. You know it.*

He barely felt Julia's lips brush his face before she disappeared to work, mumbling something about him getting out of bed and getting his arse in gear, whatever. Didn't matter. He didn't have to, anyway. This world, this new world—free of consequences, free of fear—belonged to him. True power. Every day a new delight, a new treat. This was what Carrington had never explained, what he had hidden with smiles and excuses. This was his secret. And now it was Adam's. He swung himself out of bed and pulled on a hoodie, heart racing as he headed down the stairs.

The basement had probably been a coal cellar originally; it wasn't like American basements from the movies. Julia had done it up so they could use it for storage, and it was full of metal shelving and Rubbermaid tubs and big trunks that she'd collected from antique markets, to put things in that he'd always thought she should get rid of. He snorted, involuntarily. Total pack rat, that woman.

When he reached the basement door, he paused, hand on the doorknob and listened. Nothing. Weird. Had Brown staged the whole thing? Maybe he, Adam, had made a mistake. Maybe he'd imagined the bag and the boxes. He pulled out his phone and looked again.

Nope, he was pretty sure it was his storage basement. He listened hard, ear against the door. Not a peep. He turned the handle slowly, opened the door, and flicked on the light. The smell of bare wood and stale air hit him along with a waft of cool air. It wasn't heated down there. He was grateful for the hoodie. He went down the wooden stairs in his bare feet. They creaked slightly under his weight. He peered over the edge of the handrail. Couldn't see anyone.

He stepped onto the concrete floor of the basement, barely noticed the cold.

"Hello?" he said, craning his neck. No reply. He looked at his phone again.

Look for the bag, idiot. Of course. Of course. He scanned the shelves and the piles of boxes. *We really need to get rid of this crap,* he thought. Couldn't see the bag anywhere. Another rack of shelving.

Fool! The voice in his head was vicious, and he flinched. *In the corner!*

Adam turned. There was the bag; he didn't know how he'd missed it. And sticking out from behind a stack of boxes was a bare foot.

He was shaking. He didn't know why.

"Hello?" he said again. "Hello?" He moved toward the stack of boxes and the foot.

And there she was. He hair was long and dark blond and tangled; it was falling out of a ponytail across her face. Her feet were bare but she was wearing a hoodie and filthy jeans; they were encrusted with mud and something rust-coloured. Didn't smell good. Blood? Adam's stomach rumbled. Her eyes were open, but her head lolled to one side. Adam watched her for a moment or two. She was breathing. Still alive.

"Hello?" he said, for a fourth time. The girl didn't respond. He snapped his fingers a couple of times by her ear; nothing. Drew a finger back and forth in front of her face: no response.

He stretched out a hand, fingers splayed, and ran them lightly and slowly down the side of her face. She shuddered almost imperceptibly. Adam exhaled slowly.

Wow.

"Your desires are still so limited," said a voice behind him. "You could have so much more. Even from her."

Adam whirled around. It was Brown. He froze. How could he have got in without Adam hearing him? Adam stared.

"More?" he croaked.

"This is Catherine Greenwood," said Brown. "The daughter of Richard Greenwood." Adam felt his breath catch in his throat. The only connection between him and the death of Richard Greenwood was right here in his basement. If anyone…

No one will find her.

"Then why is she here?" he managed.

"For you," said Brown, simply. "Sir." His silver cufflinks glinted in the bare bulb's light.

Adam looked at the girl. She was catatonic.

"For me?" he whispered. He turned her chin to face him. She couldn't have been more than seventeen.

Brown sighed.

"There is so much more available to you," he said, "than you even bother to try to imagine, Mr. Carpenter." He picked an invisible piece of lint off his suit. "She was present for the brutal deaths of her mother, her father and her brother. She is out of her mind with misery. With *misery*, Mr. Carpenter. Her pain is exquisite." A muscle in his face twitched. "And it is yours, sir."

"I don't understand," Adam croaked.

Fool! The voice in his head roared. Adam watched in shock and terror as his hand moved to the girl's forehead. *Feed!*

Feed.

FEED.

Adam felt the familiar sensation of his mind opening up. *Like with the Minion,* he thought, before he was overwhelmed by Cat's misery.

It was—

It was—

He gasped. It was beyond words. He knew it intimately, everything that she had been through, everything that she had felt: the horror, the shock, the crippling fear, the grief, the numbness, terror, loss, uncertaintylonelinessfearfearfear…

It felt good. It felt better than anything he had ever experienced. Money, Julia, Anna and Mila all faded away. He wanted more. He heard Brown, miles away—some kind of warning, but he kept his hand there, pressed against the girl's forehead, kept riding the waves of the sensations rushing through him.

Brown was calling his name.

"Mr. Carpenter!" he said. "Mr. Carpenter!"

The sensations began to fade. Adam pushed harder at the girl's forehead.

"No!" he said. "No! Don't stop!" He willed more of the feeling into him. The girl coughed and went limp.

"Carpenter!" shouted Brown.

Adam shoved Cat's head against the wall. His hand pushed through her face; her head collapsed into dust. His eyes grew wide and he drew his hand back in terror. He stumbled over a box that he had forgotten was behind him, and sat down with a bump.

He looked around him. He was still in the basement. He felt a little dizzy. When he turned back to the girl, he saw that her body was fast crumbling into something that looked like ash.

He looked at Brown. Brown looked disappointed.

"What happened?" Adam managed.

"Misery," said Brown. "It is what we live for. You drained her at a point when her entire existence was pain. Hence—" he gestured toward the pile of ash.

Adam looked at the ash-covered hoodie and jeans. "Oh," he said.

"Bear in mind, Mr. Carpenter," said Brown, from behind him, "that mercy is generally not one of our priorities."

"Mercy?" said Adam, turning.

"Of course," said Brown, patiently. "She is no longer in pain. Mr. Carpenter," he went on, "you could have kept her here for *years*."

He turned toward the stairs.

"How are you feeling, sir?" he asked.

Adam found himself speaking before he had had a chance to truly consider his answer.

"Good." His voice rasped in his throat. "Hungry."

• • •

"My God, you get through a lot of tea!" Jake looked at the basket full of packets of teabags that Sarah had thrown together, along with three cans of baked beans and a loaf of Mother's Pride.

"S'how stuff gets done," said Sarah, with a good deal more energy than she felt. "Doing a lot of clearing out."

"Oh, ar," said Jake, amiably. "Lot of that to do, I imagine."

"Auntie Dot liked to save things," said Sarah. It was partly true and as long as she didn't explain that "things" were mostly occult weapons from the four corners of the globe, it was a useful piece of small talk. "How are you? Keeping busy?"

"Can't complain," said Jake. The electric insect zapper behind him buzzed and flashed. Jake tsk'ed. "I thought that thing was on the blink," he added, turning. "Bloody thing won't stop going off. You wouldn't expect that in October."

"That's odd," said Sarah, looking at the small pile of bottle-green corpses that had built up underneath the electric coil.

"You're telling me," said Jake. "I think something must have died in the bushes at the back. Tons of the bloody things. Big buggers as well. I'll have to have a look later. It's been getting worse all week." He started taking the boxes of tea and cans of beans out of the basket that Sarah had placed on the counter and tapping numbers into the ancient cash register. He beamed at Sarah. "Still. Mustn't grumble, eh?"

"Got to keep cheerful," she said. *Here goes.* "I have a question for you, Jake. Do you know where Adam Carpenter lives? Dot wanted him to have a couple of bits and pieces." It was a risk—she had no idea if her great-aunt had even met Carpenter, but given the size of Crowsbrook, it was worth a shot.

Jake snorted. "Really? Then your aunt was a saint. Bit of a Hooray Henry, that one. His father was all right, but Adam's a flash bugger, excuse me for saying so. Oh, I'm sorry." He stopped himself. "Your Auntie Dot obviously liked him. How on Earth did she know him?"

"No idea," said Sarah. "Maybe he kept to himself as well."

Jake shrugged. "I think they do," he said. "Him and his lady. She's some sort of doctor, I think. They live in that big house down on Sycamore Lane. House with the fancy gate. Worried about burglars or something, they are." He put the loaf of bread in a plastic bag. "That'll be five pounds fifty-seven, please."

Sarah pulled her change purse out of her bag. "Which house is it on Sycamore Lane?"

"You'll know it when you see it," said Jake. "Got a big black metal gate. Fancy, like. You going round there today?"

"Might try," said Sarah. "Get these things over to him." The story was getting lamer as it got longer.

"Oh, ar," said Jake again. "Car working out all right?"

"Oh, yes," said Sarah, turning to go. "No complaints at all. It's tougher than it looks."

She was still thinking about it as she walked out of the shop's door—the bells hanging from the frame jangled—and back toward her cottage. She'd have to call someone, find a garage. Maybe on the weekend. Maybe Sam could ask his parents if they knew anyone, a mechanic or someone who didn't mind working on old cars. The bodywork and the bonnet were both scratched on top of everything else. She'd have to get a respray. God, this was going to be expensive. And she'd almost got used to the lime-green paint. She didn't see the black car with tinted windows pull up alongside her.

The rear door opened just in front of her.

"Sarah Trevelyan," said a man in an immaculate suit and silver cufflinks. He got out of the car and held the door for her, smiling. His eyes were bottle-green and hard. Sarah drew in her breath sharply.

"Yes?" she said.

"Brown," said Brown. "I work for Asilida. Get in the car, please."

"No." She turned to walk away, back in the direction she had come, and felt a hand shoot out and grasp her upper arm in a steel grip. She tugged away, but had no luck. She looked straight at the man holding her arm. "Didn't I kill you the other day?" she asked.

"Sarah Trevelyan," repeated Brown. "Get in the car. Please."

"Or what?" retorted Sarah.

Brown lifted his other hand into view; the sunlight glinted off a shining, serrated hunting knife.

"Or we will dissect you like a frog in a laboratory, leave you to die as slowly as we know how, and then make sure the evidence disappears like a stone thrown into a pond. No tricks of the trade. Just metal and human flesh," said Brown. "It will take a long time. The choice is, of course, yours to make."

Sarah nodded slowly. Then she pushed her hand down to lock the arm that Brown was holding, and slammed her shoulder into his chest, bringing her other hand up to punch him in the face. Quick as a snake, he brought the knife up and drew it across her forearm; she gasped in pain and dropped her hand as the blood welled up through her clothes. Brown pressed the blade of the knife to her neck, just under her jaw.

"Miss Trevelyan," he said. "Just get in the car."

With a sinking heart, Sarah complied. There was another man sitting in the back seat on the far side. When she was seated, and Brown had climbed into the car behind her, a hand clamped a strong-smelling cloth over her mouth and nose, and in a moment, she lost consciousness.

Brown smiled. He saw a spider the size of a fifty-pence piece quivering on Sarah's coat sleeve. Still smiling, he crushed it between the thumb and finger of his left hand. Then he ate it.

Three other spiders burrowed deep into Sarah's clothes and stayed there, trembling.

Chapter 18

"You okay?" Sam asked Jez, as the cab pulled into the hospital car park. It was the first time either of them had spoken since they had climbed into the car outside Sarah's. The hospital looked prosaic and unthreatening in the daylight, old red bricks and dull glass in the overcast October morning light.

"I don't know," said Jez. It was true. "I don't—I don't really feel anything. Just numb."

"I know what you mean," said Sam. "I mean, obviously it's not my family they attacked. But the whole thing is just completely mental. Unreal. I always thought that 'it felt like a dream,' was just an asinine simile. But that's what this feels like. None of it makes any sense, and yet here we are in the middle of it."

Jez nodded slightly toward the driver, meaning *shut up, you never know who's listening.* As the cab came to a stop, Sam handed him a note, and they climbed out of the car.

This was it. She stared at the hospital door and realized that the one good thing about the chaos and violence of the night had been that it had exhausted her, stopped her thinking about her father's life hanging in the balance while she worked to save her own, worn her out so she had been able to sleep and return to the hospital stronger than she had been even last night. The world worked in a weird way. But now she had to face up to what she had been putting off, all those *what-ifs* that had haunted her on her first journey to the hospital. Now she would know. She swallowed.

"Come on," said Sam. "Let's do this."

He put his arm around her and they walked toward the glass door of the hospital.

"I'm scared, Sam," muttered Jez. "I'm really, really fucking scared."

"I know," he said. "But, I dunno. It'll all work itself out."

It'll all work out. What a stupid thing to say. Jez pulled away and glared at him. "How? How will this work itself out? How does this end in a good way?" she hissed. "I don't need your stupid clichés right now."

Sam stared at her.

"Jesus," he said. "I'm just trying to help. Whatever happens, you—we—will work something out. And whatever that thing is, next year, you'll move to Manchester like you planned anyway." He shrugged. "Yeah, it's horrible. But if you don't die, you'll probably cope. And I'll help you."

Jez's anger deflated; her shoulders slumped. She looked at the glass sliding doors of the hospital. "I don't want to go back in there," she said.

"I know," said Sam. "But you have to. We're big kids now. And I'll come with you."

They walked in silence toward the doors, which slid effortlessly apart, and then closed behind them.

• • •

He was still alive. It could go either way. Sangeeta had ended her shift and gone home. The doctor who had taken over told them that Jez's dad was still in a really bad way.

"But he's come this far," he said. "He's strong. That's good."

"Can I see him?" asked Jez.

"In a bit," said the doctor. "Wait here, and I'll find someone to come and get you." He disappeared down the sterile corridor. Jez and Sam watched him go in silence. Jez swallowed hard.

"Do you want a drink or anything?" Sam asked eventually.

"Nah," said Jez. "No, you're all right." She looked around and sat down on a grubby plastic chair and stared at the floor.

Sam knew that look. "I might go for a walk," he said.

• • •

The hospital newsagent and gift shop was pretty lame. Sam wasn't expecting a full range of satirical print media, but complete thoughts that couldn't be expressed in monosyllables would have been a start. He looked at the newspapers on offer. The *Daily Mail*, he thought. *For when* telegraph *has too many syllables.*

Nothing to read, nothing to be done. No way of propping Jez up. He'd said they'd get through it, but he really wasn't that sure. He felt as though he was living minute to minute, and it wasn't thrilling. It was depressing. Dying horribly, without having left the town you grew up in for longer than two weeks at a time (and then only to go to Majorca)? Jesus Christ. His eyes rolled involuntarily. *The things I do for you, Elliot,* he thought.

His eye fell on the local rag. Twice a week, it came out. Not enough happened for it to publish more often. Last week had been—

Well. It wasn't last week anymore. This week it was—

He frowned and picked up the paper. MEETING OVER LOSS OF FOUR JOBS IN ARDENCOTE screamed the headline. *Guess they needed a break after the blood and guts of last week,* thought Sam. *Not like there's any following up to do, especially if the supernatural people have anything to do with it.* What had caught his eye, though, was the small story below the fold. LOCAL LAWYER DISAPPEARS, it whispered, much more subtly.

Sam skimmed the story. *Disappeared... family missing... pools of blood discovered...* His heart skipped a beat. Greenwood.

It was Cat's family. The story was about Cat's family. But it didn't make any sense. Cat had been at school the day before, hadn't she? The paper only came out once a week. He looked at the date on the paper. It was that week's.

This is insane, Sam told himself. *Part of the dream. Sleep deprivation taking over.* But he knew. It was the same feeling he'd had when he saw the message on the bottom of his essay. The likelihood of him or Jez ever seeing Cat Greenwood again was extremely slim. *Pools of blood.* It was all wrong.

Sam pulled out his phone and tapped "Catherine Greenwood Arden" into Google. The results threw up her Facebook page and a list of petitions she'd signed in the past year. Nothing more.

He looked again at the paper. Almost immediately the ink of the story pooled and reformed.

You think you're pretty smart, don't you? it read. *You were warned. You're fair game now, you know that?*

"Yeah," said Sam, out loud. "I know that." The cashier in the shop looked up at him and glared.

Was Cat dead? Had they killed her family, too, and then made it appear as though nothing had happened? He felt suddenly cold. The ink snaked across the page.

This is how things are now, it read. *You should get used to it. Quickly.*

Sam dropped the paper and walked quickly out of the shop.

● ● ●

Sarah opened her eyes.

She was in a circular room. She looked up. A *cylindrical* room, she corrected herself. She couldn't see the ceiling. The walls stretched upward as far as she could see, petering out into darkness.

She didn't want to look down.

The room was filled with mirrors—framed mirrors—floating around the walls and in mid-air. She was lying on a couch, which was also floating.

Odd.

She sat up carefully. Her body felt numb and as she caught a glimpse beyond the edge of the couch, her stomach lurched. The room seemed to extend as far down as it did up. She couldn't see a floor. Just walls and mirrors.

Everything was slightly fuzzy. She rubbed her eyes, and it didn't help.

"Hello, Sarah," said a voice behind her.

She turned around and saw an elderly woman standing behind her in the mirror on the wall. She was short, with shoulder-length curly grey hair and sharp ice-blue eyes. She reminded Sarah a little of her grandmother, more in her manner than in her appearance.

Sarah turned around and looked. There was no one there. The woman only appeared in the mirror.

"Auntie Dot?" she said, not quite sure.

"No," said the woman. "Try again."

"I don't think I have a lot of time," said Sarah. "Who are you?"

"Nan," said the woman, raising her chin. "Nan Trevelyan."

"Sarah," said Sarah, extending her hand. "Sarah Trevelyan. We must be related. I don't know who you are." She looked around her again. "I don't know where we are, either."

"The Crowsbrook Witch," said Nan. "I was."

Sarah's eyes widened. "You imprisoned the demon in the Foxglove Pond."

"I did," said Nan. "For a while."

"For centuries," said Sarah. "Nice work." If this woman was truly a Trevelyan, she'd appreciate the value of understatement.

"Not bad," said Nan. "It's out now, I reckon?"

"Yes; how did you know?"

"Rumblings," said Nan. "In the Earth. You know well about witches and land. We're connected. Especially if we're buried in it," she added.

Sarah realized something, and her mouth dropped open. "You're buried on the north side," she said. "Of the churchyard. It was your gravestone, wasn't it? The one that cracked?"

"Ar," said the old witch. She seemed slightly smug.

"I'm pretty sure you're not supposed to do things like that. The world of the living and the world of the dead are separate. Once you cross, you're in the Ethereal world. You don't come back, except under very specific circumstances. Or you shouldn't. That's what they taught me." She paused. "That was what my grandmother taught me."

Nan snorted. "I were never much of a one for rules," she said. "But I needed you to *know*, missy. That something were up. Bloody spiders couldn't tell you."

"You know about the spiders? How did you know about the spiders? You're not supposed to have any contact with the world of the living except..."

Nan grunted. "Badgerley. That youngster couldn't keep his mouth shut if his life depended on it. Lucky for him," she added, "it *doesn't*."

Sarah's mind was racing. "He told you about the spiders," she said. "You broke the gravestone. Why did you break the gravestone?"

"Warning," said Nan. "That thing was coming back. Deals with the Devil aren't so shiny when they can't offer you every-thing and the slop bucket for your worldly pleasure. But when they can, well." She sniffed. "Better watch out."

"We killed the demon," Sarah said. "It's done. It won't come back again."

Now it was Nan's turn to look surprised. "Killed it?" she said. "How in the name of Christ did you kill it?"

Sarah explained about the weapons, and her great-aunt's drive to trade and collect. Nan grunted again.

"Worked," she said, shrugging. "That thing's dead: all that matters. But that's not the end of it, you know. Dot was—" She looked over her shoulder. "I can't talk about it," she said. "It's not that I'm forbidden; I don't give a ploughboy's fart for that. But they can *hear*. Even in here. All I can say is that Dot *knew*. You've got to be ready, my girl. And that thing wasn't running around wreaking chaos of its own accord, either."

"Yes," said Sarah. "Someone's controlling it. *Was* controlling it," she corrected.

"Someone signed a pact with the Devil," said Nan. "What you did doesn't make that go away."

"No," said Sarah. "I know that." She looked around her. Her head hurt. "This place isn't real, is it?" she asked.

"'Real'?" said Nan. "You know better than that. 'Real.' Don't make me laugh."

Sarah felt as though her mind was slipping away from her; she struggled to find purchase. Something her grandmother had mentioned in passing came back to her.

"This is the Astral Plane, isn't it?" she said. "Somewhere in between 'real' and 'not.'"

"Don't try and explain it," said Nan. "You don't have time, and neither of us needs to know."

"Why am I here now?" asked Sarah. "I've been doing astral work for years. I've never managed anything this vivid." Her grandmother's books had promised intense visions, transcendent scenes. Sarah had managed to make her dreams more vivid with herbs; the dreams were mildly prophetic. But she had always assumed that visions on the scale of what the writers were describing was tinged heavily with poetic licence. And yet everything around her looked as real as it would be if she were awake. There was a certain softness to it—a lack of focus around the edges of the mirrors, for example—but the impossible room that went on forever was as prosaic as her living room in the earthly world.

Nan shrugged. "You're a witch," she said. "You work it out. What have you never done before?"

Sarah went cold.

Harm only as you must.

"It was self-defence—" she began.

"*They* know that," said Nan. "And here you are."

"This is a *reward?*" shot back Sarah. "For *killing?*"

"Nope," said Nan, her lips tight. "For trying to stop the goons. Giving it your best shot and all that."

Sarah frowned. "That doesn't make any sense," she said. "Why now?"

"You're in trouble, my girl." Nan sat next to Sarah on the couch in the mirror. Sarah turned to look beside her; there was no one there.

"What do you mean, 'in trouble'?" she said.

"Unless you get a message to someone out there," said Nan, "you're going to end up in the same room as an ex-human who's enjoying a symbiotic relationship with one of the Seven Princes of Hell, and when you killed that demon, you took his favourite toy away. And they're both *cross*. And no one knows where you are." She coughed. "No one on your side, anyway."

"I'm unconscious," said Sarah, mostly to herself.

"Well done," said Nan.

"How can I get a message to someone else when I'm unconscious?"

"You're talking to someone who's *dead*," said Nan. "I'm sure you can work it out."

A small flash of irritation flickered in Sarah. There were times when it would be so much easier if her family would just help her out directly. *Talking to someone who's dead* wasn't a great help.

Or was it? She had spoken to Badgerley, and he was dead, but that had been in the churchyard, one of the gates between the living and the dead. This was more like a dream. This place...

This place was different. Suddenly she understood.

"This place isn't a gate between the living and the dead," said Sarah. "It's a gate between different levels of consciousness. Or unconsciousness. If you want to reach the living, they have to be unconscious too." She had it now. "Asleep. Knocked out. In a coma. Something that shuts off the conscious mind."

"Good girl," said Nan, nodding approvingly. "Make a proper witch of you yet, we will. But you need help and fast. Who can help you?"

Jez and Sam, thought Sarah. Except Jez and Sam were at the hospital, without a driver's licence between them and no access to a car. Perfect.

"Two people," she said. "But there might be problems."

"All you can do is get a message to them," said Nan. "You'll have to trust them to do the rest. Oh, and don't forget the spiders." She turned to go.

"Wait!" called Sarah. "You can't go yet! How am I supposed to get a message to Jez? What about the spiders? How does this work?"

The Crowsbrook Witch faded from sight in the mirror and was gone.

Sarah yelled in frustration. Her reflection screamed back at her silently from a hundred reflections.

FUCK.

Why did everything have to be such a big mystery? Why couldn't anyone just show her how to do something? Give her a couple of tips instead of a cryptic message when she was already in trouble? She hated that about the supernatural world: the secrecy, the obscure texts, the constant mystification.

Her eyes fell on her hands. Suddenly, she found herself checking her arms, running her hands through her hair, looking in the cuffs of her shirt. For the first time in days, there was no spider to be found. She was completely alone.

I NEED HELP, she screamed silently. For a moment, she thought she heard an echo. *Help, help, help.*

"Why?" she yelled out loud. "Why will no one help me? Why does everything have to be such a big secret?"

Because if everyone could do what you've learned to do, Sarah, she heard her grandmother say—in her mind or out loud?—*the world would end.*

It was poor comfort. She was just one person after all. For all she knew, she was the only one left. For miles, at least. She fell back on the couch, overwhelmed, her throat tight. She would not let herself cry.

She couldn't. She had to get a message to Jez.

She stared into the nearest mirror and began to try to connect.

The room around her faded into darkness. Her mind stretched out toward the mirror. Her eyes and her mind's eye became one. The mirror darkened, clouded, and cleared; Sarah saw before her the hospital, from the car park. Like a shade, she floated through the main doors.

Holy shit. So this is the Astral Plane.

The place was deserted. It was uncanny. For some reason, she had expected it to be bustling with life and energy and careful, quiet, occult efficiency. But the place was deserted.

She tried to run down the hall, forgetting she was floating. Her legs thrashed wildly under her and the corridor swam. She searched frantically for signs—any signs—of life.

Was this the real hospital? How could it be? She tried to swear in frustration; no sound came out of her mouth.

How was she supposed to contact anybody when she could barely move and couldn't speak? In frustration, she threw herself against a wall but felt only soft resistance, as if it were a mattress.

When she looked up, there was a man standing in the corridor.

He was wearing a hospital gown and he was looking straight at her.

"I can see you," he said. His voice was muffled, but discernible.

Sarah's head jerked up.

"You can see me?" she said. "Who are you?"

"Where is everybody?" said the man. "They were here. Where are they now?"

Oh, no. The truth dawned on Sarah.

The man was already beginning to fade.

"Where are you going?" he called. "Come back! What's happening to me? I don't understand..." His voice faded into silence. Sarah stared at the space where he had recently been standing.

The unconscious mind. She could only see people who weren't conscious. For whatever reason.

Fast, she thought. *I need to move fast.* Every part of her willed it. Without thinking, she broke into a run and set off down the corridor.

Rooms to the left of her. Rooms to the right. Many of them empty. The temperature changed as she ran: the air around her was cool, punctuated by warm spots.

People, she thought. *I'm running through people.* People she couldn't see or hear. She wondered if they felt her as she moved through the hospital, what it would feel like: a cold spot, the feeling of being watched, a goose walking over your grave, as her grandmother would have said. Every so often, she could hear calling from the rooms: desperate voices calling for help, calling to be recognized, for company.

She couldn't stop. She had to find Jez and Sam. She had to find someone who could help her. And she was working against the clock; she had no idea how long she'd been out cold. Did time even work the same way, on the Astral Plane?

Shit. If only she had more information.

She slowed to a walk and threw herself against a wall in anger, sliding down it until she was sitting on the floor.

Think. Think.

She couldn't think. She was all out of ideas. She put her head on her knees.

When she looked up, she saw a familiar-looking green bag lying on the floor next to an empty chair through the doorway of the room opposite. And lying in the bed next to the chair was a man staring at the ceiling.

Sarah recognized the blue eyes and dark hair as well.

"Hello?" she said, getting to her feet and approaching the doorway. "Hello?"

The man didn't move.

"Hello?" said Sarah again. She stood next to the bed and looked down at him.

He was a mess. His face was cut and bruised, and he had stitches holding together a gaping wound on the side of his head; they'd shaved part of his hair away in order to patch him up, and there was a bandage hiding some presumably worse injury on his forehead. But there was still enough of a family resemblance for Sarah to be certain that the man was Jez's father.

He was struggling to speak. When he managed it, the words came out as a croak.

"Who are you?" he managed. "What happened?"

"You're in the hospital," said Sarah. "You were in a car accident."

The man tried to clear his throat. "Not an accident," he muttered. "Attack. Something horrible."

"Yes," said Sarah. Her voice was grim. "It's dead now."

"Dead," said the man. He tried to clear his throat again and failed. "My daughter—"

"She's okay," said Sarah. "I'm taking care of her." She decided not to get into Jez's role in offing the slave-demon.

"Who are you?" said the man in the bed again. "You're the only person who's come."

"No," said Sarah. "No, I'm not. Your daughter came, she's here, she's probably here now—we just can't see her. But she's here. Her bag's here. Look." She pointed to the bag lying for-lornly on the floor, and then realized that he wouldn't be able to see it. Without thinking, she tried to pick it up. Her arm went straight through it.

"Her bag is here," she said, aware of how lame it sounded.

"Never leaves home without it," muttered the man. He winced in pain, and Sarah realized that he had attempted to smile.

"Sometimes," he said. "Sometimes I think I can hear her."

"You probably can," said Sarah.

There was a faint hiss behind her. She turned.

There was a faint, yet unmistakable outline in the chair. A mist. A form, taking shape, like smoke filling a glass.

Jez.

"She's falling asleep," said Sarah, out loud.

"What?" muttered the man lying on the bed. "Who? What?"

"She's falling asleep!" said Sarah. "She's knackered! She's falling asleep!"

She stepped toward the chair, calling Jez's name.

• • •

"Wake up!"

Jez started. Sam was shaking her shoulder. She stretched and winced, turning her head from side to side.

"Ow," she said, stretching her legs out from the hard plastic chair that stood next to her father's hospital bed. "My neck hurts." She looked hard at Sam. His face was grey. "Shit, what's the matter? What happened?"

"It's Cat," he said, under his breath and glancing at Jez's father. "It's really bad. It's horrible. That thing—the thing from last night—I'm pretty sure it killed her family before we..." He trailed off. "Her mum, her dad, her brother—"

Jez's face creased in horror. "Jamie's *nine!*"

Sam shook his head. "I know," he said. "All they found was blood. Lots of blood. They didn't find Cat or her family, but they're probably dead. We were too late. I've got nothing left, Jez," he said, and Jez noticed that, for the first time since she had known him, he had tears in his eyes. "I don't know what to say."

Jez put her hand on his arm. She felt sick with grief and terror. The room was silent, except for the beeps and hums of the machines monitoring Jez's father.

"Sorry I woke you," said Sam after a long time. "Do you want to get some sleep? There's a waiting room down the hall with a couch in it. I don't think anyone's was using it when I went past."

"Thanks," said Jez. "But no thanks. I should—" She paused. "I can't. Not after last night." She looked at her father. He lay still, breathing evenly.

"Yes, you can," said Sam. "It's just up—"

"I know where it is," said Jez. "It's okay. Thanks."

The machines carried on humming and beeping.

· · ·

The image of Jez had vanished. There for a brief moment, and then gone.

Damn it.

Sarah's concentration broke and she fell back on the couch. The hospital faded around her until once again, she was staring at the mirror that hung motionless in the air. She felt as though she had been exploring, searching for hours. And it was pointless. She hadn't found Sam. Or Jez. Or anyone else who could help. She had only found a dead man, who had faded away almost as soon as he had appeared, and a man in a coma who couldn't help her.

She didn't know where she was, physically. She didn't know what time it was, if it was morning, if it was evening. How likely would it be that Jez or Sam would be asleep? She didn't know. Since she had seen Nan in the mirror, she couldn't even be sure that she was still alive.

As a witch, she had a less confrontational relationship with death and its inevitability than most people. But she was still well aware that being alive was infinitely preferable.

Could she wait for Jez to fall asleep again? She would have no idea where to look for her. And she didn't have time. She needed to speak to someone in the real world right now. Someone in the real world. Someone unconscious, but someone who could get up and move. Someone who could come and find her.

There was no one.

Her stomach churned with rage. She had killed the fly demon, and seriously incapacitated an Asilida Ethereal, whatever he was. She had been determined to defeat them, and she had killed and intended to kill in order to do that; she had broken one of the few taboos that her grandmother had instilled in her, and in spite of it, in spite of the risk she had taken, she had failed. She felt sick. And now, no one would help her.

No. No one *could* help her. Jez and Sam *would* help, if they knew.

That's all you've got left? sneered a voice in her head. *Two kids without a driver's licence or a lick of common occult knowledge between them? Good luck.*

They *would* help, though, she thought.

She had sworn she would never work with other people— she had to stop herself referring to them as *civilians*—again. It was too risky. Too dangerous. Her conscience couldn't take it. She had been born to this, raised for it. No one had ever explicitly told her, but it had always been the elephant in the room: Trevelyans either died very old or *young*.

There was no one who could help her.

Would help her.

Could help her.

The words echoed in her mind, bouncing off the inside of her skull, sparking the ghost of a thought that her mind couldn't quite catch.

Who would? Who could?

There was someone. There *was*. It was a shot in the dark, but she knew where to find this person. And the chances that this person would be unconscious right now were high.

She stared into the mirror and cleared her mind. The mirror room faded around her and was replaced with a scruffy living room with a threadbare carpet and a packet of open cigarettes next to a full ashtray and an ancient leather armchair.

The friar lay in front of her, snoring.

• • •

She stared at him for a moment, waiting until the room was as clear as she could make it. Then she stared at the burning cigarette.

Concentrate. Would what she wanted to do even be possible?

Fall. It needs to fall.

The cigarette wobbled crazily back and forth and then fell into the lip on the edge of the ashtray designed to hold it.

Damn it!

She focused all her will on the unlit end of the cigarette.

FALL.

The ember at the end of the dog-end seemed to lift for a moment. Or had she imagined it?

FALL, DAMN YOU!

She took a deep breath and willed it with everything she had. The smouldering cigarette tilted upward, and then flipped over onto the carpet. It rolled a short way, and then began to burn a hole.

Stage one: complete.

"Hey," said Sarah. "Hey! Father Dominic!" She hoped she wouldn't wake him up in real life and have to watch him disappear, like she'd watched Jez. That couldn't be possible, could it?

"Hey," she said again. Without thinking, she put her hand forward and shook him.

He was solid. She had made contact. She drew her hand back in surprise.

Learned something new about the Astral Plane, did we? Nan's voice rang in her mind. She pushed it aside.

"Father Dominic," she said. "Father Dominic. I need your help."

The old priest grunted and opened his eyes. Then he frowned and squinted at her.

"The witch," he said. "Sarah. What are you doing here?"

Sarah had to think on her feet.

"I'm not here," she said, speaking quickly. "This is a dream. Just a very vivid one. I need your help, and this time, you're going to give it to me."

The priest made a sound that was part sigh, part grunt.

"I already told you," he said. "My hands are tied."

"How about a deal then?" said Sarah. "When you wake up—and you will wake up in time, because I'll make sure of it—you're going to find your carpet on fire. A fire started by one of your dog ends. You shouldn't smoke if you're about to fall asleep." She stood back to reveal a small tongue of flame rising from the edge of the bone-dry rug.

"Threaten me with fire, would you?" said the priest, frowning like thunder and raising his chin.

"You're too deeply asleep to wake up by yourself," said Sarah, hoping blindly that it was true. "Are you going to help me, or am I going to walk through the wall and let you burn?"

Behind her, the flame grew, silently.

"All right," said the priest. "What do you want?"

"You drive, don't you?" said Sarah. "There's a forty-year-old Morris Minor in front of the church."

"Yes," said the priest. "I drive. Just. They keep threatening to take my bloody licence away. But they haven't yet."

"Good," said Sarah. "I need you to go over to the hospital, find Sam—the boy who was here with me the other day—and a girl called Jez. She'll have a green bag with her. You need to give them a lift to Crowsbrook. To—" *To where?* she thought. They must have taken her to Carpenter's. Where was that again? "Take them to the shop. Tell them to find out where Carpenter lives, because that's where I'll be. Tell them I'm trapped. Tell them to stop Carpenter. Tell them it'll be really dangerous."

"That's quite the message," said the priest, looking her up and down. "How am I supposed to find these two children in a hospital of that size?"

"Her dad's there," said Sarah. She could feel the heat of the fire behind her. "Elliot. Their name is Elliot. One of them will be in his room. I have to go. Promise you'll do this for me."

"Apparently, you're about to save my life," said the priest, drily. "Under the circumstances, it would seem churlish not to."

"It's just a dream," said Sarah. "You can make up your mind when you wake up." She stared into the face of a three-foot-high statue of the Blessed Virgin, smiling beatifically from the mantelpiece.

Nothing personal, she thought, and willed for all she was worth.

The statue fell to the hearth with a crash. The priest woke, coughing; the room was full of smoke. He waved his hand in front of his face as he got to his feet and began stamping out the fire on the carpet, spluttering all the while until the fire was out. Then, he pulled some dead flowers out of a vase on the windowsill and tipped half a pint of filthy water onto the burned patch on the rug, just to be sure. There was a hiss, and some steam, and then silence.

Father Dominic stared at the rug for a long time. He looked up, just to make sure the room was empty. Then he looked at the pieces of the Blessed Virgin's statue on the hearth. Then the hole in the rug again.

"Witch," he muttered to himself. He picked up his walking stick from the side of the chair and went to look for his car keys.

The carpet steamed for a bit and then went out.

• • •

Sarah fell back on the couch, exhausted.

"Not bad." Nan's voice. Sarah's eyes sprang open. But when she looked around the room, she found she was still alone.

• • •

"So now what?" said Sam, closing his tatty copy of *Brideshead Revisited.*

They were still in Jez's father's room. Hours had passed, and he was still unconscious. The machines droned around them.

"I don't know," said Jez. "I'm exhausted. I want to sleep. But I have to stay here."

"You don't have to," said Sam. "And they might not let you stay overnight."

"I don't know how I'm going to get home," said Jez. "I don't even know if I should go home, if he's not there and they know—" She swallowed. "I don't want to be there by myself. I don't know what they'd do. What they'd send."

"We can go to Sarah's," said Sam. "I'll tell my mum we're at yours. She doesn't have to know what's going on. And Sarah said that the wards on her cottage could stop a—" He found himself lost for words. "Well. A really big occult thing, anyway."

"I don't have any money, Sam," said Jez. "You want to start walking now?"

"I could call my mum," said Sam. But they both knew he wouldn't.

"I can't leave him," said Jez. "I don't have anyone else. Relatives, I mean," she added, catching the look in Sam's eye. "There isn't anyone else. No one's close by."

There was a loud explosion from outside. They both looked up. Muffled swearing was coming from the car park.

"—on a *mission*," came a voice from the corridor. "Man of the cloth. Park where I want…won't be a minute. God bless you."

"I know that voice," said Sam, incredulously. Jez looked at him blankly. "That's the friar."

The two of them peered through the doorway to see the friar, in full habit, wheezing down the corridor at a surprising clip, pushing furniture out of his way with his cane and apparently oblivious to the coterie of nurses and security guards still trying to persuade him that leaving a Morris Minor in front of the emergency entrance was very much Not What Jesus Would Do.

"I need to find Mr. Elliot," he bellowed. "Where's Mr. Elliot?"

"In here," said Sam. "Hello, Father."

The friar grunted. "Ah. You. We have to go. And her. To Crowsbrook."

"What?" Jez stared at the ancient priest, who was coughing and spitting into a grubby handkerchief. "Why? Who *are* you?"

"He's the friar," said Sam. "The Franciscan. And he's been no bloody help at all, so far."

"The witch sent me," said Father Dominic, struggling to catch his breath. "She's in trouble. She needs you to go back to Crowsbrook. Now. I'm supposed to give you a lift. Pain of death."

"Did she phone you?" said Sam. "She doesn't have a mobile. Or a car."

"She wasn't even there," said the friar. "But she made me *promise*, damn her. My car's outside. You need to come with me."

Chapter 19

Sam looked at Jez. Jez looked at Sam. They both looked at the friar, who glared back at them.

"What do you mean, she made you promise?" said Sam. "Where is she? Why was she with you?"

The friar cleared his throat. "She wasn't," he said shortly. "I don't know where she is. She's somewhere in Crowsbrook."

"Crowsbrook isn't *that* big," said Jez. "Wait. Wait, wait. Wait. She spoke to you, although she wasn't there, and made you promise to give us a lift and told you to come here?"

"She said she needed help," said the friar. "Are you going to help or not?"

"Who are you?" said Jez, baffled. "Father." She turned to Sam. "Sam, who's your friend?"

"This is Father Dominic," said Sam. He looked even paler than usual. "He's a Franciscan friar. We were visiting him to ask for help when you were here the first time and the thing came after you."

The three of them stood there in confused silence. Sam broke it.

"You wouldn't help her before," said Sam. "Why now? What changed?"

"My house nearly burned down," said Father Dominic. "I was asleep. She woke me up. On the condition that I help her."

"She visited you in a dream?" Jez looked incredulous.

The friar sighed. "Something like that. You're not a Catholic?"

Jez snorted.

"Did *the Firm* change their minds?" said Sam, in a voice that could have frozen lava.

"The Firm doesn't know," said the friar. "Forty minutes ago, I was asleep. Thirty minutes ago, I was putting out a fire on my living room carpet. I'd have been here ten minutes ago if my housekeeper didn't keep moving my damned keys. We have to go. The witch said it was urgent."

"She is *alive*, though?" said Jez.

The priest shrugged and coughed back a pellet of phlegm. "Don't know. Let's go."

Jez stayed where she was. For the second time in twenty-four hours, she was being asked—or was it forced?—to leave her dad's side. She wanted to be with him. *Needed* to be with him. She had no one else, and neither did he.

"What if he wakes up," she said to Sam, "and I'm not here? What if he—"

She had to stop. She couldn't think it, let alone say it.

"What if I'm not here?" she said again.

She thought of Sarah. Sarah who had shown her that even her boring, awful home town could be worth protecting. Who had come back for her when the slave-demon had come after her. Who was ready to give up everything to protect people and places she didn't know, people that didn't care about her, didn't even know she existed. Because it was the right thing to do, even though she resented it like hell.

Who was up against Hell. And on her own.

Jez turned back to her father, lying peacefully on the bed.

"I'll be back soon," she whispered, and kissed him on the forehead.

The other two were silent.

Jez stood for a moment and then turned.

"Right," she said, her voice shaking. "Let's go."

Father Dominic, it turned out, could move with surprising speed when he had to, cane and mild limp notwithstanding. Within minutes, they were outside the hospital staring at the friar's elderly Morris Minor.

"This," said Sam, "has to be the only car on the planet more embarrassing than Sarah's Allegro."

Father Dominic drew himself up to his full height, three inches shorter than Sam's six feet.

"*This*," he rumbled in fury, "is a *far* superior car to the Austin Allegro. Pull your head out of your bloody books and watch some bloody *Top Gear* once in a while, boy. Now get in."

Jez and Sam did as they were told, scrambling into the tattered but clean back seat of the Morris. The car reeked of cigarettes. The friar pulled a packet of Player's out of a pocket hidden within the folds of his robe and lit one before throwing his cane into the passenger seat and manoeuvring himself painfully behind the wheel, triggering a coughing fit that resulted in much gasping and spitting into his handkerchief. Jez and Sam exchanged glances.

"If she's still alive now," muttered Sam, "I hope she can hold out for another decade or so."

The car spluttered into life and Jez and Sam were thrown back against the back of the seat as Father Dominic dropped the hammer and shot out of the car park.

The contrast between this and their last drive to Crowsbrook was stark. Before, they had anticipated their return to the village would equal safety; the danger lay in the darkness, in the woods and on the road. In daylight, the road was clear, if equally empty, and the danger, they both knew, lay in wait for them when they entered the village's boundaries once again. As they passed under the trees that marked the beginning of the woods, both of them shuddered internally; both kept a look out, among the trees, for signs and marks of the epic battle that had taken place there the night before. But other than a couple of skid marks on the road—marks, Jez thought, that Sarah's car might not even have made—there was no sign of an accident or a confrontation. Even the broken glass next to the tree where the Allegro had finally come to rest had vanished.

Perhaps, Jez thought, they were just going too fast to see it. It was certainly feasible. Father Dominic drove in silence, with a look of harried determination on his face. Whatever had happened to him to make him change his mind about helping Sarah, it had clearly rattled him deeply.

And they still had to find Sarah. And then help her once they'd found her.

"Sam," whispered Jez. "What do we do next? How do we find her? How do we help her?"

Father Dominic sniffed. "You have to go to the shop," he said loudly. "She said to tell you to go to the shop."

"How did you hear me?" said Jez, at her normal volume.

"Years of teaching catechism classes," said the friar with a sniff. "She said you had to go to the shop and find out where Carpenter lived, because that's likely where she'd be."

"She didn't *know?*" said Jez. "How could she not know?"

"I don't *know*," said the friar, testily. "Wandering about the county without using one's body is not actually my field of expertise. Ask me an easy one, about transubstantiation or something. I'm just passing on the message."

"Carpenter's place would seem like a good place to start," said Sam. "What the hell do we do once we get there? If he has her, how *can* we help her? Aren't we basically talking Prince of Hell, plus Ethereal goons, versus two sixth-formers, a friar, and a clapped-out Morris Minor?"

"Car's in excellent condition," muttered Father Dominic. It backfired, and lurched forward.

"Get you," said Jez, to Sam. "'Ethereals.' Were you in her library again?"

For a moment, it was as if the witch, the friar, the hospital, Cat, Jez's father, were all in another dimension—Jez and Sam grinned. Then Jez pulled herself together.

"Weapons," she said. "We'll need weapons. We'll go to the shop, find out where Carpenter lives, go back to Sarah's, go through the trunks, and then—"

She stopped.

"And then," said Sam, "we do what we have to do."

• • •

Adam was sitting in his kitchen. Brown was sitting opposite him. Adam had made two cups of tea, which sat in front of them, full. Adam stirred his compulsively with a teaspoon.

"Was there something about which you wished to speak to me?" asked Brown.

Adam cleared his throat. There was. The girl, the—whatever it was that had happened in the basement, Greenwood's death, the existence of the Minion; he could *accept* all of it. He was living a different existence now. He had power. People who said money was power were wrong. Power got you beyond where money could get you. Power could get you *anything*.

Brown worked for the most powerful organization that Adam had ever encountered. For the first time in his life, he felt as though he had *access*, access to whatever he wanted. He understood why Carrington was different, why he smiled in the way he did when his friends at the bar were guffawing over some outrageous stroke of luck. It was because he knew that it wasn't luck. Carrington lived a life without risk, because he had power. And now that power was Adam's too.

What he didn't understand was *why*. He'd read the contract. He was "hosting," yes, fine, whatever that was. But whatever it was went beyond payment in money; sure, Brown's lot would reap part of the benefit from the facility they were building, but that payoff seemed minuscule compared to what *he* was getting. Why would they work with *him?* Why did they need to?

It was bothering him. Sure he could brush off the nagging question, tell himself that he was just trying to sabotage himself, that he was as worthy of success as any of those other guys, that he *deserved* everything that Brown and his lot were bringing to the table. But the question remained.

"Brown," he said, "there's still some stuff I don't understand."

Brown inclined his head slightly.

"The contract.I read it. Looks great. Can't argue with your organization's effectiveness."

Brown inclined his head again.

"What is it, Mr. Carpenter," he said, "that you are having trouble understanding?"

Adam cleared his throat and looked Brown in the eye.

"What do you get out of all of this?" he said "Hosting. I host. I am the host. We established that. What is it that you get?"

"Is it of consequence?" said Brown, evenly. "You get your success either way."

"You guys are amazing," said Adam. "You can do anything. I've seen that. What I want to know is, why would you? Why work with people like me—" he winced internally as he said it "—when you could easily just operate on your own?"

Brown ran his tongue around the outside of his teeth.

"That," he said, "is something of an assumption." He smiled, and Adam was left with the impression that Brown needed the practice. "This is somewhat irregular," he continued. "The practices of our organization, outside of what we have outlined in your contract are, as I am sure you will understand, highly confidential under normal circumstances."

"Of course," said Adam. "Wouldn't do for everyone to be that effective, eh?" He attempted a smile. It was less effective than Brown's.

"Indeed," said Brown. "It would not. We are—" he tapped his finger twice on the countertop "—*highly* competitive."

Adam looked at his tea. He was starting to feel dizzy again, and he didn't want to think about what had happened the last time he'd…well, got sick. Brown was fudging? Whatever. He'd tried. He'd just have to wonder.

"Your material presence," said Brown. "Your existence."

Adam looked up sharply.

"Please understand," said Brown, "that these circumstances are highly exceptional. The loss of the Minion is, I understand, an inconvenience for you, but please trust me, Mr. Carpenter: it is a far greater issue for us." He drummed his fingers on the countertop, and then stopped, abruptly. "Our ability to operate in—" he seemed to think for a moment "—the world effectively is predicated on consent. Without consent, we are—we can only ever be—excluded."

"Consent?" said Adam. "Whose consent?"

"Human," said Brown. The word hung in the air like a predatory bird.

Adam felt a jolt of panic. He knew—of *course* he knew—that the things that had been happening weren't…normal. But this—

He looked at the man sitting in his kitchen, stirring a now-cold cup of tea.

Not human.

"And you—" he started.

"No," said Brown with a note of irritation in his voice. He checked himself. "We are—" He stopped. "Mr. Carpenter," he began, "since we are having a frank discussion about these matters, it behoves me to inform you that it is necessary, since the Minion is lost, to alter the terms of your contract slightly. We will need you to increase your contribution to the agreement by a small amount."

"What?" said Adam. "Why? How?"

"We needed the Minion," said Brown. "More than you did. And now, in its absence—"

"What?" said Adam again. "What do you need?"

At that moment, both of his knees dislocated with a popping sound. Adam screamed in agony. Brown remained calm.

"A slightly greater proportion of your physical manifestation," he said. "Your body."

The upper halves of Adam's legs were being pulled upward and compressed by an invisible force shrinking the hard tissue. He could feel the metatarsals and phalanges of his toes pulling out and twisting together, the bones cracking and creaking as they broke, lengthened, and reformed. He howled. The pain was at the threshold of what any human body could bear. He could feel his consciousness becoming fuzzy.

"You will, of course," he could hear Brown saying, "retain a portion of control…"

Oh, God. Oh, God. Nausea overcame him and he sank to the ground.

"You will need to eat soon," he heard Brown say, from far away.

"My legs," moaned Adam. "My legs."

"Do not worry, Mr. Carpenter," he heard. "We will deal with the world outside from now on."

Through the fog that was smothering his conscious mind, he heard a familiar *click*.

Front door…

The front door?

The front door.

Julia…

"Adam?" she called. "Adam? Darling?"

He whimpered in pain. His last coherent thought when he heard her walk into the kitchen and scream was that he hadn't wanted her to see him like this.

Then, driven by instinct, hunger, and preternatural strength, he pulled her toward him, and, for both of them, everything went black.

• • •

Brown watched Adam feed, and then poured his tea down the sink and washed the cup. He left it on the draining board.

• • •

In the mirror room, Sarah was trying desperately to stay awake. Her eyelids were heavy and her mind kept wandering.

Focus. She couldn't even tell if it was Nan or just her inner monologue anymore. *What else do you need to do?*

The door. Jez wouldn't want to go to Carpenter's place unarmed. Neither of the kids were stupid.

She looked into the mirror for the last time. The room faded around her, replaced by her own living room. Using the last vestiges of her willpower, she stared at the deadbolt and willed it to move.

The bolt twitched, and then flipped open with a quiet *click*.

The living room faded into the mirror room. And then the mirror room faded into darkness.

• • •

The Morris screeched to a halt in front of the village shop. Sam and Jez leaped out of the back and shot through the shop door, setting the bells clanging.

"Slow down, kids!" bellowed Rose from the back. "School out early, is it?"

"What day is it?" Sam hissed at Jez.

"Yes!" chirped Jez. "Free period. Extra study time, because of exams. We thought we'd get more done at home."

"Whatever you say," said Rose. "But they never used to let you out at half time in my day. You looking for study food?"

Sam picked up two Double Deckers and a Toffee Crisp. "Yes," he said. "Good for the brain, this stuff. Takes your mind off what you're doing." Jez could tell he was frantically searching for a way to ask where Adam Carpenter lived in the village without looking awkward.

"Actually, I've got a question for you," she said, scrabbling equally frantically. "I'm doing a project on soil samples and property development, and I wanted to talk to someone who knows about it. Adam Carpenter still lives in the village, right?" She could see Sam looking at her, baffled. *Oh, shut up*, she thought. *We don't have time to be convincing.*

"Soil samples?" said Rose. "God, the things they teach you in school these days. I don't think Adam does any of that stuff himself, though. He has people doing it for him. Probably sends it to labs and stuff. Why does he need soil samples?"

"But he'd know the processes, right?" said Jez, ignoring the question, her voice growing desperate. "It'd be really helpful to speak to him. I need an A in—" she floundered "—geology." Sam was looking at her as if she were out of her mind.

"Well, I suppose it couldn't hurt," said Rose. "Although I'd just look it up on the Internet, if I were you. Is that cheating? Do you need geology to be a doctor?"

"Yes," said Jez. "Absolutely, these days. Does he live close to here?"

Rose pursed her lips and exhaled. "He's not *too* far away," she said. "He's on Sycamore Lane. In the big house, behind the wall. You know the one, right? With the gate."

Sam slapped down a couple of pound coins for the chocolate. "Yes," he said.

"Thanks!" Jez added, over her shoulder. The bells clanged madly and the door slammed behind them.

Rose stared after them, mouth slightly open.

"Kids," she said out loud, eventually. "Bloody mad, the lot of them."

• • •

"This is crazy," said Sam, as they crashed through the door of Sarah's cottage. "How in the name of God are we supposed to know what's an effective occult weapon against one of the Seven Princes of Hell?" Father Dominic had stayed in the car, keeping the engine running; Jez and Sam moved as quickly as they could up the wrought-iron spiral staircase, which wobbled dangerously. "Where did she say the trunks were?"

"In the spare room," said Jez, putting her hand on the door. "Just look for anything sharp and pointy and uncomplicated." She pushed the door, which creaked and swung open.

Myriad spiders froze momentarily in their tracks.

Jez's mouth dropped open in horror. Her eyes went wide.

"*Je*-sus," breathed Sam.

The room was a tangle of giant cobwebs. The ceiling was covered by layers of grey gossamer at least six inches thick. The spiders, almost as one, headed for the corners in a scrambling, scattered mass.

Sarah had been taking good care of them. The exodus to the upper corners of the room revealed a heap of dry bones on a plate on the floor, picked clean.

"Chicken?" said Sam. "Spiders eat chicken?"

"How many flies would you have to catch to feed this many spiders?" said Jez, absently. She put her hand up and brushed away the sticky silk covering the doorway, then wiped her hand on her skirt.

The spiders didn't react. But she had the distinct sense that they were watching her. As she stepped into the room, the remaining spiders on the floor scuttled away before her feet.

"Sam," she said. "Get in here. We need to look in the trunks."

"Yeah, no" said Sam, holding up his hands. "No. No spiders. That's fucking mental." He stepped back, out of the room, and closed the door hard behind him. "Try not to pick anything cursed," he yelled through the door.

The spiders shivered collectively at the bang.

The room was stuffy and the smell of the chicken bones was slightly rancid. There was a trunk under the window, and two along the wall adjoining. Jez flipped the nearest one open. It was full of things wrapped in brown paper. She started unwrapping.

Try not to pick anything cursed. That'd be the last thing they needed. Although most of this stuff looked like the kind of crap you'd find at an occult flea market.

Shrunken heads. A severed paw that looked as if it had come from a bear of some sort. A rope made out of some soft hair. A music box. A crystal ball that was surprisingly heavy for its size, along with a stand for it. A brass snake. *Goddammit.* She rummaged through the other two trunks. All the obvious weapons had been in Sarah's blue bag. God knew where that was. She swore again and headed out of the room.

"Thanks anyway," she said to the spiders, before closing the door.

Sam was waiting for her downstairs. He was holding something wrapped in a tea towel.

"Kitchen knife," said Sam, brandishing it. "Sharp and pointy and uncomplicated. Let's go."

• • •

Sarah opened her eyes. It didn't make a difference. She couldn't see anything. Wherever she was, it was pitch dark.

Was *this* real?

Her muscles ached. They had ached in the mirror room, though. She was lying on her side. On something hard. And her head hurt like hell.

She wriggled, as an experiment. She felt a ligature cut into her wrists, behind her back. She twitched her feet: her ankles were bound together as well.

This was reality. She was alive.

It was a start. But it wasn't good.

• • •

"Now what?" said Sam. They were back in the car and heading toward Sycamore Lane.

"What do you mean, 'now what?'"

"How do you break in somewhere without everyone knowing? How do we know that this place won't be crawling with Asilida people and neurotoxic flies and more giant killer slave-demons shaped a bit like flies? We don't. And it will be. So what do we do that doesn't result in us dying horribly within about ten seconds of trespassing—trespassing!—on Adam Carpenter's property?"

"I think," said Jez, "that we're pretty much going to have to make stuff up as we go along. I hope he doesn't have a crazy security system or anything."

"This is Crowsbrook," said Sam. "Not L.A. He probably has a burglar alarm at most."

"You'll drive yourselves mad," said Father Dominic, his eyes on the road, "trying to guess. Might as well wait until you get there and see what's what."

"There's nothing you can give us for protection?" said Sam. "Because it would be really helpful." For once, he wasn't being sarcastic. "I mean, anything. Spare crucifix or something."

The friar sighed. "I don't think," he said, "that a crucifix would help you, at this juncture. It's a symbol of faith. Faith you don't have. It won't do a damn thing. Excuse me." He picked up the crumpled packet from the dashboard and lit a cigarette, steering with one hand; the car wobbled on its course as he inhaled. "I can say a prayer for you," he offered.

"Can you say lots?" said Sam. He could practically hear Jez fuming, but it made him feel better.

They turned into Sycamore Lane. It was on the edge of the village, though the opposite edge to the Foxglove Pond. It was a quiet road, where the rolling fields of the Ardenshire country-side began; the houses grew fewer as they progressed.

Adam Carpenter's house was the last one.

Jez's heart was beating wildly as they pulled up outside the wrought-iron gate that imposed itself over the gap between the high fence around the property.

"This is where she is, then?" she said.

"I don't know," said the friar. "She said this was where she thought they were taking her. That's all I know."

Jez looked up at the house that loomed behind the fence. The curtains were all closed. Through the gate, they could see a large, black car parked in the driveway. The windows were tinted.

"Looks like someone's home," she said. "Now what?"

"We have to go and look for her," said Sam. "Jesus. Breaking and entering."

"You're kids," said the friar. "It's not the earthly authori-ties you have to worry about this time. Look at the house," he went on. "All of the windows that overlook the gate have their curtains closed. That's a good sign, no? No one's looking at the driveway, for a start."

Jez and Sam said nothing.

"I would come with you," said Father Dominic. "But I don't think I'd be the best person to have along on a break-and-enter expedition." He coughed, and the phlegm rattled in his lungs. "I can stay here with the engine running."

"Thanks," said Jez. In her heart, she suspected that if either of them came out of the house, that kid would come out walking—not running—or wouldn't come out at all. "You don't have to do that."

Father Dominic nodded slowly. "Yes," he said. "Yes, I do. It's the least I can do."

Sam looked at him. "You wouldn't help us, earlier," he said. "And you did what you said you would do for Sarah, even though there was no real reason for you to do that. You had a dream? Please. Even if you did have a dream, why would you change your mind? Why would you help us?"

Father Dominic was quiet for a long time. Finally, he took a drag on his cigarette and tapped the ash out of the car's window.

"Because," he said. He crushed the cigarette into the car's overflowing ashtray. "Dorothea Trevelyan was, essentially, a good woman. Now," he said. "good luck. I'll be round the corner if you need me. In case this thing goes off bang again. Bugger off, before you lose your nerve."

The two of them climbed out of the car, and then stood and watched as the ancient friar in his vintage car drove off along the twisting asphalt of Sycamore Lane until he headed around a bend and disappeared out of sight.

"First things first," said Sam, staring at the wrought-iron gate. "We have to get over that thing."

It was surprisingly easy, although noisier than either of them would have liked. The gate was chained shut, but rattled and clanked on its hinges as first Jez and then Sam found toe- and handholds in the elaborate metalwork. As Sam dropped the last two feet and landed on the gravel drive with a crunch, Jez looked nervously at the house. But none of the curtains twitched.

"Christ," she said. She felt as if there were a vise around her heart; it was difficult to breathe. "We have to find a way in."

"It's an old house," said Sam. "What do you think? Eighteenth century? It probably has a coal cellar or something."

From the direction of the house, they heard a distinct crunch of gravel. Jez froze. Sam shot between the fence and a bush, pulling Jez with him.

"Get *down!*" he hissed.

They peered through the leaves of their hiding place. A young man in an impeccable suit was talking in a low voice on a mobile phone in front of the shiny, black car.

"Have you seen that guy before?" whispered Sam. "Is that him? Is that Carpenter?"

"No," said Jez. She thought back to the demonstration, and Carpenter's fight with Cat's dad. *Oh, God. Cat's dad.* "Carpenter's shorter. Less skinny. Like, not fat, but like he works out a lot."

"So that guy is from Asilida?" said Sam, under his breath.

"I don't know," breathed Jez. "Probably. Let's assume yes and be careful, right?"

"Okay," said Sam. "So if Asilida are here, Sarah is probably here. And they don't have a fucking giant murdering flying demon thing on side anymore."

"No," said Jez. "They have one less. And that doesn't mean they're not dangerous."

"No," said Sam. "But they might be *less* dangerous: I'd be surprised if that guy can fly, for a start." He peered round the bush. "Also, it's 'one *fewer*.'"

Jez punched him on the arm. The man in the impeccable suit finished his phone call, slipped his phone into an inside pocket in his jacket, and crunched back toward the house. Sam breathed deeply.

"Okay," said Jez. "Let's try going around the back. On the grass." She pointed to the turf beside the gravel. It was wet and muddy, but it would be quiet.

"On three," she said, "we run, and we aim for *there*." She pointed to a space beside one of the first-floor windows, with a large wisteria vine growing up the side of the house next to it. It overlooked the garden. They wouldn't have to go back onto the gravel, and the vine would hide them as they looked around the back of the house.

"Gotcha," said Sam. "One. Two. *Three!*"

They broke cover and ran. The grass was slippery and the mud sucked at their feet; water splashed up over Jez's boots and soaked her calves. Sam was loping ahead of her, looking grim and pale. She lost her footing and momentarily slid knee-first into the mud, spitting a silent curse into the ground. She stumbled to her feet and made it to the vine, where Sam was waiting. He tried to cough with his mouth closed and ended up spluttering quietly.

"Cigarettes," he mouthed. "Gotta quit."

"Father Dominic seems to do okay," said Jez. "For a two-hundred-year-old friar." She crouched down beside the vine, making herself as small as possible, and twisted to look around the side of the house. Behind the house, the land fell away into a garden, and then a paddock, with a horse quietly munching wet grass in it. Jez looked at the building. French doors. Bay windows. And, at ground level, a few feet away, a small window.

"There's a basement or cellar or something," she whispered, turning back to Sam, who was still spluttering quietly. "Just around the corner. There's a window. It's small, though."

They crept around the corner of the house. Again, on the ground floor, curtains covered the windows. But there were no bushes back there to cover them.

"We'll have to be quick," said Jez. "If anyone spots us, we're toast." She looked at the window. It was the sliding kind. She tugged at the panel; it shifted slightly, but didn't open.

"What did you expect?" hissed Sam. "This is Crowsbrook. Everyone's middle-class and paranoid. Everything's nailed down."

"Give me a moment," Jez whispered back. She pushed the pane up, and it moved within the frame. There was a gap between the frame of the pane and the slide runner in which it sat. She fished in her pocket and brought out a pocket knife. She flipped open the blade and stuck it in between the frame and the slider. Her hands were shaking.

"Are you sure you've never done this before?" whispered Sam.

"I haven't done *anything* yet!" whispered Jez. She lifted the pane gently and twisted the blade of the knife. The frame quivered for a moment, and then the blade snapped. Jez swore.

"Well, that's that," said Sam. "And the Swiss army goes to war with these?"

"It's not a *real* Swiss Army knife!" hissed Jez. "It's a knockoff." She made a mental note that, if she survived, she would save up for the real thing.

She looked over her shoulder, breathing hard. They wouldn't have long. In a moment of panic, she opened the can opener on the knife. "Let's try again," she said with grim determination under her breath. The can opener was shorter than the blade. She slid it between the gap and twisted hard. Her knuckles went white and the handle of the knife dug into her hand, leaving imprints in the flesh. The can opener twisted a little. *Please hold*, thought Jez. The metal creaked.

"It's not long enough," she said. "I don't have enough leverage."

"Shit!" said Sam. He looked up. Still no one. They could hear voices, muffled, just around the corner. Sam sucked in his breath sharply, and rummaged in his jacket. "Kitchen knife," he said. "Try the kitchen knife." He pulled it out of his jacket. "It's longer. Try the kitchen knife."

There was a creaking and a scratching of metal as Jez levered the window out of the slider with the longer blade; Jez's hand slipped as it came free and drove the point of the blade into her other palm. She yelped in pain, then immediately stifled it.

There was a crunch of gravel from the side of the house.

"Crap!" whispered Jez. She pulled the window out of the frame and leaned it against the wall next to the now-open window. The blood was running down her wrist. "Crap, crap, crap! You go first." She pulled her sleeve down over her hand, trying to stop the bleeding. Sam didn't argue: he turned around and wriggled feet first through the small opening. It was only just big enough; he had to twist around in order to get his shoulders through, and there was a ripping sound as the sleeve of his jacket caught on the catch of the window. He dropped into the cellar and disappeared out of sight.

"Is it far?" whispered Jez through the gap. "Is the drop far?"

"Further than you'd think," Sam whispered back. "Be careful."

Jez turned around and began to manoeuvre herself feet first through the window. Her feet found no purchase on the smooth wall, and she couldn't tell how far away the floor was. Her hand burned with pain; the blood was sticky on her palm and wrist.

"Get in as far as you can," advised Sam in a whisper, "before you jump."

Jez wriggled backwards further into the room. The window pane dug into her stomach and the further back she moved, the more she could feel gravity pulling her into the basement room.

"Try now," whispered Sam.

She pushed herself backwards from the windowsill and into the void. It *was* further than she thought, and she landed awkwardly, twisting her already-sore ankle. "Ow!"

"You okay?" said Sam.

"Yeah," said Jez. "I think so." She looked at her hand, which was still oozing red. "Shit. I'm leaving a trail here." Without thinking, she wiped her hand on her shirt, leaving a bloody swipe over her stomach and side.

"Well, that's glamorous," said Sam. "Do you have anything to cover it up? Oh, wait." He pulled a cotton handkerchief out of his pocket. "You can try this for a bit. It's clean."

"Everyone else uses tissues, Sam," said Jez, but she took the piece of cloth, wrapped it around her hand and secured it the best she could. "We should move quickly. That window pane isn't exactly subtle, leaning against the side of the house. We have to find Sarah." Their eyes adjusted to the darkness of the cellar and they looked around.

"Okay," said Sam. "I guess that means going into the house. Up there, I mean." On the far side of the room was a wooden staircase leading upward to an unfinished door with a brass knob. The room they were in had clearly been converted from a coal cellar into a storage space. The place was lined with metal shelves on which myriad heavy-duty plastic storage containers were standing.

"What's the worst thing that could happen?" said Jez, in a small voice. Both of them tried not to think about it.

Sam went over to the staircase and started to climb. It wobbled a little and creaked. Jez followed. Sam reached the top and turned the door handle.

Nothing happened. The door had been locked from the outside.

Chapter 20

"Shit!" spat Sam. "It's locked! It's fucking *locked!* Now what?"

Jez looked back up at the window. "We could climb back out," she said. "But we'd need a lot of boxes to stand on. And then we'd be in the same position as before." She leaned past Sam and turned the handle herself. The mechanism was well oiled and ran smoothly, but when she tugged at the door, it wouldn't budge.

"Okay," she said. "Okay. Let's think about this."

The gravel path crunched outside the window. The two of them flattened themselves back against the wall, instinctively.

It was easier to see out into the light than it would be to see into the darkness, Jez reminded herself. She crouched down to look across the room and out of the window.

A pair of legs in impeccable trousers and highly polished shoes walked past the window and stopped. Jez froze.

The legs bent, and the figure crouched. She couldn't see the man's face. His fingers touched the ground and he lifted his hand to look at it.

"Shit," whispered Jez. "Sam, I bled on the ground!" Sam's eyes were wide. He didn't say a word; he remained frozen, staring.

The man paused for a moment, and then moved the window back into position without replacing it. He stood up and walked away.

Jez exhaled sharply. "That's it?"

Sam was still staring at the window. "Maybe he thought it was an animal. An animal's blood, I mean," he said, but he didn't sound convinced.

"We can't get out through this door. We need to get back out the window and find another way in," said Jez, standing up. Her heart was racing and she felt sick. They'd just wasted at least twenty minutes, and they were no closer to finding Sarah than before. And she still had no idea what they were going to do once they did. What if Sarah was injured? What if she couldn't walk? Jez realized the extent to which she had assumed that, once they'd found the witch, she would take charge and know what to do. With a sinking feeling, she realized that Sarah probably wouldn't be in a fit state to do that.

Even if she's still alive.

Jez tried to push that thought out of her mind. But it kept coming back. What if Sarah were already dead? They were walking into a house full of beings who didn't have to obey all the rules of physics and chemistry that humans did. And they were under the command of someone who was part human and part demonic prince. One of the most infamous and dangerous Princes of Hell, in fact. And this organization of hellish creatures had the power to bend reality, to shape it to their will, for their own best outcomes.

What on Earth had she thought the best possible outcome would be for her, in this scenario? For any of them?

The crunching gravel brought her back to the moment. She dropped into her defensive crouch again, eyes glued to the window.

The legs were walking *backward.*

Jez looked at Sam. "What the hell?" she mouthed.

There was a thud, and the room went dark.

"What the *hell?*" whispered Jez again. She moved carefully down the stairs, trying to keep the creaking to a minimum, and stepped gingerly across the room to the window. The path to the stairs had been relatively clear, but the amount of light in the room had dropped dramatically.

Jez reached the window, and looked up. Her heart sank.

A large crate had been placed in front of it. She could see the rough wooden slats through the paneless gap.

"Sam!" she hissed across the room. "They've put something in front of the window!"

"What is it?" he whispered back. She heard the stairs creak as he moved toward her.

"I don't know. A crate or something. Maybe we can move it?" She felt sure, even as she said it, that whatever was in the crate wouldn't shift easily. Whoever had put it there knew that the house had been broken into. And, chances were, that person also knew that the basement was locked. Sam and Jez didn't have much time. "We need to try. Can you get some of those boxes down?"

Sam pulled one of the plastic Rubbermaid bins off the industrial shelving. "Jesus," he said, exhaling with effort. "This is heavy." He lugged it underneath the window and put it down with a crash. Jez winced. She stepped up onto the box.

"It's not high enough," she said. "We need at least one more."

Sam grabbed another Rubbermaid from the shelves and placed it on top of the first. "Can you still get up?" he said. "Do you need a leg up?"

Jez climbed gingerly up onto the top of the two containers. They wobbled dangerously. "This is really unstable," she said. "And we need another one on top of this." She climbed down in stages, searching tentatively for the floor with her feet.

Sam pulled a third Rubbermaid off the shelving. "Another heavy one," he said. Jez lifted up the lighter box, and they put the heavy box underneath it. Jez climbed to the top of it, and it shifted precariously.

"I can reach the crate," she said. She put her hands against the wooden slats. The wound on her palm screamed through the handkerchief dressing. She tried to ignore it and pushed experimentally, testing the weight of the crate and the stability of the tower.

The crate didn't move.

"Shit!" she spat. "It's too heavy." She put her hands on the crate and tried again. But it wouldn't budge. She pushed harder and felt the boxes move under her feet. "I can't do it." She climbed down. "You try."

Sam clambered up the tower of boxes and reached out of the window. He strained against the weight of the crate, but it wouldn't budge. There was a rasp of plastic against concrete as the tower of boxes scraped against the floor. He tried again; nothing. Finally, he slapped the crate hard, in frustration.

"*Fuck*," he said. "Nothing." He climbed off the tower of boxes and hurled himself against the wall in frustration. "All we can do is wait until they come and get us. After all that, we couldn't help her." In the shreds of light, Jez saw he was angry. "She's a *witch*, for fuck's sake. How come she couldn't help herself?"

"I don't know" said Jez. "I don't know. She did what she could. She got a message to Father Dominic. I don't know how any of this stuff works." Sam was right, she thought. There was nothing that they could do but wait.

In despair, she sat down on one of the large crates. Like the crate outside the window, it was made of rough wood, but it was solid and seemed heavy. They sat in silence. Minutes passed.

And then, they heard a thump. Jez jumped and looked at the staircase. Nothing. The door handle hadn't moved.

"What was that?" she whispered to Sam. He was sitting on the floor, with his knees pulled up and his back against the crate. A moment later, the sound came again. Sam turned around.

"It's inside the box," he said. "Whatever it is, it's inside the box. And we're stuck in here with it." Slowly, he lowered his head into his hands.

"Why would they keep a demon in the cellar?" asked Jez.

"I don't know. I'm not a demon-keeping expert." Sam leaned back against the crate and glared at her. "Sure. Go ahead. Open the box. Worst-case scenario: we die horribly of some hellish demon-related cause. Our best-case scenario right now is that no one ever finds us and we die horribly of dehydration down here in about ten days. So go for it."

"I'm not making that decision by myself," said Jez. "I'm not opening the box unless you're okay with it."

"Why not?"

"Because you're my best friend," said Jez. "Because I got you into this in the first place."

Sam sighed.

"I wish you hadn't," he said, eventually, through his teeth.

"Yeah, well," said Jez. "I wish I hadn't, too."

There was a long silence, eventually punctuated by another thump from the box. Jez caught Sam's eye. She knew that he was thinking the same thing.

"What if it's her?" said Jez. "It might not be. But what if it is?"

Sam looked away. "Just open it," he said. His hands were balled into fists. "We've got a kitchen knife and beyond that, whatever happens, happens."

There was a catch on the front of the crate. Jez slid it to the right and it clicked. With trepidation, she put her hands under the lip of the lid.

This could be it, she thought. *Again. This could be the end.* But what choice did she have? If Sarah was trapped in the box, they might have a better chance of surviving, at least for longer. If it wasn't Sarah, then they were probably going to end up like Cat's family.

Pools of blood. The mental image sickened her.

No, she told herself. *Don't think about that.* She took a deep breath and pushed at the lid of the crate. It was on a hinge at the back, and it was surprisingly heavy.

"Help me out, Sam," she said. He turned around and the pair of them leaned the lid against the wall of the cellar. They peered into the box.

Jez and Sam struggled to make out the supine figure in the darkness. Sarah blinked in the cracks of light. She hummed loudly through the gag.

"It's her!" said Jez. She reached into the box and fumbled with the gag around Sarah's head. Sarah gasped and coughed as it came away.

"Hands," she spluttered. "Hands and feet." She rolled onto her front to make it easier. Jez grabbed the kitchen knife from where they had dropped it while climbing through the window, and sawed through the plastic ties binding the witch. Sarah wriggled and sat up.

"Alive," she said. "Alive and...ow." She rubbed her temple. "My head hurts."

"Are you okay?" asked Jez. "Did they hit you?"

"Drugged me," said Sarah, with a sniff. "Chloroform or something, I don't know. I have a headache. You didn't bring aspirin, did you?"

"No," said Sam. "When the elderly friar picked us up at the hospital and told us he'd had a dream where you told him to come and get us so we could rescue you, we didn't think to stop at the chemist's first." Jez caught the edge in his voice.

"Shit," said Sarah. She blinked and looked around. "Dark in here," she said, groggily. "Where are we? At Carpenter's?"

"Yes," said Jez. "That's how we found you. You told the friar to tell us to come here."

"I was guessing," said Sarah. "Why are we in the basement?"

"This was how we found our way in," said Sam. "We came in through the window, and then we discovered the door over there—" he pointed "—was locked, so we went to go back out, but by that time, the Asilida guys had put something heavy in front of the window. There's no way out."

"What happened to you?" asked Jez.

"I went to the shop," said Sarah. "I asked Jake where Adam Carpenter lived, and he told me, and I left the shop and got picked up by a bunch of goons from Asilida who chloroformed me. *Chloroform*," she added, pressing her lips together and shaking her head. "Not impressed."

"Well, that's good," said Jez. "Right? They said that you wouldn't be able to stop them, but they're obviously scared enough of you that they tried to stop you. Right?"

Sarah shrugged. "Or," she said, "they wanted to make an example of me, because I was being a pain in their bums. Or they wanted to bring me to their overlord because he's a Prince of Hell and enjoys torturing living souls on a...what day is this? Anyway. Recreational torture. *Fuck*," she added. "I'm really sorry it came to this." She leaned forward and rested her head on her hands.

"Yeah," said Sam. "So are we." He turned away. Jez saw his shoulders moving silently in the dark.

"It's not your fault," said Jez. She moved toward Sarah and put her hand on her arm. "Sarah. It's not your fault."

"Of course it's her fault," snapped Sam. "If she'd been more careful, we'd never have got involved."

"No," said Jez. "But Gareth and Marina would still be dead, wouldn't they? We just wouldn't know who was behind it. And that thing that killed them would still be running around the countryside burning everyone who got in its way with acid. Cat and her family would still be dead. Sam, we had to try and stop them. We partially stopped them. We killed their demon thing." She felt a tightness in her chest and stomach.

"We're going to pay for it now, though, aren't we?" snapped Sam.

"There must be something we can do," said Jez. She looked at Sarah. "There's something we can do," she said again. "Isn't there? You called us to come and get you. There must be something."

Sarah shrugged again. "Unfortunately," she said, "most of my plans involved at least one person-sized aperture leading out of the place the box was in." She rubbed her head with her hands. "I'm sorry."

"You're a *witch*, for fuck's sake!" yelled Sam. "Are you seriously telling me there's *nothing* you can do to get us out of here? You can't magic a lock open or move the stupid crate?"

Sarah glared at him in the dark. "Magic doesn't work like that," she said. "I'm not Harry flaming Potter."

"Then how *does* it work?" demanded Sam. "Because it's been bugger-all use so far. What do you actually *do?*"

From the top of the stairs came the sound of a key moving in a well-oiled lock.

"Right now," said Sarah, "I'm really not sure."

The door at the top of the stairs swung open silently and they heard the sound of feet clacking slowly down the rickety wooden stairs. Light flooded in through the open doorway.

Something's wrong, thought Jez. Her heart was pounding again. *Something doesn't sound right. No shoes in the world sound like that.* She glanced toward the staircase. The feet had paused on their way down. Jez could hear heavy, laboured breathing as whoever it was stopped on the stairs. Over the breathing, she could hear a distinct buzzing noise.

Clack. One foot moved down onto the next step. Followed by the other. *Clack.*

Jez's face froze in horror. The feet were—had originally been—human feet; large human feet. She could see the toes, painfully bent underneath the foot. The metatarsal bones had been bent out of shape, curled as if around a cylinder, and there was a weird fleshy growth, new growth, around the part of the foot that hit the ground. Thick cartilage. And hard.

 A hoof.

Clack. Whatever was coming down the stairs grunted in pain.

Clack. The stairway creaked. Jez shot a terrified glance at Sarah. She was staring at the thing coming down the stairs, chin raised and lip curled.

Clack. Whatever it was, it was big. And it was heavy. The buzzing grew louder.

Clack. The thing made it down the final step. Jez peered at it, squinting; the light from behind it made it difficult to see its features.

It stepped forward. Adrenalin shot through Jez's body; it felt as though something were squeezing her chest; she fought for breath.

The thing that had once been Adam Carpenter was still traceable in the body of the monster before them. It was much taller than Adam had been: seven, maybe almost eight feet. His eyes were human, but the front of his face had collapsed; his nose was missing and his sinus cavity was open; part of his lower lip looked as though it had been burned away by acid.

And his face was full of flies.

They crawled in and out of the hole where his nose had been, surrounding him like a halo, and partially covering his face like a shimmering green mask. As Jez watched, two of them crawled out of his mouth and joined the throng around his head.

His legs had been broken and reformed. They were still recognizably human, but the bones had been snapped and reformed into familiar, backwards angles. Goat legs.

The host. Carpenter was the host. And whatever he was playing host to had almost taken over the whole party.

Almost. But not quite. Jez looked at the eyes. Something in there, a spark, a flicker, told her there were rags in there that had once been human.

Adam was staring at Jez. Then he looked at Sam.

Sarah was jerked away from her racing thoughts by the voice. It was hideous. It emanated partly from the distorted and broken body in front of her, and partly echoed in her head, as if it were taking over her very thoughts.

"Sarah Trevelyan," it rasped. "The witch. I knew your ancestors."

"What the hell is that?" whispered Sam.

"It's Carpenter," muttered Sarah. "Plus guest."

"Carpenter is the host," croaked the voice. "I am the host."

"Sounds crowded," said Sarah staring at him directly. The creature looked at her for a moment and then broke into a phlegm-filled, rattling laugh.

"Witty," it managed eventually. "You know we have *won*. We told you you could not do anything. We told you to leave. You did not listen." The thing that had been Carpenter kicked at the wooden stairs twice, knocking. Within a moment, two Asilida Ethereals were clattering down the stairs and standing behind it, awaiting instruction.

"I am still in control," croaked the voice. The eyes blinked.

"No, you're not," said Sarah, looking at him directly. "You're paying for the bargain you made. An evil bargain."

"You are a true Trevelyan," croaked the creature. "You still believe in good and evil. We have waited a long time for revenge."

"Revenge?" burst out Sam. "What has she done? She hasn't done anything! She hasn't stopped you. You still have everything you want. Why don't you just let us go? You're way more powerful than we are."

"There's no fun in that," muttered Sarah through her teeth.

"Indeed," rasped the creature. "We have waited a long time to take our vengeance upon the Trevelyan family."

"What did they do?" asked Jez. "Sarah hasn't done anything to you."

The creature coughed. Flies shot out of its mouth and buzzed angrily. It spat on the floor; maggots crawled amid the oyster of phelgm lying on the ground. Jez swallowed, feeling nauseated.

"They trapped us," it growled. "They trapped us in the pond."

"What?" said Sam, looking at Jez.

"That must have been Sarah's ancestor," she whispered. "She was a witch too. She trapped a demon in the Foxglove Pond. The demon that killed Gareth and Marina. The one we—" She stopped, realizing that she was about to incriminate them all. *Did it know?* she thought. *Did it know that they were responsible?*

"Centuries," Carpenter snarled. "We were trapped for centuries."

"How is this even possible?" whispered Sam. "I thought that was the other thing that was trapped? This thing was trapped too? *What the fuck?*"

"Symbiosis," said Sarah, not taking her eyes off Carpenter for a second. "Oh my God. It's symbiotic."

"What the fuck?" breathed Sam. His voice was barely audible.

"The fly demon was in the pond," said Sarah. "We killed it. And now this thing is saying *it* was in the pond. And that bloke, the one that brought me here... I met him in the office, and I stabbed him, and he disappeared." She spoke as if a fog in her mind was lifting and she could see clearly for the first time in a long while. "Except he was up and running again by this morning. Everything it controls is a part of it. The flies. The agents. The demon. They're symbiotic." She stared at Carpenter's eyes. "You're still in there, though," she said. "Aren't you? When we killed that thing, that was when you changed. Because it needed a physical demonic presence as well as a spiritual one." She looked the thing in front of her in the eyes. "You're still part human."

The creature looked back at her for a moment, locked in her gaze. Then it jerked its head toward her.

The agents moved more quickly than Jez would have thought possible; they grabbed Sarah and forced her onto her knees in front of Carpenter. Sam tried to pull one of them away; the agent broke his arm like a toothpick, with an audible *snap*. Sam screamed in pain and turned pale.

"Sam!" yelled Jez, eyes wide. She shot over to him; he was moaning on the floor. She looked at his arm; the broken bone distorted the line of his sleeve. Jez felt dizzy and a little sick. What were you supposed to do with a compound fracture? She couldn't remember. Stop it moving. Call nine-nine-nine. Automatically, she pulled out her phone. Dead. Of course it was dead. *Shit. SHIT!* She grabbed Sam's other hand, and he gripped it tightly, breathing heavily.

"We can get through this," she muttered to Sam. "We can get out of here. Get you to a hospital." His breathing was ragged. She knew you didn't die from a broken bone—not immediately, anyway—but shock, shock could kill you. Shock and fear.

And demons.

The creature coughed and spat again. Jez grimaced and looked at Sarah. She was kneeling on the floor, held there by the two Asilida Ethereals, but her chin was raised and she was looking straight at Carpenter. One of them fastened a new plastic cable tie around her wrists.

"So now what?" she spat. "You're just going to kill me?"

The creature snorted. "Of course not," it snarled. "We are going to make you suffer. And then, when we have had enough, we will leave you to die. On your own time. Who knows where you are? No one. Who cares? No one. We will have our revenge. We will succeed in this world. You have failed. You have failed generations of your family. You are the last of the Trevelyans, and with you, the family will die. And—" it nodded toward Jez and Sam "—more innocents will die because of you. Because of your actions. Your failure."

Sarah swallowed, but she kept her cool.

"How did you come to this, Carpenter?" she asked. "This can't have been what you had in mind. You'll get your factory. You'll get your worldly wealth. But look at you. You're a collection of cells supporting a parasite. How did you not see this coming?"

The creature blinked and put its hand on Sarah's head. The nails were yellow and thick.

How could this have happened? Jez watched Sarah stare deep into the creature's eyes. They flashed with hideous malice. There was a growing darkness there, a coldness characterised by a profound lack of compassion. Its hardness was terrifying.

"Why did you *do* this?" asked Sarah. "How did you not know?"

Jez couldn't bear the sight of the creature any longer; the dripping larvae made her stomach churn. She turned away, longing for something familiar, some comfort that would take her out of this; she wanted to go home, not to die in a cellar. Her eye fell on her green bag.

And the doodles. *Digitalis.*

Holy shit, she thought to herself.

"How did you not know?" repeated Sarah. There was despair in her voice, and Jez knew that she had resigned herself to death.

"Because someone told him it worked," said Jez, quietly. "Didn't matter why. Or how. Just that it *worked*." She sat up straight and stared at the creature's eyes one last time. Briefly, finally, the last remaining dregs of humanity flared desperately and then went out.

"You didn't see this coming," she said, thinking quickly. "Did you? Someone told you about Asilida. Someone told you what they could do."

Jez looked at Sarah and saw the Asilida Ethereals tighten their grip on her shoulders. She couldn't move. But the beast in front of her was momentarily frozen.

"Who told you?" Sarah asked, looking Carpenter straight in the eye. "Who set up this deal?"

The creature tilted Sarah's head back. Carpenter's eyes stared back at her. For a moment, she saw that they were grey, with flecks of brown in them and bloodshot.

"Carrington," the beast whispered. Sarah went cold.

"Nicholas Carrington?" she managed.

The creature responded with a barely perceptible nod. The eyes turned black.

Nicholas Carrington. The man whose greed had led to Eleanor's death.

She had promised herself she would take revenge on Carrington and, because of him, she was about to die. And he didn't even know. He would be free to carry on abusing people, stepping on them, crushing lives in order to feed his own ambition and greed. Free to carry on living. And he would never know that she had been looking for him, determined to make him pay.

She exhaled. The anger that had driven her to Crowsbrook after the fire, that wouldn't let her give up in the face of those two kids' murders, dissipated. There was nothing left she could do. It was truly hopeless.

The creature drove its thumb hard into her right eye. She felt the pressure, felt the edge lacerate her eyeball, felt the burst of pressure released and the vitreous fluid well up and run down her cheek. Felt pain. She cried out.

Watching her from across the room, Jez shuddered and moaned.

The creature's nail caught Sarah's lower eyelid, and tore it, adding a thread of blood to the fluid coursing down her cheek. It fell in a long, viscous drip to the ground. She was breathing hard; her remaining eye was screwed shut.

"We will leave you one," murmured the creature. "For now. We have business with the children. You will watch." It turned its head to look at Jez, and then, looking at Sarah's left foot, resting on her toes as she knelt in pain on the floor, stomped on it hard. The bones cracked audibly, and she cried out.

She was shaking. From pain, from rage. *Carrington*. He would live free. There would be no consequences for him. And she would die alone and in agony in the cellar, and Asilida would arrange reality so that no one would ever know. No one would ever miss her.

She had failed. Failed utterly.

The creature let her go, and the Ethereals pushed her to the hard floor. She could barely see out of her good eye; her face was screwed up in pain.

The beast was moving again. She heard the *clack* of its malformed hoofs on the concrete floor. It was moving toward Jez, who was still kneeling over Sam.

It turned its broken head to one side and looked her up and down. Steadily.

"No," whispered Jez, staring back. "NO!" she yelled more loudly. She backed away toward the wall, looking for something, anything to use as a weapon. The kitchen knife was on the floor; she couldn't get to it. Another rush of adrenalin hit her; she pulled the lid off one of the Rubbermaids and held it in front of her like a shield, swiping at the creature with it as it advanced toward her. She was faintly aware of a rushing sound in her ears, like wind through grass.

"Fuck off!" she yelled. "Don't fucking touch me!" She swiped at it with the box lid. The creature knocked it away easily.

Jez's back was against the wall below the window. The beast stretched out its hand and stroked her hair.

The rushing noise grew louder.

And then they arrived.

Spiders.

Thousands of spiders.

They poured in like a wave, scuttling like a leggy tide through the cracks between the crate and the window, down the walls, down the stairs, through the shelves, through cracks in the ceiling, through the gaps in the skirting boards. It was as if the entire fabric of the room had come alive. They poured over Jez; she felt the gentle tickle of a thousand delicate legs moving fast against her skin.

They passed over her as if she wasn't there.

Forward. They surged forward, almost as one. They swirled around the Ethereals like water, heading straight for the creature that had once been Adam Carpenter, pooling around the hoof-like feet and crawling up his broken, misshapen legs, covering his flesh in a living, ever-moving blanket of arachnids. The creatures burrowed beneath the ragged clothes that covered him; as Jez watched in horror, she saw smaller spiders disappear into his sinus cavities.

The creature was screaming, trying to brush them away, but they kept coming, large and small, until he was entirely covered. The flies crawling in and out of his face dissipated like gunshot, and the spiders poured in. Into his face; in through the creature's burned lip.

A million spiders. A million spider bites. A million pricks of paralyzing venom shot into Adam Carpenter's body. His abdomen was shot through with cramp and he felt his lungs slowly freezing up, diaphragm stiffening. He gasped for air, desperate to pull oxygen into his body, overwhelmed with a rage and frustration that wasn't his. He gagged.

His movements became slower, stiffer, and he sank to the floor, looking Jez straight in the eye. She stared back, for a long time. Eventually he stopped blinking. Then moving. Then, finally, breathing.

The corpse of the thing that was half demon and half human lay desiccated on the cellar floor.

There was a noise like a roaring wind, as if a hurricane had become trapped in the house; nothing moved, but the two Ethereals guarding Sarah faded in front of Jez's eyes, began to splash and drip into dark water, pooled on the floor, drained away as though through invisible cracks, and vanished. A dry pattering followed, like rice grains falling on paper. Jez looked around, and saw dead flies dropping out of the air.

The corpse before her crumbled into a heap of dust that grew finer and finer until there was barely anything of it left.

Then, everything was still.

• • •

A moan from Sam tore Jez from her reverie of fear.

"Christ," he groaned. "Hurts... it fucking hurts. Help me... somebody, help me."

Jez got to her feet. Her whole body was shaking.

"I'll do it," she said. "I can help. I'll go and get help. I'll be back in a minute." She made her way unsteadily up the stairs, which trembled under her weight; she still felt dizzy and sick.

The house. She was in the house. She stumbled from room to room until she found the front door. She struggled with the handle, until she realized it was bolted from the inside; sobbing, she shot back the bolt and hauled the door open. The light flooded in, and she ran through, out of the door, feet scattering the gravel, toward the gate and the road, screaming.

"Father Dominic!" she yelled. "Father! *Faaaaaaaatheeeeeer!*"

Chapter 21

Greg Jarsdel pushed his chair back from his desk, stared at his story and grinned.

It was big, this one; oh, it was big all right. Multiple murders! Forced confinement! Government corruption! Well, the last one was a bit of a stretch: it wasn't national government, obviously, but there *were* a lot of photos floating around the picture desk (a.k.a. Midge Appleton and a laptop) of Norman Bastable looking *very* uncomfortable. Apparently he couldn't remember how a large file regarding a laughably illegal planning application had ended up being partially processed. Greg rolled his eyes. He had thought it was only people in the House of Commons who were capable of that level of selective memory loss, but he wasn't too fussed about the details: Bastable's saving grace was that neither he nor any other member of the council had appeared to receive *any* kind of perks regarding the file, and it was, in Greg's opinion, a lot more likely to be basic incompetence, which was a lot more credible, frankly. And no one would care about the council being idiots, anyway: everyone was reeling from the revelation that local property mogul Adam Carpenter—you could be a mogul in the provinces if you'd had a hand in a couple of well-designed shopping centres— had disappeared, leaving behind a trail of horrors and Christ knew what kind of a mess for the lawyers to clear up. Just disappeared—*poof!*—and left the mangled remains of his girl-friend in the kitchen, and three locals in the cellar...

He imagined Rusbridger calling him *personally*.

He looked at the picture of the people who had managed to escape from Carpenter's house. Frowned. He'd never seen them before. There was something he couldn't quite put his finger on; they didn't really look like they were from around Arden or Crowsbrook or Castleton. They were too...well...*glamorous*.

• • •

Mrs. Bastable chatted to her new Jack Russell puppy as they walked through the centre of Crowsbrook. She didn't like to speak ill of the dead, not her, but the pup—Pip, she'd called him—was a lot more tractable than Joey had ever been, God bless him. Her headaches were getting better too. Ah well. Perhaps it had been Joey's time. Everything worked out for the best in the end, didn't it?

Ryan Ogden picked up the ringing phone, and only heard the words *good news* and *false positive* before he zoned out. Things were looking up.

Sally Jensen watched her daughter stacking building blocks and knocking them down with a crash, and not for the first time thanked her lucky stars that she finally seemed to have shaken off the bug she'd had in October. Had Sally really worried, that did. There were times when she'd thought the worst, though she hated to admit it. Horrible. Still, all was well that ended well, wasn't it?

The blocks came down with clatter, and she smiled. It was all right now.

• • •

The spiders were busy.

A spider whose web has been damaged will usually wait until the danger has passed—a storm, a predator, an errant feather duster—and will then venture out to repair it, rather than abandoning it to rebuild.

If you wish to live and thrive, let a spider run alive.

Sarah's spiders began to weave the threads of reality back together.

Chapter 22

Slade were on the radio, even though it was only December 1. Sarah hummed along with Noddy Holder while she made a cup of tea.

Steady. Steady.

She lifted the kettle and tilted it. The water missed the cup and splashed over the hob, putting out the burner. The smell of gas drifted upward.

Crap. Sarah turned off the hob. Still, she was getting better at it. Hadn't done that in a while. She decided to have a can of pop instead.

She limped into the living room and sat down. Her ankle was getting better. They hadn't been able to save her eye, but they'd told her that she could get along just as well with one, that she'd lose some depth perception, but she'd adapt and get used to it, that she'd still be able to drive, even. Well, she would be after Jake and Rose's son, Alan, had fixed her car. It would take a while, but she wasn't in a rush.

She didn't care. There was a reason they called it *second sight.*

She had work to do. She turned to the pile of books on the table, her great-aunt's notebooks, and sat back down. She still had a lot to learn, and a lot of what she was finding out wasn't pleasant.

There was a knock at the door. Sarah looked up.

"It's open," she yelled. She already knew who it was. Jez slunk round the door, green bag on her hip.

"Hello," said Sarah, eyebrows raised. "Been a while. How are you? How's your dad?"

"All right," said Jez. "Better. Lots of physio. He and Sam are seeing the same doctor. Sam's mum's been driving them. How are you?"

Sarah shrugged. "All right," she said. She could tell Jez was trying not to stare at her face. She pointed to her black eye patch. "Looking better, no?" she said. "Used... you know. Bit of... Just to hide the scarring."

"Glamour," said Jez. "That's the word, right?"

Sarah nodded. "You can have a seat, you know." Jez looked around the room; all the chairs were covered in books. She heaved a pile onto the floor and sat down.

"Sorry I haven't been round," she said. "Lot going on. Exams. And my dad." She looked at the carpet and tried to fit the tip of her shoe into one of the crazy, threadbare swirls. "I've got so many questions," she said.

"Yeah," said Sarah. "Me too. But I'm working on them." She gestured to the giant pile of books in front of her. "It's taking a while."

"Did you find out about the spiders?" said Jez. "What happened with the spiders? Why did they...do what they did?"

"I'm not sure," said Sarah. "I'm still going through the books." She gestured toward the pile on the table. "I think, though—I think they were left to me along with the house."

Jez felt an expression of incredulity trying to creep across her face. She fought it, and bit her tongue.

"*Left* to you?" she said. "How does that work?"

"Familiar spirits," said Sarah. "You know the old thing about witches and black cats? Or frogs or bats or whatever? They're familiar spirits. Sort of like personal helpers."

"Four thousand of them?"

Sarah shrugged. "I guess. Or if Asilida can manifest as one spirit in many forms simultaneously, there's no reason that they should be the only ones. One." She rubbed her forehead. "Jesus. I have so much to learn."

"They saved us," said Jez. "Why did they save us?"

"They're very protective," said Sarah. "Traditionally. Familiars."

"Right," said Jez, slowly. "So they weren't saving us. They were saving you."

"Collateral survival is still survival," said Sarah. "I'd take it."

"I'm not complaining," said Jez. "But how did they know?"

Sarah rummaged through the stack of old, leather-bound books on the table and found one with a hot-pink Post-It note sticking out of it. She flipped to the page. "'The connection between a witch and her familiar is a complicated one and ancient,'" she read, "'but it seems that when the witch feeds the familiar, a contract is created that can be passed down the generations; a contract in which the familiar will serve in return for food and care.'" She closed the book. "That's all I've found so far."

Jez thought for a moment. "They didn't come when the goons kidnapped you," she said. "They only came when they hurt you. When you were bleeding. Maybe that had something to do with it."

Holy crap, thought Sarah. *She's right. The kid could be on to something there.* "Well," she said, "that sounds like a reasonable theory to me. I'd really rather not test it out, though."

Jez nodded. "Yeah," she said. "Gotcha. Are they all still upstairs?"

"Some of them are," said Sarah. "Not as many. They're not hiding from toxic flies anymore."

Jez nodded. There was a silence for a minute or so that verged on awkward.

"So what are you doing now?" she asked.

Sarah shrugged.

"Getting better," she said. "Reading. Jake said I could work in the shop for a bit when my ankle's healed. Alan Pound's fixing my car." She looked at the pile of papers in front of her and then back at Jez. "Got a lot of studying to do," she repeated. "Some of the things that happened—" She paused.

You can tell her, she told herself. *After everything that's happened, you can tell her.*

"There are a couple of things I can't figure out," she said. Her voice was low. "My grandmother taught me that seeing the future was always problematic, that you could only ever make educated guesses. I mean, in our line of business, you have more 'education'—" she made quotation marks with her fingers "—about the future than most people. But she taught me that everything was amorphous. Subject to change." The prospect of articulating her fears made them more concrete to her; she felt a familiar clenching in the pit of her stomach. "My great-aunt not only saw the future, but was able to leave us messages to guide us," she said. "She left me a letter here, and she left me a letter at Father Dominic's house. That shouldn't be possible. I'm used to dealing with things that shouldn't be possible, but that—" She swallowed. The implications were terrifying. "I don't know how she did it," she said. "But I'm sure that it wasn't just lucky guessing. And if she was right about that—"

If she was right about that, there are dark times ahead. Malevolent Ethereals in league with humans, and not for the greater good.

She sighed. "You've got exams coming up," she said. "You don't need to be bothered with all this."

Jez frowned. "Yeah, I do," she said. "I want to know how it works. Are you still going after that bloke?"

Sarah swigged from her can of pop. "Jez," she said. "The last thing I got from Adam Carpenter was the name of the guy who set him up with Asilida. It was the same name. Carrington. I have to. And I have no idea how."

"What do you mean, you have to? Why?"

"Because he's in league with malevolent Ethereals," said Sarah, "and if he's allowed to operate unstopped, things will get really nasty. You saw what they attempted to do here; if Adam had succeeded, we'd all be generating high-grade depression for Hell to get high on for evermore. And that would be our lives. And Adam was small fry. Carrington's the big fish. God knows what he's up to."

Jez frowned again. "What are we going to do?"

We?

Sarah crushed the pop can, and sent it flying in the direction of the waste-paper basket. It missed, and she shrugged. "You're going to take your A-levels, move to Manchester, hang out with Sam, become a doctor, and cure cancer," she said. "I'm going to read a lot of books, harbour thoughts of bloody vengeance, cure warts for the locals, and probably die before my time in a stupid, magic-related accident."

"You just said that no one can see the future," said Jez. "It might not work out like that."

"It might not," said Sarah. "You're right." *Damn it.*

Jez stood up. "I should probably go and do some revision," she said. "But I'm glad you're getting better." She paused. "Er. Say hi to the spiders from me. And thanks."

"I will," said Sarah. "I'm sure they'll appreciate it."

"Cheers," said Jez. "See you later. You should put that in the recycling." She pointed toward the can lying on the floor, and let herself out.

Yeah, thought Sarah. *I probably should.*

She picked up the pop can and limped into the kitchen, where she dropped it into a white plastic box. She looked at her watch.

Her physiotherapist said she was supposed to go for regular walks. She got her coat.

. . .

The leaves were all gone at the Foxglove Pond now, and the foxglove leaves had decomposed into mulch, the plants dormant beneath the topsoil, waiting. The branches of the trees jutted starkly into the air, black against the soft grey of the overcast winter sky. The sun was low in the sky, glowering coldly through the trees. Sarah stood at the edge of the pond, shoes sinking into the soft mud, watching the water.

The barbed wire had gone. The red string had gone. It was safe now. She could feel it.

Something caught her eye, in the shallows at the edge of the pond, catching the remaining threads of light. Sarah frowned, bending to look closer.

A silver cufflink with a complicated sigil engraved on it rolled gently back and forth under the water.

Sarah clenched her teeth and reached slowly into the water. It was icy cold. She picked up the cufflink and placed it on the flat of her hand. She looked at it for a very long time.

Then she closed her fingers around it, drew her arm back and threw it as hard as she could into the centre of the pond, and watched the ripples circle outward silently. She pictured it falling slowly through the water, down through the depths where the light couldn't reach it, on and on, falling into an eternity of darkness.

She turned to go home. A crow cawed high above her.

* * *

The stairs were getting easier and she'd been told by her physiotherapist that they'd be good exercise for her ankle. Still, after the walk to and from the Foxglove Pond, she was relieved to get to the top and take the few extra steps across the landing to her bedroom.

She lay down on the bed and began to connect. She could feel the spiders in the house, in the garden, in the fields beyond. Thousands of them.

Come. She called to them silently. *Feed.*

The rush was becoming familiar; they flowed into the house through every crack and covered her body, her face, her hair; the air crackled with magic as the witch fed her familiars.

They needed everything she could give them. She had work to do.

SARAH TREVELYAN WILL RETURN—
visit www.welcometocrowsbrook.com to find out more...

Acknowledgements

I wouldn't have been able to write and publish *The Crowsbrook Demons* without the hard work, help and support of a fantastic group of people, most of whom are listed below. Huge thanks to all of them. If I've missed anyone out, my apologies!

My wonderful team of beta readers and support gurus provided invaluable feedback and encouragement: thanks to April Bially, Christine Gilbert, Paul Kendal, and Jen Lockie for much feedback, support and encouragement (special thanks to Jen for Sam's observation about Rilke and Ikea). Thanks to my editor, Heather Martin (**www.heather-martin.com**), for her eagle eye and editorial expertise; any remaining typos and infelicities are all my own work. Heather is exceptionally multi-talented; she also built the wonderful website at **www.welcometocrowsbrook. com**. Thanks to Janet Weldon Murray (**www.beaconsfieldcards. com**), Jennifer Leung (**http://www.be.net/jenniferleung**), and to Nelson Gonzalez for their stellar work on the cover, interior and typesetting respectively. Thanks also to the following people who contributed expertise, advice, and encouragement: Susan Calvert, Natalia Denesiuk Harris, Stephanie Doig, Jennifer Hare, Joanne McNeil, Ken Phipps, Imoinda Romain, Daina Schreiber, Vicki So, and Lenore Spence. Thanks to Michael Mandarano for formatting the ebook (**http://www. michaelmandarano.com/**). A big thank-you to Andrew Sutherland, who helped me negotiate the brave new world of social media and marketing. And huge thanks to everyone at and around Rue Morgue magazine, especially Dave Alexander and Monica S. Kuebler.

And if you've made it this far, thanks to you, too.

About the Author

Claire Horsnell grew up in a small English village and maintains that it would have been a lot more interesting with witches and monsters in it. She now lives in Toronto. You can read her blog at www.bloodandvegetables.com, and follow her on Twitter at @bloodandveg.